Praise f

"Near-future science-fiction crim⋯⋯⋯⋯⋯⋯⋯⋯⋯⋯⋯⋯⋯⋯ries later in a wildly imaginative ge⋯⋯⋯⋯⋯⋯⋯⋯⋯⋯⋯⋯ . . . Although this narrative provides ⋯⋯⋯⋯⋯⋯⋯⋯⋯⋯ for more about these unlikely allies. Excruciating, cathartic, and triumphant."
—*Kirkus Reviews*, **starred review**

"*Latchkey* is explosively imaginative. This narrative shimmers with rich characters and a nuanced mythology. Weaving throughout it like a trail of ink is a heartbreaking exploration of trauma and how we engage with the scars left behind by history. Readers will leave this world feeling as if they've drawn new breath."
—**Roshani Chokshi**, *New York Times*–**bestselling author of**
Aru Shah and the End of Time

"I loved *Archivist Wasp*, and *Latchkey* surpasses it in every way. Everything about it moved me to tears and wonder: the girls who used to be mortal enemies amicably dividing up chores; Isabel's tender hopes for community alongside her aching loneliness; the tentative expansion of her world's horizons to other starveling towns. *Latchkey* reads like a parting of *Archivist Wasp*'s mists: clear, sharp, taut, with an angry, singing heart, this is a book that refuses categories by embracing everything it loves."
—**Amal El-Mohtar**, **Hugo Award-winning author and critic**

"*Latchkey*'s prose is elegantly self-effacing: smooth, easy to read, and full of adroit turns of phrase. Kornher-Stace has a gift for creating atmosphere, from the familial closeness of Isabel's small community of former upstarts in the Catchkeep-temple, to the ominous claustrophobia of the tunnels beneath Sweetwater, and into the hectic chaos and turmoil of battle. And underwriting every moment is a core of kindness, of compassion—of choosing a path away from cruelty, even when it's hard: a core that makes this book, for all its darkness, somehow fundamentally uplifting. If I had to choose one word to describe this novel, it would be *compelling*: in its pacing, its characterisation, and even in its genre-blending approach to worldbuilding, it compels attention. I really enjoyed *Latchkey*. I can't recommend it, and *Archivist Wasp*, highly enough."
—**Liz Bourke**, *Locus*

"Kornher-Stace understands that the best sequels don't retread old ground; they use what you know to build something fresh, something both natural and unexpected. *Latchkey* peels away the layers of its past while pushing its characters into the future, offering the hope that out of the wreckage of old cruelty might come new dreams. Like a ghost caught in a loop, you'll find yourself drawn in, not to escape until it's done."
—**Marie Brennan, Hugo Award-nominated author of**
   A Natural History of Dragons

"Like Catchkeep's harvester knife, *Latchkey* will cut you up. Wasp, now Isabel, may no longer be the Archivist, but her force and fire remain undiminished, even in the face of raiders, amnesiac ghosts and her own psychic wounds. I adored *Archivist Wasp* for its unerring vision of an atavistic mythos-ridden future and its dangerous heroine, but *Latchkey* ups all the antes as Isabel struggles to create a new future for herself, her fellow villagers, and the ghosts—whose past traumas might be the key to everything. Kornher-Stace's action is precise and razor-sharp, and her talent for bringing her characters—and her readers—to the brink is unsurpassed. Oh, and her world-building! *Latchkey* leaves other dystopias in the dust wallowing in More-of-the-Same. Kornher-Stace doesn't do More-of-the-Same; she's a strictly leave-her-readers-in-palpitations type of writer. Prepare to palpitate, and to read the entire novel in one go. I did. Like the ghosts that just won't leave Isabel alone, I'd follow Kornher-Stace anywhere. After reading *Latchkey*, you will too."
—**Ysabeau S. Wilce, Andre Norton Award-winning author of**
   The Flora Trilogy

"Nicole Kornher-Stace's *Latchkey* is a little like retracing a war veteran's scars with a scalpel and asking, 'So. Does this hurt more than the original?' It does, of course. Hurts good, hurts deep, this almost-familiar world that bleeds right into ours, where the only thing fiercer than ferocity is tenderness—though both talk equally as tough. After reading *Latchkey*, one starts seeing ruins superimposed over currently thriving structures. Every struggling patch of city lawn becomes a garden of ghost grass; every breezy puff of leftover winter holds the possibility of frostbite and vertigo and seeing the face of a long-lost friend once more. Has there ever been such longing, fueled by such darkness and adrenaline? Has there ever been such satisfaction, and at such a cost?"
—**C. S. E. Cooney, World Fantasy Award-winning author of**
   Bone Swans

"As lean, dusty, and haunted as the overgrown ruins of a greyhound racetrack, *Latchkey*, like its predecessor, is a beautifully written ode to friendship, survival, secrets, and memory. Wildly inventive, saturated with grit and guts and a wistful, calloused ephemerality, this is a book that lands with all the sting and palm-tingling impact of two partners joining hands before facing down impossible odds. It refuses classification. It laughs grimly at the concept of labels. It tests boundaries and kicks the door in with a quirked lip and a sad glint in its narrowed sunset eye.

"Nobody else could have written *Latchkey*. More than anything else I've ever read, this is undiluted, 110% the vision of one author. Nicole Kornher-Stace is her own genre entirely, and if you're anything at all like me, you are the target audience."

—Brooke Bolander, Hugo, Nebula and World Fantasy Award -nominated author of *The Only Harmless Great Thing*

"Nicole Kornher-Stace's *Latchkey* is equally gorgeous and spooky. In this sequel to *Archivist Wasp*, Isabel and her companions must save their home by unearthing the secrets of the past. *Latchkey* vividly asks so many of the right questions about what memories linger after an apocalypse, for worse and for better. Surreal, beautifully rendered cross-genre action-adventure."

—Fran Wilde, Andre Norton-winning and Hugo-nominated author of *Updraft*

"*Latchkey* is the opposite of escapist: it is, instead, horror for people with the courage to benefit from beholding actual horrors. Building on the deeply-realized *Archivist Wasp*, in *Latchkey* we are given a world even more fallen and brutal, for now even the old order of the archivists is broken. Here, when heroes are hurt, they stay hurt; here, the survivors must endure trauma without the words to describe it; here, knowledge itself is both deeply suspect and humanity's only hope. History itself, embodied by blood-hungry ghosts, by turns cannibalizes the living and provides the only way forward. And yet, for all the loss and bodily pain, *Latchkey* shows us the power of community and the worth, greater than diamonds, of courage. Cathartic, feminist, explosively imaginative and masterfully told, Kornher-Stace gives us a second-world fantasy that transports our minds while, time and again, it emotionally arrives."

—Carlos Hernandez, author of *Sal and Gabi Break the Universe*

"What a great read! This surreal dreamscape of a book delves deeper into the unique world of the Andre Norton Award finalist *Archivist Wasp*, continuing a resilient heroine's unusual friendship with a super-soldier ghost amid a far-future dystopia they both struggle to survive and understand."
—**Beth Cato, author of *The Clockwork Dagger* and *Breath of Earth***

"Nicole Kornher-Stace's *Latchkey* is a completely unique and enthralling story. A blend of fantasy, paranormal and more that defies categorization, I couldn't put it down. Highly recommended!"
—**Jennifer Brody, award-winning author of *The 13th Continuum***

"The sequel to Nicole Kornher-Stace's *Archivist Wasp* is a breathless rollercoaster ride through hope, despair, narrow escapes, and a history that refuses to die, built on a bedrock theme of community and friendship. All the characters are individual, convincing, and alive—including the dead ones. I've never read anything like it, except *Archivist Wasp*. If you're looking for a fresh voice in dark fantasy, you've found one."
—**Delia Sherman, Andre Norton Award-winning author of *The Evil Wizard Smallbone***

"Spine-tingling ghost encounters and tension sharp as razorwire make this a sequel well worth waiting for. You will not want to miss this, but you might need to sleep with the lights on and plant a protective circle of ghostgrass around your bed!"
—**Tiffany Trent, award-winning author of *The Unnaturalists***

"*Latchkey* has the fierce heart of *Fury Road* and the kindness of *Station Eleven*—a deliriously readable future ghost story sewn through with action, healing, and hope."
—**Leah Bobet, award-winning author of *An Inheritance of Ashes***

"Nicole Kornher-Stace is a goddess of grit and heartworn heroes. In *Latchkey*, the reader is hurled into a world of ruins, raiders, and lost tech. It's a severe setting, and Kornher-Stace could've gone full grim future, but instead, she manifests character friendships that just may get the reader through the long dark of troubled times."
—**Patty Templeton, author of *There Is No Lovely End***

"Fierce, blazing, brilliant. The mythic and brutal world of Nicole Kornher-Stace's *Latchkey* is so richly realized, you don't step into it, you fall."
—**Jacqueline West, *New York Times*–bestselling author of The Books of Elsewhere**

LATCHKEY
NICOLE KORNHER-STACE

Also by Nicole Kornher-Stace

LATCHKEY
NICOLE KORNHER-STACE

Book Two of the Archivist Wasp Saga

Mythic Delirium
B O O K S

mythicdelirium.com

Latchkey
Book Two of the Archivist Wasp Saga
Copyright © 2018 by Nicole Kornher-Stace.

Cover art copyright © 2018 by Jacquelin de Leon, jacquelindeleon.com.
All rights reserved.

ISBN-10: 0-9889124-8-1
ISBN-13: 978-0-9889124-8-9

Library of Congress Control Number: 2017919480

FIRST EDITION
July 10, 2018

Published by Mythic Delirium Books
https://mythicdelirium.com

Our gratitude goes out to the following who because of their generosity are from now on designated as supporters of Mythic Delirium Books: Saira Ali, Cora Anderson, Anonymous, Patricia M. Cryan, Steve Dempsey, Oz Drummond, Patrick Dugan, Matthew Farrer, C. R. Fowler, Mary J. Lewis, Paul T. Muse, Jr., Shyam Nunley, Finny Pendragon, Kenneth Schneyer, and Delia Sherman.

Chapter One

She clashed with Lissa, blade to blade, then grabbed the wrist of Lissa's knife-hand and yanked. As Lissa's knife slid free of Isabel's, she stumbled forward and was promptly hauled down and in toward the elbow Isabel was firing at the hollow of her throat. Isabel pulled the strike a quarter inch shy of a crushed windpipe, paused in demonstration, then let go.

"In a real fight you'd follow through." Isabel aimed her voice back over one shoulder, toward the twenty-odd people gathered there. Regulars of her weekly training sessions, most of them. A few new faces. Several ex-upstarts of the Catchkeep-shrine, whose stares still made her skin crawl. A duel was a duel, after all, wooden knives or no. Three years of not having to watch her back against them was, apparently, not enough to quite erase the three years when she had. "So that's Lissa done. But maybe she brought friends."

On cue, Bex took a swing at her. Isabel got the wooden knife in a backhand grip, dropped her weight to pivot down and under the punch, then tensed her good leg and shot upward, twisting at the hips, hissing pain through her teeth. Again she froze a split-second before she would've smashed the butt of the knife-handle into Bex's temple. She could hear the gathered caught breath of the onlookers.

So easy to imagine she was right back where she'd come from. Blood on the sand, the Catchkeep-priest on his high seat, Catchkeep's up-self twinkling overhead. The smell of the ancient dogleather Archivist-coat, in which countless girls had died. The crowd surrounding, betting on the Archivist-choosing day's outcome. Which girl would leave the lakeshore walking on her own two feet. Which one would leave in pieces. A skull for the shrine, some blood for the fields, meat for the shrine-dogs' dinner. Not so much as a name left behind.

They weren't on the lakeshore now, and the stars weren't out. It was a beautiful summer afternoon, and they were training on the reclaimed grounds of the Catchkeep-shrine after the death of the Catchkeep-priest, and the nightmare of the Archivist-choosing system—four centuries of slaughter—had died along with him.

Yet the memory remained. If anything it intensified.

She was an Archivist again and they were upstarts, they wanted her Archivist-coat and her harvesting-knife and her blood, and the Catchkeep-priest was peering down on her from his high seat, smiling pityingly, because he knew where an Archivist's road dead-ended and he knew hers didn't have far to go before it got there. The upstarts all smiled too, but their smile had no pity in it, only patience.

Her hands had gone sweaty. No sure grip on the wooden knife. Her mouth went dry, her throat tightening. Pure flight instinct crackled down her spine, her legs, her knife-hand. To flee this place. To fight her way out if she had to. To—

No.

She had to anchor herself. Get a deathgrip on the here and now. Quickly, calmly, she started listing towns in her head. Her own village and others on its north-south trade route, places where people had managed to carve their footholds into the ashy emptiness of the Waste. *Sweetwater. Sunrise. Grayfall. Refuge. Chooser's Blindside. Last Chance. Lisbet's Rest. Here.*

Sparkles dropped slowly through her field of vision like grains of sand through water, taking the nausea and dizziness with them. Then she realized she was still holding on to Bex and let go.

Intellectually she knew better, but even now, years later, some part of her still occasionally got confused. It would hit her, maybe once or twice a month, for no particular reason she could discern. Heart slamming in her chest, hands shaking, breathing like she'd just outrun a bear. It felt like a waking nightmare, or a memory, but stronger than either. A souvenir of the ghost-place, she guessed, like a scar on her mind. Ghosts were *made* of memories. It made sense enough to her that she, having been part-ghost herself, could be so easily overpowered by her own.

"Plenty of ways to do damage without drawing blood," she said firmly, wiping her palms. Clearing her throat. Drawing a steadying breath. "Next."

This time Glory charged her. Isabel knocked Glory's knife-hand aside, grabbed her arm, planted her good leg and tried to ignore the jolt of pain that shot up her bad one when she used it to sweep Glory's feet out from under her. It hurt like hell, but Glory dropped hard, harder than intended. Distantly Isabel observed her own sudden petty spike of satisfaction. *I could still hurt you if I want to.*

"In a real fight you'd kick out her knee," she said. "Wouldn't be much of a fight after that. But still." She reached to help Glory up, slower than necessary, taking advantage of that moment to quietly catch her breath. "No blood. This is important." She raked her gaze over the ex-upstarts, their steady eyes like candle-flames, their holy scars that all matched hers. "Tell me why."

"Ghosts," several ex-upstarts said at once.

"I know *you* know." She scanned them until she located Onya, the brew-mistress's daughter. Ten years old, and one of the training group's newest additions. Isabel nodded to her. "You. Tell me why."

"Blood pulls ghosts," Onya answered. "Salt too. But blood more."

"And can you put a ghost down?"

"No."

"Do you want to have to try?"

Wide-eyed, Onya shook her head. "Slag that."

"Any of you?"

Silence.

"Neither do I."

Even now, a couple of the youngest glanced up at this, surprised. Isabel couldn't blame them. All they knew of Archivist-work was stories. Hunting ghosts for clues about the old dead world Before probably looked like a fun game from a distance, and in hindsight, with somebody else's neck on the line.

"You don't remember before the ghostgrass barricades," she told Onya, as gently as she knew how. "When the Catchkeep-priest was alive. When I was Archivist."

Onya eyed her skeptically. "The barricades were there when I was little," she said. "I used to get in trouble for going up close to see."

"You were little *yesterday*," Sairy said, poking Onya in the ribs.

"Used to be," Isabel explained, "only the Archivist got ghostgrass. Just enough to hang a bundle by the door of the Archivist-house, and burn some to draw a protective ring on the ground outside."

Which made her remember the last ghost she'd caught, and the only one to ever have walked into that house on its own power. Hastily she shoved that thought away.

Keep moving forward, she warned herself. *Like a stone skipping across water. You keep moving or you sink.*

"Well, if I had ghostgrass," Onya announced, "I'd share it."

"And that's what we do now," Isabel said. "We cultivate it and make sure everyone has a share. Because now we don't have any Catchkeep-priest making sure that you can't protect yourselves, that you need an Archivist to do it for you."

"Screw that," Onya said, and a number of the others nodded agreement.

"Exactly," Isabel said. "We've put this in place and now it's our job to make sure it works. The problem is it's been working so well that some of you are forgetting what happens when it stops. You think: *I'm safe here, this is just practice, we're in the middle of town, what will happen.* But what about when you're on perimeter? What about when the ghostgrass barricades fail? You think: *they're strong, we planted them well, they keep the ghosts out and they've never been breached,* which stays true for exactly as long as we take steps to maintain them. We only stay safe if we stay smart. Vigilant. Lucky."

Several of them gestured automatically to the One Who Got Away, whose plaything luck was.

Isabel nodded to Glory. It was a thank-you and a dismissal. Glory nodded back and joined the others. "I've seen a number of you come back from training these past few months with cuts, scrapes, bloody noses," Isabel told them. "That's a problem. Bruises, sprains, broken fingers, fine. Annoying, and you'll need to call in favors on your chore rotations for a while, but you'll survive. No blood. Whatever issues you think you have in a fight, they are going to seem very small very quickly if you bring a pissed-off hungry ghost down on you. Believe me when I say you do not want to learn that the hard way."

A few of the ex-upstarts, Sairy and Kath and Bex, were nodding grimly. Others like Onya, who'd never had to stare down the barrel of that work, didn't know well enough to be afraid. With luck—and a lot of effort—they never would.

"Pair up," Isabel told them. "Practice. Blocks and counters. Get creative. You never know what's going to happen until you're up to the eyes in it. So what do you do?"

"Be ready for anything," they recited.

"When?"

"At any time."

"What else?"

"Work together," Onya said.

"Trust each other," Glory added. "Until the end."

"It's worth risking two to save one," Bex finished.

"That's right," Isabel said. "Hold on to that. There's a reason why we go over it so much. Keep it in the front of your minds when you practice. And remember: these tactics are what you use on people. Don't try this on a ghost. You're in a fight, you're breaking up a fight, someone starts up with you, you're standing perimeter and something goes bad. Okay? Now work until I say stop."

They paired off and went to it. Isabel circulated among them for a while, making suggestions, giving advice. Here and there she reached in to fix someone's attacking or blocking angle, or told someone to go harder or lighten up a little. Refusing to be envious of the ease and grace of their movement.

Back from the dead, she thought for the millionth time. *Of course I walk like a ghost.*

When her leg started complaining too loudly she sat on a rock and watched them in silence until Squirrel padded out from the back door of the Catchkeep-shine and sat at her feet. He'd been a tiny puppy when he'd lost the job he would've grown into, but somehow the idea of trailing her around was coded into his brain from generations of breeding toward that very purpose. Or maybe he just liked her. It was probably a good thing then that he didn't know she'd had to kill his parents.

Sairy had named him Squirrel. She'd thought that after four hundred years of upstarts and Archivists being chased down and terrorized by the monstrous shrine-dogs that were his ancestors, it'd be funny.

"Look at them," Isabel murmured, giving Squirrel a scratch behind the ears before setting to work massaging the knots of scar tissue in her bad leg. The ex-upstarts never ceased to amaze her. In the three years since the Catchkeep-priest's death, they'd been like plants moved into the gardens after too long spent in too-small pots. They'd stretched and grown and thrived. It was amazing how well and how smoothly they worked together when nobody was strategically, systemically setting them at each other's throats.

Do the work, the Catchkeep-priest used to tell her. *You were entrusted with the tools to do the work, and you will do the work.*

This, she thought, *is what the work is now.* Trading for apple-grafts and altar-candles. Chopping vegetables. Sweeping floors. Teaching people how to protect themselves. It was satisfying, honest, exhausting work, and in some ways it fulfilled a sense of purpose of which her Archivist-work had only ever skimmed the surface. The things she lived in fear of now were bad harvests, drought, running out of basic medicines, trade agreements with neighboring towns falling through. What others feared in her now was no worse than her displeasure if they shirked their chores. Nothing that would end up with somebody's blood on the lakeshore, somebody's skull on the shrine-wall, a dozen survivors wondering which one of them was next.

She enjoyed the work. She enjoyed the routine. She enjoyed the soreness in her muscles at the end of the day, not from dueling and murdering the living, or hunting and exploiting the dead, but from gardening, hauling water, making paper, harvesting ghostgrass, chopping firewood, drying herbs, pounding grain. Sometimes it felt like there was a hole in her and she was filling it, chore by chore, project by project, day by day. Sometimes it felt like it was working.

She sat and watched the ex-upstarts spar with townspeople and with each other, repurposing their combat skills for self-defense and the defense of their town, a small green place carved into the vast and ashen Waste under the heel of nobody. That had to count for something.

By now the sun had risen fully, the day's heat a damp weight on her head. On the edges of the field, younger children had gathered to watch the training. Periodically they were shooed away, only to scatter and regroup like crows. More than a few of them were busily whacking each other with sticks in imitation.

Isabel took off the Archivist-coat and folded it over one arm. Ran a finger idly over the stitched holes in the dogleather of it. Even years later, no trouble at all to remember which holes she'd put there, which holes she'd scrubbed the blood from and sewn shut. But there were countless more. In some places—over the heart, between the shoulderblades—the coat was more thread than leather, more mended than whole. How many Archivists must have died in it? It was less a coat than a graveyard. Despite or because of this, she hadn't yet been able to bring herself to throw it away.

"That's enough," she called, and the sparring pairs broke off, stuck their wooden knives into their belts and wiped their sweaty faces on their sleeves, awaiting further instruction. Under the awkward burden of all those expectant stares, she paused. Going from mortal enemy to mentor was a weirdness that would probably never have the edge completely ground off it. "That all looked good," she told them. "Any questions?"

"So what happens," Onya asked after a moment, "if we do pull ghosts?"

Isabel blinked. "You know, you're right. We don't really ever go over that." *We don't really ever need to,* she could have said. *Because I—*

"That's my mistake," she said instead. "We'll go over that next week."

"What if I see one *today?*"

"Grab some ghostgrass. Run like hell. Come find me and I'll deal with it."

"With that?" Onya pointed at the harvesting-knife in its sheath at Isabel's hip.

"Not if I can help it," Isabel said.

"Then how do you know if it still works?"

Isabel paused. Then, in a sudden access of honesty: "I don't."

"Then why do you still have—"

"Next week, okay?" Cutting her off fast because it was either that or ignore her. Answering that question—genuinely answering it—wasn't an option. Isabel struggled to soften her tone. "I promise."

"Here," Sairy said. "I got this." She reached in and tied a long braid of ghostgrass blades around Onya's ponytail. "See? Nothing touching you like that. I could *throw* a ghost at you right now and it'd bounce off."

Onya lit up like a warn-fire. "*Can* you?"

Sairy swatted her. "No."

"Can I see the knife then?"

"Fine," Isabel said, relenting. "Stand back." The harvesting-knife had a blade the length of Isabel's forearm, more of a hilt than a handle, and a guard like a sword. Because it used to *be* a sword, she knew now, and long ago it had been broken, tapering the remaining blade unevenly.

"What's this?" Onya asked, poking at the shiny blue-black synthetic wrapping of the grip.

"Before-stuff," Sairy said.

"It's so *smooth.*" She ran her finger back and forth, then withdrew.

Isabel glanced over the others. "Nothing else? Okay. Dismissed."

They broke and wandered off in ones and twos, and when they all were gone Isabel stood and made her way across the grounds toward the shrine, Squirrel padding along beside her.

Halfway there, she slung the Archivist-coat down on the sun-bleached grass and stopped to tie up her hair. She hadn't cut it in a while and it was just long enough to be gathered in a string and kept off her neck. There'd been a few years when she'd almost forgotten what color her own hair was, it was so interbraided with the shorn-off hair of every upstart she'd killed, and the Archivist she'd defeated even before that—and besides, it wasn't like she'd had a mirror on her wall to see herself in. She'd cut off her braids down in the ghost-place and never missed them once. Her own hair had come in thick and brown. It could've been piss-yellow and glowing for all she cared. She hadn't seen her reflection in ages.

She picked the coat back up and kicked her way through a late patch of suns-and-moons overgrowing the path. Too close to autumn for suns, but the moons went up in an explosion of silver-white fluff, almost the exact color of a weakened ghost. Ignoring the spike of pain in her leg, she kicked them toward the grassy side of the path. More fluff meant more seeds, more seeds landing on viable ground meant more edible leaves next spring. *They say people used to wish on these things,* she thought, and kicked harder, sudden anger driving off the pain. *They should've known better.*

Chapter Two

Dinner was flatbread, soup, hard-boiled eggs, and their tiny daily ration from the town garden's plum tree, sliced and passed around and supplemented with the double pocketful of wild blackberries Meg had gathered on her way back from her chore rotation in the town gardens. Usually there were apples, but lightning had struck Sweetwater's prized orchard last spring, and it was a couple acres of blackened stumps and scorchweed now. Nothing they could eat.

It was Sairy's and Isabel's turn to stay in the Catchkeep-shrine common room and set that long table, which they did while the others trickled in from their afternoon chores. All seven ex-upstarts that remained in Sweetwater, along with a few of the townspeople from the training session that afternoon. Onya was there, a couple of kids her age in tow. Isabel recognized Andrew, the songkeeper's grandson, but not the other.

"Ugh," said Lissa, sniffing as she walked in. "Onion soup."

"At least it's not bug soup," Jen said, and that shut her up. Lissa knew what happened when a harvest ran low, and with the apples gone, it would be a hungry winter.

"Or dog soup," Sairy added. "Cover your ears, Squirrel."

Now they all went quiet, as they still did three years later at any reference to any aspect of their lives under the Catchkeep-priest. They all still remembered drowning those extra puppies, the ones that didn't make the cut to become shrine-dogs.

"I'll go check the bread," Meg said loudly, and normalcy resumed.

Isabel stood sweating by the fire, ladling soup while bits of the ex-upstarts' conversation skidded over her. Glory complained about the

10

weather. Bex had heard a rumor about some bit of Waste-relic stuff someone had left as an offering at the Catchkeep-shrine. Kath was trying to negotiate a preemptive trade of tomorrow's chore tokens because she had a freshly sprained ankle and orders from the midwife to keep her weight off it. Lissa was convinced that Catchkeep was trying to warn her of something important, because when she'd been on shrine duties that morning, the candles in Catchkeep's statue had blown out, one by one, in no wind at all. Jen had a bit of news about the high seats of Sweetwater trying to replant the burned orchard with grafts traded up on a barter run from Grayfall. Sairy hoped the grafts would bear red apples. Jen hoped for green. Friendly debate ensued. Then Meg came back in with an armload of flatbreads and got practically mobbed.

"We should get one of those grafts when they come in," Bex said through a mouthful of food.

"I nominate you," Sairy said, leveling her little garlic-peeling knife at Jen.

Jen choked a little on the hot pepper stem she was chewing. "Okay, first thing? Unlike some of us, *Sairy*, I'm pretty busy with harvest inventory."

Sairy looked elaborately unimpressed.

"Second thing—"

"She likes you."

"She doesn't like any of us," Lissa said, spidering her fingers at Onya and her friends. "We're *scary.*"

"Jen got her to send people over to build the new oven that time," Sairy said. "Didn't you, Jen."

Lissa shrugged. "True."

Jen dropped her face into her hands, began massaging her temples.

"What would she want for it?" Meg asked.

"Paper," Jen muttered. "That's my best guess anyway."

Meg groaned.

"Well," said Sairy, "how bad do we want that graft?"

"Our own apples?" Bex said, making a face like Sairy was asking her how fond she was of breathing. "Bad enough."

"Eggs?" Kath suggested, drumming her fingers on the table-edge. "Honey? Wine?" Sairy and Lissa both turned to her in horrified unison. "Okay, okay," she said. "Not wine. Isabel? Thoughts?"

They glanced over at Isabel, who was busily decimating a plum with slow ferocious precision. Perfectly uniform slices slivered from her knife-blade. It was a moment before she felt their eyes on her and glanced up. "Hmm?"

"Where the hell were you?" Sairy demanded in mock outrage, but her eyes were sharp with concern. She wasn't Isabel's second-in-command for nothing, but some days she felt to Isabel more like a caretaker. She was the one who'd told Isabel to recite lists in her head when the memories threatened to overtake her, who tried to rig Isabel's chore rotations with easy work on days when the ghost-place's toll was too much for her to lightly bear. When Isabel was Archivist, Sairy had been the only upstart who'd ever shown her kindness.

But there was so much that Isabel couldn't bring herself to tell anyone, second-in-command or no. She couldn't even begin to explain how she'd traveled into the ghost-place, and to what purpose, and in whose company, and why she'd come back out alive. All Sairy or anyone knew was that Isabel had vanished, out on the edge of the Waste, in the dead of winter. By the time she came back, on foot, across the snow, she'd been within spitting distance of starvation, dehydration, exsanguination, death by exposure. Horribly wounded, though the wounds had been closed by some unrecognizable means, and showed no sign of turning septic. Nearly bled out, nonetheless. And she wouldn't talk about what had hurt her, or who had healed her, or where she'd been. But she'd come back.

Which in itself was a puzzle. She'd tried to escape several times before, and failed—but this time, she'd finally succeeded. And, for some often-guessed-at reason, she'd *chosen* to return.

Not only that, but she'd come back knowing the truth behind the upstart-Archivist system. Secrets she had no way of learning out in the Waste. And armed with that truth she'd torn the system down.

She's heard them talking, from time to time, in voices they thought were beyond her earshot. Among their theories: she'd run off with a scav crew; she'd discovered a town unknown to Sweetwater; she'd died out there that winter and was now actually a ghost, returned among them to atone for her bloodyhanded past.

You're not a ghost, went a voice in her head. *You're in-between.*

"Apples," she said, ignoring it. "Right?"

"Right," Sairy echoed, side-eyeing her like the world's most suspicious hawk.

"I don't care what you people say," Bex said. "I want that graft and I'm going to get it."

Jen produced a pad of brittle paper, its handmade stitching frayed. Finding the page she wanted, she ran one fingertip down it. "Well, we have surplus vinegar, beeswax, nettle-yarn, and a whole jug of that corpseroot ink that didn't really take. We—"

"We won't have surplus nettle-yarn when we need it for winter clothes," Meg pointed out.

Jen's pointer finger blurred through her notebook. "That," she said, "is a thing that needs to go on the rotation *yesterday.*"

"On it," Glory said. She'd already brought over the bowl from the rotation wall and was carefully charcoaling something onto a blank chore token that looked like a thing the baker's cat might cough up.

"That's *yarn?*" Sairy asked.

"Oh look," Glory said, lobbing the token at her. "Our first volunteer."

"Like hell."

"I'll figure this out later," Jen said. "What's in the bowl for tomorrow?"

"Nettle-yarn," said Sairy, dropping the token in the bowl.

"Give," Kath said. "I can do that with my foot up."

"I call perimeter," Sairy said.

"Full or half?" Jen asked.

Sairy rooted around until she came up with a token. "Half."

"And?"

Sairy made a face and blind-grabbed another token from the bowl. Looked at it. "No."

"Well?"

Sairy heaved a sigh and tossed the token on the table. It had a little drawing of a log of firewood. Except that, now that the orchard was gone, there *was* no firewood, and flammable alternatives must be sought. Sometimes that meant surplus ghostgrass. Sometimes it meant dried goat shit from the cheesemaker's yard. Grumbling theatrically, Sairy hung the token from her hook on the chore rotation wall. "Best luck," Kath sang sweetly after her.

Glory drew water-hauling and paper-making, Meg drew shrine duties and food-preserving, Lissa drew full kitchen, Kath drew gardens and promptly traded it for Meg's food-preserving token, and Isabel drew bread-baking and ghostgrass. Jen did not draw a token. She was head of barter and inventory, and her chores were unchanging.

Everyone went to hang their tokens on the rotation wall. Isabel was a moment in joining them. As always, her attention snagged on that ghostgrass token, its symbol like five long knives bundled. Odd that such a tiny thing could make her feel such keen—displacement.

Sudden cramping in her chest, where a thread had once connected her to her own half-dead body and been severed. As if Isabel was not so much her true self as she was the husk her true self had ripped free from. As if the Wasp part of her remained down there, in the ghost-place, tearing itself into crumbs, scattering itself into a path that no one would ever follow.

"Trade," Sairy said, appearing beside her. It didn't sound like a question.

"For *firewood*?" Isabel said, snapping out of it. "No chance. Enjoy."

"No, I'll . . . " Sairy eyed the rotation wall. "I'll get someone to trade with you. I'll call in a favor. I'll figure it out. Keep the bread one. Give me the ghostgrass one. Do, I don't know, do nettle-yarn with Kath."

"You do know I can still walk, right?"

"It's not that." Sairy pulled a long-suffering face. "Look, you want perimeter instead? Plenty of walking."

"I'm fine."

"You also haven't done ghostgrass in a while."

"So?"

"So it makes you weird."

"It—"

"Watch this." Keeping her eyes on Isabel, Sairy raised her voice to reach the room. "Does doing ghostgrass make Isabel weird?"

General assent.

"See?"

"Listen, I'm fine," Isabel said. "In fact, I'm going to get it out of the way right now so you stop worrying. Deal?"

"In the *dark?*"

"The moon's out."

"Not a full one."

"She can walk, she can see—what *can't* she do?"

"I'll come with you."

"No."

Something in her voice stopped Sairy dead in her tracks. "It's just," Sairy said quietly, "we work together now, right? Worth risking two to save one? Aren't you the one who taught us that?"

"You don't need to save me, Sairy." *You couldn't if you tried.*

Alone, she made her way around back of the shrine, across the field where they'd trained that afternoon, along the path that skirted the western edge of Sweetwater near the burned orchard, heading out along the ridge toward the Waste.

It wasn't Catchkeep's time yet. Unlike the others She was visible year-round, but right now the sixteen stars of Her up-self were halfway hidden behind the Hill across the way and out of sight. In a couple of months She'd swing down slightly, visible from Sweetwater but not from here, lashing Her tail to bring the autumn winds over the lake, and in years past it was then, when She was Her lowest and closest over the water, that Her Archivists were chosen. By that time, the leaves would be drying on the branch and rattling like the Chooser's cape of bones, and the Chooser Herself wouldn't be far behind.

The Ragpicker was setting now, hanging upside-down as if suspended by one foot, His head dipping down into the Waste where it belonged. And the One Who Got Away had gotten away, not to return until next winter's collapse into spring.

Carrion Boy stood ascendant, partway turned toward where Ember Girl was just beginning to climb up out of the Waste and into the sky. He reached out to Her one-handed, either to assist Her in Her climb or strike Her down. On that point the stories were unclear.

Isabel walked on.

There were four places in Sweetwater where ghosts were known to appear. Four of the silvery ghost-passages Isabel had come to think of as *waypoints*.

Around the well. Beside the snapped bridge where the suns-and-moons grew thickest. Surrounding the heavy round door leading down into the old Before-tunnels beneath town. And up Execution Hill, where Isabel's journey into the ghost-place had begun. Places where two worlds rubbed thin against each other, rupturing into something like doorways, passable by the dead and—as she'd learned—if conditions were exactly right, the nearly-dead as well.

It had been a job of some weeks to find, uproot, and transplant enough ghostgrass that each one of these waypoints now stood behind its own waving knee-high sea of silvery gray grassblades, a field at least ten long paces by two. The local wildlife—deer and squirrels mostly—seemed pretty uninterested in those tough gray grassblades, so the major problem with maintaining the transplants was erosion and desiccation as day by day the Waste fought to reclaim its own.

The Execution Hill waypoint had proven the hardest to barricade, cut as it was into the sheer face of a cliff almost eighty yards up, accessible only by a busted path and a narrow ledge. But the ex-upstarts had relayed dirt up there dutifully and spread it on the ledge so the ghostgrass could take root.

If she tilted her head back and squinted, Isabel could just make out that waypoint from the fields below. Among all that black rock, a lonely silver glimmering. Blades of ghostgrass waved before it in the breeze, eclipsing and returning that pale cold light.

No way could she get up there to check on that one. The path was much too hazardous. She'd nearly died climbing up there before, and that was years ago, without all the scars the ghost-place had laid on her. The bone-deep stab wound in her right calf. The shoulder that'd been yanked from its socket with huge force and hadn't been quite right since. The slash that nearly disemboweled her. The pale pink starburst on one brown forearm where the deliquescing sludge of a dying ghost had left a spray of chemical burn straight through the skin and into the meat below, tracing the vague outline of the ghost-teeth that had dissolved there. The place over one temple where something nearly crushed her skull. Not to mention the unseen internal damage from having left her body behind while she wandered the ghost-place—at the top of Execution Hill, for solid weeks, in the dead of winter. Exposure, dehydration, her body digesting its own proteins for lack of food.

She wasn't climbing the Hill today, but that still left her three barricades she could check. The hatch to the tunnels was closest, then the bridge, and she could hit the well on her way back in toward town.

So she followed the path around toward the town gardens. Around the garden fence, past the gate, and toward the mountain of rubble that marked the southernmost corner of the perimeter.

She hadn't been out here in months, but it looked much the same as she recalled. Fence, weeds, seventy-foot heap of metal and brick and heat-fused glass, and the raggedy hem of the Waste beyond, the ash of it rendered plush and blue and peaceful in the moonlight.

Wasn't fooling her. That way was death. The path from town dead-ended at the gardens for a reason.

She reached the ghostgrass barricade around the far edge of the ruins and stood a moment, struck by the tarnished silver color of the ghostgrass by night. Weird that a plant so dead-looking could smell so green. She really hadn't been out here in a while.

Impossible to get a better look at the actual waypoint from here, but no matter. This was the only one of Sweetwater's four waypoints that was not within actual sight of its barricade. Instead it lay below. Past the ghostgrass barricade, buried somewhere under corpseroot overgrowth, was the ancient heavy round hatch that led down into the busted tunnels under Sweetwater.

That used to be a ghosthunting spot, though never one much frequented by ghosts, and so mostly avoided by Archivists as well. But if a ghost did wander through the waypoint, down the tunnels, and up the ladder to the surface, the barricade still stood between it and Sweetwater, and the ghostgrass would burn it down to shapeless silver slag before it so much as set foot on the path. Never mind that most ghosts were shapeless silver slag to begin with. She'd only ever seen one ghost strong enough to even think of attempting a stunt like that.

This barricade was nearest the Waste of the four, and the one that needed the most regular shoring up with new transplants, so she made sure to inspect it carefully. First she paced out the length of it and noted the distance—twelve paces—then stood at the near edge of it and took three long steps in among the grassblades, which brought her to the other side. There the ruins opened out into a kind of little cave of fallen brick and ancient trash and thickly growing corpseroot, its thorns the length of her fingers. Not about to venture in there and scratch her legs to bleeding so near a ghost-place waypoint, she retreated. Pulling out her notebook, she charcoaled in *ruins barricade twelve by three looks solid.* Then she pocketed the notebook and charcoal and began to walk away.

And stopped. There was someone behind her.

Slowly, carefully, knife-hand on the hilt, she turned.

Nothing there. Just that sea of ghostgrass, dead still now that the breeze had gone, and the bunched shadow of the ruin above.

Still, the back of her neck was prickling. Her palms had gone pins-and-needles. No—not *palms*—only the one holding the harvesting-knife. She had the weirdest most sudden compulsion to walk back through the barricade and toward the hatch beyond, corpseroot or no.

She glanced down at the harvesting-knife. She knew, though she couldn't begin to explain how, that it had been trying to turn her around.

It wasn't *moving* exactly. It wasn't *really* rattling in its dogleather sheath, tapping at her hipbone, prodding her to draw it. It wasn't *actually* trying to get her attention. It only *seemed* like it was, in a way she couldn't begin to describe. Her fingers itched to pull it clear of her belt and—what? Follow it around like some kind of slag-for-brains until it brought her—where? Around in circles, like a dog chasing its tail. *Like ghosts*, she thought. *Like stars.*

Down in the ghost-place, that knife had helped her find the ghost of Catherine Foster. Its methods for doing that were strikingly similar to whatever the hell it was doing now. Mysteriously vanishing from its sheath and appearing yards away, impossibly, where a passage through the ghost-place had been hidden. Falling to the ground where a passage could be made. Catching on things to stop her from walking past a passage she couldn't see. Getting her to where she had to go.

She knew the knife was Foster's broken sword, buried for countless centuries before being given to the first Archivist. Maybe now, she reckoned, it was trying to compel Isabel back toward those ghost-passages, back to Foster, wherever she was in the ghost-place. For all the sense that made.

But Isabel wasn't in the ghost-place now. And she wasn't mostly a ghost herself. This was just a memory she carried, the way your hand would cramp after gripping something too tightly too long. A thing to make note of, maybe, and move on.

Isabel let go of the knife, scrubbing her palm on her pant-leg until the prickling subsided. Took out the notebook again. Flipped to a different page, on which she'd drawn a crude map. The C shape of the ridge encircling Sweetwater with the lake in the opening. Town, orchard, gardens, ruin. Four Xs marked barricades. The whole page was littered with dozens of dots, a nonsense constellation. Now she added another, just before the X of the barricade nearest the ruins.

Under her notes on the barricade she considered adding *harvesting-knife doing its thing again,* then thought better of it, pocketed the notebook, and walked back toward town. She'd check the barricade by the well and save the one under the broken bridge for tomorrow. Exhaustion was slamming into her now in huge soft waves and three barricades in one night was more than her body was going to handle without full-on mutiny.

It was the middle of the night by the time she'd finished checking the well barricade, and the streets of Sweetwater were empty. Isabel dragged ass back to the Catchkeep-shrine and let herself in as quietly as she could.

Past the long table she went, past the chore rotation wall, down the double row of curtained sleeping-alcoves and into hers, the next-to-last on the right before the big room at the end of the hall that once housed the Catchkeep-priest's chambers and now served as a public common room for townspeople who needed someplace to stay. It was full dark inside the Catchkeep-shrine, but she'd walked this hallway so often she could do it blind.

She was practically falling over anyway by the time she collapsed onto her cot. But there was something she had to do before she slept. Something she did every night, no matter how busy or tired or sick. All her life had been steeped in four centuries of ritual, after all. This was one that was hers alone.

So she got up, and lit the lamp, and opened the chest of field notes.

She'd destroyed the original field notes long ago. In an attempt to sabotage the Archivist-upstart system in her absence, she'd smashed all the ghost-catching jars and burned four hundred years' worth of field notes before venturing into the ghost-place to earn her freedom.

What was in this chest was what had come after. The notes she'd taken on her own terms. After the Catchkeep-priest's death she didn't capture or destroy ghosts anymore unless they left her no options, but until she'd fine-tuned the ghostgrass barricades she'd still sketched the ghosts that wandered in through Sweetwater's waypoints. Like most ghosts, once they'd pushed through they hadn't done much. Just pace their circuits, or mindlessly repeat their dying words over and over. They'd looked very different and very alike, and she'd sketched them all and recognized none.

And then the barricades had gone up, and there were no new field notes, because no more ghosts ever made it through.

She liked to study those old notes sometimes. Some of them she'd taken herself. Some of them had the names of other ghostgrass-rotation regulars—Kath, Lissa, Bex—signed at the bottom.

When she'd been Archivist, the oldest sheet of paper in those field notes had been a list of questions she was supposed to ask a ghost, if she ever found a specimen that could answer them. *Name of specimen. Age of specimen. Description of surrounding environment during specimen's lifetime. Place and manner of specimen's death. Manner of the world's death, if known, in as much detail as possible.* And so on.

The oldest sheet of paper in this new box of field notes was dedicated to the only two ghosts she'd ever found who could've answered almost every question on that list, if it'd occurred to her at the time to ask them.

She didn't want to pull that page out now. Really she should have burned it when the ghostgrass barricades went up and nothing on that page was allowed to matter anymore.

Looking at it now made her feel gutpunched. So she made herself look.

Around the margin were little sketches, no larger than an inch or two. A creature that looked like a dog, but was not a dog. A broken sword, and a whole sword next to it. A bridge over a black river with a meadow beyond. A crossroads of wide streets like a canyon bottom between the sheer cliffs of buildings taller than ten Sweetwaters stacked up. An open door with nothing through it. A whirlwind or cyclone. A tiny house in a sea of grass, its chimney throwing a scarf of smoke. A round metal door set into the ground in the middle of a snowfield. A maze made of thorns, hung with faces and hands. A wispy thing that looked like a spiderweb. A smooth thing that looked like a pill.

In the center of the page stood two figures, identically dressed: dark pants, dark jackets, dark boots, a belt with a sword and a gun in it. A man and a woman. He was a little taller than she was, and her hair was a little shorter than his. Isabel's years of sketching field notes still hadn't prepared her to exactly capture the expressions on their faces, so she'd given up and they just looked out at her blankly, as if waiting for her to do better.

Above the woman's head she'd written *catherine foster*. Above the man's head she'd written nothing.

She sat and looked at that page for a few seconds, rubbing at the old wound in her leg. "Not today," she said to the drawing, or to herself. Slowly, deliberately, she turned the paper over and slid it under the bottom of the pile.

"Can't sleep either, huh?" Sairy said from the doorway.

"Not really," Isabel said, lowering the lid of the chest and smoothing it unconsciously with both hands. There was too much in her head. It wouldn't all fit. Somewhere, something had to give. She wished she knew where the plug was so she could pull it out and let it all drain away.

"Still not going to tell me who they are," Sairy said, raising her eyebrows at the now-closed chest, the field notes within. How long had she been standing there? "Are you."

"You know who they are," Isabel said tiredly. "They're in the field notes. They're ghosts."

"You know what I mean. It's the most detailed drawing in that box. You drew all that . . . *stuff* around the edges." Sairy made an exasperated gesture toward the chest. "You wrote their *names*, for Chooser's sake."

One of their names, Isabel thought. A twinge in her chest where the thread used to be. Not as bad as it'd been earlier, and anyway she was used to it.

"Fine," Sairy said. "Just . . . if you want to talk. About anything. I'm here, okay?"

"Don't worry about it," Isabel said. "I'm . . . " She trailed off, re-alizing she had no idea how to accurately finish that sentence. "Don't worry about it."

"Sure."

"I'm just tired."

"Then go to sleep," Sairy said, and left.

Isabel cast one last glance at the chest of field-notes—*idiot*—and blew out the lamp. In the dark she dropped into sleep like a stone into deep water.

At first she didn't realize she was dreaming, only that she was still walking in the moonlit fields outside of town. Making her looping circuit between waypoints in the exact manner of a ghost pacing out its last moments, walking the length of the same invisible tether.

In the dream she was holding the harvesting-knife out in front of her with both hands, following it across the fields like some Before-story's water-witch. Like the knife was dragging her out of the safe zone and out into the burnt-out heart of the Waste, and in the dream she never once glanced back.

She'd had this dream before, and all at once she recognized it. Soon there'd come the part when a voice would startle her attention up from the knife and the dust at her feet. It was a voice she'd know anywhere, a voice she'd long since blown her chance to ever hear again.

What is it exactly that you're doing? that voice would ask her, and then she'd know she was dreaming, so she'd wake up and pull on her boots and stick the knife in her belt and throw herself so hard into her chores that she'd be too tired to dream again tomorrow.

What—the voice began to ask, and then there came a noise like the whole world being crumpled like a sheet of paper in a fist, and she woke up to the sound of screaming.

Isabel had hurled herself out of the sleeping-alcove and into the hall before she'd given conscious thought to getting her legs under her, let alone spent time preparing her injuries to bear her weight. Her knees felt rubbery. No—there was something wrong with the floor?

It was too dark to see. Something in the kitchen was crashing noisily. Like Catchkeep's Hunt was barrelling through, leaving nothing standing as it swept on by. Somebody—Kath?—was praying loudly to the Chooser, her voice wrung strange with terror. Somebody else was crying.

"Sairy!" Isabel called. Toppling against the wall. Hanging onto it as it *shook* like it wanted to be rid of her. Stones grated together, then went still. "Jen! Somebody report!"

"Isabel!"

"Sairy?"

"What the shit just happened?"

"I don't know. I'm going to find a lamp."

"Stay put, I'll come to you."

"I'm fine. Is anyone hurt?"

Something else fell over with a splintery crash, this time from the direction of the altar.

"Jen?"

"I'm here," Jen called from down the hall. "Kath, stop it, it's okay." Then, louder: "I think it's over!"

Isabel hitched up breath. Her legs were jelly. In the wake of the adrenaline dump, her everything was spent. "Everyone report!"

"I've got Kath and Meg here," Jen called.

"I'm good," Lissa shouted. "What was that?"

"I don't know," Isabel yelled back. Feeling her way along the wall, back into the alcove, she lit her lamp on the fifth try with trembling hands. "Where's Bex and Glory?"

"I think Bex ran outside," Sairy called. "Bex!"

"Got the lamp," Isabel said. "Glory, report?"

Nothing. Just muffled crying, coming from farther down the hall.

"Glory, are you hurt?"

No reply.

"Stay there, Glory, I'm on my way."

"I've got her," Sairy called from the direction of the Catchkeep-priest's old chambers. "Her arm's hurt but she's in one piece."

They all converged in the common area by the light of Isabel's lamp. The long table hadn't moved, but everything else looked like

Ember Girl had taken the room between Her hands and given it a shake. Chore tokens had scattered to the far wall. Probably half of their clay bowls had broken. Drying bunches of whatnot—garlic, come-what-may, ghostgrass, wild mint—had fallen from the ceiling. Something unseen crunched underfoot. There was a general smell of vinegar.

Sairy sat Glory at the table, then lit a second lamp from Isabel's and proceeded to inspect Glory's arm, the elbow of which was already swelling. "This is nothing," she said brightly. "Look, the bone's not even popping through."

"You're a world of help," Glory gritted through her teeth.

"I try." Sairy beamed at her. "Seriously, let's give this a minute, make sure it's stopped. Then I'll walk you to the midwife. She'll get you fixed right up."

Meantime, Jen was making the rounds of the room, squinting into her notebook and moaning in agitation. "This jug of vinegar is cracked," she announced. "And some of the wine, and—what *is*—there are *seeds everywhere*." She bent down and raised something miniscule to the light, then dropped to her knees, aghast, and scrabbled at the floor. "My *carrots*—"

"Not too bad in here," Bex called from the altar-room.

"I thought you were outside!" Sairy said.

Bex emerged from the altar-room, a chipped skull and a green stone in her hands. "A few of them fell off the wall," she explained, failing to fit the stone back in behind the skull's teeth. "Sorry," she muttered at it.

It came to Isabel that they all were unconsciously touching their scarred cheeks as they watched this operation.

"And the altar?" Lissa asked.

Bex shrugged. "Couple candles broke, and I had to pick up the offerings. The statue's okay. What the hell was that anyway?"

"Earthquake, I think," Jen said. "I've never . . . been in one before." She shivered. "I didn't like it."

They fell silent, and Isabel realized she could hear noise from the town now. A general yelling and rushing. Something large and distant let out one long slow creak and fell. The Catchkeep-shrine was one of two sturdy stone buildings in all of Sweetwater, and even here she'd felt the stones of the wall grinding as the earth cracked and buckled under—

Her veins ran ice. *The ghostgrass.*

She was halfway out the door before she realized she'd gotten up. She turned and Sairy was holding her sleeve.

"Isabel," Sairy was saying. "Isabel, wait."

Isabel shook her off. "I have to check the barricades."

"You sit," Sairy told her. "I got them. Kath, you're in charge of Glory."

"But you can't—"

"I'm just going to check them." Already tying braids of ghostgrass around her wrists and ankles, already stuffing more bundled grassblades into her pockets, already checking her hands and arms for scratches. "If there's trouble, I'll get you."

It should be me, Isabel wanted to say. *If ghosts came through, I need to see them, I need to know if—*

She clamped down on that thought like it was a wound and she was trying to stop it bleeding. "Report anything unusual," she said instead.

Something in her voice betrayed her. "Anything in particular?" Sairy asked.

"Anything unusual." Watching Sairy go through a brief series of stretches, preparing for the run to come. "And be careful."

"Always am," Sairy replied, and was gone.

Isabel stood a moment staring into the dark outside the shrine. Like she could see the waypoints from here. The damage to the ghostgrass barricades. Whatever might be pushing its way out of those silver slashes from the ghost-world into this.

If you want to come with us, went a voice in her head, *it'll be—*

"Well," she said briskly, louder than necessary, "let's get Glory to the midwife and see who else needs our help." *Keep moving or sink,* she commanded herself, and lifted the lamp. "Looks like we start early today."

They left the shrine in a group. Isabel leading, Meg and Kath walking Glory, Lissa and Jen pushing Jen's market-cart. Bex stayed behind to tidy the altar and ready the shrine for the townspeople who would doubtless arrive later to pray before the Catchkeep-statue, as they always did in time of calamity.

They stuck together, traveling in a weird small straggly pack, not knowing what they'd find. At least the nearly full moon meant that they could leave the lamp, and the sun would rise soon.

On Jen's cart were some bandages, a jug of water and a cup, and as many bundles of ghostgrass as they could gather. Also a recent experiment of Glory's: a little pot of ghostgrass crushed with oil into a paste. The barricades had made it pretty much impossible to test the efficacy of that ghostgrass salve, but they'd all smeared a little on their skin for protection before heading out into the dark.

They got Glory to the midwife. Hung fresh ghostgrass bundles from damaged houses. Helped the cheesemaker rescue a goat trapped beneath a fallen shed. Bandaged a cut on the songkeeper's arm and tied a five-strand ghostgrass braid around it in accordance with open wound protocol. Assisted injured townspeople back to the midwife's, clearing space on the cart and pushing them one by one. Gave the water-boilers fresh ghostgrass bundles to ensure safe passage to the lake. Let Onya walk with them so that her mother could help her neighbors repair a wall. Jen tasked Onya with filling the water-cup for anyone who looked thirsty, which she did until the jug ran dry. There wasn't much to fix, for which they all gave thanks to the One Who Got Away.

Isabel buried herself in the work, and by midday Sairy was back. "Everything looks good," she told Isabel. "Nothing to report."

"No ghosts?"

Sairy shook her head. "No anything. The barricades are sound." She gestured at the hills that cupped Sweetwater in their center. "I think the ridge protected us from worse."

But the sun was high by then, and Sairy was drenched with sweat and breathing hard, so Isabel sent her back to the shrine for food and water and rest.

"I'll take her," Jen said. "I have to check on something anyway."

"Everything okay?" Isabel asked her.

"I think so?" Jen replied. "Trade run from Stormbreak was supposed to show at dawn. Maybe the quake hit them too." She looked momentarily confused, which was a very un-Jen-like expression. She glanced at Isabel questioningly. "As far as that? And still reach here?"

Isabel had no idea, and shook her head.

"I have to talk to Ruby. One of the other high seats if I have to. Someone might've heard something."

Obviously fretting, which was also unlike Jen. Though it made sense. Sweetwater and Stormbreak traded heavily in all seasons. Jen and the other trade supervisors would have to scramble fast to open new lanes of barter with other towns if Stormbreak failed.

After Jen left, Isabel thought no more of it, and for the next couple of days Jen didn't bring it up again. There was a sense of watchful waiting about her, though, and the next day when Isabel asked after the Stormbreak trade run, Jen looked so distraught that Isabel didn't ask again.

Then, a few days after the earthquake, Jen arrived late for dinner. Stealthily, quietly, looking like she was being tracked by something she'd have to sneak her way past to live.

Even more alarming, Ruby was with her.

The high seats never set foot in the Catchkeep-shrine's common room. The relationship between Sweetwater and the ex-upstarts and -Archivist just didn't work that way. The town and shrine coexisted peacefully, trading and helping each other in small ways. This—Ruby herself walking behind an ex-upstart into the shrine common room in full view of everyone—was new.

"Jen?" Sairy asked. "Where were you? What's going on?"

"We don't know yet," Ruby answered for her. "Jen, show them."

And Jen led them all back through the common room, back down the hallway of sleeping-alcoves, into the large room that used to be the Catchkeep-priest's chambers. That room had a window that opened off the back of the shrine and commanded a clear view across the shrine-yards: past Meg's berry-garden, Kath's chicken-coop, the little lean-to shed where they made paper, the clay oven for their flatbreads, all the way to Lake Sweetwater, which was now sparkling orange in the setting sun.

Jen pointed at something. Isabel squinted.

Off in the distance above the low buildings she could just make them out, across who knew how many miles of rock and ash and nothing, almost invisible against the sunset. If she hadn't been looking for them, she'd never have noticed them there.

Plumes of smoke, or dust, thin as threads at this distance. Easily a dozen, probably more, breaking up to nothing before they vanished against the last of the early-evening stars.

"Raiders," Jen said.

Chapter Three

R uby was waiting for her in the altar-room, accompanied by the
other two high seats, Jacen and Yulia. With them was a woman
Isabel didn't recognize until she mentally subtracted the dirt and
dried blood from her face, mentally added several pounds of water weight lost to dehydration. Cora, the trader due from Stormbreak, arriving late. Late and, oddly, alone. Usually traders traveled
in groups. Greater carrying weight, safety in numbers. Yet here was
Cora, no sign of her party in sight. She looked like she'd been tied
to the back of a cart and dragged through the Waste. *Maybe*, Isabel
thought, thinking of those fires in the distance, *she was.* Cora was in
the process of gulping down what was probably not her first cup of
soup when Isabel came in.

Squirrel was already in the altar-room when Isabel arrived, sitting before Cora and eyeing her and her soup clinically. Isabel had
been on the receiving end of that stare before. It was nearly at eye-
level and deeply disconcerting.

Sairy and Jen entered with her. She told the others to stay in
the common room. They were up to their eyeballs in some kind of
trouble, that was clear enough. She just wasn't sure yet how much
deeper it was likely to get. Raiders or no, what were the high seats
doing *here?*

"Wasp," said Jacen, and nodded to her in greeting.

Ruby stared at him.

"Right. Sorry. Isabel. Old habits."

Isabel ignored this. "Tell me," she said, "what you know."

"First," Ruby said, "not a word of what we are about to tell you
leaves this room. Is that clear?"

High seat or no, she said this carefully. The atmosphere of the Catchkeep-shrine still carried that weight of expectation, like it was holding you to a certain standard that you'd fall short of at your peril.

Nonetheless, Sairy bristled. "Isn't it you who should be asking for our trust?" she asked. Gesturing to the altar-room around them, its scavenge-statue and wall of skulls, as if to say: *this is our roof you're under.*

"Not now," Isabel told her. To Ruby: "Must be one hell of a raiding party." She made herself smile. "If you're after *our* help."

Cora glanced up from her soup. "Raiding party?" Her laugh was more like a choke. "Well. Aren't we optimistic. Try a raiding *army.*"

Ruby shushed her with a gesture. "That earthquake a few nights ago? We only caught the edge of it. It hit . . . other towns . . . much harder."

Sairy's eyebrows shot up. "That was the *edge* of it?"

"That was nothing," Cora said. "You had to fix what, a couple houses?"

"Other towns," Jacen said carefully, shooting Cora a look, "aren't going to be able to be fixed."

"First the orchard, now this," Yulia said as if to herself, shaking her head sadly.

Isabel wasn't used to seeing the high seats like this. Like there was something they'd be chasing the Chooser's cape just by saying. "Other towns." She shook her head, confused. Looked at Cora. "We're talking about Stormbreak, yes?"

"No." Ruby seemed, alarmingly, almost wistful. She took a deep breath like a lake scrap-diver and spoke. "Clayspring."

This tore from Sairy a sound of pure alarm. Jen, apparently not having been brought up to speed on that detail of Cora's news, gasped. Even Isabel was taken aback a second.

Not every town was sworn to Catchkeep. Each constellation in the sky, each god's up-self, had at least one town that kept its worship. Grayfall to Ember Girl. Last Chance to the One Who Got Away. Sunrise to the Chooser.

Clayspring—

"Carrion Boy's people," Isabel said.

Ruby nodded. Her face was like the midwife's, confirming an awful prognosis.

"But what—"

"Their town's gone," said Cora. "Their shrine, their crops. There were fires. We could see them from a half day's walk. What do you *think* they're after?"

"Good," Yulia spat. "Let it burn. Their *shrine.*"

Cora shook her head. "They'll take yours. And your gardens. And your houses. And when the garden runs out, and winter comes . . . "

She didn't finish that sentence. She didn't need to. They'd all heard the stories. What happened to a town claimed by Carrion Boy's worshippers. What happened to its people. Especially in a starving year.

"Wait," Isabel said. "Who's *we?*" Then it hit her. "You lost the rest of your party?"

Cora flinched. Unconsciously she fidgeted at a thing around her neck. Some scrap of Waste-salvage, maybe, hanging from a cord, catching and sparking at the light. "One of us went to Three Hills, one to Chooser's Blindside. Warn people off the Waste-road between Clayspring and here. Keep an eye out for trouble. Pretty standard stuff for when Carrion Boy's people go roaming. Nothing special. Me, though." Cora sat back, crossed her arms. "I came here. To warn you. Because that's where they're headed."

"You're sure," Jen said.

"Unless there's another town south along the Waste-road inside two weeks' hard journey out of Clayspring," Cora said, "that I somehow don't know about? Then yes. I'm sure."

"How far out?" Isabel asked.

"It's a week on foot from Clayspring to here if you're marching hard, which they are. They mobilized the day after the quake hit, which puts them here in . . . " Her face went slack and hazy, like she was remembering something she rather wouldn't. Back went her hand to her scrap-necklace. "Two days if the weather holds. A storm might buy you a third, but that's it."

"But we can fight them," Sairy said.

"You can try. I've seen what's left of towns that try and I don't recommend it. But I'm just here to tell you what's coming, not what to do when it gets here."

"Carrion Boy's up-self is ascendant," Jacen added. "While Catch-keep's is behind the hills." Then, hastily, as if remembering where he was: "May She soon arise."

"May She soon arise," the others replied, the reflex momentarily overriding their fear. Catchkeep never set, but She was nearing Her lowest station now in the sky. She wouldn't be at Her highest and most auspicious until spring. At which point they might all be long since slaughtered and eaten. Or left alive, and ritually mutilated, and conscripted.

"Wait a second," Sairy was saying. "So it's fine when it's Catch-keep asking for upstart blood," she told the high seats. "But when it's Carrion Boy asking for yours, *now* there's a problem." She coughed a derisive little laugh. "That you need *our help* to fix."

"Sairy," Isabel said warningly, and Sairy shut up, glaring daggers.

"Listen," Yulia said. "I was living up at Lisbet's Rest when Car-rion Boy's people came down on it out of Shelter nine-ten years ago. They didn't take many of us. The midwife and all her healing sup-plies. All the children old enough to hold a spear. They made us tell them where we'd buried the food stores. Nobody wanted to tell them, so they grabbed my little cousin out of my brother's arms, and they . . . " She trailed off. "We couldn't stop them then. We can't stop them now. When they get here, believe me, we want to be gone."

"Gone where?" said Sairy. "We're just going to go take over someone else's town? Isn't that what we're trying to avoid happening to us?"

"If you see another option," Yulia said icily, "do enlighten us."

"We fight," Sairy said. "We keep what's ours."

"Like you fought to retain Catchkeep's favor?" Yulia said. Gave Sairy a slow once-over. "For a while."

Sairy opened her mouth and Isabel wheeled and bore down on her like a glacier. "Enough," she breathed, and Sairy backed down, staring holes through the high seats' heads in silence.

Isabel turned to Cora. "Say you're Carrion Boy's people. From Clayspring you'd come through Stormbreak along the Waste-road to get here. Long walk for little reward. Why?"

Cora shrugged. "Stormbreak's guarded. Too risky. They burned half the night going off-road around the walls."

Isabel thought of Lake Sweetwater to the north edge of town, the ridge and the Hill encircling it southwards. The Waste-road only ran through Sweetwater proper one way. "*We're* guarded."

That half-laugh again. "That's not what they say."

"Who the hell is *they?*"

Cora smiled. Started counting on her fingers for her benefit, very slowly, as if to a child. "Stormbreak. Clayspring. Lisbet's Rest. Here. Word travels far through the Waste. You're lucky it hasn't come back to bite you before—"

"Apparently it is *believed,*" Ruby interrupted, choosing her words with care, "that in order for Catchkeep's priest to have been overthrown, Catchkeep Herself must no longer hold us in Her favor."

"Or else," said Jacen, watching Isabel closely, "that She too is dead."

At this point Sairy hit her limit. "Her priest was an asshole," she shouted, and Isabel felt an awkward rush of gratitude. But she knew whose fault it was that the Catchkeep-priest was dead. At whose feet all this trouble fell.

"Be that as it may," Ruby was saying, "She let Her priest's death go unpunished. Nobody knows why that is, and this isn't the time to argue it. All we need to know is that people think Catchkeep no longer protects Sweetwater, that She has abandoned us, and that we are easy prey."

Isabel bristled. "So we'll prove them wrong."

Cora stared at her. "Did you not hear what I just said? Clayspring raider army on the march. Three days out at best from your front door. Look, you do what you have to, but I *strongly*—"

"We'll be ready."

Yulia snorted. "We don't even know what's coming. Ready for what?"

Beside Isabel, Sairy was grinning the grin of a person backed into a corner in a sea of enemies. "For anything."

"We need a *plan.*"

"And that," Ruby said, turning to Isabel, "brings me to the part where we need your help."

* * *

Everyone else went back into the common room, shutting the door behind them. Isabel stood alone for a moment in the clammy dark, absorbing the humid silence of the place, before beginning the once-arduous task of lighting candles blind.

One at either end of the altar. Huge pillars of golden beeswax, stuck to the stone slab with their own past meltage, still tall enough that Isabel had to reach up with the flame. The little dish of oil between Catchkeep's massive front paws was lit next, throwing weird shadows from the mismatched salvage-angles of Her statue, the offerings heaped in the darkness of Her underbelly. A little bouquet of three-eyes, tied off with a blade of grass. A chunk of acorn-flour bread. The sand-colored husk of a molted cicada. A cairn of blackberries perched on a rainstealer leaf. Bits of whatnot from Chooser-knew-where, out in the Waste: fragments of bone, metal, plastic, most unidentifiable. Even a coin, silvery and worn as a ghost, both faces rubbed blank and glistening from the ash burial from which some scav crew had salvaged it. A sun-dried whole apple, tiny and riddled with maggot-holes: somebody's hoarded ration from last fall's harvest, when there'd still been an orchard to harvest from. Whoever'd put it there had already, wildly optimistically, cored it for the seeds.

Next was the worst part. Sixteen stars in Catchkeep's up-self, so sixteen points of light on Her image that must be lit. The hard part was keeping them all going at once in that drafty open space. The good thing about a muggy summer evening was that it didn't lend itself to breeze.

When all was finished, Isabel stepped back. In the dimness of the shrine, if she stood square in front of the altar, and balanced on her tiptoes a little—whoever had slapped the statue together out of Waste-salvage had clearly had a couple inches of height on her—the points of light described Catchkeep's constellation almost exactly.

She opened her mouth to say the words that would call the goddess down out of the sky—*I am the Archivist. Catchkeep's emissary, ambassador, and avatar on earth. Her bones and stars my flesh; my flesh and bones Her stars*—and stopped, the words caught in her throat. None of that was true anymore. What was she supposed to say instead? She had no idea. Nobody had asked her to do this for years. And never in a situation quite like this.

"Um," she said. Cleared her throat. On the wall, the skulls of fallen Archivists grinned down, green stones in their mouths, shadows where their eyes should be. She belonged up there with them. She was living on borrowed time. She knew it. Catchkeep knew it.

The room hadn't seemed quite so dark a minute ago.

"So, uh. Remember me? The high seats sent me to ask You something. We're in trouble. There are raiders coming. When they get here, it's going to be bad. We have to fight them. Or run away. So the high seats want to know what You think we should do. Stay or go. Fight or run. They're waiting for me to come back and tell them what You say, so. Whenever You're ready. They said they won't move until You . . . "

She trailed off, feeling stupid. Talking to a lump of Waste-scraps, fitted together into the shape of a dog, with candles hidden in its eyes. After the things she had seen, it was hard for her to find a trash-statue duly awe-inspiring.

She stood in silence, waited a fifty-count. Nothing. The skulls grinned down. Here and there, the candles picked out green glints. Among them, something shifted. A spider? A moth? Some lost ghost? A moth would have gone for the candle-flames. A ghost would have gone for the salt in her eyes. She swallowed, one hand dropping to the harvesting-knife. It wasn't doing anything this time. Of course it wasn't.

"Come on. I'm not asking for much. Let's say this. If the light in Your left eye goes out first, we go. Right eye does, we stay. Sound fair? Left, go, right, stay. I'll wait."

She parked herself on the stone floor, blinking sleep away, and stared at those two little flames until her eyes stung.

Stay or go. Defend or flee. Build walls or burn bridges. At a glance, she wasn't sure which was the least of evils. Two hundred-odd people on the run through the Waste, on foot, carrying their harvest on their backs, or two hundred-odd people, unarmed, unarmored, standing their ground? It was a choice between a bloodbath and a slow starve. Isabel didn't feel qualified to make that choice herself, or bear the fallout if she happened to choose wrong.

In her head, a voice said: *We bring our own monsters with us. It looks like these are yours.*

Isabel started. Had she fallen asleep?

Catchkeep's left eye had gone dark. Isabel got up and leaned in close to be sure. Not so much as an ember, though the right side's flame stood at full strength, flickering as she breathed.

"Going then. I'll tell them."

With every step toward the shrine-door and the outside and the town hall, though, she became less and less sure. A few years ago, all she wanted in the world was to escape this place. If the lake had reared up and swallowed Sweetwater whole, it wouldn't have been anything to her. But now? Now these people were her responsibility, whether she liked it or not. And sending them out into the Waste, a few months of slow starvation with winter at the end of it, was sending them out to die. She may as well line them up and slit their throats herself.

And then there were the ghosts. The ghostgrass barricades. That was wholly her responsibility. What would happen when the people of Sweetwater left and the ghostgrass barricades eventually failed?

Not my problem, one part of her thought. But another part was thinking about the ghosts jostling at those barricades, bursting forth one day in a blare of silver light, overrunning Carrion Boy's people and sending them all to Catchkeep's dominion. It was a pleasant enough notion until she considered what would happen after. How far could ghosts travel from their waypoint of origin? She didn't know. But the idea of setting Sweetwater's ghosts loose on the Waste at large was not an option she was prepared to entertain.

No effort at all for her to picture it, ghosts pouring out of those unguarded passages, tearing through the streets like wind. From every corner of Sweetwater they'd come. Everyplace there was a passage, a place where the fabric between worlds was porous and threadbare, only her ghostgrass barricades holding that onrushing in abeyance. The ledge, the oldest bridge, the tunnels, the well—

She stopped so fast she almost went facefirst into the door.

The tunnels.

They were ancient, and crumbled, and mainly unexplored, apart from one short stretch beneath the town gardens where ghosts were known to appear. There were no people down there. No light. Nothing in the field notes about expeditions sent down there for salvage. It was probably only Archivists who knew they even existed.

She'd just been out to the entry point a few days ago. Behind the ghostgrass barricade, under the corpseroot overgrowth, that weird round heavy door with its drop down into the dark. It was half a mile outside of town. Under a pile of rubble the size of a small mountain. Not even most townspeople knew that door was there.

She wouldn't have to go far in. Not much space had to be cleared. Just enough to hide the few dozen people who couldn't fight—the children, the elderly, the injured—while the rest defended the town. Yulia had said that Carrion Boy's raiders took children for their armies. Isabel could hide a lot of children in those tunnels.

She'd been in those tunnels before. There was a ghost-passage down there, but it was where one arm of the tunnels dead-ended in a collapsed brickfall. Even back when she was Archivist, ghosts hardly ever came through there. It was the least-trafficked waypoint in Sweetwater and she mostly avoided it. And the ghostgrass barricade around it was solid. She'd checked on it before the quake, and Sairy after.

It was a Ragpicker's gambit, of course. But it was the best option she could see. This way the townspeople wouldn't have to take off on a hopeless slog through the Waste. They wouldn't have to abandon their food supply, their water supply, their shelter. They wouldn't be standing an excellent chance of being caught out in the open miles between towns for winter or worse to find them.

When Isabel went back out into the common room, all seven ex-upstarts and all three high seats were there, waiting. Their faces turned to her like flowers to the sun.

"So. What was Her counsel?" Ruby asked her. "Do we stay or do we go?"

Isabel meant to tell her the truth. How could she possibly know better than Catchkeep what the proper course of action was? This wasn't the time to be going rogue, indulging her own authority at the expense of the town's safety. Nobody else even knew those tunnels existed, and she hadn't been down there in years. They could well be a deathtrap. They were well on their way to deathtrap last she'd seen.

On the other hand, she couldn't protect anyone out there. Here she at least knew what they'd be up against, and she could fight it on her own terms. They already knew which direction Carrion Boy's people were approaching from, and that they'd be caught between ridge and lake along the one Waste-road. Meanwhile the townspeople could stockpile supplies in the tunnels. The ones who were able to defend the town could protect the ones who weren't. The ex-upstarts in particular, she knew, would fight tooth and nail for the place they'd carved out for themselves, the roots they'd sunk in the Waste. Alone if they had to, and to the last one standing.

In any case it was out of her hands. She was the mouth of a goddess, and she would let the goddess speak.

"Catchkeep's up-self never sets," she found herself saying instead. "She watches over us always. Until Her stars fall from the sky, Catchkeep will never turn Her back on us. Not here where Her house is. Not here where Her ways are kept."

None of this would have even been happening if she'd just kept her head down, stayed Archivist, let the Catchkeep-priest live. She had dug this hole herself, and nobody was going to fill it for her. She looked Ruby dead in the eye and swallowed her second thoughts.

"We stay."

Chapter Four

So Ruby threw a party.

It would start at first light and was set to carry on until around midday. That gave Isabel's team a few hours to clear the tunnels while the high seats worked with the perimeter guards to coordinate the town's defenses. Then, when the tunnels were ready, Ruby would make her announcement to the people of Sweetwater. Some would begin training, some would relay supplies to the tunnels, some would prepare to hide for the fight's duration.

To that end, Isabel and the ex-upstarts grabbed a few hours of sleep before the long day to come. Then at dawn they gathered ghostgrass to bring into the tunnels and readied themselves for the descent.

Meanwhile, Ruby bought out the brew-mistress's supply. She tasked the baker's whole family with baking the last of the summer fruits into the kinds of sweets that usually only appeared on high holidays. She had someone set up games in the grass outside the meeting-hall. She sent people to pick all the more delicate vegetables from the garden, everything that couldn't be stashed in the tunnels.

Isabel had no idea what Ruby had told these people. Whatever it was, it wasn't the truth. Not that she really had any room there to complain.

"What," Ruby said, amused. "You think I don't know how to have fun because I'm a high seat? Or because I'm older than you?"

"Both?" Lissa said.

Jen punched her on the arm. "Mostly," she said, giving Lissa a *just-shut-up-already* look, "we thought it was a weird time to be celebrating."

Ruby nodded. "Chasing the Chooser's cape. You thought."

Jen hesitated, visibly suppressing the reflex to gesture *Chooser-look-away-from-here*. "Yes."

"Well, we're not celebrating," Ruby said. "We're using up some food we can't store in the tunnels. I don't know about you, but I call that resourcefulness." But she caught Jen's eye and winked.

"I call it distracting people," Lissa said. "Giving them something shiny to look at while they get stabbed in the back."

"Or how about," Ruby said, "letting them enjoy a beautiful summer day in peace, without troubling themselves with what's to come."

Lissa snorted.

"She wants to prevent a panic," Sairy told her, not taking her eyes off of Ruby as she spoke. "She doesn't want to tell everyone until she can give them something useful to do. So they don't feel so helpless when they get the news."

"You catch on fast," Ruby said admiringly. To her credit, she didn't say *for an upstart*. "You should've been a high seat."

"I get to a point where all I want to do is sit in a fancy chair in the meeting-hall and listen to people complain about their neighbors all day," Sairy said, "I'll let you know."

"I look forward to it," Ruby said.

"Give us a few hours to clear a space," Isabel told her. "Then send down the supplies. I want everything ready before we have to fit people down there. Get me an accurate head count."

"I have forty-one so far," Ruby told her.

"Plus a couple of mine to watch them? It's going to be tight."

"But you'll manage?"

"We'll manage."

When Ruby had gone, Isabel gathered the ex-upstarts.

"This party is a terrible idea," Sairy said, launching into her best impression of Ruby's voice. "*So, everyone, here's some food and wine and games. Enjoy them! Because you're about to die.*"

"I don't know," Kath said. "It gets people fed, keeps their energy up."

"And she's right," Jen added. "We can't store the whole garden in the tunnels. Better they eat that food than the raiders do."

"That's not our concern," Isabel said. "Most of you are going to work with the perimeter guards and train people. You need to be ready to receive the people Ruby sends you. They're going to be scared. They're going to be pissed off. They're not going to want to need your help, and they're probably not going to thank you for it." The corner of her mouth quirked. "Remember," she said, "the idea is to train them. Not break them."

They laughed.

"Be efficient. Think: if you had two days to learn how to fight, what would you want someone to teach you? Nothing fancy. The dirtier the better. And no ghost stuff. They'll be fighting people. We know Clayspring is coming from the north, so they'll hit us where the road passes between the western edge of the lake and the top end of the ridge. The high seats will have some kind of strategy to defend that stretch and the town itself. Whatever we do, we do within the framework of that plan. Don't do Ruby's job. Do your job. It comes down to it, you can't find me, your orders come from Sairy. Argue with me later if you have to, but listen to her then. We can't protect the people in the tunnels if the town above is overrun."

She gestured toward the table beside her. Where the vegetables and chopping-boards had been yesterday there was now a bundle, partially unwrapped, glinting where the light caught on its angles. Jen, who had brought that bundle out of long storage, untied the twine and pulled away the rest of its blanket wrapping.

Thirty- or forty-odd knives, given over to Jen for safekeeping when the Catchkeep-priest had died, taking the Archivist-upstart system with him.

They lay in a jumble of salvage scrap and glass and filed bone. The weapons of all the ex-upstarts were here, and the weapons of a number of dead upstarts before them. Many were rusted or chipped, or snapped entirely in two, but others were whole, and yet others could be repaired.

The ex-upstarts stood before them in silence. Several of them, Isabel noted, were looking everywhere and anywhere but at that pile of knives.

There are other exits, deeper in, said a voice in her head. *But this door is not one of them. And I can't open it for you.*

"I know," she told them, as gently as she knew how. "But it's not like it was before. We don't owe these people anything. If you want to leave, this is the time. Nobody will come after you. But if you want to stay, you fight. Because you choose to. Because if Carrion Boy's people catch you, they *will* conscript you. You know the stories. You're too useful to kill. They'll break you until you have to fight for them, their way, on their say-so." She looked into their faces, each in turn. "You want to go back to that?"

Silence.

"Fuck no," said Sairy.

"Never again," said Kath.

Meg shook her head, mouth pressed into a line.

"No way," said Jen.

Glory shuddered, like she'd touched something unclean.

"They'll have to kill me," Bex said. "I'm not doing shit for them."

Lissa was staring at the pile of knives like it was first-apples day and she'd just found the winner's token in her slice of pie. "Let them come at us," she said. "I'm ready."

"Clean the blood off of them," Isabel said. "Add the kitchen knives and sharpen everything. Broken ones go to Kath." She raised an eyebrow at Kath, sitting with her sprained ankle elevated on a stool.

Kath gave the knives a once-over and nodded. "Some of these are completely trashed, but I'll fix what I can."

One of Lissa's old knives lay near the top, and she ran a fingertip along the flat of it. It had one notch cut into its handle, old sweat and blood dried into its grip. She reached to take it up, but then a thought hit her and she looked up at Isabel instead. "There's going to be a lot of blood."

"Carrion Boy's people won't come at you with wooden knives," Isabel told them.

"And if we pull ghosts?"

"We take precautions. You draw a ghost down on a crowd, it goes for the person who's bleeding. The person who doesn't have ghostgrass to protect her. Don't let that person be you." Isabel paused to let that sink in. "You're right. Normal days, yes, we play it safe, we train with wooden knives. But whatever this ends up being when Clayspring gets here, it won't be a normal day."

They nodded. Some with resignation, some with focused calm, some already spoiling for the fight to come. These girls might've been domesticated, but it'd be a good long while before they were anything like tame.

"You, and whoever is up here fighting alongside you, you're the first and middle and pretty much last line of defense. So put away everything you're thinking about these people. You don't need to make friends with them. You need to keep them alive. You need to teach them how to help keep *you* alive. Anything less than total cooperation and this goes straight to shit *very* fast."

"What about you?" Jen asked.

"I'll be on the front lines with you. Once the tunnels are cleared, Sairy and I will join everyone aboveground. Glory and Bex, you'll be in charge down there. All you have to do is keep them quiet and keep them still. No wandering. Nothing stupid. No matter what you hear up here, you keep those people locked down."

Bex and Glory exchanged a glance. "Sounds easy enough," Bex said.

"Good. Now. Sairy, Glory, Bex, you're with me. Jen, gather all the ghostgrass we have. Make sure everyone has some, and the houses are protected too. Lissa's right—there's going to be blood. Let's not make more problems for ourselves than we already have. The rest of you, get ready to teach these people how to cut something that's not their dinner."

I sabel, Sairy, Bex, and Glory made their way out of the Catchkeep-shrine, carrying sacks of ghostgrass. They had to move fast, travel light, and, most importantly, get to where they were going without being seen.

Easy enough when everyone was occupied. Whether or not she agreed with it, Isabel almost had to admire the sneaky efficacy of Ruby's plan.

Their path to the hatch was a new one. It avoided the Waste-road entirely. As per Sairy's idea, it turned away instead through the sparse grass at the Waste's edge, tacking back and forth to avoid leaving too clear a trail.

"This'll be more important when the supply runs come later," Sairy said, walking backwards to kick ashy soil over their footprints. "But it takes ten seconds to test it for them now."

They made their way around the far side of the ruined building so as to avoid the gardens and the workers hastily picking vegetables for Ruby's party inside.

"All right," Isabel said, stopping at the edge of the ghostgrass barricade. Breeze went sighing through it, tousling it like hair, and an awful thought occurred to her. What if the earthquake had collapsed the tunnels, bringing the ceilings down like a rotten log, and she'd open the hatch onto a cave-in? Why hadn't she thought of that earlier? Why hadn't Ruby? Or the other high seats?

Even worse, she understood why nobody had brought up the possibility. *Because Catchkeep wouldn't have told us to stay if it wasn't safe.*

She sighed. Already the day was weighing on her like a stone around her neck. "Go easy," she instructed the others. "Don't trample the ghostgrass. Pick a few fresh blades to put on yourself. Just a few. The freshly-growing stuff is more potent."

"What about the bundles we brought?" Glory asked.

"It comes down with us. That's our perimeter."

Quickly, efficiently, they tied the long strands of ghostgrass around their wrists, ankles, necks. Bex and Sairy had hair long enough to have grassblades braided into, and they all wrapped some around their belts and bunched some in their pockets. Isabel took one blade and wound it around the hilt of her harvesting-knife, over the shiny synthetic grip that'd remained when the secondary dogleather one had been removed.

That done, she took a deep breath and picked her way in. Through the ghostgrass barricade, up against the corpseroot overgrowth where she'd turned back the other day.

There she stopped to consider it. It grew waist-high and filled the cave of the brickfall completely, burying the hatch. All jaunty crimson blossoms and clustering thorns, undaunted by the dark. There was no way around. There was no pleasant way through.

This gave Isabel pause. The thorns were inches long and curved like reaching claws. And she was supposed to herd children and injured people through this without drawing blood?

At least the brickfall hadn't collapsed onto the hatch. She was fully prepared to take her good news where she could get it, and that was good enough news for now.

Carefully, she began to work her way through. Stepping on the brambles to crush them, shoving through them in a kind of sullen fury with which the corpseroot was wholly unimpressed.

After a moment of hesitation, she drew the harvesting-knife. Even after these years of disuse, it cut through the corpseroot like butter.

The others joined her, slashing with their newly-reacquired knives, but Glory hung back, visibly pale. "There was death here."

"No shit," said Sairy, grunting as she sawed through a bramble the thickness of a wrist.

"I've never seen so much corpseroot."

Isabel straightened. "You do realize what we're standing under."

She pointed at the ceiling of the brickfall and all three gazes followed. From the look on Glory's face, Isabel could well believe that Glory, in fact, had not realized until she stood before it now. Most of the bricks themselves were eroded to gravel, but long spider-legs of twisted metal remained. Impossible to guess how tall the thing had stood. The pile of its ruins alone was taller than any five buildings of Sweetwater stacked up.

"It's a building," Bex told her, voice hushed in the presence of the dead. "From the way way back Before. It's even bigger than it looks from out where we planted the ghostgrass."

"Buildings died in the Before," Isabel said. There was more irritation in her voice than she wanted there to be, and much less of it was directed at Glory than Glory probably assumed. "People in them. Dead buildings, dead people, corpseroot, ghosts."

At *ghosts* Glory stopped cutting. "But it's safe?"

"It's dead empty down there," Isabel said. "There's a waypoint in the—"

Sairy blinked. "A what?"

It was a moment before Isabel realized her misstep. "A ghost-place passage. It's—"

"What did you call it? I've never heard that word before."

"Something somebody else called them once," Isabel snapped. "It's nothing. Anyway it's empty. I think it used to be more populated—it's in the field notes—but every time I went hunting ghosts here there was nothing to find."

"But you have the kit?" Glory asked.

Isabel's ghost-destroying kit, a relic of her Archivist days. To draw holding rings around a ghost in water, fire, milk, and blood. And speak the words that would reduce a ghost to nothing, sending it on to Catchkeep's jurisdiction. Like the harvesting-knife, she hadn't used the kit in years, but she carried it with her all the same.

She patted the pocket of the Archivist-coat.

"Still, we want to be careful," Sairy said, aiming her voice back over one shoulder at Glory and Bex. "No salt on you. No scratches."

"How stupid do you think we are?" Bex asked, affronted.

"Relax. I'm just saying there's no room for screwups. We have a job to do."

"It won't be nice down there," Isabel said.

Bex snorted. "Nice."

"No, I mean it. I brought you because I can trust you. No running off. No backtalk. No heroics. I don't care what you see down there, or what you think you see. We stick together and we get it done. Yes?"

They nodded.

"Which brings me to: we're going to double-check ourselves for scratches once we get out of these thorns, before we so much as touch that hatch. I brought bandages."

They kept clearing ground, making a path just wide enough to walk through single file. After a while Isabel's heel came down on something that clanged dully, from which the overgrowth was more easily cleared.

It was a metal circle, roughly four feet across, set into the frame of a slightly wider metal ring, with a raised wheel in the center. Bex reached for the handle, but Sairy stopped her. "First we check for blood, remember?"

It proved too dark in the deep shade of the brickfall, so they went back out into the light, picking single-file along the path they'd made. Hugging the edge of the brickfall so the garden sentries wouldn't see them, they checked each other over. Sairy and Glory had some minor scratches, quickly wiped dry, but nothing that Isabel deemed dangerous. Bandaged, they ducked back in.

Isabel gripped the wheel, braced her feet, and tugged sideways. Pain sizzled up one side of her body from the leg to the back wall of her skull, but the wheel wouldn't budge. She stuck one foot on the outer ring and tried again. Nothing. Sairy came and grabbed on too and when they tried to turn the wheel together it made a paint-peeling grinding sound, which was better than nothing, so they caught their breath and tried again, and the noise got worse, so they hauled harder on the wheel, and at last it popped loose with a shriek of protesting metal. Six full turns of the wheel and the door was ready to open.

"Ready?"

Glory gave a little nod. All worried eyebrows and determined jaw. chewing the inside of her cheek. "How far in?"

"The passage? A couple hundred paces maybe. There'll be dried ghostgrass all around it. Bundles and a perimeter. And this whole field of it we planted up here, that'll be weakening anything that as much as thinks of coming through. Seriously, when the raiders get here, this is going to be the safest place in town." Isabel raised one finger. "But. You want to turn back, go help the others with training, it stays between us. Same goes for all of you."

They weren't upstarts anymore, and weakness no longer meant death, but their pride in their strength was entrenched, alive and well. Isabel saw no reason not to respect that. It wasn't like she'd come through her own transition to normalcy unscathed.

"Turn back?" said Sairy, smiling sweetly. "Sure, why not. You first."

Glory laughed, and the clench in her jaw relaxed, and it was settled. They lifted the hatch door and peered into the dark belowground. It was like looking down into the way way back Before. Or it would have been if they could see anything.

But it was dark, which meant it was empty. The ceiling hadn't fallen in. For a moment Isabel felt like she might faint with relief.

"Do this," said Isabel, and squeezed her eyes shut, buying time while she recovered. "Hold it and count thirty. Then open. It helps."

Obediently they shut their eyes and counted. On *three* Isabel opened hers. On the off chance that there was a ghost wandering around down there, she didn't want it spilling out onto four slag-for-brains squatting in the trampled thorns with their eyes scrunched shut like little kids playing seek-and-find.

But she knew that was stupid. A ghost strong enough to even *approach* this part of the tunnels, so near the ghostgrass barricade, would have a presence they could feel from here. Frostbite and vertigo, unmistakable. A smell like someone had left a window open on an early spring morning. And a ghost *that* strong—

Glory was staring down into the dark. "We jump?"

"There's a ladder. It's bolted into the wall."

Already Sairy was lowering a lamp as Bex scattered ghostgrass down the hole.

They climbed down the ladder and stood in the circle of lamplight, casting around half-blind. Not much daylight made it in under the brickfall and through the hatch. Most of what Isabel's senses reported to her was a smell of ancient damp, the distant rustling of what was probably mice, and an impression of trackless dark receding before her. When the rustling stopped, the silence shouldered in, absolute. Without sound at least to anchor her, the darkness irised open at her feet. She felt like there was a pressure at her back, compelling her forward, and she was one wrong step from falling forever.

Beside her, she could hear the others' breathing quicken. *They've never been underground before,* she realized. *None of them.* She might be the only person alive in all the world who'd ever set foot in these tunnels, and even she was acutely aware of the depth of their descent and the weight of the earth above their heads.

"Get the lamps lit," she said, and they began igniting the other wicks off the one that was burning, while Isabel stood by, one hand on the harvesting-knife, on full alert for silver flickering in the deeper dark. But there was none.

The widening of the light revealed no ghosts, no anything. Wide halls. White walls gone greyblack with lichen and mold. Ceiling topping out a few feet above her head. The floor looked to have been tiled, once, with some kind of synthetic that didn't rot, just broke apart in shards and lay like that, like chunks of eggshell mortared together with mud.

Whatever this place was built of, the earthquake apparently hadn't been strong enough to touch it. More fallen bricks and stuff on the floor than there had been the last time she'd come here, but there was no evidence of further cave-ins. *Just hold on a few more days,* she asked the tunnels silently. *That's all I need.*

"Now we're going to fan out a little. Gradually. See what we see, and secure a perimeter. Bring the ghostgrass."

"Already got mine," Sairy said, shouldering a bag. The others each took one and awaited further instruction.

Isabel raised her lamp. A few long strides from where they stood, the shadow of an opening yawned. The toppled remains of a thick white door, busted off its hinges from either great force or great age. The massive dent in the middle of the fallen door strongly suggested the former.

Isabel took point, gaining the slope of the fallen door and stepping into the darkness beyond. She'd been down here before, so that part wasn't new. What *was* new this time was a tingling in the backs of her hands like she was plunging headlong into a trap. She didn't know what she was expecting to be different. The half-ton of door to leap back up into its frame, slicing her neatly in half as she stepped through. The floor on the far side to drop away into a sinkhole the moment she put her weight on it.

Neither of those things happened, but that weird feeling didn't go away. She'd never felt it down here before, years ago when she'd *been* down here, but she knew at once where she'd felt it recently. Then she realized that the sensation was more or less localized to her knife-hand, that her knife-hand had unconsciously dropped to the hilt of the harvesting-knife, and that the sensation was buzzing its way up into her hand from there.

"Careful," she said, lifting her hand deliberately away. "Ground's uneven here."

She could hear the ex-upstarts' caught breath as they passed through that doorway, as they paused to stare as they stepped over the dented place in the door. That door was solid metal, thicker than Isabel's torso, and probably weighed well more than all four girls combined. Whatever'd made the dent had plowed into that door like a fist into bread dough, and it gave them pause. Recognizing significance, unknowing what it signified.

Bex's hushed voice at her back: "What did this?"

"No idea. Something a long time dead, anycase. This place is older than anywhere you've been."

"You know what else is a long time dead, though?" Glory said. Glancing around nervously. "Ghosts."

"You realize you're practically more ghostgrass than person right now, yes?" Sairy told her.

Isabel cleared the rubble on the far side of the doorway and swung the lamp in a slow half-arc, assessing the space beyond. "Clear," she said. "Come on through."

She held the light for them. Glory swatted a grinning Sairy on her way though. Bex followed in silent concentration, visibly assessing and cataloguing everything her calculating gaze fell upon.

Through the doorway the tunnel branched off, left and right, the lamplit view down each direction dissolving in the grainy dark.

There was something set into the wall behind them, beside the doorway. A black rectangle made of a different synthetic than the floor, about the size of Isabel's hand, its purpose indeterminate. Long since smashed, anyway, maybe by whatever had wrecked the door.

Isabel had seen such rectangles beside doors before, in the ghosts' memories. Locks that you touched in certain patterns to open.

On the hatch side there'd been nothing. This door, all however many pounds of it, was only designed to open one way.

Glory gaped, taking in what the light was showing her. "What *is* this place?"

"What you see," Isabel said, straining her eyes at the middle distance. Not wanting to risk getting snuck up on by something she was too light-blind to notice coming. "A Before-place. Long dead."

She wished she could pause to think without raising suspicion. She couldn't shake the feeling that she'd been here more recently than she actually had. Which made no sense.

"This place is *weird*," Bex said. "Like—" she shook her head— "like it's watching us."

"It smells bad," Glory added.

"We're breathing the Before," Sairy said.

They all fell silent.

No surprise to Isabel. Sweetwater being built on tunnels wasn't news to them, but the sheer age and size and Before-ness of the place, once you were down in it, was staggering. Even in this little closed-off section, lamplit and full of activity, it felt to Isabel like they'd all been swallowed by something vast and silent, something that was now holding its breath to see what they would do.

"Come on," she said. She raised the lamp leftward. Light glanced off those long white walls, furred with lichen. The tunnel didn't look any less pounded deeper down. "That way's the ghost-passage. About fifty paces down, like I said."

Sairy was squinting down the right-hand hall. "And that way?"

"Not our concern." *Your guess is as good as mine.* "The left dead-ends. Easy to secure."

Glory looked dubious. "At a ghost-passage."

"At a *contained* ghost-passage."

"We're good," said Sairy, elbowing Glory hard in the ribs. "Let's do this."

Isabel led them down the left-hand passage.

"Said something here once," Glory was saying, facing a section of wall. A good third of the outward-facing bricks had come out, mostly off to one side. It looked like the mouth of someone who'd eaten the solid right hook that lost them a fistfight. "Under this mossy junk. The bricks are a different color."

"Not now," Sairy said, pulling her away. "Keep up."

"What about all this mess on the floor?" Bex asked. Looking down at the rubble and edged shards of busted floor-stuff. "It looks like the Ragpicker threw up in here. Where're they going to *sleep*?"

Isabel stopped. "You three work on that. Be quick but not too quick. Don't cut yourselves on anything. I'm going to check on that ghost-passage."

They set to work immediately.

"You need a hand?" Sairy asked her.

"You stay here. Really this is more to scare bored kids away from messing with the ghost-passage than anything. If it was still active, with actual ghosts going in and out of it, we'd know."

She held her lamp high. Its glow reached a little way before her field of vision dissolved into a slurry of darkness and what small glints the lamplight picked out on something farther in.

One of the glints moved.

Isabel narrowed her eyes down the tunnel. Raised and lowered the lamp and the light slid up and down the length of something silver. Again the slight small movement when the light touched bottom. *The hell?*

Closer, she found that she was right. It was no ghost at all.

At least not anymore.

What she stood before was a four-foot-long streak of what looked like dull silver paint, if paint were the texture of honey and Isabel didn't know better.

The ghost-blood ran down the wall in tacky rivulets, thickest around the height of her chest, and sprayed up from there and outward, as if—

Seized by a sudden surmise, she glanced down at the thing lying at the bottom, the size of Isabel's hands put together side-by-side, less silver than the rest. As though the silver had drained from it, leaving a grayish residue.

She picked it up—it felt not *quite* like loose skin, but not *quite* like slightly cool, slightly clammy fabric either—and shoved it in a pocket of her Archivist-coat before Sairy found some excuse to come back and noticed the empty eyeholes and the gaping mouth and the fact that it wasn't made of fabric at all.

But first she couldn't resist giving it one quick glance. The gray of it was tinged faintly orangeish where its hair would've been, and there were still a few faint lashes around where the eyes belonged.

The place where the stump of its neck ended was cleanly severed and—from the look of the spray on the wall—with some force. The rest of its body was gone.

Quickly, Isabel grabbed a cloth bandage from her pocket and scrubbed the silver from the wall. It didn't come off so much as smear around. Then she shouldered the bag of ghostgrass and walked the rest of the way down the hall.

There, as expected, was the waypoint.

In Isabel's experience, each ghost-passage looked a little different. Most of the ones that actually resembled doors were the ones she herself had made to look like doors. Left to their own devices, to be formed by whatever forces usually were behind their creation, they might look like anything. Places where the fabric of the world, for whatever reason, ripped. The one up on the ledge at Execution Hill was a crack in the cliffside. The one at the dry well was the well itself. The one under the fallen bridge was a perfect ring of suns-and-moons growing in a field of them, easiest to spot in winter when all the other surrounding flowers died.

This one was a place in the tunnel where, by all rights, the tunnel should have continued, on and on into the mazy dark. Except that at some point the ceiling had caved in, leaving a fall of broken bricks, all painted white, or white's remainder, on one side.

Gray light shone through the cracks from nowhere, pulsing faintly.

No sign of any ghosts.

"All clear down here," she called up. "Keep working up there. I'm going to set up this end of the perimeter, then work my way back up to you. I want to put ghostgrass the whole way across the hall to mark the cleared area on both sides. Ghosts or no, we may as well give people a line to stay behind. It—"

She froze.

There'd been more ghostgrass here before. She knew there had. It wouldn't grow underground, so she'd scattered plenty at the waypoint, and hung bundles on the projecting bricks of the cave-in, before planting the barricade above. Most of it was still there, no question, but at least three bundles had walked off somehow, and something prickled down her spine to look at those empty places. Nobody came down here. Not since the ghostgrass barricade had gone up. Years ago.

Then again, this place was probably crawling with mice. Mice made nests out of grass. She'd have to keep a close eye on their supply and their perimeter once they moved the townspeople in. Couldn't be too careful.

"Isabel?"

"Nothing. Thought I forgot to bring my ghostgrass," she lied. "Never mind."

Hastily she began hanging the ghostgrass bundles over some of the bricks, doubling down on the ones that were already there before. When that was done she'd go back up to the others and mark out the other edge of the perimeter.

After a few minutes she realized she was still stuffing ghostgrass in amid the rubble of the cave-in. So she stopped. Put the rest of the ghostgrass back in the bag. She was weirdly dizzy, both hands tingling and her stomach in knots.

On her way back up the tunnel, Isabel glanced over her shoulder despite herself. The waypoint remained empty, dim and gray, shimmering gently like a candle afloat in a bowl of water, throwing shadows off of collapsed little cairns of brick. That sense of waiting watchfulness intensified.

Suddenly, Isabel didn't want to have that ghost-passage at her back. At all. She dropped her hand to the hilt of the harvesting-knife—and jerked it away, startled to find the knife practically quivering in its sheath. As always, to look at it, it didn't seem to be moving. But how else to describe the compulsion it laid on her? It was like when Squirrel would stare at her for table-scraps, drilling his gaze into the back of her head until she turned around. Like that, but a whole lot stronger.

Under the ghostgrass bracelets, Isabel's wrists began to itch terribly. Her ankles. Her neck. Her palm, where it was set to the hilt of the harvesting-knife. No—to the ghostgrass wrapped around the hilt of the harvesting-knife.

"Shut up," she told the knife, clamping it white-knuckled until it went—or seemed to go—still. Her whole hand went pins-and-needles with it, which she decided to ignore. "I know. I see it." She gestured at the waypoint. "I don't care."

Screw this place, she thought, and powered her way back up the hall.

The length of tunnel where she'd left the ex-upstarts was almost wholly unrecognizable. They'd almost completely cleared a section that was about eighty strides long. The floor was clear of sharp-edged debris and all the junk they'd picked up was piled out of the way for later sorting.

When Isabel arrived, Bex was hauling bricks. Glory was stomping tiny shards of synthetic tile deep into the mud of the floor where they couldn't cut anyone. And Sairy was in the middle of laying the other end of the ghostgrass perimeter.

Isabel picked up a few chunks of broken brick and went to add them to Bex's pile, which stood to waist-height all along a stretch of wall. Metal, plastic, glass, bits of whatnot from Chooser knew how long ago. Relics, every one.

"Jen made me promise to go through whatever we find," Bex said, dropping off another armload of rubble and pausing to wipe sweat from her forehead. "See what's worth keeping."

"Of course she did," Isabel said. "We get through the next few days, she can come down here herself."

"That's what I told her you'd say."

Sairy picked up an orange plastic cylinder, some kind of little bottle with a white plastic lid. Like everything else down here, it was grubby with an unguessable accumulation of dust but not brittle the way it'd be if it'd been exposed to sun. "Hey, Isabel. If Glory sees a ghost, you can catch it in this."

Sairy tossed her the bottle, which she went to drop on the heap. And stopped.

Wedged behind the pile of rubble was a flat flexible sheet of plasticky synthetic. It was scratched up, and smudgy, and sideways, but Isabel knew a map when she saw one.

She pocketed the bottle absently and pulled out the map. It was about the size of two of Meg's flatbreads laid side to side. Beneath the dirt she could just make out snaky lines of color, the suggestion of little squares. The songkeeper had some old maps like this, collected by Sweetwater scav crews and years of barter. Isabel made a mental note to bring him this one after—

Dislodged by her rummaging, something else rolled free of the pile and fetched up against her foot, and she forgot the map entirely.

A tube-shaped device about the size of Isabel's thumb. One side was surfaced in black Before-stuff, dull and dented now, but Isabel knew that it'd once been shiny and smooth, because she'd seen another of these things before.

Standard issue, went the voice in her head.

Isabel replaced the map and picked up the device. Carefully, thumb-and-forefinger, like it'd burn her.

No effort at all to remember the noise one of these things had made as it powered up, its beeping just barely scraping through the smeary film of her consciousness, and then the searing pain of being put back together, cell by outraged cell.

Sairy was at her elbow. "What'd you find?"

"A Before-thing," Isabel said. Turning the thing over and over in her hands. "They used to use them to heal people."

Weirdly, it didn't look too banged up. The tunnels had protected it from the ash and wind of the Waste for longer than Isabel had any way of guessing at. Not enough visible metal on it to rust.

Sairy was narrowing her eyes at the healing device doubtfully. "What, like it has ointment inside it?"

"It's a Before-thing. You touch it and it works."

"And does what? Heals you? Like in 'Ember Girl and Carrion Boy Fight the Metal Men?' Just like that?" Sairy lit up. "We can use it in *our* fight!"

"It's been down here since the Before, Sairy, it's broken. Look."

Isabel pressed one fingertip to the black-film side of the healing device, as she'd seen the ghost do, back in her little Archivist-house, forever ago.

They watched the device expectantly, but this time the film didn't light up. Not so much as a blink. Not so much as a fizzle. Not even the mournful little beeps these things made when they powered down and died.

"Your hands are shaking," Sairy observed.

"Just cold." Isabel made herself shrug. "Hey," she called, and tossed the healing device over to Bex. "Relic for Jen," she said. "We done here?"

Glory checked the lamp-oil. "Done *early*. This hasn't been burning more than two hours."

Sairy glanced over their work. "I think we're ready to report."

When they reached the hatch, Isabel went last. She stood, one foot on the ladder, looking back over her shoulder into the unanswering dark. Then climbed.

"Well," Glory said, as they shut the hatch and turned the wheel, "that was nothing."

"Told you," Sairy said, swatting at her. "This was the easy part. Tomorrow you get locked down here with *forty children.*"

Glory made a face. "I want to help fight."

"Seriously, the raider army will be coming for the children," Sairy reminded her. "Protecting them means telling the raiders to shove their plan up their ass where it belongs." She pulled Glory in sideways and kissed the top of her head. "Now let's go see if they left us any wine."

Chapter Five

They found Ruby in the meeting-hall, where the party was still underway. Bex and Glory made a beeline for the wine and sweets, but, tempted or no, Sairy insisted upon staying with Isabel, helping her shoulder through the packed room.

Not that Isabel needed the help. Even after all this time, crowds parted before her like water. Isabel didn't know if this was due to all the bloodshed in her history or all the ghosts, or both, but *something* seemed to have left an invisible, indelible stain on everything she touched, and there were still those in the village who wouldn't so much as set foot in her shadow.

Isabel shooed Sairy toward the wine. She didn't need much convincing.

Reaching Ruby's high seat, Isabel stopped. She knew better than to say anything here in this crowded room. So she waited for Ruby to climb down and together they went outside.

"I miscalculated," Ruby said. "My latest head count is forty-six."

"We can fit them."

"And the supplies?"

"You'll have to be picky about what you send down," Isabel said, "but yes. Food. Water. Bandages. Enough for a week."

"If we haven't solved the problem up here in a week, I'm afraid it'll be beyond solving," Ruby said grimly. "What about the town relics? The songkeeper's histories? The statue in the shrine?"

"The songkeeper's things we can fit. The statue is way too big to move, and it has sharp edges. I'm not risking their safety down there. It's going to be hard enough keeping forty children still without having a bunch of metal teeth and claws around for them to stick themselves on."

"Nothing you can't handle," Ruby said.

Isabel blinked. "Nothing *I* can't—" Then she realized what Ruby was saying. "No. Not happening. I'm staying up here to fight. I'm not herding a bunch of—"

"Walk with me," Ruby said.

"No. This is stupid. We prioritize people who can fight and we put them up *here*. We send a few down into the tunnels to keep the children quiet, but that hatch is unfindable. You probably don't even know where it is."

"Be that as it may—"

"Did you put me in charge of this or didn't you? I'm telling you the people in those tunnels do not need to fight. Glory with her broken arm goes down. Bex goes down because she physically *cannot touch a weapon* without puking everywhere. Now ask me *why* she can't. I'll wait."

Ruby wasn't a high seat for nothing. Abruptly, she changed tactics. "Isabel. Listen. The tunnels were your idea. They were a good idea. We might well look back on that idea and say *this, right here, is what changed things for us. This plan, Isabel's plan, is what saved the town.* If that were my idea, I wouldn't want to leave it in the hands of someone else to screw it up. I'd want to be there supervising it myself. Don't you?"

"If I'm of more use up here? No. I don't." Isabel lowered her voice, hissing: "You do know what's going to happen to the people in the tunnels if the town is overrun? Maybe eventually they come back out and Carrion Boy's people find them. Or they'll hide down there until they starve. Neither will be quick."

"And now you understand," Ruby said gently, "why that's exactly where we need you."

It was like being slapped. After everything she'd done over the past three years, this was still what the high seats looked at her and saw.

"I'm sorry," she said tightly. "You're going to have to elaborate. I'm not sure I understand what you mean."

But she understood. She understood all too well.

Ruby looked more uncomfortable than Isabel was used to seeing her. "Believe me, it isn't what I—"

"You want me," Isabel said, keeping her voice slow and soft because it was either that or shouting, "to slaughter a bunch of sick people and children. Just—" she gestured, furious— "sit down there with my feet up, sharpening my knife, waiting for my signal to start cutting throats. And you waited until *now* to tell me."

"I want you to do what you alone of all of us have extensive experience doing," Ruby said. "Yes." Then, to whatever she saw in Isabel's face: "Don't think of it in those terms. Think of it like this. Those people are counting on you. You are their last line of defense. You are their only hope of mercy. Because you're absolutely right. Every other option is slow, and painful, and unnecessarily cruel."

Isabel stared at her.

"You could send a guard then," she said at length. "You're going to tell me they haven't killed before?"

Ruby opened her mouth to answer, but Isabel didn't give her the chance.

"But you won't send them," she said. "Because they're part of the town, and you trust *them* to fight for it. And you *can't* trust them to kill their own people. But they're not *my* people, so *I* can do that no problem."

"Isabel—"

"No. You know, you're right. They're not."

She stormed away a few steps, then stopped short.

"I'll stay in the tunnels," she said, her voice abruptly colder. Calmer. It backed Ruby up a step. "But on one condition. When the fight starts, Sairy is my voice. The other girls from the shrine answer to her above you or anyone else."

"Isabel, there are extensive plans in place already for—"

Isabel plowed over her, her tone unchanging. After all, it'd been the voice in her head for three years. "That is not negotiable. They are a unit, and that unit moves on her command. And I'm not sure you even *begin* to deserve to have them at your service. So when this is over and I get Sairy's report, the only thing I expect to hear about you is the *extent of your gratitude.*"

Ruby was looking at her like the Ragpicker Himself was clacking His teeth at her heels.

"Send them whenever," Isabel said flatly. "I'm ready."

She strode away, fists jammed into her pockets to hide the shaking in her hands, and didn't stop until she found herself back at the hatch, pacing furiously back and forth along the length of the ghostgrass barricade. The old wound in her calf was screaming at her, and the one in her side felt like someone had reached in and knitted a scarf with her guts, but she had no choice. She had nowhere else to go, and she couldn't stop moving. If she stayed still she presented a better target for all her thoughts to settle on her fully.

Eventually, though, her bad leg made the decision for her. She followed the path they'd cut in the corpseroot earlier and sat on the shut wheel of the hatch, elbows on knees, her face in her hands.

It wasn't that far in, but all the sound seemed to die at the edge of the brickfall cave, and she couldn't even make out the noise from the town. She was struck by a strangely uncomfortable sense of perfect balance, caught in that bubble of space between the collapsed building above her and the hatch below. A poisedness between the now and the Before, which she found herself mentally prodding, the way she'd poke a sore tooth with her tongue.

After a while she heard footsteps, picking their way through the ghostgrass. She'd been tailed by them often enough to recognize whose they were by sound alone.

"Not feeling like a party either?" Sairy asked, ducking into the cave. There came a distinct sloshing sound as Sairy plunked down beside her on the hatch-rim. "Lucky for you, I brought the party with me."

She nudged Isabel with her shoulder and passed over a wine-jug. Isabel didn't move. "I'm good, Sairy, thanks."

"Like hell. Come on. This is the brew-mistress's finest. There's peaches in it. All the way from Chooser's Blindside."

Isabel lifted her head. "I thought she was hoarding that batch."

"She was."

"She sold it to *Ruby*?"

"She *gave* it to *me*." Sairy was grinning outright. "What can I say, I'm very persuasive. Here."

Isabel took the jug. Went to put it down. Found herself taking a sip instead. It was delicious.

"Oh. I brought these too. Sorry, they kind of stuck together."

Sairy wrangled a couple of sweet buns out of her pocket and pried them apart, then passed Isabel one. It was full of what were very likely the garden's last blackberries.

Isabel wasn't hungry, but made herself eat with Sairy anyway. Not for the first time her friendship with the ex-upstarts struck her as something like a very soft, very warm, very cozy garment that just happened to not fit her quite right.

"How long do you think this has been here?" Sairy said eventually. Pointing up with the last corner of her pastry at the ceiling of the brickfall cave.

Isabel shrugged.

"Maybe the earthquake the other day loosened it up," Sairy went on. "Maybe it'll come down on us while we're sitting here. Stomp us like Ember Girl's own bootheel." She clapped her hands together once, then picked up the jug and drank. Laughed. "Squish."

Isabel took the jug from her and hefted it in one hand. It wasn't very heavy. "How full was this when you—"

"I remember my family," Sairy blurted. At Isabel's incredulous look, she laughed a little, bitterly. "I know, we're not supposed to, we got taken too young. But I see them sometimes when I dream. Until you figured out the truth about how we got here, I thought that's all it was. Just dreams. We're in a different town. It's in, like, a bend in a river, so the water wraps around the whole front of the town." She gestured widely: a broad ribbon of water, curving. "In this dream there's fire on the river, something burning. Whatever it is, it smells like the Ragpicker's own crapper, and it burns green." Sairy paused. "I think maybe I had a brother? I don't know. Some boy. He put me in a basket and hid me on a cart. Told me *hush*. When I'm dreaming I can see his face, but when I'm awake and try to remember it, he turns into Aneko. And I'm forgetting *her* face too."

Despite herself, Isabel flinched. Aneko, the upstart Isabel had tried to save. Had tried to spare during the last Archivist-choosing fight, thus breaking the system and freeing them all. And failed.

"We had a plan," Sairy said. "Aneko and me. To escape together. Steal a map and try to find a town along a river. See what we see. I don't know. Stupid, probably." Then, her tone brisk: "Obviously we never got up the guts to *do* it, and now she's dead." When Sairy broke the ensuing silence her tone had changed again. "Sometimes in the dream it's her burning, pushing me down into the basket while her hair goes up like a warn-fire. Brightest green you ever saw."

She took the wine-jug back and drank. "I used to want to kill you, you know."

"To avenge her," Isabel said. "I kind of figured."

"Partly, maybe? Mostly just so I could become Archivist instead and find her."

There was so much Isabel could say to that. "If you found her," she heard herself saying instead, "she wouldn't know you anymore."

Sairy's smile wasn't a smile, not really. "It took her a long time to die. She didn't know me by the end of that either."

After a moment's hesitation Sairy pulled a folded paper out of her jacket and handed it to Isabel. "Don't get mad at me," she said. "Here."

Isabel didn't have to unfold that paper to know what it was.

"If the town gets trashed tomorrow," Sairy said, and stopped. "I thought—I don't know—you'd want that kept."

"I guess," Isabel said, or meant to. No sound came out. She turned the folded paper over and over in her hands.

"All I want to know," Sairy said softly, "is if they're the ones who hurt you."

Isabel looked at her sharply. "No."

Silence raveled out between them.

"They healed me," she made herself say, and she heard Sairy's breath catch. "I would've died."

A pause, and then, delicately: "When you were gone that winter."

"That's right."

"With one of those healing things! That's how you knew what—"

"Yeah."

Visibly, Sairy tried to drop it. But she couldn't help herself. Three years of silence was a long time. "You should've seen the Catchkeep-priest's face when the dogs couldn't starve you down off the Hill," she said all in a rush. "He told us Catchkeep had gotten sick of your disobedience, stepped down out of the sky and swatted your useless ass dead, but you could see in his face that he didn't believe it. He knew you finally got away, and he knew we knew it, and that's the part he *really* didn't like. He'd whip us if he heard us say your name. He—" Sairy trailed off. Closed her mouth. Braced herself. Opened it. "Isabel, what *happened* out there?"

Isabel thought about what it must cost Sairy to reach out, over and over again, despite what Isabel had taken from her. Thought how maybe, if both their lives had gone very differently, it might cost her nothing to reach back.

So Isabel unfolded the paper. Looking at that sketch made her feel like she was trying to puke up something bigger than her whole self.

"This one—" a jab toward the page, pulled just shy of contact— "came to me. Wanted my help. I wanted out. We made a deal."

"Deal how? Ghosts can't—"

"Talk? Think in a straight line? Interact with the living? Yeah. Well." Isabel wasn't even trying to lift her gaze from the sketch anymore. Like Wasp was this whole separate person that Isabel used all her strength to hold underwater, and every so often Isabel lost her grip, and Wasp came up gasping. "This one could."

It took Sairy a moment to process that. "What did it want?"

So, went the voice in her head. *I take it you are in the business of hunting ghosts.*

In response Isabel tapped the other figure in the sketch, the one that had *catherine foster* floating over its head like a halo. "To find his friend."

"In the Waste?"

"In the ghost-place."

None of this was squaring with what Sairy had been taught. She was blinking hard, shaking her head like she could physically shift the information into place.

"Wait. To *find*—but. They don't *remember* any—"

Isabel looked at her.

"Don't tell me," Sairy said. "This one did." Then, when Isabel didn't refute it, even more skeptically: "From the *Before*."

Nobody knew how long back the Before even was. When it had ended. How long it had taken people to scrape the residue of their lives back together and push it, over untold generations, into the shape of something new. It was a question that not even four hundred years of ghostcatching and field notes had been able to answer. Isabel watched as Sairy's mind threw itself at those unknowable numbers, gained no handholds, slid off. "But *why?*"

Isabel couldn't begin to explain to Sairy what little she understood about the Latchkey Project. How it turned children into living weapons. Its four percent survival rate.

"They fought in a war together." The voice in her head: *when there were twelve of us left, they partnered us up. Not to help each other. To inform on each other. It didn't work out quite the way they wanted.* "They . . . took turns saving each other. They weren't supposed to, but they did. Foster's last turn got her killed. To protect him."

"From what?"

"Bad shit." Isabel didn't even have to close her eyes to see the little room where they'd tried to break Foster, again and again, healing her up just to give them more to cut into. Three days and they couldn't crack her. And then—

Isabel dug her nails into her forearm, bringing herself back. "Very bad shit."

Sairy shook her head slowly, awed. "Making deals with ghosts. Making *friends* with ghosts. It's—" She had an upstart's upbringing, so she knew what would've been expected of her as Archivist in the off-chance she drew the short straw and managed to not get herself murdered. Catch ghosts, study them, destroy them, go catch more. It was a short list, on which bargaining and befriending did not appear. "This is crazy. What are they like? Where are they now?"

"Gone."

"How do you know?" Hard to tell if Sairy was still thinking of Aneko or if she was just terminally optimistic.

"Because," Isabel said. Hating how her voice was rising unsteadily. Wholly unable to stop it. Briskly she folded the paper back up and shoved it into her pocket. "They came back for me."

"Really?"

"And I sent them away."

Sairy blinked, absorbing this. "They might—"

"No," Isabel said shortly. "They won't."

It took a second for that to sink in. Even without watching Sairy's face, it was easy to know when it had.

"No," Sairy said, aghast. "No way. You—"

"It was the best way to protect the town," Isabel said softly.

They gazed out at the silver sea of ghostgrass.

"But if you—" Sairy began, and then jumped off the hatch as Jen and Bex exploded into the brickfall cave. "Don't *do* that!"

"Oh thank the Chooser," Jen panted. Had she run all this way? She gestured breathlessly at the hatch, where Bex was already getting her grip on the wheel. "Help me get that open."

"Now?" Isabel asked. "But—"

"Perimeter shot a scout a quarter hour ago," Bex said, cranking the hatch-wheel. "Raider army's not two miles behind him."

"They're not supposed to be here yet," Sairy protested lamely.

"Well," Bex replied, "you're going to have plenty of chance to tell them that. Real soon."

"Oh shit," Sairy said. "Oh *shit*."

"The kids are right behind us," Jen said. "A few adults. Glory's showing them the way."

"And the supplies?" Isabel asked.

"Let's just say we'll have to wrap this fight up fast," Bex said.

Sairy froze. "*What?*"

"There's what they could grab on foot," Jen clarified. "It's not much." She tilted her head, listening. "Here they come."

"On three," Isabel said, and she and Bex heaved the door open. "Tell me you at least brought lamps."

"I have one," Glory said, appearing at the edge of the cave.

"One," Sairy repeated. "One lamp."

"Lin has another, I saw it."

Isabel flung a staying hand back toward the field of corpseroot. "Keep them back! One at a time, and not until I say. There's thorns." Then, as Glory's words sunk in: "But Ruby's not sending guards down."

"Lin's not here as a guard," Glory said as Jen lit the lamp. "She's nursing babies."

"She only has one baby," Sairy said.

"She's nursing *all* the babies. This is ready to send down."

"On what?" Bex said. "Give me a rope."

Glory froze. "*Shit*—"

"Don't worry," Sairy said. "I got it." Scrambling one-handed down the ladder with the lamp.

"Okay," she called up. "Bex, get down here so you can keep the kids in line. I can't watch the ones in the tunnels and the ones on the ladder at the same time."

"I'm sending Glory," Bex said. "Her arm's busted. There's at least one sick person up here who needs to be lowered, and Isabel can't—" She bit off the rest of that sentence. "You're getting Glory."

Bex helped Glory down, then situated herself at the hatch with Jen while Isabel took over the bottleneck at the cave entrance. There was a crowd of people there, mostly terrified children. Isabel picked out a total of three adults, one of whom was too sick to walk and was being carried by the other two on a litter. One cart of supplies. As far as Isabel could see, two jugs of water. Some random bags and bundles and loaves and baskets and whatnot held in arms. That was all.

It wasn't near enough. Not for this many people, not for any length of time.

But it was going to have to be.

"Everyone quiet." *Now there are two ways we can do this,* said a voice in her head. *Calmly or the other way.* "Line up and come along the path one at a time. Don't touch the thorns."

Isabel gestured to the adults bearing the litter. The songkeeper and one of the water-boilers, it looked like.

"No," the songkeeper called back. "Children first." He waved at Onya, who was hesitating at the edge of the ghostgrass barricade with a sack of acorn flour hugged in both arms. "Go."

"Here's how we're doing this," Isabel said. Gesturing for Onya to come forward. "We're going to toss down any supplies that won't be damaged in the fall. Then you go down and relay that stuff back to the cleared area. Glory will show you the way. Then—" Isabel pulled a couple more older kids out of the crowd— "you two help her. You three are on supplies duty. Glory!"

Glory's voice echoed up. "Yeah?"

"You make sure they're putting that stuff where it actually belongs and not just dumping it wherever."

"Got it."

"I'm going to lower some really little kids down," Jen told Glory. "Can you reach them?"

"Broken arm?" Glory reminded her. "Bex, get down here!"

"Little busy."

"I'll go," said a woman from the crowd. Lin the guard stepped forward, two babies strapped onto her, front and back. She handed them off to the songkeeper and climbed down.

One by one, townspeople disappeared into the hole after her.

Ten down. Fifteen. Twenty.

At twenty-eight there came a horrible noise from below. A long metallic screeching, followed by a crash.

"Whatever that was," Isabel called over one shoulder, "it better have been on purpose."

"Ladder gave way," Glory yelled back from below. "The rest will have to lower themselves down."

"Prop it back up," Bex told her.

"It's in about twenty pieces all over the floor. They're gonna have to jump. Give me a minute to clear a space for them to drop to."

"I still have some busted-up person on a stretcher up here," Isabel shouted. "We need a rope."

"There's no time," Jen said. "We'll figure it out. Keep sending them."

They got the children all lowered down, and then worked together with Lin and the songkeeper to get the sick person—a man Isabel didn't know—readied for lowering.

"Put him apart from the others," Isabel said.

"He's not catching," Jen said, voice hushed. "I know him. That's David. He got hit by lightning out in the Waste on a scav run a week ago. He almost died."

"He *did* die," Bex added. "That's what I heard. His heart stopped and they were going to bury him but he woke back up."

As Isabel stared after the man, he began coughing. He hacked up a mouthful of pink froth and spat to the side of the hatch.

Alarm brought her up a little straighter on her feet. "That's blood."

"Barely any. Look, what do you want us to do, leave him up here?" Jen read Isabel's face and shook her head. "We're not leaving him up here."

"I want you to go *bury* him in ghostgrass," Isabel told Bex. "But don't draw attention to what you're doing or why. Understand?"

Wordlessly Bex swung down into the hole. At the bottom, Isabel could just make out one of the kids, struggling with the last armload of supplies. Bex shouldered half of the load and they disappeared into the dark together.

Isabel gave the situation until the count of ten to present another catastrophe on the order of the collapsed ladder. Nothing came. Voices echoed out from the cleared area. That was all.

"That's the last of them," Jen said. "Let's close it up."

"I'm not coming with you."

"What? Why?"

"Because this was my plan," Isabel said, "and I have to stay to see it through."

Jen took this in. "But the fight—"

"The guards can fight. *You* can fight."

"Not like you."

"Maybe a few years ago," Isabel said, "that might've been true."

Then, entirely unsure how to say goodbye for what might end up being rather longer than just a day or two, Isabel found herself brusquely giving Jen advice instead.

"Watch your footprints," she said. "Keep ghostgrass on you."

"Ration the supplies," Jen replied. "The water and lamp-oil especially. Have them eat the really fresh stuff first before it spoils." Her face twisted. "Not that there's much of it."

"Fight dirty. But don't fight stupid. And when you come back to let us out, I guess we don't have anything to climb up now. Bring ropes."

"Bex and Glory get themselves killed on your watch, I've instructed them to send their ghosts back to haunt you."

"You get yourself killed, I'm going to take the barricades down so I can beat your ghost's ass personally."

"Deal," Jen said, and Isabel climbed down into the dark.

Chapter Six

I n the tunnels, at first everything was chaos. Kids yelling, kids crying, babies crying. The injured man David moaning in pain, presumably from the less-than-gentle descent. Bex and Glory hustling to move the supplies to a corner of the cleared area where they could be guarded and rationed and kept safe from accidental spillage.

Isabel got to work. She had a clear sense of what to do and how to do it, and it gave her the same weird sense of peace that she got from loading up on chore rotations at the Catchkeep-shrine. Alongside her, Bex and Glory pulled their own weight and then some. Gradually, things calmed.

First thing: make sure everyone else stayed busy and out of their own heads. They'd all watched that hatch close, watched their light dwindle to what they carried. It wasn't just her that could use the distraction.

There were only three adults plus the sick one.

Lin, the perimeter guard, who was healthy.

The songkeeper, sworn to the Chooser, whose faith did not permit him to fight. The father of one of the kids who brought boiled lakewater to the shrine every morning, slowly organizing rations with a bandage on his head. Another earthquake casualty like Glory, Isabel guessed.

She made sure everyone knew not to touch the ghostgrass for any reason whatsoever. She set older children in charge of keeping the smaller ones away from the perimeter she'd staked out the day before.

"I have to check you all for cuts and scrapes," Isabel said. "Anyone who knows they're bleeding, or sees someone bleeding, come to me. I'll get around to all of you but those ones are first."

Nobody came, so she collared Onya and gave her a quick once-over. Found a scrape on her upper arm and bandaged it. "You're my eyes," she told her. "Anyone's hurt, bring them here."

In between checking people, she surveyed the pile of supplies. There were half a dozen big jugs of water, which turned out to be most of what the supply-cart had been holding. A couple sacks of acorn flour, one of dried meat, two of black walnuts, one of dried plums. A few loaves of bread. A basket of carrots, still dirty from the garden. A basket of raw eggs, some broken. A roll of bandages. A jar of lamp-oil. Three lamps.

It would be enough for a few days. They'd be hungry, and thirsty, and uncomfortable, but they'd live.

As she worked, Isabel kept glancing over at David. Bex had stashed him off in the corner of the ghostgrass perimeter nearest the waypoint. More bundles of ghostgrass lay at the head and foot of his blanket, and some of Glory's ghostgrass paste was smeared around his mouth. He lay there, muttering feverishly, tended by the midwife's apprentice, an eleven-year-old girl named Rina.

Commotion behind her as the songkeeper began to unpack his puppets. Isabel caught a glance of The One Who Got Away with His/Her arms sewn into a position of time-biding patience, Carrion Boy and Ember Girl all in black, and the Chooser with Her good eye and blind eye and little scaled-down cape of mouse- and bird-bones stitched together.

Within five minutes the songkeeper had drawn a crowd, two dozen pairs of eyes now staring enraptured at his recital of "Catchkeep's Favorite Children."

He could've grabbed some food instead, Isabel thought, but then realized how quiet the tunnels had become and changed her mind.

Out of the corner of her eye, a couple of older kids about Onya's age were rifling through the debris piled along at the other edge of the perimeter.

"Hey," she called out. "Leave that stuff alone. Glory!"

"You two! Over here!" a voice barked out. The perimeter guard, Lin. She had her daughter slung sleeping across her back and was adroitly nursing two other babies as she summoned the kids with her eyes. Onya and Andrew, the songkeeper's grandson.

"Everybody has a job to do," Lin told them. "Your parents would be really proud of you if you help with the babies and little kids down here. They're really scared and they don't understand what's going on and they're way too little to take care of themselves. Or," she continued, "I can tell them you were causing trouble. Or I can just deal with you myself." At their look of terror, Lin's face softened. "But I'd rather not. See that tall lady over there with the spiky hair?" Nodding across the way at Glory, crankily wrangling a swarm of toddlers into the songkeeper's circle. "I bet she could give you some important work to do."

They ran off and Isabel mouthed *thank you* at Lin.

"So this is turning out to be an interesting day," Lin said. "Straight from a party to a lockdown."

Isabel hesitated. It was a rare thing, someone from the town talking to her. Someone not of the Catchkeep-shrine, someone not Ruby when she wanted something.

"What's it like up there?" she asked. Carefully not asking: *did Ruby even explain what was coming before it got here?* Not asking: *was anyone ready for it?* Or: *were the ex-upstarts the only ones who even knew?*

"I don't know," Lin said. "They rushed us down here first thing." Then, quieter: "Yulia and Jacen assembled the guards earlier and told us. Some of us went to ready the defenses while the people were distracted."

Somehow, Isabel wasn't surprised. "That sounds familiar."

"They'll be fine," said Lin. "Perimeter will spot the raiders miles off." Lin attempted a gesture that might have been the beginning of the drawing of a bow, before realizing her arms were full. She adjusted her grip on a protesting baby and grinned. "Target practice."

Isabel made a noncommittal sound. But Lin was just warming to her subject.

"Plus we still have a few surprises stashed in the guardhouse for just such an occasion. These slag-for-brains are only getting in along the Waste-road, unless they've grown wings or they plan on swimming. We'll mop them up by dinnertime."

"Well," Isabel conceded. "I hope you're right."

"I saw some of yours up there keeping pretty busy too," Lin said. "Lissa and Meg made this one thing with tripwires and some old broken knives that looks pretty nasty."

"That sounds like them. Listen, do you need me to get you anything? Water? Did you eat?"

"Bex took care of me. I'm good."

"Okay. Yell if that changes."

Lin nodded. "Will do."

She didn't even realize the midwife's apprentice had come up behind her, the girl was so quiet. When Isabel turned she almost tripped over her.

"David says his skin is stinging him," Rina said.

"His *skin* is stinging him?"

"And he's dizzy."

"Okay," Isabel said. Trying not to let her exasperation show. "What do you usually do about that?"

"I don't know. It just started. When we came down here."

"Keep him comfortable. We'll be out of here soon."

Glory came up to her, looking troubled. "Isabel."

"*What.*"

"Where are they supposed to pee."

Isabel turned to stare at her. She hadn't even thought of it yesterday, and now their options were pretty limited. For one second she entertained the notion of sending the kids down the hall to squat with that glowing ghost-passage at their backs. No chance.

So she took a lamp and a bundle of ghostgrass, set Glory in charge, and went off to clear the space directly on the other side of the hatch entrance.

Before she'd even made her way back over the dented fallen door, she could hear noises coming from the hatch. No: from directly below the hatch. Instinctively she ducked out of the open doorway, curling her body around the lamp to hide its glow in the wide wings of the Archivist-coat. Making sure the harvesting-knife was within easy reach. Running through scenarios in her head, none of them good.

She left the lamp, tiptoed through the doorway in the almost perfect dark. Somebody was frantically trying to jam the broken rungs of the ladder back into the holes it had ripped from the wall.

Isabel snuck up on the figure, grabbed it, spun it around.

"Isabel?"

"*Sairy?*" Sheathing the harvesting-knife. "What the hell—"

"I was trying to—"

"You're not even supposed to *be* here."

"I *know*. I was helping settle people in. When I went to leave, the hatch was already shut, and the ladder . . . " In a fit of frustration she hurled a broken rung at the wall. "There has to be a way to fix it. There *has to*."

Cursing under her breath, Isabel fetched the lamp. Raised it toward the hatch. It was easily six feet above her head, and it weighed more than any three of the ex-upstarts combined. For all its weight it opened surprisingly easily on its hinge—but only if they could reach it.

"This is a problem," she said.

"I know. I screwed up. I thought Jen would *wait* for me—"

"Go find me the strongest person in there who isn't Lin."

Sairy took off and returned with Bex. After several minutes of taking turns boosting each other upward on interlaced hands, they fell back defeated. They hadn't even managed to so much as brush that hatch-wheel with their fingertips.

"It's right there," Sairy wailed, gesturing violently upward. "It's *right there*."

"Okay," Isabel said. "Get Lin."

Bex went and got Lin and they still couldn't reach the wheel enough to grip and turn it.

"We need a ladder," Lin observed.

"No shit," Sairy said.

"You were trying to push the pieces back into the wall?" Lin said. "Some Before-people tool put them there, you can't just do that with your *hands*."

"We had a whole *plan*," Sairy wailed. "Me and Lissa and Meg and everybody, we were going to work together, they don't trust the high seats, they'll—" She trailed off, horrified. "All hands in the fight. *They said we need all hands in—*"

"*You* need to breathe," Isabel said, because now Sairy was eyeing the tunnel wall like she was planning to dig her way out through that and twenty feet of dirt beyond. "Jen knew you were supposed to be up there. She'll come back for you. Or she'll send someone. They can open it from above."

But a very different thought was running through her mind.

I told Jen I was staying down here. And Sairy's been shadowing me for years. Jen must have thought—

And I told Ruby that the ex-upstarts only take orders from Sairy.

"And what if she doesn't? Or she can't? What if she's pinned down in the fight and *I can't get to her?*"

"Sairy. Listen to me. Right now you need to calm down and you need to—"

A distant cry came from behind her, way up the hall in the cleared area.

"That's Glory," Bex said, and took off running, Sairy right behind her.

"What the *shit now,*" Isabel hissed under her breath, following them as best she could. "Ragpicker take this day and every—"

She stopped when she saw Glory's face.

"Please tell me," Glory was saying, "that Onya and Andrew are with you." Looking around the cleared area like maybe two ten-year-old kids were hidden under a brick she hadn't checked yet. "I just saw them a minute ago."

"Well, they didn't go that way," Bex said, nodding down the hall in the direction of the waypoint and cave-in.

"And they sure as hell didn't go *up,*" Sairy said.

Glory caught sight of her. "Sairy? Aren't you supposed to be—"

Sairy blew out a frustrated breath, throwing up her hands. "Surprise."

"If you just saw them, they're not far," Isabel told Glory, already walking backwards down the hall, away from the waypoint. "Nobody moves. Nail them to the floor if you have to. I'll just be a minute."

"Bring them back safe so I can kill them," Glory called after Isabel's back. A pause. Then, incredulous: "Did they take a *lamp?*"

After a few steps Isabel caught sight of someone approaching her shoulder. "Sairy, what part of *nobody moves*—"

"This is my fault and I'm going with you and that's just how it is so let's go."

For one second Isabel considered this. It'd probably be easier to push a Sairy-sized boulder back to the cleared area, by hand, uphill, than it would've been to talk her out of it.

"Then you get to hold the lamp," she said, and together they headed into the dark.

Soon they'd gone far enough that the collected lamplight of the cleared area beyond the hatch couldn't reach them. The sounds of the townspeople could only be heard faintly, wavering, like murmurs at the bottom of a well. Ahead was black. Behind was black.

No sign of Onya or Andrew.

Isabel's wrists began to itch.

"I get to help Glory kill them," Sairy was muttering. "She can hold them down."

Ten more paces and they'd reached the first door.

It was made of some kind of metal that had only barely begun to rust, which amazed her, given the humidity of the tunnels and the sheer age of everything in them. It was rectangular, as heavy-looking as the hatch door, with a small opening at eye level set with the remains of what used to be a tiny window, glass layered with a very resilient-looking synthetic mesh.

There was a dent in the center of the door like someone had catapulted a boulder at it.

Isabel didn't like the look of this door one bit. It didn't look like a door for going in and out of. It looked like a door built in the same spirit as an Archivist's ghost-catching jars. For locking something up and taking field notes on it, and eventually letting it out into some-place even worse.

Sairy shouldered open the door on shrieking hinges and shoved her lamp-arm in. Nothing.

There was an identical door beside that one, and another beside it. Another across the hall. Another next to that. And so on. Several had been dented by some great force. Some had been ripped straight out of the wall and flung an improbable distance. Like someone at some point had gone to considerable trouble to trash this place to hell, and had gone about it methodically, systematically, door by door by door.

"Well," Sairy said, shining the lamp down that field of doors. "That's creepy."

Isabel didn't reply. The nervous itching on her wrists was getting truly awful now, and spreading to her neck and hands. She scratched under the ghostgrass bracelets covertly.

They investigated the next room together, and the next, and the next.

Inside each room was nothing. Same floor, same walls, same ceiling. All apparently once white and white no longer. Isabel couldn't even imagine what it must've looked like, all that white. Like staring down on the Waste from a height when fresh snow was on it, so bright in the sunlight that it hurt the eyes.

Each little room itself was empty but for the remains of where something had once been bolted into the wall in two places before the bolts rusted through. A bed of some kind, maybe, a narrow metal slab. On the other side of the room there was a hole where a pipe had gone into the wall, attached presumably to something else, now collapsed into rubble or missing altogether.

It came to Isabel that each door had a handle on the outside, but the inside was smooth.

No Onya, no Andrew. They moved on.

By the eighth room, Isabel was starting to get dizzy. When had she last eaten? Her vision was going weird around the edges, like she had a migraine coming on. And it was taking every crumb of her willpower not to scratch her itchy wrists to bleeding.

"What do you think did this?" Sairy asked, voice hushed. Raising the lamp at a door that, to all appearances, had been thrown so hard that the edge of it had embedded itself in the wall.

Despite herself, Isabel reached out and touched it, and Sairy gasped.

"Isabel, what the *hell*."

"What?"

Sairy grabbed her hand and dragged it by main force into the light. There was an angry red rash on Isabel's wrist and palm.

"Isabel, are you okay?"

"Of course I'm okay." Reclaiming her hand. Shoving it into a pocket. Her conversation with Rina earlier was returning to her uncomfortably. *His* skin *is stinging him?* "Come on. They can't be far. You go on ahead." Swallowing her pride. "You're faster."

"There's one lamp."

"So I'll follow it. The longer we wait the farther they get." Isabel gestured up that endless corridor of rooms. Chooser, she was dizzy. "I'm right behind you."

"I'm going to *kill* them," Sairy muttered again, and hauled open the next door.

Isabel locked her focus on the ground at her feet, shutting out the migraine aura edging in on the sides of her vision, and started walking.

No problem at all to trail Sairy. Her lamplight was easily close enough to safely follow. Nothing on the floor was likely to trip Isabel up even if she wasn't staring at it. Just the same even field of broken tile both ways, like the thin ice on a puddle that somebody had stomped. Broken tile and mud squelching up between.

Isabel had gone a few steps like that when she slipped on a patch of ice where that broken tile should've been and her feet shot out from under.

She went down in a heap and sat there. She felt, and probably looked, like somebody had just tried to brain her with a brick.

Ice?

In the middle of summer?

She hitched in a steadying breath. It smelled wrong. The only parts of it she could identify were winter air and smoke, although she couldn't guess what would smell like that when burning. There was another smell almost like metal left out in the summer sun, at odds with the general smell of cold. And another like a sudden burst of improbable flowers as someone brushed past her and kept on walking, unseen, a shadow dissolving in the dark.

"Sairy?" she whispered.

No answer.

She scrambled back and hit a smooth glass wall. Which had about as much business being in these tunnels as the ice. Too startled to shout, she gave a kind of squeak and recoiled hard enough to almost flop over sideways and stared up and up and up at what used to be the low-ceilinged side of the tunnel, last she'd checked.

It was a building. A very tall building. Taller than any building, any tree, any *thing* she'd ever seen, short of Execution Hill—except in the city she'd entered in the ghost-place, the memory of a city from a time not her own. Glass and metal flashing blue in the low-slung winter sunlight. People walked past her, over her, through her. They didn't say anything or notice her there. They didn't smell like the people of Sweetwater. Their coats flapped against her like crows' wings.

It was a hallucination. Had to be. Bad air in the tunnels. Maybe that's why she'd been so dizzy.

Catchkeep, she thought. *The Chooser. Ember Girl. Carrion Boy. The Hunt. The Ragpicker. The Crow. The One Who Got Away. Catchkeep's Tower. The Grave. The First to Die.*

Even listing constellations wasn't cutting through this one. She felt like the tunnel had flipped sideways, not worming just under the surface but boring straight down for miles, and she was tumbling into the dark. Frantically, she marshaled her senses to anchor her.

It was silent, so if she was silent too she'd hear Sairy walking ahead. If she looked down she'd see the broken-eggshells-and-mud patterning of the tile floor.

She was quiet—and heard the footsteps of the not-there-people all around her. She glanced down—and froze.

There was a faint pale light coming from somewhere, and in it, she could just make out an even fainter silver thread, flickery but definitely there, emerging from her breastbone and fading to nothing as it fed out away from the light.

Strange, that light. It was a cold phosphorescence, like what was thrown by a ghost-passage, or a ghost—

She clung to the thread as something behind it, deep in her chest, lurched into freefall.

The light was coming from *her.*

"Not possible," she whispered. She wasn't in the ghost-place. She hadn't left her body.

Possible or not, the thread pulsed almost invisibly along with her heartbeat. It moved—the tiniest bit—in her breath. She plucked one dull flat note on it and did not dare touch it again, because she knew what it was, what it had to be, and that nothing good would happen to her if it broke.

In that instant, the sound cut out, and all was quiet.

The silence scared her worse than the noise. The noise was something she could track. She had a horrible feeling that the silence hid something that was tracking *her*.

She found her feet and tried to dart off through the crowd—and the crowd wasn't there. Mildewed walls, busted floor, slimy pond-smell, the warm humid stillness of the tunnels like a clammy hand laid across her face.

There was a person lying sprawled on the tile a few feet away. It wore a long brown coat and had short brown hair. The other end of her thread was sticking out of that body's chest. It was a moment before she realized it was her.

It was like startling yourself awake from a nightmare. She snapped back into her body so fast that for a moment it felt wrong, ill-fitting, unresponsive.

"Sairy?" she croaked. Unsure what she would say when Sairy answered. *Can you see me? Did I disappear just now? Am I back?*

Shakily, she stood. No more glow. No more thread. The dampness of the floor hadn't soaked through her pant-legs. She must've only been lying there a second or two at most. But it'd felt like many minutes had passed.

That unsettled her almost as much as the thread. She knew quite well where she'd experienced both of those things before.

Took two steps and stopped, splaying her hands at hip level as if the ground had just trembled underfoot. A weird feeling gripped her, one she couldn't begin to name. It felt almost like that untethering sensation she'd get when she was almost asleep. It put her in mind of soft mud being pressed through a loose-woven basket, or one stack of papers being shuffled into another. If she were the mud, the paper, pressed through or shuffled into . . . what?

So, she thought drily, because it was either that or lose it entirely. *This is new.*

"Isabel." Sairy sounded farther off than she should've. "Think I found them."

One quick look over her shoulder—nothing tailing her—and Isabel set off toward the bright radius of Sairy's lamp, shaking her head to clear it.

Sairy was standing in the middle of the hall, gesturing with the lamp toward another door a little ways ahead. No—Isabel realized—not the door but something on the floor in front of it.

"At least they weren't *completely* stupid," Sairy was saying. "I'm still going to kill them though. You open the door and I'll go in and give them hell."

Then Isabel drew level with Sairy and saw what she was looking at. Ghostgrass.

Dried, bundled ghostgrass. Visibly older than what they'd brought with them into the tunnels. Paler, more brittle, less potent. Entire bundles, three of them, carefully laid to overlap end-to-end across the foot of the door.

It looked a whole lot like what had gone missing from the way-point at the cave-in.

"This," she said carefully, "isn't ours."

"Huh?" Sairy said, turning. "Then what—"

Away up the hall, Onya's voice. Laughing. Then she and Andrew emerged from one of the farther rooms, spilling lamplight before them. Caught sight of Sairy and Isabel and froze.

Sairy fishhooked them with her eyes. "Get. *Over.* Here. *Now.*"

They obeyed. At least they had the good grace to look sheepish.

Sairy strode ahead to meet them partway. As she walked past the ghostgrassed doorway, she stopped. Seemed to lose focus. She was shifting her weight from foot to foot, rubbing her arms, looking lost. "What is that?"

Isabel looked from Sairy to the ghostgrass to the shut door beyond.

"All of you," she said, keeping her voice as calm and even as she was able, "come here."

"We're sorry," Andrew called down the hall as he and Onya approached. "Really sorry," Onya added. "Please don't be mad at us. We were just exploring."

Sairy didn't seem to hear them. "No, seriously, what *is*—"

She staggered sideways like something had pushed her. But nothing had.

Then Isabel realized she felt it too. Frostbite and vertigo. The exact unmistakable sensation of touching a ghost.

Except she wasn't.

Three years Isabel had been Archivist. She'd encountered many hundreds of ghosts and was thoroughly familiar with the wide variation of every class of specimen. From the silver wisps too weak to coalesce, all the way up to the enraged blinding blurs of light too pissed off to coalesce. And, of course, the ones in between. Able to coalesce but not do much else.

The pissed-off ones had mindlessly attacked her, from time to time, and done worse to several Archivists before her. But even with the strongest of those, the frostbite-and-vertigo sensation only came when she picked one up, or one grabbed hold of her ankle like a baby, or when one's fist slammed into her face hard enough to loosen teeth.

It came on contact. Only on contact.

But there was nothing there.

Was that a flicker of light across the darkened little window of that door? There and gone, darting past like a fish in the shallows, leaving her questioning whether it'd been there at all. It might've been nothing more than their lamplight reflecting. But it'd looked too silvery for that, and Isabel's luck had never been that good.

If it came down to it, could she still fight a ghost? Or would she meet with that occupational hazard described with such horrified fascination in the field notes by the Archivists next in line? Shredded, bled out, flayed for the salt of her fear-sweat . . .

"Stop," she said, throwing up a staying hand toward the approaching light of Onya's lamp. Her mind was whirring back and forth between Sairy and the children in desperate calculation. None of them were going to be any help to her here. She'd have to hold this together with both hands, alone. *Should've covered this in training after all.*

"Stay there. I'm going to come to you."

"What's wrong with Sairy?" Onya called back.

"I said *stay there.*"

Already dragging Sairy away from the door. She looked like she was about to be sick. This close to the doorway, the frostbite-and-vertigo sensation ramped up and went through Sairy like a boot through rotten wood, and Isabel held her up bodily. Pulling

ghostgrass out of her pockets. Shoving it into Sairy's hands. Barely registering how it felt like it was frying her fingers. "Don't put
that down. Not for anything. I'm going to go get them. You turn
around quietly and start walking back the way we—"

The silver light whipped past again and faded, shuddered and
came back brighter, and the last dregs of her patience shriveled
abruptly up and died.

"*Sairy*, Ragpicker slag you, back it up or I will put you down."

Sairy didn't seem to hear her. She was frozen in place, gazing toward that little window in the door. "Isabel," she slurred, "something
in there just *moved*—"

Shivering violently now, Sairy swayed a few steps forward and
stumbled. Went down on one knee. Threw a hand out and down to
catch herself. There came a dry rustling sound as her fingers caught
on the end of the nearest ghostgrass bundle, shifting it ever so slightly out of line.

"*Run*," Isabel breathed, yanking Sairy by the shoulder as from
the doorway there came a sound of metal tearing.

Sairy had hardly turned from the door before it blew off its hinges, barely missing her as it shot across the tunnel and cratered the far
wall.

What stepped through that doorway wasn't featureless and silvery, like a ghost that hadn't been deliberately strengthened for questioning. This ghost was plenty strong enough on its own. It stood
there, large as life, looking like it'd just wandered in out of the Before, fully dressed and vaguely bewildered.

Automatically Isabel grabbed Sairy, dragged her back against the
wall. *Stay put*, she thought at Onya and Andrew up the hall. Hissing
at Sairy: "Don't move."

Then she really looked at that ghost, and all the strength ran out
of her like water.

It was female, around Isabel's height, with olive skin and
brown hair pulled back in a ponytail. It wore a uniform, basic
and dark, with clean lines and black boots. A gun and a sword
were stuck in its belt. It looked to have died not too much older
than Onya and Andrew were now. Blackish silver light steamed
gently off of it.

Isabel stared at it, a kind of hollow-seashell rushing sound in her ears.

She knew those clothes. She knew that gun and that sword and the way it was *radiating* strength, tendrils of visible energy shooting out of it like lightning. She'd seen all of that before.

But only once.

At that time, with the salt, and the kit, and the knife, and far fewer injuries, that other ghost had still nearly murdered her. Isabel looked across the roil of silver-black light at this specimen and knew that if it went after her, or Sairy, or Onya and Andrew, she was going to have to fight her way through it if she wanted to live. And knew, with equal certainty, that she would lose. Badly. This thing could probably spread her in an even layer across the tunnel floor without breaking stride.

Plastered in ghostgrass, Sairy was just about able to hold herself up now. "Is that a *ghost*?" she whispered. "It looks so . . . so *real*." She narrowed her eyes. "Wait. Isabel. It looks like—"

"Shh."

"It looks like the ones in your drawing."

"*Quiet.*"

Quickly, silently, she assessed. The ghost hadn't noticed them, or Onya and Andrew. That much was obvious. Sudden movement might draw it down on them, but thank the Chooser, the kids had some sense.

She had to think. But it was hard to. The frostbite-and-vertigo sensation was flowing freely out from the ghost, miring Isabel's thoughts. Waves of dark light lifted off of it, getting denser every minute, flaring and mantling like wings. The smell of it was like the lakeshore after lightning struck. The sound of it was one clear pure glassy note, shattered and reformed, still ringing, but with all its edges grinding one against the other.

It was pacing back and forth before the doorway like a shrine-dog on a too-short lead. Two steps and turn, two steps and turn. Seemingly agitated, staring at nothing from the open sores of its eyes. Blind as it was, Isabel had the distinct sensation that it was *aware* of her there. That if it turned her way it would see her. Not the space where she stood, which was all most ghosts seemed to be capable of. *Her.* Which should by no means have been possible.

But it didn't. It kept on pacing with its hands in its pockets as a comet-tail of dark silver light raged around it, brushing the ceiling.

Whatever had killed this ghost hadn't been pretty. An open lesion covered half of its face and tracked down its neck in weeping craters, and there was blood crusted around its nose and eyes. Patches of its hairline oozed where the hair had come out, taking scalp with it, and what little of its skin Isabel could see looked bruised.

She recognized it. She'd seen it years ago when she'd read Foster's memories. Coughing up clots, half its nails fallen out. Caught in the jaws of the illness that Isabel knew had been its death.

Salazar, she remembered. *Her name is Mia Salazar.*

The longer they stood there, the closer Isabel's flight instinct got to bypassing her brain and going right for her legs until it slingshot her back up that tunnel and away from the slag-pit of Salazar's face. But the Archivist-part of her was driving now, and it knew better than to turn its back on this caliber of specimen. And seeing a ghost in that uniform, with that sword and gun . . . complicated matters in ways she didn't have time just now to unpack and examine.

Salazar reached the end of her circuit and spun on her bootheel to stalk back the other way.

"Why isn't it killing you?" Salazar was repeating, over and over. "Why isn't it killing you?"

Sairy's voice in Isabel's ear. "Is it *talking?*"

"Stay still."

Every ghost had a moment it couldn't move past. Its death, usually. A choice it made wrong. A screwup it regretted enough to imprint upon. In any case, a loop it couldn't break free from. It stayed caught there like a leaf frozen into a block of ice, neither drifting nor landing.

It didn't escape Isabel's notice that Salazar's inability to break free of her loop was very possibly the only thing keeping her and Sairy—and everyone else in the tunnels—alive.

"Are you going to capture it?"

Another tight shake of Isabel's head. There was no way she was getting this thing in a jar. Besides, it'd been three years. Did her knife even still work?

"Are you going to destroy it?"

Her ghost-destroying kit was still in the pocket of her Archivist-coat. But part of that ritual involved lighting a fire. Outside was one thing. But in the tunnels?

"Only if she makes me."

"Did *you* put that ghostgrass in front of the door?"

"No. Hush."

Sairy took this in. "Then who—"

Eyes glued on Salazar, Isabel clapped her hand over Sairy's mouth.

Over by the doorway, Salazar had began nosing at the air, scenting like a predator. Suddenly, viscerally, Isabel wished Salazar still had eyes. Her slow blind triangulation of their position was extremely unnerving. It made Isabel uncomfortably aware that she was, at best, a slow-moving bag of blood, and it would take precious little effort on Salazar's part to unzip her.

Isabel's brain chose that moment to remind her of something she was far happier forgetting. Something she'd heard Foster say, when Isabel had read her memories.

We're not special, Foster had told what few of her fellow operatives had survived their treatment so far. *Martinez was special. Tanaka was special. Salazar was special. You know what we are? We're just* the ones who didn't die.

Martinez. Tanaka. Salazar. The best and brightest operatives that the Latchkey Project had to offer. And one of them, Chooser knew why, was here.

Had Salazar lived out her treatment, her strength and abilities might've surpassed the ghost's, surpassed Foster's. This was distinctly terrifying. Isabel had to focus on the *had she lived* part. Because if Salazar had already surpassed them despite dying so young, Isabel might well be staring across fifteen feet of empty space at the strongest ghost she'd ever seen.

But this old bundled ghostgrass, however it had gotten there, had held Salazar in that room. Even when she'd met the other ghost on Execution Hill three years ago, she'd had to remove the bundled ghostgrass from her door before he could enter.

As plans went it wasn't her first choice, but it wasn't nothing.

"Stick to the wall and head back the way we came," she commanded Sairy. Talking low and fast under her breath. "Slowly. You don't stop til you get over our ghostgrass perimeter and then you make sure everyone stays put. I don't care what you hear, you keep moving." Nodding toward the silver raging of Salazar's light. "I'm going to put her back where we found her. Then we—what are you doing?"

What Sairy was doing was pulling the rest of the ghost-grass from her pockets. Brandishing it in front of her. "Helping."

"Not happening. You're getting out of here."

"It's what, a dead thirteen-year-old girl? You get it back in the room. I'll fix the ghostgrass. Done and done."

Isabel stared at her in horror. *You really have no concept of the depth of what we're standing in, do you?*

What Sairy saw in Isabel's face decided her. "Fine," she whispered angrily. But she set her face and began backing away.

One down, Isabel thought. *Okay.*

She waited until Sairy was almost out of sight up the hall. Then, ghostgrass held out in front of her, she took a tiny careful step toward Salazar. Then another.

"Why isn't it killing you?" Salazar was still whispering to nobody Isabel could see. "Why isn't it killing you?"

Still sniffing vaguely at the air, and all at once Isabel knew what she was looking at.

She wasn't hunting at all. Stuck in that memory like quicksand, Salazar was *crying.*

A sound from way behind her, and she turned just in time to see Sairy stumble, tripped by something in the rubble. Saw her land neatly, one hand one knee. Heard her curse softly under her breath as she lifted that hand into the lamplight and stared at it, horrified, as the blood started trickling down.

Isabel spun back toward Salazar—and Salazar was no longer there.

Chapter Seven

Isabel didn't think. She moved. Somehow, gracelessly, bad leg screaming, she closed the distance. Already, with the proximity to blood, even from up the hall she could *feel* Salazar gaining strength. The color of the ghost-energy radiating off of her had condensed to a depthless, radiant black, like the space between the stars. The sound of it, that glassy keening, was now a shriek Isabel heard mostly in her teeth.

Sairy had popped up off the floor and was brandishing her fistful of ghostgrass at arm's length with two shaking hands, keeping Salazar—for the moment—at bay. "Isabel?" she asked uncertainly.

Salazar, however the hell she'd gotten there so quickly, had halted a few inches from the ghostgrass and was staring across that invisible barrier at Sairy, wrecked gaze drilling into her face. "Why isn't it killing *you?*" she screamed.

It was exactly here that Sairy hit her limit. She broke and ran.

"No—Sairy, *no*—"

Salazar lifted her head after Sairy, tracking her with something that could not possibly have been her eyes. *Blurred*—and reappeared in Sairy's path, reaching out for her.

So fast, Isabel thought wildly, *so*—

"Sairy, *look out!*"

At the last possible second, Sairy's brain seemed to accept what her eyes were showing it. She did what Isabel guessed anyone would do, seeing someone magically appear twenty feet from where she'd left them. She skidded to a startled halt so fast she nearly fell back over. Got hold of herself quickly enough to whip the ghostgrass into position, swinging it between herself and Salazar like a child beheading suns-and-moons with a stick-sword.

Salazar drifted back a step, though languidly, not obviously impressed. Ghostgrass or no, the blood had her attention now. It was going to be a hell of a job to shift her focus.

"Stay there," Isabel told Sairy. Working her way up the hall toward them. "Do—*not*—move."

"It's still bleeding," Sairy said, voice small. "I don't know how to make it stop. I think there's a piece of something stuck in there—from where I fell—"

"Don't panic," Isabel told her. "If there's something stuck in the wound, do *not* pull it out. Just put your hand in your pocket and back slowly—toward—me." *And,* she could've added, *start praying to the One Who Got Away that I can pull her attention off you before you get yourself eaten from the hand up.*

"Little further. Don't turn around. I'm right behind you." Grabbing a length of bandage fabric from her pocket. "Reach back and take this. Get that bleeding stopped, but keep the ghostgrass between you and her *at all times.* Okay?"

"Okay."

Isabel came up beside Sairy, holding out her own bundle of ghostgrass to give Sairy cover while she wrapped her hand. Fascinating how Salazar's ghost-energy died back to a dark fuzz of light around her, thinning out to nearly nothing the closer she got to the ghostgrass. Around Salazar's glove it was nearly invisible.

Isabel looked up from there to see Salazar staring into her face with a curious intensity. It wasn't the right word for something with no eyes, but Isabel didn't have a better one. Unnerved, Isabel drew the harvesting-knife, and an instant wave of fresh ghost-energy poured off of Salazar like mist off the lake, all of it visibly yearning toward Isabel.

Isabel had no way of interpreting this beyond *time to go.*

"Now we back her into one of those rooms," she said evenly, "and we ghostgrass her in. Just like we found her."

"Got it."

Isabel looked around. They'd gone back past the little rooms and were at the T junction that led out to the hatch. If Salazar got past them here, it was only another few dozen yards until she'd be within sight of the townspeople, and that was not a risk Isabel planned on taking.

"We're going to walk her back toward the rooms. First one we reach, we hold the ghostgrass out front, we direct her in. Slow and steady. Yes?"

Sairy nodded, and they backed Salazar up the hall one step, then another.

All at once, Salazar drew herself up, like a dog catching sight of a deer. Snapped her attention *away* from Sairy. Away from Isabel. Back down the hall, toward where they'd found her. Toward where they'd left Onya and Andrew.

No, Isabel thought. *They wouldn't.*

"Hey slag-for-brains!" Onya's voice piped up behind her, and Isabel froze. It was the worst kind of gutsy, misguided, Ragpicker-taken—

"What the *shit*," Sairy hissed, half-turning. "Get *back.*"

As she turned, there was no ghostgrass covering her shoulder, her back, her whole right side.

Too fast to track, Salazar's hand shot out and grabbed Sairy by the exposed arm. Spun her around easily, with such careless strength that Isabel could hear Sairy's shoulder pop. Sairy immediately began beating Salazar over the head with her ghostgrass bundle, but the blood was pulling on Salazar too hard now. She brought Sairy's hand to her mouth and began to feed.

Onya and Andrew swarmed Salazar, yelling and pelting her with bricks, but Salazar paid them about as much attention as she would a couple of buzzing flies. She didn't even notice when the ghost-proximity proved too much for Andrew and he threw up on her boots.

And Isabel—remembering a fight with another strong ghost a long time ago, and what'd happened when those crackling arcs of dark light had reached and exceeded its capacity to contain them, and what else strengthened a ghost besides blood—drew her knife and opened her mouth to say something she would almost certainly regret.

"Your name," she said clearly, "is Mia Salazar."

Salazar froze for a three-count. Then dropped Sairy, instantly forgotten. Again she blurred, too fast to track—and the next thing Isabel knew, Salazar had reached out and taken her by the shoulders. The frostbite-and-vertigo sensation was an icicle in her eye, a lightning strike down her spine, nerve pain in every nerve she possessed.

Salazar was tilting her face toward the knife, toward Isabel's face, as if she was having a hard time squaring one of those things with the other.

On the verge of blacking out, Isabel waved feebly at Sairy and the others. "Go," she mouthed.

And Sairy, Catchkeep blast her, didn't run. She popped her shoulder back in with the speed and clenched-jaw grit of someone accustomed to sustaining training injuries, then came around behind and began digging for something in the voluminous pockets of Isabel's Archivist-coat. Emerged with the vials of water and milk, the firestarter, a few scraps of bandaging-fabric. Hurried back over the broken doorway into the empty space of hall beneath the hatch, dropped to the floor, dipped a finger in the milk and started drawing the overlapping rings of a ghost-banishing circle on the broken tile.

Salazar let go of Isabel and stepped back. Even for a ghost her movement was stilted and juddering, not with a fading of energy but an overload of it. She stood there a moment as if recalibrating herself for that sudden influx, spewing silver light.

The blood had strengthened her, Isabel realized distantly. The blood had strengthened her a *lot*. But wherever a ghost's limit was to bear that dark light without bursting into silver shrapnel, Salazar was certainly teetering on the edge of it now.

"You," she said.

Hazily, Isabel blinked. Had she just caught Salazar on the last word of her loop? It sounded different. Almost like—

Then Salazar drew her sword, and it was all Isabel could do to get her harvesting-knife in hand and jump out of the way.

Salazar came at Isabel in stop-motion bursts, a jerky here-and-gone movement that was on some visceral level awfully disturbing to look at. Flickering in and out of reality as the blood lent her strength, the strength gave her memory, and the memory pulled on her hard.

She swung her sword at Isabel, blaring blue-violet light in an audible arc before it.

Lucky for Isabel, the harvesting-knife was itself a broken sword, with a sword's hilt and guard, and she just managed to turn Salazar's strike aside, just managed not to shatter both wrists while doing so. Backed a step and Salazar drove forward, an overhead blow that Isabel darted to the side of, already repositioning the harvesting-knife in a reverse grip. Paused a split second, dumped tension down her legs and out her feet and sprang at Salazar with all she had, slamming the end of the hilt into whatever passed for her temple.

It was pretty much a controlled fall back two more steps from there while Salazar hacked at her again. Hoping Salazar didn't realize she was being baited toward where Sairy was using her ruined hand to paint a ring of blood on the floor, was tracing over that with the strips of fabric, was fumbling with the firestarter above them.

Salazar wasn't fighting like a Latchkey operative, Isabel noticed as she defended against her next two strikes. Too wild, too sloppy, too desperate. Swinging her sword like a club.

Then she realized exactly where she'd seen this before. In the memory she'd read, twelve-year-old Mia Salazar training with twelve-year-old Catherine Foster, Salazar had fought exactly like this. Until the treatment-sickness had doubled her over, choking up ropes of her own tissue before they'd carted her away. Turning to Foster, terrified and enraged: *why isn't it killing you?*

This might be the last clear memory Salazar had ever had.

Back by Sairy, the ring of fabric began smoldering weakly.

"Done!" Sairy shouted, and got clear as Isabel backed into the circle and Salazar followed.

The dark light encased Salazar fully now, pulsing out from her in waves that Isabel had to brace against or be knocked back by. In the grip of it Salazar's face was going featureless, reverting to a howling mask the color of lightning. Around her, the bricks of the tunnel were beginning to vibrate, attuned with Salazar's energy flares.

"I need her inside the ring," Isabel shouted. "And both of us out of it."

Somehow.

But she *had* frozen Salazar in place. Briefly. When she'd spoken her name. And Isabel now had a pretty clear idea of what memory Salazar was stuck in. Strengthening that memory would strengthen Salazar, yes. But first, if the One Who Got Away smiled upon Isabel, for a few precious seconds it might also overload Salazar into staying put.

It was a Ragpicker's gambit, but one that'd kept Isabel alive once before.

"Why isn't it killing you?" Salazar asked her, almost mournfully.

And, in the memory, Foster had replied—

"I don't know," Isabel said.

And for a split second Salazar froze, flickering, and the uprushing of light froze above her, like a waterfall of black ice.

Isabel didn't hesitate. She stepped back out of the circle, leaving Salazar within. Even now, the words rolled off her tongue like they'd always been there, waiting for her to choose again to speak them.

"I am the Archivist. Catchkeep's emissary, ambassador, and avatar on earth. Her bones and stars my flesh; my flesh and bones Her stars. I am She who bears you, She who sustains you, She to whom your dust returns. You have lived well. You have died well. I release you. Do not ghost my way."

She knelt to plunge the blade of the harvesting-knife into the overlapping circles Sairy had drawn—and just managed to scramble free as Salazar's sword crashed down, spraying tile.

Too late, she thought inanely, *too—*

"Isabel! Get your ass out of the way!"

Sairy and Bex had appeared from the direction of the cleared area, each with a huge armload of ghostgrass and a terrifying light in her eyes. *No,* Isabel thought, *no no no—*

They charged.

It was all Isabel could do to scramble out of the way as they came barreling through, hollering at the top of their lungs, driving Salazar back and pinning her to the far wall a few feet from the hatch.

The dark light of Salazar's ghost-energy was spraying outward like blood from a slashed throat, making a sound like hot oil spitting on a pan. Isabel went and joined Sairy and Bex and together they shoved the bundles in place around Salazar's feet, her own personal ghostgrass barricade. Behind it Salazar writhed and twisted, hooked like a fish.

They backed off quickly as the black light shot up from her, raging but contained by the invisible half-cylinder of the ghostgrass semicircle, eclipsing Salazar completely. All that energy focused to a point now like sunlight through glass.

Focused—toward the ceiling.

Which started to shake.

Isabel wheeled on Sairy and Bex. But they were already backpedaling, eyes on the ceiling, which was now throwing bricks.

The pitch of the light and the noise—both piercing—redoubled until Bex winced and cried out and put her hand to her ear and brought it away red.

Sairy grabbed her and dragged her bodily away from Salazar as that funnel of dark light began to bore a hole through the ceiling. Bricks rained down, then dirt, then the rubble of the ruined building above. It fell through the hole, pattering the floor, slowing as larger pieces plugged the gap from above. But the light kept drilling through.

It's going to push its way out, Isabel realized. *Straight through and up into the sky.*

A perfect beacon to lead Carrion Boy's people directly to the tunnels.

"Get out of there!" Sairy was yelling behind her. "It's going to—"

"Leave me and go!" she yelled back. "I have to contain this."

But how? Reaching through that storm of ghost-energy would be like sticking her hand into a grinder. She couldn't expect to be able to pull it back out.

She took a step forward.

Then she was moving backwards rapidly, gracelessly, dragged between Sairy and Bex as the rest of the ceiling gave up and fell in. Salazar's ghost-energy kept drilling upward, taking chunks of the ruined building down. Isabel could hear it dropping into the tunnels like thunder.

All three stood there a minute, coughing up dust, eyes streaming. The inside of Isabel's head was making a noise like she had mosquitoes stuck in both ears.

"No," she whispered, staring at the glowing hill of rubble that used to be the exit to the hatch.

"How are we supposed to get out now?" Bex said, voicing Isabel's own thoughts. "How are they going to let us out?"

Down the hall, others were heading over, alerted by the noise. Sairy herded them back across the ghostgrass perimeter into the cleared area, cursing at the top of her lungs.

Isabel didn't need to turn in order to be aware of all those scared eyes tracking her. Waiting to see what she would do.

She set one hand to the new cave-in. It was solid. Tonnage of tunnel-stuff and the brick and whatnot from the building above. It must have filled that stretch of hall entirely. More fell as they stood there, shaking the ceiling even through however many feet of dirt.

It's like the earthquake, she thought dully. *Except upside-down.*

Salazar's purplish silver light leaked steadily through the cracks in the rubble. Frostbite-and-vertigo came with it like air through an open window.

What Isabel really did not need right now was Ruby's voice in her head, but it looked like she was getting it anyway. *Every other option is slow, and painful, and unnecessarily cruel . . .*

There wasn't a person in here whose gaze she felt remotely ready to meet. She fixed her stare on the ground.

It fell upon a pale silver thread. It emerged from the cave-in, slack and loose against the floor, and continued in the direction of the room where they'd found Salazar to start with. Toward the unexplored reaches of the lower tunnels. In the torrent of ghost-energy, Isabel hadn't noticed it until now.

But she's been dead since the Before, Isabel thought. *She has no body to connect to. What's she doing with a thread? And where the hell's the other end of it?*

Even as Isabel studied Salazar's thread, the slack seemed to be slowly, almost imperceptibly reeling up out of it, like whatever was holding the other end of it was drawing it taut. And then the thing down in the tunnels, whatever it was, would follow the thread up toward—

Before she let that scenario play out fully in her mind, Isabel drew the harvesting-knife and quickly slashed the thread. She watched as it began to dissolve into silver sparks and felt an unaccountable sense of relief, probably misguided.

A moment passed.

"Do you hear that?" Sairy said.

Isabel didn't look up. "What?"

"It's quiet." Sairy set her ear to the cave-in, where the tendrils of light were fading. The frostbite-and-vertigo sensation was still discernible, but dialed way way down. Like Salazar, improbably, had worn herself out.

Sairy straightened, her whole face shining with cautious wonder. "It stopped."

Chapter Eight

They spent a few minutes picking at the cave-in, lifting rocks and setting them aside. For each piece of debris they moved, several others fell, raining gravel and pulverized brick for many long seconds on end. Bex deadlifted a bigger chunk out of the edge of the landslide and the ceiling began to grumble ominously. It backed them up several steps and they stood staring at the ceiling until the rain of dirt and Before-junk had stopped just out of sight. Then they backed quickly away.

It felt like a long walk back to the cleared area and the gathered townspeople. Onya and Andrew had run ahead and Lin could be heard from some distance, ripping into them for running off. Even she fell silent when Isabel stepped over the ghostgrass perimeter.

They all had a million questions, that much was obvious. And there wasn't a single one of them that Isabel was ready for. So she took Sairy aside and sat her down to clean and rebandage the cut on her hand. That much she could do.

Chooser knew what kind of Before-germs had been rubbed into the wound by whatever Sairy'd cut her hand on—or from Salazar's *mouth* for that matter—but at least it wasn't a huge cut or a deep one. Rina dug into her apprentice satchel and came out with a pot of ointment. "Rainstealer salve," she explained.

"Tell me that keeps infection out," Sairy said.

Rina shook her head, holding it out. "Stops bleeding."

"I was hoping it did both."

"The good stuff is at the midwife's," Rina said. "She said we'd be safe enough down here." Leveling a critical eye at Sairy's hand: "You cut yourself on *what?*"

"Bricks. Ghost teeth. You know. This and that."

"Ghosts have teeth?"

"Well, I mean, maybe not ghosts of babies, or really, really old—ow!"

Isabel packed salve into the cut as Sairy winced and swore under her breath. "Move your fingers," Isabel said, and Sairy gestured at her rudely. "At least it's not your knife-hand."

Lin came to sit beside them. "Is it true?" she asked.

Isabel knew what that meant. Lin would have heard everything from Onya and Andrew. The ghost, the capture, the cave-in.

But word had spread that Sairy had been ghost-bitten, and children had gathered to stare. If they were on the edge of panic, Isabel didn't want to push them over now. "It's okay," she said. "We'll figure it out."

Sairy was watching her closely. Uncharacteristically quiet all of a sudden, her face still spoke volumes: *we will?*

Finally Lin seemed to notice the children to either side of her. She stood, mouth pressed into a grim line, and went to whisper something to the songkeeper. Immediately the songkeeper was gathering the children back into the story circle, launching straight into "Ember Girl at the Crossroads."

Isabel tied off Sairy's bandage and leaned back against the wall. Catchkeep save her, she was tired. She listened to the songkeeper a moment, waiting for—she didn't know what. Lin to return and come up with a plan. The hatch to magically unbury itself from the cave-in. This all to be over.

"So," the songkeeper was saying. "This one time Ember Girl got in a fight. Ember Girl got in lots of fights, because Catchkeep told Her to. Because Ember Girl was so good at making ghosts for Catchkeep to carry, and Catchkeep, like any smart dog, hated being bored. You know how when a dog gets bored it starts chewing on the chairs? Well, a dog the size of Catchkeep gets bored, you can see how things get ugly fast."

"Lots of little ears," Lin explained, plunking down beside Isabel. "Now. What's the plan."

Isabel blew out a breath. "We still have enough food and water for a few days if we stretch it thin."

"And then what?" Lin whispered. "I just went to look at the cave-in. They're not digging us out of that in time. It'll take weeks."

"Do we have enough air?" Glory asked, arriving with Bex.

"The *plan* was to shut us in here," Sairy said. "Remember?"

"The tunnels are full of air," Bex added reassuringly. "That's the one thing we have plenty of."

But Isabel was thinking about the hallucination that had landed her on her ass in the mud earlier, and she wasn't so sure. She must have breathed something. The air had gone bad. There was some kind of Before-chemical in it. *Something.*

"And ghosts," Lin said. "Apparently."

"I don't know," Isabel said. "We only ran into one, and she was nowhere near the ghost-passage."

"It only got out because we were careless," Sairy admitted. "We know better now."

"She responded to ghostgrass," Isabel added. "She was strong but it still held her off." Not saying: *she was the second-strongest ghost I've ever seen.* Not saying: *I still have no idea who ghostgrassed her into that room.* Nodding instead at the perimeter. "If there were more ghosts down here, you'd know it, because they'd be trying to get through that."

"Okay," Lin said. "So we stay behind the perimeter. That still leaves us stuck down here with three days of supplies."

"I'd say more like two," Bex said.

"There's not much lamp-oil left," Glory said. "A day at most."

At this they all fell silent, eyes on the place where the lamplight pushed up against the encroaching dark. Isabel let the songkeeper's voice cut a welcome swathe through her thoughts.

" . . . Ember Girl said yes, because yes is what you say to Catch-keep. But on the inside you can still think different, and so on Her inside Ember Girl was busy scheming. *I've made a million million ghosts for You, Catchkeep, and now I'm bored too. Maybe today's the day I put My stuff in My backpack and go find something new to do instead.* So when Catchkeep left, Ember Girl put on Her shiny boots and went to find Carrion Boy, and They—"

Isabel started. "I think I can get us out."

"What?"

But Isabel was scrambling to her feet, hurrying to the pile of debris they'd cleared from the tunnels.

Sairy surveyed this moodily, her curiosity not quite defusing her frustration. "Please tell me that somewhere in there is some Before-thing for opening hatches."

Isabel fished out the plastic map.

"How about," she said, "a Before-thing for *finding* hatches?"

"What is that?" Lin asked. "That's the tunnels?"

"Yeah," Isabel said, scrubbing at the map with a sleeve. "I think it has to be. I had it set aside for the songkeeper's collection, but . . . if I can just . . . " The dogleather of the Archivist-coat wasn't doing much to clean it, but she didn't dare waste the water. She spat on the plastic and tried again. When she sat to tilt the map into the lamplight, angled lines and little labeled boxes stared back at her cryptically.

Sairy gave a low whistle. "Ragpicker take me. All *that* is down *here?*"

"It's like a whole other Sweetwater," said Glory. "But underground."

"A bunch of Sweetwaters squished together, more like," said Bex. "Like Grayfall, or Here."

"The lines will be the halls," said Lin, leaning in to see. "I think the squares are rooms."

"And if even our shrine and meeting-hall have back doors," Isabel said, scanning those colored lines with a furious intensity, "something this big is going to have another way out."

"Okay," Glory said, "but if this whole mess is the tunnels, then where's us?"

"Near a hatch," Isabel said. "Near where the halls are shaped like a T near a hatch."

They all leaned in to look.

Upon closer inspection, there were four separate mazes, blue-green-orange-red, one for each quarter of the map.

SUBLEVEL A
SUBLEVEL B
SUBLEVEL C
SUBLEVEL D

Interspersed among those lines were little squares and rectangles, more palely colored. Each one labeled tinily.

CAFETERIA

QUARANTINE

MEDICAL BAY

There was a red star on a length of blue straightaway branched with especially small squares.

OBSERVATION CELL 27

OBSERVATION CELL 28

OBSERVATION CELL 29

Bex appeared with the songkeeper. "I figured if anybody knows how to *read* one of these things . . . " she said.

"I'm not entirely sure I do," the songkeeper said. "I have twenty-seven Before-maps, and they're all different. Some of them aren't even—oh. Look at that. This is a beautiful piece. May I?" He took the map and scanned it briefly, then made a sound of surprise. "All *this* is here under the town?"

Sairy looked like she was about to companionably elbow the songkeeper, then thought better of it. "That's what I said."

"Well," the songkeeper said, recovering himself, "these will definitely be rooms. Look, they're all labeled. *Training Hall. Reception. Generator Room.*"

"I understood, like, two words of that," Bex said.

"Classroom 1," Sairy said, reading over his shoulder. "Classroom 2."

"Laundry," Bex added. She made a face. "Laundry in a *room?*"

"Archive," said Glory.

Isabel blinked. "What?"

Glory poked a tiny square in the lower left quadrant where a tangle of orange dead-ended. Isabel read that label twice, convinced she must've seen it wrong.

"Weird," Sairy said.

Isabel tore her eyes from the *ARCHIVE* label.

Hatch, she told herself. *Halls shaped like a T.*

"I don't see a hatch," Lin said.

"I don't either," said Bex.

Neither did Isabel. There was absolutely nothing that looked remotely like a big round door set with a wheel in the middle.

If she set out blind there'd be miles of ground to cover, and the lamp would only last so long. Even down by where they'd found Salazar, already the tunnels had felt different. Smelled different. Her voice hadn't echoed there. It'd dropped like a weight, dull and deadened. Isabel found herself picturing the deeper tunnels as somewhere sound didn't carry right, light didn't go far, the halls never connected up, and there was nothing down there but uncharted miles of suffocating, lake-stinking, ghost-infested dark for her to die in.

Not uncharted, she reminded herself grimly. *Map.*

For all the good it was doing.

After a moment the red star dragged her attention back to it. It was the only one on the whole map. And stars were something she knew better than to ignore.

Then she saw it.

A little ways from the star, that blue tangle made a T shape with no branching squares. The bottom leg of the T continued a short distance toward the bottom edge of the blue quadrant, was crossed by a thick black line, and went on a little farther before terminating at a weird little symbol like an X inside an O.

Beyond that there was nothing. Just the grimy whitish background of the map.

Fixing what little she knew of the tunnels in her mind, she followed that blue squiggle back upward. She had to be sure. Symbol, space, black slash, bigger space, then that long-armed T with no rooms. Hatch, hall, broken door, hall, and the branch in the tunnels. It matched.

"Here." Isabel tapped the symbol. "That's where we came down. So if we can find another—"

Bex was already poking another spot in the tangle. "There."

Another X-in-O symbol. It was way up the side of the blue tangle, near the upper right-hand corner. Almost the whole way across that endless maze of halls.

Impossible to gauge how long it would take to reach it. If she could get there before the lamp went out. If the ceiling wasn't somehow caved in around that hatch too. If it had a ladder. If that one didn't break when they tried to climb.

If. Such a little word. Like a rock you throw at a plan over and over until the plan shatters.

"I'm going to scout ahead," Isabel said. Going over to the water jug and drinking two careful swallows even though she was still horrifically thirsty after. She picked up the jar of ghostgrass paste, then put it down. The way her wrists and neck and ankles already felt, she'd rather let the ghosts at her than smear that stuff on her skin. But she did make herself pick up the last sack of bundled ghostgrass, even though it felt like a fistful of nettles. "If the hatch is viable, I'll set up a perimeter. Then we relocate." *Before we lose the lamps and have to walk this maze in the dark.*

Lin was looking at her dubiously. "By yourself?"

"No," said Sairy.

"No," agreed Isabel, stowing the map under one arm. "Sairy, you're with me."

"What?"

"You heard me. Check your ghostgrass and get ready to move out."

"But—" Sairy drew Isabel aside. "My hand. I'll draw ghosts."

"And if you do," Isabel said softly, "I want you doing it out there. Understand?"

Sairy looked around the cleared area, and her eyes widened a little. Swallowed. Nodded.

Isabel pushed the sack of ghostgrass into Sairy's arms. "Good."

Louder, including the room: "Lin's in charge until we get back. Bex and Glory are her hands." The ex-upstarts took one look at Lin's armload of babies and nodded. "There's danger, you find Bex. You're looking for work, you ask Glory. She'll find you something to do."

Last, she drew Bex aside. "If you do see a ghost," Isabel told her, "you do not engage. You stay behind the ghostgrass and you *wait for me.* Got it?"

"Got it."

"Everybody say good luck to Isabel and Sairy!" Lin told the children, and they all hitched in a huge breath to yell with. "Quiet voices," Glory added, with a hasty glance toward the ceiling.

"Good luck, Isabel and Sairy!" they whisper-shouted at her, and Isabel stood aside while Bex and Glory hugged Sairy hard and clapped her shoulders and hung their good-luck charms around her neck and whispered things in her ears that Isabel couldn't make out from her distance but weren't meant for her anyway. The ex-upstarts would always all have each other, no matter what, and Isabel could only stand on their periphery, one step removed. She'd spent too long being their monster to reasonably expect anything different.

Chapter Nine

They got as far as the room where they'd found Salazar and stopped to get their bearings, holding the lamp out at arms-length toward the further dark.

"Straight down past this bank of rooms," Isabel said, "then left between *OBSERVATION CELL 14* and *16*. Then it looks like a lot of little turns, so stick close. You see anything that looks like stairs or anything leading down, stay clear. One cave-in for today is plenty."

They walked in silence. Isabel carrying the map and lamp, Sairy one-arming the ghostgrass bag with her bandaged hand crammed as deep as it would go in the pocket of her coat. All they could hear was a low unsteady dripping, coming from somewhere further off, deeper down. Slowly but steadily the mud between the floor-tiles was getting wetter, and Isabel gave up quickly on trying to gauge whether they were getting nearer to the lake or farther from it.

"Who builds a bunch of underground tunnels beside a lake any-way?" Sairy whispered.

Isabel just shook her head in response. They were both breathing like people trying to conserve their air, though they'd never specifi-cally agreed to. They were also breathing like people trying to move quietly, so as not to catch the attention of whatever their lamplight might discover next.

Here and there they passed areas of the hallway where the bricks were different colors, spelling what might've been words stenciled straight onto the wall. Whatever they'd used to paint with, it must've been with an eye for preservation in the damp, or something, be-cause the darker coloration remained. It was only because a number of the bricks had fallen out of the wall face that the words were no longer legible. Not a map, not by a long shot, but maybe better than nothing. Once Sairy picked up a few bricks, slotted them into gaps in the wall, stood back, inspected the result, gave up.

They'd been walking for maybe fifteen minutes when Isabel started feeling that very specific weirdness again. She tried to brush it off, ignore it, but she couldn't deny that this place was getting under her skin. That inexplicable sensation of being sieved through something unseen hadn't quite returned to her but she felt constantly as if she were caught in the split second between a shove and a stumble. She wasn't off-balance *exactly*, and it wasn't *exactly* that she thought something was going to come up behind her and give her a push. It felt sort of like a stuck sneeze, that pinch in the back of the nose, except everywhere.

Worse, the ghostgrass bracelets had upped their game and gone beyond raising welts on her exposed skin. Where they touched it was now beginning to blister.

I'm not a ghost, Isabel thought at them, like she could will braids of grass to comprehend. *Leave me alone.*

In those twisty halls the squares on the map were farther between and less uniformly-shaped. According to the map they passed *ELEVATOR,* and *EMERGENCY MEDICAL SUPPLY,* and *KITCHEN.*

Rounding a bend in the hall toward *DORMITORY A,* Isabel flung an arm out, nearly clotheslining Sairy. Lifted her chin in silence toward an open doorway. There, on the floor, laid along the threshold—ghostgrass. Not as much as on the room Salazar had been contained in. Not by far. But someone had put it there, and it wasn't Isabel.

In the black cutout of that doorway, the faintest possible silver glow.

Isabel's outflung arm turned palm-down, made a gesture like she was pressing something unseen toward the floor. It only occurred to her afterward that she used the same gesture on Squirrel. *Stay.*

But she needn't have bothered. Sairy had already set the ghostgrass bag aside and was holding one bundle out like a weapon. She pointed with it, eyes narrowed in the dim light, at something at the doorway's edge.

Isabel glanced down, and sure enough there was a thread, even fainter than Salazar's, so fine and pale she'd write it off as a trick of the light if she hadn't just seen this same pattern a little while ago. Doorway, ghostgrass, silver glow, thread.

Optimistically, she raised and lowered the lamp, altering the angle of the light. No such luck. That was definitely a thread.

So frail though, like Isabel's own thread had been right before it'd been cut. Like when Sweetwater sugared its five stunted maples in the early spring, and left the boiled syrup to chill until it thickened to the texture of honey, of ghost blood, and the children would dip their fingers in and pull them out trailing dripping strands. Where those strands terminated in sugary wisps almost too fine to see, that was what this thread looked like.

They retreated a few steps and Sairy watched the doorway while Isabel consulted the map. "No good," she said. "It's this way or nothing."

"So we go quiet," Sairy whispered back. "Avoid the ghostgrass. Maybe we add more even? There's hardly any there."

"If we're lucky," Isabel replied, "maybe that means a weaker ghost."

Shaky logic, she knew. She'd feel a whole lot more confident in that ghostgrass if she knew how it'd gotten there to begin with.

Glued to the far wall, they approached.

As they came level with the doorway, Sairy stopped dead and stood staring into that room, one hand over her mouth. Isabel squinted into that soft silver light—and found herself looking at one of the strangest-looking ghosts she'd ever seen.

It was totally silver, and nearly formless: no hands, no feet, no head, just the vague noodly shapes of arms and legs stuck into a blob of torso. It was lying on the floor like a piece of pale fabric that some-one had dropped.

"That's a ghost?" Sairy was hissing. "Where's its head?"

"It's just weak," Isabel whispered back. "That's our first good news all day. Let's not question it."

But Isabel had never seen a ghost in the living world that was this weak but still this *big*. In the ghost-place you could cut a ghost into pieces and the pieces would keep moving. Mindlessly squirming, like a worm cut in half, for eternity. *Here*, though, this ghost would've shrunk as it weakened, it should've been small enough to sit in her hand. But this one was as big as Onya.

That thread, Isabel surmised, was the only thing keeping this ghost from melting into a silver puddle of slop on the floor. First Salazar's awful strength had dropped out of her immediately when her thread was cut. Now this.

But what were they? Not tethers to a half-dead body, certainly, as Isabel's had been three years ago. At least Salazar's couldn't have been—she'd been dead since the Before, she was dust somewhere in the rumored green beneath the Waste.

No—Isabel pictured these threads more like puppet-strings, or fuses a fire could travel along. Increasingly, she didn't reckon she wanted to run into whatever was holding the other end of them.

She drew her knife to cut the thread—and jumped, startled, as the ghost twitched hard and began to move. Flopping weakly like a fish trying to wriggle its way back to water, sand in its gills, hopeless. For a three-count Isabel watched it. Then she sheathed the knife.

"Come on," Isabel said, giving Sairy a nudge as she walked by. "That one's not going anywhere."

But Sairy didn't move. "Is it *bleeding?*"

Despite herself Isabel paused. Glanced back in.

The silver ghost had edged up to the near wall now and was bumping up against it rhythmically with the place where its head should've been. Tangling in its thread, which kept spooling out from wherever to accommodate it. It fumbled its way vaguely toward the open door, depositing a silver trail as it went.

So it wasn't that it hadn't fully formed a head. It was that its head had been *removed*.

Isabel went still. That spray of silver blood on the wall back by the ghost-passage. That rag-like thing on the floor beneath.

She needed a second to piece this together. Someone had decapitated a ghost back by the ghost-passage. Left its head there. Moved its body down the tunnels and stashed it in this room. Attached a thread to it, fed it just enough strength to maintain its form, but not enough to bust through the ghostgrass that they'd laid so carefully across the door.

Systematically, meticulously, and all for reasons unknown and pretty much incomprehensible from where Isabel was standing.

And, apart from the decapitation, they'd done the same with Salazar.

It was like an Archivist's shelves of ghost-catching jars, if that Archivist had figured out how to expand that operation on a much larger scale.

Except that the idea of an Archivist who could handle a specimen like Salazar without being reduced to a drag-trail with a splatter at the end of it was . . . unnerving.

Sairy was staring into the room in a kind of unsettled fascination. "I wonder who it used to be."

Keep moving forward, went the voice in Isabel's head. *Even if it doesn't get you anywhere.*

"I'm going in there for a second," she said. "Stay here. It won't hurt me."

Stepping over the ghostgrass, she pulled that silver rag out of her pocket. Ignoring Sairy's shout of surprise when she realized the rag had a mouth and eyeholes and was squirming slightly in her grip.

Eventually Sairy found her words. "This shit," she declared, "did not come up in training."

"Yeah." With slow care, Isabel knelt. "Mine either."

The silver ghost's body bumped its way along the last few feet of wall and heaved up against her, slick and cold, too insistent to be mindless, lashing her soggily with boneless arms.

This is a terrible idea even for you, Isabel thought, and held the rag against the stump of the silver ghost's neck.

And the thread emitted a single faint pulse. Began glowing brighter and brighter, vibrating like a plucked string as it siphoned power out of wherever until the shape of the silver ghost began to sharpen off and brighten and saturate as color bled in.

"Is—" Sairy began, then stopped. "Is that . . . normal?"

"Blood will strengthen a ghost like this," Isabel murmured back. Not taking her eyes from the silver ghost as the paddles of its limbs began to sprout hands, feet, then fingers, toes. "Just . . . not this fast."

Not only that, but whatever this thread was, it was repairing damage that no amount of blood would ever fix. The gap between the head and body began to fill with slow silver like a scab. The changes were rapid and dramatic, like a come-what-may unfolding from bud to flower in the moonlight.

Isabel let go, took a step back, and watched, hand on knife-hilt in case of trouble.

The silver of the ghost's body began to loosen in pleats and folds, suggesting clothing, which darkened rapidly through grayscale to pitch black. The vague silver flap of its hair brightened to an orangey brown. It was definitely a child, maybe seven or eight years old.

"Oh," Sairy breathed. "It's so *detailed.*" Then she seemed to realize what she was saying, and her voice sharpened. "Like the last one."

"If it was like the last one," Isabel said, "I wouldn't be in here. We'd've dumped ghostgrass all over this doorway and run like hell."

Slowly, the child-ghost pulled itself to a sitting position. Same stuttering quality of movement that Salazar'd had—that any ghost had in the living world. Flickering like a candle in a draft.

There it turned its back to them and sat like it'd been caught misbehaving and was being punished. It squirmed with impatience, rocking back and forth, tugging on its thread each time it shifted forward. From behind it was impossible to tell whether it was a boy or a girl.

"What's it doing?" Sairy whispered.

What it was doing was humming to itself. A simple little tune, but it sounded oddly familiar.

Then it turned, wiping blood out of its eyes, and with a shock like a slap, Isabel knew where she'd seen this ghost before. The blood had been red then, not silver, but everything else matched up. She'd seen this child-ghost the same place she'd seen Salazar. In the ghosts' memories, in the ghost-place, on her search for Catherine Foster. *A dead kid, bleeding out every hole in its head.* A casualty of the second or maybe third wave of the Latchkey operatives' development, of that *four percent survival rate* that in the end had left only two standing. Gone in its sleep, bled out, strapped to a cot, while that Ragpicker-taken lullaby played on, relentless.

That was the tune the child-ghost was humming now. The same one they'd play to the youngest Latchkey subjects at lights-out. Strapped down to tiny cots in an open observation area, hooked up to machines, with a statistically significant chance of bleeding out in their sleep. No wonder they'd needed a lullaby.

It had played for them in mechanical beeps, looping endlessly. All night, every night, well past when they'd outgrown such a baby-ish thing. It didn't sound as soothing as it was probably meant to. Isabel'd heard it in one of the nameless ghost's memories, years ago, and still woke up some mornings with it stuck in her head, humming it to herself as she got dressed for the day.

It came to her that it might be the only song any of the opera-tives knew.

The child-ghost was swaying back and forth a little, wearing a kid-sized version of the Latchkey operatives' uniform, sleeving at the bloody mess of its face.

For some reason the little uniform made Isabel think of snakes shedding their skins. She wondered who'd made all the new copies of those uniforms, a little bigger every year, for those that survived. Until they didn't have to make any more.

The child-ghost was blinking in her vague direction, hers or Sairy's, but didn't really seem to be seeing either of them. Whether that was because it was a ghost trapped in the world of the living, or because its eyes were full of blood, Isabel didn't know.

Nor could she have really said why she did what she did next.

She started to hum the lullaby.

And when she did, the child-ghost drew her into focus and *saw* her. Slowly, jaggedly, it got up and padded its way over to her, lifting its feet with effort, like it was walking through glue. *Still weak*, she noted. *Not a threat.*

"Isabel?" Sairy said, uncertain.

But the child-ghost had stopped before her and was tilting its head inquisitively. It'd died a fledgling Latchkey operative, but it'd died a little kid first. It didn't attack her. It didn't try to empty her out onto the floor. It seemed to like the look of her knife, and it made a grab for it.

It didn't move with the same ridiculous speed as Foster or the nameless ghost, or Salazar for that matter. Its development hadn't made it that far. If it had been, Isabel wouldn't've so much as seen it move before it had hold of the harvesting-knife with one hand and probably broken her neck with the other. As it was, she was running on pure reflex when she jumped back and slashed out, more warning than intent.

And the child-ghost's hand closed around the blade, and Isabel was ripped from reality like a patch from a quilt. And into—

I sabel was in a room she'd seen before: the wide open space where she'd seen Foster and Salazar sparring, as children, in Foster's memories. But now it looked different. Gone were the racks of wooden swords, the bins of padded gear that even Isabel knew would make no difference if those operatives swung at each other with anything more than minimal effort. Even the walls were bare and gray, not yet painted brilliant white and padded for impact. The floor matched them.

The gray room was packed with children. None younger than five or six, none older than maybe eight. They looked tired and grimy, some visibly injured with the kinds of wounds Isabel had seen on people pulled from broken buildings in Sweetwater's earthquake a few days ago.

Most of the kids didn't look too happy to be there, though there were some who'd formed up into little groups to chase each other around the room, shrieking, weaving between the ones miserably slumped on the floor.

A wash of sound. Half plaintive despair, half oblivious joy.

A little team of adults had split up and fanned out among the children, squatting down before each one in turn, checking the little cards pinned to the children's shirts, writing on a kind of handheld light-up panel with a pen-like thing.

One of them, a tall woman in a blue skirt, clipped across the floor in crisp-sounding shoes and stopped before a little boy leaning against a wall, hugging himself and staring at his feet. He had the same wavy orangey-brown hair as the child-ghost in the tunnels, before it had turned silver. He was about the same height, too. No uniform though. No uniforms on any of them. Not even the jumpsuits they'd been given in the early stages of the project. All their clothes were mismatched and filthy, like they'd just returned from a long march through the Waste.

"Let's see here," the woman said, and glanced at the tag on the boy's shirt, then at the panel in her hand. Nodded. Jotted something on the panel. Smiled. Too many teeth in that smile for Isabel to trust. The boy looked like he'd probably agree. "Good morning, Zachary," she said.

Over the smile, the woman's eyes were calculating. They didn't look as tired as they had when Isabel had seen her before, in other memories, in which the operatives had addressed her as *Director.* Here she looked confident, optimistic, but with a strange grim determination behind it, like she was preparing to break a whole lot of eggs to make a very small omelet. It put Isabel in mind of upstarts drawing straws on the eve of the Archivist-choosing day. *Four percent survival rate,* she thought, and looked across this sea of children, and swallowed.

The Director was strafing her gaze back and forth over the boy like she was capturing and indexing his every movement, mannerism, expression. *Field notes,* Isabel thought. She stood for a full half-minute apparently just to watch him fidget. Once every few seconds she'd write something else on her screen but said nothing.

Eventually she seemed to decide enough time had passed.

"I like your shirt," she told the boy, in a voice so gentle it made Isabel's skin crawl. Seemed to be counting seconds of ensuing silence. Another flurry of notes when he didn't reply. Then she raised the pen and made with it a kind of elegant sweeping gesture from her blue skirt to the boy's shirt, also blue, though his was smudged and torn, mostly gray now and a kind of muddy brown. A different blue, anyway, to begin with. "See? We match."

There was another pause, filled with joyous screeching in the background. If the adults' attitude reminded Isabel of upstarts, some of these kids reminded her of rejected shrine-dog puppies, bundled into a sack with rocks and pitched into the lake. They'd keep on thinking it was the best game ever until the moment the water closed over their heads.

The boy didn't seem to want to meet the Director's eyes. Isabel couldn't blame him. "I'm thirsty."

The smile, if anything, brightened. The Director made a note on the device. "Of course you are! You have had yourself *quite* a week.

All of you boys and girls here have been very, *very* brave." She glanced up from the screen, tried to catch the boy's eye, but he was having none of it. "Now, I have *just* a few quick questions for you and then when we are finished I will *personally* not *rest* until I have found *you* a cup of *juice*. Deal?"

His eyes darted up at her, then away. Brown. Before they'd been full of blood they'd been brown.

"Easy questions?"

"Would you like them to be?"

The boy nodded at his shoes. The Director noted that too.

"Orange juice?"

She beamed. "You know it."

"I don't like apple juice," he mumbled.

"Tell you a secret," the Director said, leaning in conspiratorially. "Neither do I."

I sabel came to, lying on her back, staring up at a shadowy ceiling beaded with condensation, gasping like she'd been kneed in the chest. Damp floor, soupy gloom, smelled like an old shoe left lying in a pond. The harvesting-knife lay a little ways away, as if it'd been kicked and clattered to rest across the tile. Ghost blood, like silver honey, still clung to the jagged point.

Sairy was leaning over her, staring into her face like the simple fact of Isabel blinking up at her was a hand-delivered gift from the Chooser Herself.

"What the *shit*," Sairy said, whole voice and face and person tight with alarm, "was *that*?"

Of course. Sairy'd never seen her read a ghost's memories before. No living person ever had.

She couldn't've been gone for more than a few seconds, but that was a few seconds too much. A quick glance revealed that the child-ghost seemed to have lost interest in her and her knife and had reverted to humming that lullaby to itself, fidgeting with its sleeves like any bored, nervous kid.

"Too damn close," Isabel said, "is what it was."

"You weren't moving," Sairy shouted at her. Down came her fist on Isabel's shoulder. "You were all *flickery*. Like a mirage or something."

"Ow. *Sairy*—" Then it hit her. "Wait. What? I was—"

"You were. Disappearing. And coming back. And disappearing again." Sairy slumped, deflated. Then she punched Isabel again, like she was trying to reassure herself of her solidity. "You looked like a ghost!"

Painfully, Isabel levered herself up to standing, picked up the harvesting-knife, and slashed the thread. It scattered into glowing ash and the child-ghost collapsed, immediately and utterly, like a stomped sandcastle. It toppled over and lay there motionless, rapidly silvering. The place where Isabel had fused its neck back together began to liquefy and separate, its head listing sideways on melty strings of silver goo.

Sairy was staring in horrified fascination. Isabel had seen enough.

"Come on," she said brusquely. Shaken and trying to hide it. This was all very, very strange.

Everything—the tunnels, the child-ghost, the healing device, Salazar, the lullaby, the map, the ghostgrass, the thread—was in pieces, sliding past each other in Isabel's mind, glancing off, trying to connect into some kind of meaningful whole. They would fit together, she was almost sure of it. She just had to figure out which way round to turn them.

All at once the story came flooding back to her. The one the upstarts learned first. The origin story of the harvesting-knife.

Catchkeep fought the Chooser for dominion over the land of the dead and won, sort of, but the last star was knocked loose from the tip of Her tail and fell, and the first Catchkeep-priest found it in a ruin deep underground, and gave it to the first Archivist, who realized that it could . . .

The harvesting-knife. Foster's sword. A ruin deep underground. Where not one but now at least two Latchkey ghosts remained. At the bottom of all the lies, at the heart of a system *built* on lies, at least some small part of at least one small story was true.

Isabel realized she'd been spending this whole time rejecting the obvious.

She knew exactly where she was.

These places she'd seen three years ago in the ghost's memories, and in Foster's—they'd been right beneath her feet this whole time. No wonder the ghost had come after so many Archivists, unsuccessfully seeking their help in his search for Foster, before he'd found her. In part because the Archivists' particular skillset had rightly seemed useful, of course, but also simply that *the ghost had been here first.*

But ghosts didn't—usually—stay where they died. What were these ones doing *here?*

All she could think was: *there'd been a dozen Latchkey operatives. Foster and the ghost had gotten free of this place, but that still leaves ten.*

Chapter Ten

Not a minute's walk farther down the tunnels, Isabel started feeling seriously wrong. She was queasy. Dizzy. Couldn't tell if she was too hot or too cold. There was a pain where her thread had been, like a long thin needle being delicately bored into her chest. She didn't have much in her to puke but her guts seemed to be pretty enthused about giving it a try all the same. It felt like opening her eyes after spinning in circles with them shut, except all she'd been doing was walking down a hallway in a straight line.

She stopped, knuckling at her eyes like that would fix anything. Took her hands away and the view of the tunnels before her was somehow melting into, interleaving with, the view of someplace else. Someplace definitely not the tunnels. The sensation came to her again of being pressed through or shuffled into something just beyond the reach of her mind to perceive. Like the skin of the world was being abraded. Like a friction burn to the brain.

Too afraid to ask Sairy if she saw it, because she knew what the answer would be. So she soldiered forward a few more steps and doubled over in startled pain as the ghostgrass wards on her wrists and ankles began to sear like oil burns. She could almost hear her skin cooking.

But no. That didn't make any sense. It was this place getting to her, it was—

Frantically, she started listing stars in her head. She'd gotten as far as the Broken Trap and the Spool before she realized she could list every star whose name she knew and it still wasn't going to do so much as take the edge off this level of weirdness.

At her side, the harvesting-knife chose that moment to begin twitching hard. It was really going berserk this time, acting up worse than it had in years. It reminded her of when it'd kept vanishing unaccountably from its sheath in the ghost-place, and she now held it tightly in place so it couldn't pull that trick again. She was taken by a sudden urge to look behind her.

She resisted. Holy or not, ancient or not, weird or not, a knife couldn't tell her what to do. If she turned around, obeying that compulsion, she'd be beginning a long slide down a slippery slope to nowhere good.

Don't, she thought at herself, *don't you dare,* and turned.

Nothing.

Shut up, she thought at the harvesting-knife, glancing down, *shut up shut up*—and there, stuck to the front of the Archivist-coat, was the thread.

It was frailer than before. Frailer even than the child-ghost's. It blinked in and out of existence, nearly invisible. Sick with dread, she tried to draw it into focus—

—and she wasn't standing on the tile floor of the tunnel, she was standing on nothingness, hovering a few inches above something roiling and swift and black as tar. Desperate, Isabel yanked her gaze back up. Kept it locked on Sairy's silhouette, toiling through the lamp-lit dark beyond. Oblivious of the walls curving back on themselves, the hallway tunneling to a point, a slowly spinning vortex which they'd soon reach and be sucked down and lost—

It's in my head. It's in my head. It's in my head.

She tottered forward one step, another. Almost caught off-balance when her foot struck tile exactly as that out-shouted, rational part of her had known she would all along.

See? It's—

She made the mistake of blinking. When her eyes reopened, the darkness ahead was wavering violently, like heat-mirage, like migraine. Blurring and sharpening, exchanging focus with—she squinted—something else, also dark, also shifting, but differently, somehow. She struggled to focus on the darkness and shifting that she knew. Push it back into the shape of a crappy dank tunnel. Slot herself back into that picture. Stitch the patch back into the quilt.

But she'd slipped through once already. Fallen on ice that wasn't there. Stared up at the buildings of a city that'd either never existed or long since fallen. Whatever this rip in the fabric of the tunnels signified, it'd already proven itself wide enough to receive her.

Staggering on, trying not to alert Sairy and freak her out worse than she was already, dragging her feet like the mud was over her ankles. Exactly the way the floor had clung to the child-ghost's feet as it'd stutter-walked up to her, half here, half not.

She wished she hadn't thought of that.

It's in my head, she told herself, and took a few more steps and went down. Unsure what she tripped over, only that her foot snagged and dropped her, arms out in front, with the sick bleary helpless knowledge that she'd go *through* the floor, through and on into—

She landed on tile. Even dizzier now, her vision reduced to pure migraine aura with one clean spot in the center like a hurricane's eye. Everything around it swirled but through that hole she could see both places clearly, interleaved, seething over each other like maggots in a ball.

She tried to call out for Sairy, but her voice had cut out on her. Whatever noise came out of her instead, though, was enough to get Sairy's attention. As if in slow-motion, as if from miles away, Isabel saw her turn, her mouth falling open even as she began to sprint back toward Isabel, holding a bundle of ghostgrass high up and back like it was a club she was going to beat Isabel with.

"Stay back!" Isabel tried to call to her, but Sairy didn't seem to notice what was wrong with the floor. Her eyes were fixed on something above and behind Isabel's head.

Her curiosity momentarily overriding her horror, Isabel tried to turn around. See what Sairy was seeing. But as she did, her focus shifted, and the not-tunnels place was brought into piercing focus.

Oh, she said to herself. *It's a river.*

And then she fell in.

I sabel splashed and spat, kicked and flailed. Water shot up her nose and washed down the back of her throat. Felt like swallowing needles. Choked and hacked and got another mouthful. Labored to stay afloat, fought herself against fighting the current. Bobbed up, was whisked around, stabilized. Breathed. Breathed. Realized her body had locked in that position, head flung back, arms flung wide.

Breathed. Couldn't move. Breathed and the river ducked her for a six-count, popped her back up like a cork. Arms still frozen. Legs still dead. All her panic on the inside. Retched. Black water, thin and murky, like diluted ink, like bile.

All at once, she knew where she was. Wished she didn't. Remembered the ghost explaining the darkness of that water to her—*it draws all the colors out from the ghosts that die in it*—and heaved again.

Move, she told herself. *You have to move.*

She forced her arms out in front of her, tried pulling at the water to slow herself down. The shore was passing fast. Buildings hunched and clustered on the riverside. Scrap-houses like the ones in Sweetwater. Mud houses. Long low pastel-colored houses with weird squarish bushes beside the doors. Those impossibly tall buildings she'd seen in the city of the ghost's memories, made of glass and metal and stuff she had no name for, daggering at the clouds. Huge houses with heavy doors and peeling multicolored paint. Log cabins. Ruins of white stone. Towers like shivs of black glass set with running lights. All mashed together with no order, no reason, piled shoulder to shoulder like they'd been dropped at random to fall where they may.

Waypoints of the dead, she knew. The ghost had taught her how to recognize them. Relics. Memories. Doorways, all. They flashed past and were gone.

She was losing strength. The river was sucking it out of her. Scanned the surface for something to grab hold of, something to float with, something by which she could get herself to shore.

Nothing. Not so much as a stick. Not so much as a drowned ghost. Not yet.

Pain lanced down her side as she tried to turn herself around, get her legs out behind her, shove her way to land. But the river would not be shoved. The river shoved back, and she went under. Came up burbling, black water streaming from every hole in her head.

There wasn't much more of this left in her. She was rapidly nearing her limit. If the thread was still attached, it was hidden beneath the frothy skin of the water. It didn't matter. If she'd already drowned, would she know? She'd seen what happened to ghosts in this river before. She knew what was coming next for her. Caught in the current, thrashing, conscious, filling with water but not dying, unable to pull herself to dry land, until it dumped her out into whatever ocean it fed, where she would drift forever, a silver bag full of black water staring up at the unchanging sky. Alive, aware, scraped clean of everything that defined her.

No. She wasn't dead. Couldn't be. She'd *know*. Just this side of dead, maybe, arms windmilling for balance as she walked that wire, almost definitely, but not right-this-minute dead and that was something worth clinging to.

She'd fight, it'd hurt, she'd die and turn ghost regardless, but there were worse things than being handed Chooser's odds and telling Her with all due respect to stuff them.

With difficulty, she brawled her way against the water, got herself aimed toward the shore, and braced for a world of pain when she showed this river she was done messing around—and the current kicked up, twirled her backwards, pushed her down and sat on her. She gasped and got a burning lungful, willed herself not to cough and suck more in, desperately wanted to cough, fought it, convulsed, cursed herself, convulsed, coughed, clamped down, convulsed, fought it, couldn't fight it, fought it, inhaled—

"**S**hut up! They'll hear us!"
"Hear *you*."
"Shhh!"
"Your dessert for a week if they do."
"Our heads on the Director's wall if they do."
"Hey, a bet's a bet."
"Tell that to the Director."
"Tell her yourself, while you're busy kissing her ass."
"Say that again."
"You heard me."
"Oh *shit*. Down! Get down!"

Four kids in dark uniforms dropped like sacks of flour, heads tucked in, huddling beneath the bottom edge of a wide thick window set into a white brick wall. Two of them were visibly ill, luminous with fever, swallowing their coughs. Maybe twelve years old, and sick, but still with that inhuman, almost-disturbing elegance of movement that made Isabel's breath catch, because it was no less clear an indicator than their uniforms of exactly who and what these children were.

One of the kids was Foster. Another was the nameless ghost.

She'd know them anywhere, dead or alive, child or adult, even surrounded by their fellow operatives and dressed the same. She'd know them with their heads cut off. She recognized them like she'd recognize a friend who'd snuck up behind her, hands over her eyes.

Seeing them here, now—even knowing it *wasn't* here and now, just a memory—it did something to her that she couldn't put words to. It caught her in the throat, behind the eyes, in the sudden clammy shaking of her hands.

She started listing plants in her head. *Corpseroot. Three-eyes. Suns-and-moons. Carrion Boy's Tears. Scorchweed. Clotweed. Ghostgrass. Come-what-may.*

She'd keep going until her heart slowed, her breathing regulated, and the unseen weight crouching on her shoulders got up and went its way.

Unseen but not unknown. She was quite familiar with it by now. She saw it every time she closed her eyes. It looked like Isabel planting ghostgrass in front of waypoints. Its name was *not today.* Its name was regret.

Listing plants wasn't working. Of course it wasn't. She advanced to phase two. Anchoring herself with her senses. What she could see. What she could hear. What she could smell.

But how was that supposed to work if she wasn't even *here*? This was just a memory, and she was just passing through.

Wait.

A memory—but *whose*?

It should worry her more than it did. She should be losing it, she should be trying to wake up, she should be climbing up the walls of this place to escape. Like a bug in a bottle. Like a ghost in a jar. Dimly she was aware that this was the reaction she was supposed to expect of herself in a situation such as this.

Instead she stood there, heart pounding, retching breath like she'd been throatpunched. And watched.

Maybe eight feet away from them and they couldn't see her. All four kids, all four fledgling Latchkey operatives, stared through her at the far wall, panting with nerves, hissing at each other like cranky geese. She vaguely recognized the other two from Foster's memories, but didn't have the first guess to their names.

It wasn't that she didn't know—suddenly, immediately—where, and when, she was. It was that she had no idea how she'd gotten there. Water, the river, the black river in the ghost-place, she'd been drowning, and—

"Is it her?"

"Of course it isn't. Foster's full of it. Like I said. There's no way." This from the ghost. His attempt at withering disdain, at age twelve, needed some fine-tuning.

His voice was still a knife in an old wound, though, and the longer she stood there the deeper in it twisted. But at the same time, calm overswept and enveloped her like the thickest softest quilt in the world, and her throat unclenched, and her hands stopped shaking, and her mind, for the first time in three years, was still.

"Foster's full of it, huh?" Foster was saying. "Quit talking about Foster like Foster isn't here. Did *you* follow them when they took Deegan away? I saw what I saw."

"Yeah," said another of the kids, "too bad nobody else did."

"What do you think you're here for *now*, genius?"

"This is so stupid."

"Oh, I'm sorry. Somebody make you come here? No? Then shut it."

"Oh my god. You know what? Forget this."

"Don't you even think about it. They'll see you."

"Yeah, but this is crazy, Foster. Think. It's freaking *Medical*. They're not gonna—"

"Will you please. Shut. Up."

"This is such a bad idea—"

Meantime the ghost had leaned back against the wall, eyes shut, silent, shaking his head in a very particular *this-is-a-stretch-even-for-you-Foster* kind of derision. Desperately trying to put himself above this. But Isabel could read him. Sometimes it was like looking into a mirror. He was closing in on himself because he was staring down into the depths of whatever abyss Foster was dragging him toward, and whatever he saw there scared him half to death.

Foster shifted to take something out of her pocket, wrapped in a long perforated sheet of some kind of flaky brown paper. Shook it out carefully into her lap. Shards of mirror, one per kid. She passed them down the line, and all four held their mirror-pieces out in front of them and a bit above, tilting them around, trying to find the angle that would show them what was happening through that window at their backs.

"We're too low down. I can't see. Way to think shit through, Foster—"

"You're not aiming at *them*, dumbass. The whole wall behind them is a two-way mirror. Aim at *that*."

"Why *is* there a two-way mirror in Medical anyway?"

"The hell I look like, the answer fairy? Did I build this craphole? Did I put it there?"

More fumbling and bickering, and then they all fell abruptly into wide-eyed silence.

Isabel, having a fine view through the window they were hiding under, saw why.

Inside, on a white table in a white room, a team of men and women in white coats were shaving away what was left of Salazar's hair. Clearing ground for a silver pen tipped with a red light that sliced through Salazar's skin and bone and brain like a hot knife through butter. Next thing Isabel knew, there was a window cut in Salazar's head and a puzzle-piece of her skull in a pink plastic tray and a woman in a white coat was working long silver tweezers out of the red-gray meat of Salazar's brain with a fingernail-sized glinting piece of something caught in their grip.

The woman turned the thing back and forth in the light, gave one tight-lipped nod, and even from her distance Isabel could see the tension in the white room lift a little.

The thing was set all around its edges with hair-thin filaments, which the woman was now in the process of very carefully detaching. Isabel couldn't really make them out, they were so fine, but from the motions the woman's tweezers made around them, they looked to each be a good few inches long.

A tiny box was brought for the remaining tiny central square, a box with a lining and padding of the exact right shape and size to receive it. The square was cleaned off and laid inside and the box was sealed and set down like undetonated ordnance, and the woman stripped stretchy blue gloves from trembling hands and dropped to a stool while another woman clapped her on the shoulder.

Isabel forced her focus to draw away, back to the hall. Bit by bit, the rushing in her ears faded, and sound washed back in.

"We gotta go. We gotta get out of here right now. We gotta go—"

A piece of mirror clinked to the floor, was kicked skittering away across the tile.

"You can't just *leave* that here, they'll know—"

"No way that was Salazar. They said they buried her. She was sick, they—they buried her, they *said* they—"

"What about all the other sick ones?" said one of the sick ones, frantic gaze darting from face to unresponding face. "*What about*—"

Somebody sobbed once, bit it off fast.

"What *was* that thing?" the ghost asked. Voice so quiet, like the question would go away if nobody answered. "Are there . . . do *we* have . . . I mean, we'd *know* if we . . . "

"I get it now, Foster," one of them said, sounding dazed. "I get it."

Foster was collecting the mirror-pieces, tucking them away into her jacket before anyone could protest. That way, any fallout from this would land square on her, and Isabel could think of nobody else more capable of carrying it. After all, she'd seen the whole long road that one-wayed straight to Foster's death, and she knew where it began.

This wasn't the first step down that road but one of many steps along it. Foster's will had already aimed and deployed itself. This was just one snapshot of the resulting trajectory.

"Nobody *gets it*," Foster said. Her whole body rigid, radiating terrible purpose. "But we're gonna keep looking 'til we do."

I sabel drifted slowly, hesitantly back to reality, her mind still trying to process what'd just happened. Tried to move, could not. Eyes shut, she mentally probed her body for damage. Disoriented as hell but alive, best she could tell. Banged up but nothing broken. Still, her whole body was one great slug of pain. Everything from her nose down her throat and deep into her chest felt like it was smoldering. A crushing pain in her knife-hand, different and deeper than the welts and blisters that the ghostgrass had left there. But she hadn't hurt her hand in the river, or in the memory she'd seen next.

But she hadn't *read* a memory. At least not that she knew of. No ghost was in evidence. She hadn't so much as drawn her knife, though there it was in her hand, she'd know the feel of that hilt anywhere. Ghostgrass burned her palm, even worse now than before.

She opened her eyes. Blinked the tunnels into focus, and the river was no longer interleaved with them. The sensation of being sieved through or shuffled into something—the ghost-place, she now understood—was gone. For the moment, she was stable. She was here.

The light was somehow different. Fainter, colder than the lamp. It wasn't coming from her.

Effortfully, she lifted the vast weight of her head.

Her hand hurt because someone was clamping it hard to the hilt of the harvesting-knife. That someone had their other hand in a black-gloved fist around the blade, thick silver blood squishing up between the fingers.

That's unlike him, she reflected blearily. Normally he held the knife with such care, such awareness of the permanence of whatever damage he sustained. He hadn't even taken off the glove.

Then she realized what her eyes were showing her.

That's it, she thought. *I'm dead.*

Her gaze winced its way past those black gloves, up the black sleeves beyond it, until it met that familiar gray stare, angled slightly aside, less coolly analytical than she remembered but instead studying her with the white-hot intensity an Archivist might accord a promising specimen. The way she'd looked at this one when first she'd caught it, a lifetime ago.

No, not the way she'd look at a specimen. More like the way that white-coated woman had looked at that shiny piece of whatever from Salazar's brain. Like someone who'd been handed Chooser's odds and told Her with all due respect to stuff them. And, against all reason, somehow gotten away with it.

It was not a look Isabel saw often on this particular ghost. It wiped his face clean of all arrogance, or most of it, leaving him eyeing her askance with a very uncertain sort of awe.

"Got you," he said faintly.

Isabel stared. Behind the ghost, beyond the edge of the silvery phosphorescence he threw before him in the living world, Sairy had slumped—no, Sairy was being restrained in the world's gentlest choke-collar of a hold by the ghost of Catherine Foster.

"Morning, sunshine," said Foster.

At long last, Isabel found her words.

"Oh," she said, "you have got to be fucking kidding me."

Chapter Eleven

"Don't say anything," she told them. "Just . . . not yet. I need a minute. Foster, let go of Sairy before she pukes on you. Sairy, listen to me, it's okay, Sairy, put the ghostgrass away, she's not going to hurt you, I promise—"

Propping herself up on her elbows as the walls spun around her. Drowning, she'd been drowning. Then, like a scene change in a dream, she'd snapped out of the river and into—

The harvesting-knife. When she'd regained consciousness, it'd been in her hand. She *had* read a memory after all. And now she knew how, and why.

And whose.

Released from Foster, Sairy immediately flung herself out of reach of another choke-hold. Stayed there, crouching behind her brandished ghostgrass bundle, glaring cagily. "Isabel, what the—how the—what the shit is going on?"

"It's fine, Sairy, they're—" She paused, mentally cycling through her options before settling on: "Just trust me, it's fine."

Sairy didn't look like she was buying it. "That one *cut* you." Utterly outraged. Leveling her ghostgrass bundle at the ghost. Her temper had torn free of her now, and bringing it back was about as likely as catching a bullet midflight and stuffing it back into the gun. "It cut you *with your own knife.*"

Isabel had no way of explaining it to Sairy. She was in the midst of trying to explain it to herself.

"It tries that again," Sairy announced, "and I'm going to end that thing myself. Ghost kit or no. I'll take it apart."

The ghost gave Sairy a look that reminded Isabel of nothing so much as the screen of leaves over a beartrap: mild enough until you test it, then the long drop and the spikes.

Foster, meantime, was grinning at her appraisingly. "She is not taking your shit," she told the ghost.

"He didn't cut me, Sairy," Isabel said. "He cut himself. He just . . . made me hold the knife . . . " She trailed off. This wasn't going to make any more sense to Sairy than . . . anything else she could be telling her, honestly.

"You *trust* it," Sairy said, aghast. "Since when do you trust *any*—" Sairy stopped short. "Did you say *Foster*?"

"I *said*," Isabel said, louder now, "he didn't cut me. Just . . . let me think a second."

Isabel dragged herself upright, eye level with the ghost. The hallway swung around her, slowly steadying. Reading a memory took a lot out of her, mentally and physically. The same went for going into the ghost-place. Doing both in short order, she was learning, was exquisitely demanding. Especially when she'd dropped into the ghost-place without warning or preparation, and reading that memory wasn't something she'd done by choice but a *tactic* that was used on her *strategically*—

It would have pissed her off a lot more if it wasn't also indisputably the only reason she was sitting here, now, alive enough to have the luxury of annoyance.

"You—wait. *You* fished me out of the river with—but—how did you even—"

As always, the ghost recovered his composure almost before she'd witnessed it fail. "Is that where you were?" Wiping his blood from her knife. Handing it back. Inspecting the silver-stained slash in the glove. All with that ridiculous fluidity and economy of motion, that studied nonchalance. If she hadn't known him as well as she did, she might've disbelieved she'd just seen him shaken. "You'd collapsed. There was a thread coming out of your chest."

"You were *flickering* again," Sairy added. "Like a—" She stopped herself just short of saying *ghost*.

Reflexively Isabel glanced down. No thread. It must've vanished when she'd returned from the ghost-place, like before.

"But *how* did you—"

"My options were limited. Some looked more favorable than others."

Isabel's eyelid twitched. Catchkeep preserve her from the insufferable dead. "How could you possibly know that would *work*."

The ghost just gave her that languid blink and stare. Clear, cold, calm. "I didn't."

"Wherever you were," Foster said, "it didn't look like anyplace good."

"Like you were having a nightmare," Sairy said.

"It was like that," Isabel said slowly. "Like waking up out of one bad dream into another. I was drowning." Looked at the ghost. "In that black river we crossed in the ghost-place." It was settling on her fully even as she said it. "I had a *thread*. I was drowning in that river and I had a *thread*. I fell *through the floor*. And then I—"

She paused. Right then she couldn't access the words to tell them about the chemical stink of that room, the blinding whiteness of its walls, the fear in the child operatives' eyes. That bloodied silver shard being worked out of Salazar's brain like a thorn.

The ghost was watching her closely. "You fell through the floor?"

"You have no idea how creepy that is," Sairy told her. "I was staring *right at you*. You didn't *go* anywhere."

"Not like through a hole," Isabel clarified. Then, realizing she had to do better: "Like when you purify lakewater for drinking, and you filter it through sand? Except I don't know which one of those things is me." She looked from face to face. "That's not helpful, is it. But even now I . . ."

She trailed off, feeling for that strange sensation that'd struck her earlier. It was dialed down, way down, but definitely there. Like it was biding its time, waiting for her to drop her guard again. "You feel that?"

The ghost snapped to stillness, gauging his surroundings with total concentration and in complete silence. Scanning the tunnel like he could see through the mold and brick and Chooser-knew-what of its construction. It was like the look the songkeeper would put on when he told Carrion Boy stories, miming Him catching bullets out of midair.

In a moment his gaze flicked to Isabel's face instead, and she knew the ghost was using her reaction as a measure for what he had not sensed himself.

They waited, watching each other, as Isabel tried to put words to what she was feeling. Words that made more sense than being-shuffled-into-something, being-pressed-through-something, being-stuck-half-in-one-world-half-in-another.

Under the knife-blade of the ghost's regard, she forced a shrug. Got up.

Too fast. The ghost-place had always had that after-effect on her. Like being blackout drunk without having touched a drop. Like the ground beneath her feet was thin ice, and she couldn't walk lightly enough for it to hold her.

Before she could so much as blink, the ghost was on his feet. He delicately pinched her coat-collar as she stumbled back, waited without comment until she'd gained her footing, then let go. All the time with that *look*. The pitch of it seemed calculated to pierce clean through with utter clarity to all the things she would rather be punched repeatedly in the face than say.

"You saw one of his memories just now?" Foster asked, frank curiosity shining out of her face. How much had the ghost told her about their journey to find her? "With the knife?"

But before she could respond, Sairy spoke.

"Isabel."

"*What*."

The ghost raised one eyebrow incrementally with what might have been amusement. "'Isabel'?"

She gestured *leave it*. "Sairy. I'm listening."

"These are the ghosts in your drawing."

"In my field notes," Isabel said brusquely. Unaccountably embarrassed. "Yes." Then, remembering what people did in circumstances like this—or at least a *little* like this— "Sairy, this is Kit Foster, and this—"

"We've met," Sairy said icily.

"And this is the ghost I traveled with before." She hesitated. "He, um, well, you know how ghosts don't tend to remember much about their lives, and—"

"You don't know your own name," Sairy said, peering up at him, which he allowed. "Weird." Then, to Isabel: "That's why you didn't put it on that sketch!"

Isabel elected not to respond to this. "And this is Sairy."

The ghost nodded once in Sairy's general direction.

"Charmed," Foster said.

"You should be," Sairy replied. Then something seemed to occur to her. "They're dressed like that one that *bit me*." When Isabel didn't answer, Sairy went on. "How do you know they won't go all crazy hungry ghost on us like that one?"

"Because they're right here and you've got an open wound and they're *not*, Sairy, okay?"

"But what if—"

"You know we can hear you?" Foster held up one hand. "Hi."

Sairy looked Foster up and down. "I don't recall addressing you," she said. Then, to Isabel: "This one tried to choke me out."

"You were choking yourself out," Foster said amicably. "I was just holding on."

"You don't *touch me*."

"Then don't start what you can't finish." Foster glanced down at something, then back at Sairy.

Isabel followed her gaze. There on the floor between them was a bundle of ghostgrass, presumably lying where it landed when Sairy had been disarmed of it.

Poor Sairy. These ghosts were uniformed and armed identically to Salazar. No wonder she'd assumed they were a threat to be neutralized. The fact that she'd jumped them, two on one, after having catastrophically underestimated Salazar's power, and with Isabel down—it spoke volumes for Sairy's grit and guts and Isabel couldn't help but be impressed.

"You two can fight this out later," she said. "For now we have to find a way out of this place."

The ghost made an indecipherable sound.

"What?" she asked him. Then, because she couldn't help it: "What are you even doing here?"

"I should be asking you the same." His tone strongly suggested there was one potential right answer and a pile of wrong ones, and he wasn't expecting her to come out with the former.

Foster was more helpful. "Come here," she told Isabel, walking back to the little room where the child-ghost was. "I'll show you."

I have to keep moving, Isabel told herself. But these ghosts were standing here before her, after all this time, and something was compelling her to linger. Like they'd vanish back into the realm of her should-have-dones the second she turned her back on them again.

So she got up and she went to join Foster. Sairy was standing nearby, arms folded, not lifting her glare from the place between Foster's shoulderblades where Sairy's knives would both vanish to the hilt if Foster so much as breathed funny.

Foster paid her no mind. She leaned in the doorway, staring at something in brief confusion. After a second she laughed. "I was wondering where that was," she said to herself. Then she called over to the ghost: "They found his head."

It was too much. "*You* put the ghosts in these rooms? *You* took the ghostgrass off my—what the hell is *that?*"

Foster straightened and glanced down at what Isabel was staring at. Threads.

Where Salazar and the child-ghost had each had one thread, Foster bristled with *seven*, each a slightly different shade: silver-white, silver-gray, silver-violet, silver-blue. All pale and dull, difficult to notice if the light wasn't on them directly. They all attached where Isabel's had in the ghost-place, where Salazar's and the child-ghost's had too—directly over the heart, or where one would be if a ghost were possessed of such. Two of Foster's threads were broken and dangled loosely down, glowing in high contrast against the pitch-black of her jacket, remaining bright until the point of termination.

"You're—" Isabel said, and trailed off, struggling to square what she knew with what she saw. Yet again, her inner Archivist's mental field notes were undergoing a sudden, rapid expansion. She knew she had to get out of here. Find the hatch. Move forward. But she couldn't help herself. The Archivist in her had to know. It had rooted her feet to the floor and was now prying her mouth open to ask: "*You're* what these ghosts are attached to?"

Foster drew her sword. Holding it at arm's length she used the point of it to nudge the ghostgrass strands out of place, giving herself a gap to step over. "Yep."

"For *what?*"

"Observation."

"You—" Isabel blinked, taken aback. "You can *see* the ghosts through those?"

"It gets harder the more of them there are," Foster said. "But I can keep track of them. Threads started breaking, going dark, and I knew something needed checking on. Didn't know it'd be you."

Two broken threads. One for Salazar, Isabel reckoned. One for the child-ghost. Did the threads dissolve back toward Foster when they were cut? Did the excess fall away like ash? She didn't know. *Fuses a fire could travel along,* she thought again, watching in rapt fascination as Foster went straight over to the vague silver shape that used to be the child-ghost and knelt beside him. Wrapped one of the two broken threads around her hand, spooling it out with meticulous care from somewhere within her. It looked like quite a process, arduous and painful. It set off a matching memory-twinge in Isabel's own chest.

When the thread was long enough to reach, Foster attached it to the child-ghost, then sat on her heels and waited meditatively until some unseen calibration was reached and the thread ignited white down its length.

Gradually, the child-ghost reattached his head, regrew his clothes, and was beginning to detail his features back in when Foster tousled the silver-orange flap of his hair. "Gotta cut you off now, buddy," she told him. "It's for your own good, I swear."

With that, the flare-like glow of the thread began to taper back until it looked much the same as it had when Isabel had first seen it. Fine and pale. The word *dormant* seemed odd to apply to a thread but crossed Isabel's mind anyway.

"The last one got stronger before we trapped her," Sairy said, still balefully tracking Foster's every movement from the doorway. "She was getting that power off of *you?*"

Foster shrugged. "Sometimes, they get strong enough, they get greedy and try to draw more. I noticed she was hitting that point so I regulated the output. You'll have to show me where you put her so I can link her back up."

The blood drained from Sairy's face. "It . . . she could've been *stronger?*"

Foster just laughed.

Beginning to dawn on Isabel was the unwelcome suspicion that cutting Salazar's thread was the only reason she, or anyone she'd brought down into these tunnels for that matter, was still alive.

She knew these two ghosts were strong, but a ghost having enough surplus ghost-energy to *power other ghosts* went sailing well beyond the limits of anything she was equipped to comprehend. She'd seen something like it when she'd first met the ghost on Execution Hill, an outpouring of power so sudden and huge that other lesser ghosts had exploded like seedpods scattering, but Foster's excess ghost-energy had been utilized, fashioned deliberately into a tool to do—what?

"They don't know who they are," Foster told her, watching the child-ghost as he crawled back into his corner and began rocking and humming anew. "They don't even remember how to talk. Some of them just say a few words over and over but that's it."

"That's all most of them do," Isabel said. "They get stuck on something. For a lot of them it's the moment when they die, but for some of them it's just something they can't move past." She thought of the ghost's memories, and of Foster's. "Usually something bad."

"They look like they had hard lives," Foster said. "I thought maybe I could help them."

"I think," Isabel said carefully, "they had lives a lot like yours."

Foster shrugged. "Maybe."

Maybe?

Isabel looked from the child-ghost to Foster and back. The threads, the oversized catchment-jars of the rooms, the ghostgrass barring exit. Strengthening the ghosts just enough to serve some purpose, not enough to allow them to escape.

She's doing my job, Isabel thought again, incredulous. All that was different was that Foster was feeding them straight-up ghost energy instead of blood, and that if she was taking field notes, her notebook was not in evidence.

"I've never even seen a ghost with a thread before Salazar," she said. "Just the one that attached me to my body when I was in the— oh." She glanced over at the ghost. "You told her about that?"

"Of course," the ghost said simply.

It took her aback. Not five minutes ago he'd saved Isabel with her own knife, turning her memory-reading tactic into a stratagem. Isabel hadn't even explained much to him about the ghostgrass before, only why it'd been hanging above the door of her Archivist-house the day they'd met, and her own thread had been something they'd learned the nature of together. And yet here was Foster, playing Archivist, claiming and shaping those threads and ghostgrass into research tools.

"Salazar," Foster echoed, thoughtfully but without recognition. More like she was mentally recording syllables in order and filing them away. The name itself had no significance.

Which was strange.

The ghost not recognizing Salazar's name—that made sense. As far as his life was concerned, he had a memory like a bucket with a hole kicked in it. Foster, though, hadn't been wandering through the ghost-place for ages, gradually losing herself. She'd been stuck in the loop of her death, the moment she hadn't been able to move past, and Isabel had freed her. Unlocked her memories. Or so Isabel had thought.

Foster had *known* Salazar. Trained with her. Isabel had *seen* it. Foster's amnesia flew in the face of all of Isabel's assumptions. It was deeply unsettling. The look of resigned disappointment on the ghost's face did nothing to make it less so.

Isabel glanced a question at the ghost and he shook his head, almost imperceptibly.

Her unease was instantly upgraded to a definite chill.

Finished with the child-ghost, Foster cleared a gap in the doorway ghostgrass, then fixed it back up behind her as before. Then she caught sight of Sairy's ghostgrass bundle, lying where it had fallen. She hooked it over with the swordpoint and flinched. "Ow." She sheathed the sword to shake out her hand, tilting her head at the ghostgrass quizzically. She squatted beside it, took off one glove and stuck an experimental fingertip directly on a blade. It hissed. Foster yanked her hand away and leaned in for a better look. "This stuff's stronger," she said to the ghost in surprise. "A lot stronger."

Foster's assessing stare was different from the ghost's, more like a predatory bird gauging how much fight its prey had left in it. It wasn't malicious, but neither was a predator's, for all the difference it made to the prey. She fixed this on Isabel now. "Where did you get this?"

"We grow it," Isabel said, flustered. "It's a plant, it grows, we *picked* it. It—"

"And you brought it down here," the ghost said. "Why?"

Isabel made a quick assessment of Sairy, who'd gone quiet again. She wasn't taking her wounded hand out of its pocket and every time that arm moved she winced. Isabel was going to feel a whole lot better about that once she had a clear exit to the midwife's.

"Walk with us," Isabel said to the ghost. "And I'll tell you. Sairy, good to go?"

Sairy lifted the map and her eyebrows in response.

"How's your hand?"

"Fine," Sairy said.

"You'd say *fine* if it fell off and you were carrying it in a bag," Isabel told her.

But Sairy kept up, and didn't go after Foster again. They walked and walked, past *COMMUNICATIONS* and *AIR/WATER FILTRATION* and *COMBAT SIMULATOR* and *COMMISSARY*, and Isabel told the ghosts about the townspeople hidden in the tunnels. The smoke rising in the distance. What would happen to a town that Carrion Boy's people invaded and took over. The plan to fight, and to protect those who couldn't. The cave-in when she'd trapped Salazar and the map they were following now.

She paused, wanting to tell them about Ruby's plan for Isabel if things went wrong. Found that she could not.

Unbidden, the thought arrived: *how am I supposed to do it exactly, if it comes to that? No ghosts down here my ass. Am I supposed to mercy kill all these people bloodlessly? Go around snapping necks one by one?*

"I feel strange down here," she said, swatting that thought away. "There's something weird about this place. I'm dizzy, I feel like I'm going to puke any minute. My knife has been doing the thing like it did in the ghost-place. Right before you found me it was almost as bad as back then." She hesitated, then held out her wrists. "And then there's this."

Sairy saw it first. "That's from the *ghostgrass*? What in the shitting hell, Isabel, you should have *said something*."

"I guess it's because I was partly a ghost once," Isabel said, because she had to say it out loud or she had no chance of normalizing it. Her whole brain felt like it was grasping at straws. "But I handle ghostgrass all the time and it never happened up there."

Foster was staring like she could read her fortune written on Isabel's face. Whatever the ghost was thinking, he gave no sign.

"You know this place," she told them. *It's probably the only place you know. Tell me why it's doing this to me.* Instead she took the map from Sairy and pointed at the symbol of the second hatch. "Do you know if the path is clear between where we are and this?"

"Not as clear as here," Foster said. "The facility is kind of a mess further in. It only gets worse."

"More ghosts?" Sairy asked.

Foster tapped the shimmering bundle of threads at her chest. "Contained."

"Can we make a space that fits fiftyish people without the ceiling dropping on their heads?" Isabel asked. "One cave-in for today is enough."

"If by *we* you mean yourself and your injured subordinate," the ghost said, "I would say it's doubtful."

Sairy spluttered. "*Subordinate?*"

"She's not my subordinate," Isabel said, at the same time the ghost said: "I'll go with you. If you like."

"Oh no," Foster told him. "You're not decapitating any more of my ghosts. I'm coming too."

Only after the ghosts had volunteered their service and their company did Isabel realize she'd been holding her breath wondering whether they would. Incomprehensibly, her hands were shaking. She felt like she'd been walking on the ridge and a rockslide had missed her by inches.

"And I need to check on Salazar," Foster said. Still with that weird hesitation, like *Salazar* was a word she'd just learned, not a person she'd lived and trained and nearly died beside. Then, tensing slightly: "You said you'd trapped her? You didn't—"

"Destroy her? No. She's safe. But she kind of brought the ceiling down on herself. It seemed stable, but if you try to excavate her while the townspeople are still so close, I don't know what will happen."

"Then she'll keep. I'll take a look at her when I can but I won't move her until we get your people relocated."

Gratitude, Isabel discovered, still made her awfully awkward. So instead she held up the map in front of her as she walked.

"We put her here," she said, indicating the space between the first hatch and the tunnels. She tried to calculate how far they'd come along that blue tangle, how long it had taken, how much longer they had to go. But she'd slipped into the ghost-place, where time ran different. If she stuck out her thumb and pinky finger as far as they would go, she could just about touch the second hatch symbol and the last room they'd passed simultaneously. "How far are we looking at here?"

The ghost glanced at the map. "Seventeen hundred sixty-odd meters, if it were a straight shot. Which it isn't."

Isabel eyed him. The ghost stuck a thumb over his shoulder, helpfully. "Miles," he said. "That way."

"Miles," Isabel echoed. Ragpicker take her, she was tired. She felt like she'd been bundled into a sack and bounced off a cliff. "Okay. Have you ever opened that hatch? Do you know if it's even . . . openable?"

Foster shook her head. "We tried to leave through the southern exit, but." She took off a glove, held her hand palm-out to Isabel.

Isabel looked at Foster's hand and her mind went white. The skin there had flaked and silvered. Never, not if Foster drank blood by the bottle every day for a thousand years, would it heal. Isabel thought of the way the child-ghost's *head* had reattached because of Foster's thread and wondered why Foster hadn't just tried to fix herself. Unless she had, and this remaining damage was all that was left. The ghost equivalent of a scar.

Foster wiggled her fingers at Isabel. "You can see how well that went for us."

The ghost watched Isabel's reaction. Without looking she could feel his scrutiny. The palpable, precise, careful weight of everything he wasn't saying.

Even after everything they're helping me, she thought miserably. *Even now.*

For a while after that it was an awkward procession. Nobody said anything. There was only the shuffle-slide of Isabel's injured gait and the dripping of the ceiling. Two sounds she'd rather not hear.

For a while now her stubbornness had worn her like a puppet, lifting up one foot at a time, moving it forward a little, plunking it down. It'd carry her a while farther yet.

Her wrists were killing her. Her ankles. Her neck. She could *feel* the ghostgrass Sairy was carrying at a deliberate distance from the ghosts, a slow-spreading smoldering like a warn-fire gone damp. One foot in front of another.

Her whole world had narrowed to a point, which was the sound of her heart hammering its ghostgrass-poisoned blood deeper into her veins. Felt like it was beating just below the surface. Like it was about to burn a hole through the fragile paper of her skin and land splat on the floor at her feet.

She tried to lose herself in thought. Certainly there was plenty on her mind. But she couldn't say most of it, not without admitting things she had no intention of saying aloud. It was all too tangled together. Any one thing she gave voice to would rip the others out of her, and the person she'd spent three years building would fall around her like a house of cards.

Get your shit together, she told herself. *Walk or fall.*

"I'm surprised you wanted to protect Salazar in the first place, Foster," she said. "Considering how nasty she was to you when you both were—" *alive*— "kids."

Foster rounded on Isabel so fast Sairy almost tripped over her. *"What?"*

"When you were kids?" Isabel repeated. Maybe Foster's earlier confusion had been temporary, some kind of ghost-glitch Isabel hadn't before encountered. Only one way to be sure. "Salazar was . . . it's, um, strange that you'd be so nice to her after . . . "

"After *what?*"

Isabel had nothing intelligent left to say to the confusion on Foster's face. She stared helplessly.

"You're saying," Foster went on, incredulous, "that I *knew* her?"

"Seriously?" Sairy said. "You realize you guys are all dressed exactly alike. Unless everybody in the Before went around wearing all black with swords and guns stuck in their belts, it's probably pretty safe to assume—"

"I know," Foster said, quieter now. "But I would have thought I'd have remembered."

Isabel caught the ghost's eye. He was giving her a complicated look from an angle that Foster could not see.

Isabel knew that look. From living in a house full of upstarts all keeping secrets from each other and from the Catchkeep-priest and possibly mostly from her, she knew it. That look said *not here, not now, but we have to talk.*

Chapter Twelve

They walked for what felt like forever. Down the long length of that hall, around a corner, down another hall, two consecutive lefts. Without the map, Isabel would've been convinced by now they were going in circles. The place was huge. She said as much to the ghost.

"It used to be much bigger," he replied. "This is just the basement." Then, apparently realizing that the word *basement* might not be one she knew: "The part that's underground. There was a whole building above this. Many, many floors."

Isabel thought of the ruined building at the corner of the garden. The brickfall mantling the hatch. For generations Sweetwater had built its houses out of what it had salvaged there. There'd've been no town if there hadn't been those provisions for shelter. Settlers would've moved on, or been stomped by the Ragpicker striding through the Waste of His domain.

Strange to think about. This place, this ghost. Her life built on the bones of his.

As they walked, Isabel explained to Foster as much as she knew about Salazar, the Latchkey Project, the facility where they were now. It was all secondhand, and based on memories that were mostly Foster's to begin with, but Foster listened in rapt silence until Isabel was out of information to relay, which didn't end up taking all that long.

After a while Sairy took point with the sack of ghostgrass, over Isabel's protests.

"Look," she said. "I'm carrying a bag of ghostgrass the size of a small child. I'm safer than you, certainly. I—"

142

Isabel grabbed her, pulled her back. "Shh." Pointing with her spare hand to something off ahead, down in the dark.

Whatever it was, Foster and the ghost had caught sight of it too. They'd both assumed a kind of quiet readiness, still and calm. All their attention was fixed on something further down the tunnel, where part of the darkness seemed to separate.

Isabel slitted her eyes at that darkness.

The darkness glinted back.

*G*reat, Isabel thought. *Another ghost.*

As its light brightened and she saw it clearer, she amended that assessment. *Worse. Another Latchkey ghost.*

This one had died several years older and so was substantially larger than the last one. It looked to have been closer to the age that Salazar had been when she'd succumbed to the treatment. Isabel, with the strength of Salazar's ghost quite fresh in her mind, would be lying if she said she wasn't somewhat disconcerted to see this one here now. Not so much blocking their way as having collapsed in it, oblivious to their presence. But what was really alarming was the look of surprise on Foster's face.

Seven threads, Isabel thought. *Twelve operatives.*

And this one had no thread.

"I thought you had this under control, Foster," she said. Not shifting an inch. Barely even moving her lips when she spoke. Like this Latchkey ghost would rush at her the second any part of her changed position.

"Count of twenty," Foster replied. Watching that Latchkey ghost in perfect stillness, like an arrow just before it's loosed. "Then see if you feel the need to say that again."

"She *does* have this under control," Sairy said to the ghost, her voice skeptical. "Right?"

But the ghost wasn't listening. He was drawing his sword. Easing a step forward. Without taking her eyes from the Latchkey ghost, Foster shook her head very slightly, and the ghost paused and stood there on full alert as Foster started making her way down the hall, stalking that Latchkey ghost in long slow silent strides. Weighing his partner's wishes against his partner's apparent deathwish, and for the moment—and likely *only* for the moment—staying put. And practically vibrating with the strain of doing so.

"It's okay," Foster was telling the Latchkey ghost. Like it was a stray kitten she'd found in an alley, not the disembodied will of a genetically modified superpowered murder machine. Isabel couldn't even make out its face. Time and isolation from the ghost-place had so weakened it that its features had gone gummy and gelatinous, worn through in places to an oily-looking gray. The awful strength of any Latchkey ghost seemed to be the only thing keeping this one from deliquescing completely, boiling itself down to a puddle of silver sludge. A framework that held up the vague shape of the thing while all of its substance fell in.

Wherever it'd come from, this ghost was lost, so lost. It obviously had no idea who or where or what or *when* it was. As Isabel watched, it kept trying to hurl up arcs of bruise-colored light, as Salazar's ghost had done before, but this one lacked the juice. Here and there, sparks of ghost-energy hovered off it, fizzled wetly. It had its head pressed against the jagged brickwork of the wall, was trying to push itself, facefirst, to standing. One cheek and one temple were slashed and silvery from the effort.

Foster, being Foster, reached in and stood with it and set it on its feet. There she got it in an elaborate hold that looked friendly enough, but Isabel knew better. Foster might be an idealist, she might be reckless, she might be stubborn—but she was about as far as you could get from stupid.

This ghost was male, about Foster's height and solidly built. Its hair had either been blond in life or was well on its way to damaged silver as a ghost. A lake-color, like driftwood or sand. Sixteen, maybe, at time of death.

Isabel took stock of the hall. They'd moved well beyond the banks of identical observation cells where they'd found Salazar and the child-ghost. This stretch of tunnel was comparatively bare. They'd passed a door that led onto an up-down set of broken staircases, which they'd avoided, and were about to come up on a very large rectangle on the map labeled *TRAINING HALL*.

In short, nowhere that looked suitable to store a captive ghost.

"We should help her," Sairy whispered.

"She caught seven already." Isabel glanced at the ghost for confirmation, but he wasn't taking a shred of focus off of Foster and he didn't look terribly at ease with what he saw. "This is nothing."

"Whatever happened to *count of twenty*?" Sairy hissed. "It's *been* twenty—"

"Foster knows what she's doing."

"This starts to look like trouble, I'm going up there."

Dead-on-her-feet spent or not, Sairy looked about ready to march up there and shove a fistful of ghostgrass down that Latchkey ghost's throat to the elbow. But it'd be sheer force of will driving her. She looked awful. The second Foster finished up here, Isabel was getting a good look at that hand, even if she had to tackle Sairy and sit on her.

"We stay put," she said. Then, teasingly, because the more she really looked at Sairy the more unsettled Isabel became: "You don't even like her."

"So? I didn't like *you* for *years*. First rule: *It's worth risking two to save one.*"

Isabel gaped at her in mortified horror.

Too late. The ghost was staring too. *"What did you just say?"*

"I *said* it's worth—" Sairy trailed off to a gasp before Isabel could strangle her to shut her up. "The shit is that *noise*?"

It was like two sheets of rusty metal grinding together, and it was coming from the Latchkey ghost. Thread or no thread, its proximity to the apparent ocean of Foster's strength was, in turn, strengthening *it*. Silver droplets of ghost-energy were beading up on it. Was it coming out of the Latchkey ghost or was the Latchkey ghost gathering it from Foster?

"We can *help you*," Foster was shouting. The rusty-metal sound went shearing through Isabel's teeth and she winced. Presumably based on what Isabel had told her about Salazar, Foster continued: "We worked together. We were kids together. We trained together."

Here Foster's reserve of extrapolation ran dry.

Admittedly, if Isabel mentally removed the gaping silver wounds and subtracted about eight years off this ghost's age of death, it—*he*—started to seem familiar. She pictured those last dozen surviving subjects, perched at little desks, raising their hands, the Director calling on them to answer—

"Ayres," she whispered, the name falling into her head and out her mouth concurrently.

Down the hall, Ayres went very still. Too late, Isabel saw her mistake.

"Oh," she breathed, "*shit*—"

Beside her, the ghost, one shadow of a provocation from blurring down the hall to bag himself another specimen's head, glanced at her sharply, then back at Ayres, who had gone dangerously still and was now staring just past Foster with a curious lucidity. "What."

"He *heard me*."

Grabbing a bundle of ghostgrass. Gritting her teeth as she felt it burning its way into the flesh of her palm like a hot coal through a snowbank. Holding it out in front of her, she broke into a run—

—and Ayres's feeble silver sparks flared up and ran together, stretching into a crackling arc of blue-violet light that whipsawed out and took Foster upside the head with a sound like a wire snapping under tension.

For the tiniest instant, Foster's grip failed the tiniest bit.

It was enough.

Ayres ripped free of her and stood there blazing, his light so intense it seemed to throw cold the way a warn-fire throws heat. Pure reflex, Isabel dug her heels in and skidded into an about-face on the muddy tile, her momentum flinging her into the core of that bright darkness that seemed to pull all other light toward it. She struggled to stop and earned herself another helpless quarter-turn, drawn inexorably in as if into orbit.

Like the story, she thought inanely, flying sideways toward her doom. *How the Chooser was stealing all the dead from Catchkeep, because the Chooser's eyes were so sharp She could see everyone's death nesting in them long before it blossomed, so Catchkeep tricked one of Her eyes into trying to look so far that it exploded, and that eye-star of Her up-self exploded with it, so bright it blocked out half Her other stars from sight, and—*

Something knocked her aside, hard, slamming her into the wall. She went down like a bag of rocks and sat there. Sairy rushed to her side, hauling her up, checking for wounds. Isabel shook her head to clear it and there was the ghost, standing between her and that blinding light.

Foster had interposed herself between the ghost and Ayres. She was positioned sideways between them, sword trained on the ghost, gun trained on Ayres. Staring at the ghost in dawning disbelief. "What do you think you're doing?"

"Minimizing risk," he replied.

"To *what?*"

He said nothing.

"What are they doing?" Sairy whispered.

Isabel shook her head. "I don't know." Whatever it was, having seen these two ghosts as living people, she wasn't overmuch surprised.

"So, what, *now* you have a problem?" Foster jerked her chin toward the threads. "All the others went down just like this and you said nothing."

"It was not," the ghost said tightly, "*just like this.*"

Because of me, Isabel couldn't bring herself to say. *Because I said his name and he heard it. The thing that went wrong here was me.*

"Then stop me." Foster tightened her grip on the sword. "Or stand the fuck down."

"Foster," said the ghost evenly, "get out of the way."

In response, Foster shifted her feet slightly, redistributing her weight. She hadn't spared a glance for Ayres this whole time and she wasn't starting now. Every iota of her attention was on the ghost. Given the raw power Isabel could plainly see radiating off of Ayres, what this suggested about the ghost's strength was terrifying.

Foster slid her right foot another couple millimeters and settled on it, beginning a long slow exhale. She stood easily, relaxed and still, her breath her only movement. Isabel had seen Foster fight before. Recognized the signs of imminent detonation. The calm before the storm.

"I don't want to hurt you," Foster replied, just as evenly. "Don't be like this. We had a deal."

Isabel wasn't sure she heard that right.

Deal? *What* deal? What could possibly be worth this?

"Move," said the ghost. "Or I will go through you."

"I thought they were friends," Sairy whispered. "They're going to kill each other if we don't do something."

But do *what*? Their code was unlike anything that Isabel had ever dealt with or had any idea *how* to deal with. It'd be like trying to negotiate an accord between two warring shrine-dogs, or storms, or stars. *Or*, thought Isabel, the stories bubbling up in her again, useless as a drink while drowning, *like Carrion Boy and Ember Girl*.

"He's one of us," Foster was saying. "Like Salazar is one of us. That little kid you *executed*, you idiot, is one of us. I am *trying* to do for them what you did for me. If I'm going to lose all my memories anyway, I need some of those memories to be of things I actually *did right*. Or there's no—goddamn—*point*."

Something in the ghost's expression snagged and was forcibly smoothed, and that more than anything told Isabel that they were running out of time to settle this—whatever it was—nicely. Not for the first time, she wondered how they'd survived each other's presence long enough to die older than her.

The ghost didn't move. Neither did Foster. They stood, sizing each other up, gauging distance, strategizing. Isabel knew that behind the blank intention of their faces the machines of their brains were on overdrive, each of them visualizing the coming fight branching out like a tree in all the possible permutations of strikes and blocks and dodges, disarmings, throws and recoveries, clinches and breaks. Each calculating a sequence of events leading to a desired outcome. Projecting damages. Compromising risk with benefit. They were, right now, easily twenty steps ahead of anything Isabel could begin to guess at.

"We have to get out of here," she yelled up at them. "We're feeding him. You two standing there having your incomprehensible little pissing contest, you are *feeding* this ghost literally everything we don't want him to have."

"So get him out of here," Foster yelled back, gesturing with a wrench of her head toward the ghost. "I'm doing this. I *have to do* this. He's—"

The light surrounding Ayres gave a single hard pulse and blew a layer of bricks out of the wall ten feet to either side. Chunks of rubble pattered around the ghosts' boots. Neither so much as blinked. They'd reached a place where Ayres was going to have to wreak a lot more havoc than that to break their focus.

"Do you need to be reminded what happened when Salazar got loose?" the ghost said. "I'm not leaving this thing walking."

"If he was hostile he'd be attacking," Foster shouted. "He's confused. Like Salazar was confused. And Salazar's been *secured*, she's—"

"And *who secured it?*" the ghost shouted back. "I'm not putting her at risk again."

There was one merciful split-second in which Foster was actually taken aback. Then she swung the blistering force of her attention onto Isabel. It felt like staring directly into the sun and Isabel willed herself not to look away.

It took Isabel a second to realize the ghost didn't mean Salazar. "Wait," she said. "What? Don't put this on me."

"It's already on you," the ghost said. "This thing is our responsibility. Like Salazar was our responsibility. You could have been killed. If you think I'm going to just stand by and watch that happen—"

"We're not in the ghost-place anymore, okay?" she said. Harsher than she intended. Like her voice was a barricade, pushing him away. Whatever this was, whatever he was doing, she didn't begin to deserve it. "I helped you, I got you back to Foster, and it's done. It's over. You don't need to have my back anymore, and you sure as hell don't owe me."

The ghost straightened. His stare was unfathomable.

"Look," she said. Why couldn't she shut up? She wanted to shut up. Instead she jammed her shaking hands into her pockets and listened to the words spill out of her, hating herself. "You just pulled me out of the ghost-place river like an hour ago. Okay? We're even."

"You actually think," he said at last, "that what this is about is me *owing you?*"

There was a pause in which Isabel had no idea what to say. She didn't want to say anything. She wanted to drop into the floor again. In her pockets, her hands balled into fists. One of them brushed against something smooth.

Ayres threw another blare of light, stripping another layer of moldy brick off the wall.

The dripping from the ceiling noticeably quickened.

And Isabel realized what the smooth thing in her pocket was. The orange plastic bottle Sairy had found clearing the tunnels.

"I can capture him," she said. "But Foster, I'm going to need your help."

"I'm listening," Foster said.

"How?" Sairy asked. "I used up the ghostcatching kit stuff back with Salazar."

Isabel fished the orange plastic bottle out of her pocket and held it up for all to see. "We're going to shrink him down and put him in here. Temporarily. Just to keep him from dropping the ceiling on us for now. But to do that I need your help. All of you." She lifted her chin at the ghost. "You keep him still. Sairy, you stand back. Keep the ghostgrass ready. He's probably not going to like this."

"Did I miss something?" Sairy asked. "Or did you skip right over the part where you say *how* we're going to shrink him?"

"I'm getting to that. Foster, you're going to link up a thread to him, like you planned. *But*—" holding up a silencing hand toward the ghost— "instead of feeding him more power, I want you to use the thread to try to draw some of his extra ghost-energy *out*. Like you did when you regulated Salazar. But I want you to *keep* pulling it out until he's small enough to put in here. That way he won't break anything or hurt anyone—" she raised her eyebrows at the ghost pointedly— "and then later we'll take him back to where the little rooms are and I'll help you put him in one myself."

Foster gave Ayres one last once-over and holstered her gun. Then, not dropping the sword or taking her eyes off the ghost, she reached down blind with her off-hand and pulled out the first few inches of a new thread. It glimmered faintly as she stretched it out. Then she stopped, pinching the thread thumb-and-forefinger and squinting at it doubtfully. "You've seen this work before?"

"Not exactly. But weakened ghosts shrink, if they're not in the ghost-place. That's how Archivists get them in jars. And I'm pretty sure if you can strengthen him, you can do the opposite."

Nobody said anything. Isabel's exasperated gesture encompassed Foster and the ghost and their whole ridiculous standoff. "I can promise at least it's a better idea than whatever the hell this is."

Foster opened her mouth to protest, then shut it. Isabel had her and knew it. Before and beneath all of Foster's anger and frustration remained the deep-rooted, ice-pure, chase-the-Chooser's-cape desire to *see what would happen.*

"Okay," she said. "Let's do it."

Then—incredibly—Foster sheathed her sword. Another pause and the ghost followed suit. It was a formality, a gesture, a joke. If they got it into their heads to pound each other into a fine silver mist, they'd do it armed or no, and the best she'd be able to do is get out of the way.

"So, what," Sairy was whispering to Isabel. "Just like that they're friends again?"

"Let's just take what we can get, okay?" Isabel replied. To Sairy's unasked next question she said: "And yeah. They're usually like this."

Foster got the thread in one hand and pinned Ayres's shoulder in the other. Readying for placement, she looked like a parent preparing to pull a scorchweed splinter from a child's foot. Sairy and the ghost flanked Ayres and stood by with ghostgrass and sword at the ready, respectively. Isabel wrestled open the bottle and slowly approached.

Ayres seemed to have stabilized, thank the Chooser. Without further provocation, the initial jolt of energy that Ayres's name had given him was wearing off. The walls had stopped shaking, and the chattering of Isabel's teeth slowed in the wake of diminishing aftershocks. Which was a wink of the Chooser's good eye, as there was already lakewater dripping into Isabel's hair.

Close up, that flickering ghost-light was giving Sairy a better look at Ayres than she probably wanted. She shuddered a little. "What the hell happened to these people?" she hissed at Isabel.

You don't want to know, Isabel thought. "Eyes in front. Stay clear of his reach."

"Don't need to tell me twice," Sairy muttered.

Light was rippling down the back of Ayres's coat in wavelets, rousing and settling like a bird fluffing its feathers in the rain. His hands hung at his sides, ungloved, with the same oozing nail beds and calcified ridges of scar tissue as on Salazar's, and his face didn't look much better. Whatever had gotten Salazar had gotten him too, though he looked to have burned out faster in its grip. Less evidence of successive rounds of strategic damage and regrowth, like a tree being pruned. He had the marks of the sickness, though, the slack gray skin and the weeping sores, blood crusted in tracks down both cheeks from the eyes, down the neck from the ears, down the front from the nose.

"Just one . . . more . . . second . . . " Foster was saying. "There."

A shudder racked Ayres as the thread connected. His light began to tremble like a stomped puddle, followed by a faint, almost-metallic thrumming as the energy siphon took hold.

"Okay," Foster said. "Here we go." As she had back in the child-ghost's room, she shut her eyes, and the thread began to glow. Dark light bled down the length of it from Ayres to Foster, flaring and quenching, slow and sure. After a moment, Ayres's light began to fade.

"Stay back," Isabel told Sairy needlessly, and they all stood and watched as Ayres' ghost-energy weakened from mostly black down through violet and blue to gray, finally bottoming out somewhere between tarnished silver and dirty white. Rounds of fat sparks went sizzling down his shoulders and arms, which shrank gradually and vanished up the thread.

It was working. It was actually working. She'd seen ghosts weakened before, of course, but not like this. The Wasp in Isabel had dragged her forward one step, then another, before she realized what she was doing and started backpedaling.

Too late. Weakened or no, Ayres's head snapped up, and he stared straight at Isabel. Not past her down the long drop of the vanished years. *At* her. Despite herself, she froze.

No reaction from Ayres when Sairy or the ghost had neared, no reaction when Foster had taken hold of his shoulder—but as Isabel approached she realized he was muttering something over and over. Had he been doing that before? Had she somehow not noticed?

Regardless, she knew what she was witnessing. The moment a ghost couldn't move past. The moment it snagged on, like a sleeve on a thorn, and stuck. Ayres's version of Salazar's *why isn't it killing you?*

But he was looking Isabel dead in the eye like he knew she could hear him.

"I got this," he was saying. "I got this."

Sairy narrowed her eyes. "What's it saying?"

Isabel shook her head at Sairy: *hush.*

"Wasp," the ghost said warningly.

"Back off, Foster," Ayres was saying. "It's okay, I said I got this."

Foster's eyes went wide. "The hell did he—"

But Ayres wasn't looking at Foster. Ayres was looking at Isabel.

"I got this," Ayres repeated, and *flickered,* the way the ghost had done three years ago on the ledge of Execution Hill, guttering like a candle-flame in a drafty room. Balancing on the knife-edge of a memory, teetering back and forth between that world and this.

With that, Foster wasn't holding onto Ayres anymore. He'd stepped free of her like she wasn't there at all. Automatically, Isabel drew the harvesting-knife.

"I got this," he told her.

Oh, she was going to regret this in short order.

"Got what?" she said.

Faster than she could react to, Ayres reached up. Put his hand on her face to give her a shove that would have launched her straight off the ground and sent her flying to smash against the far wall.

And the ghost reached the abrupt end of his patience. Before Isabel had so much as seen him move, his sword had gone through Ayres below the collarbone, pinning him to the wall.

Before all that, though, Isabel's reflexes flung her knife-hand up to block Ayres's grab. A split-second in which the knife slashed through Ayres's sleeve and found the arm beneath.

As always, a split-second was all it took.

I sabel was in a city.

It wasn't a city like the kind she'd heard about from songkeepers or Waste-walker scavengers like Cora whose rounds brought them to Sweetwater every few weeks for trade. Cities like Grayfall, away to the south, where the cliffs dropped away into a shield-wall at its back. Or Refuge, to the northwest, a month's slog from Sweetwater and to all accounts worth every step.

Isabel had never set foot in either. Even so she knew that those cities, trade-rich and grand as they were, were to this one as a puddle of mud was to the lake that had lent her own town its name.

Strange to think that she'd spent more time in this fallen city than in any that still stood. Even if she'd only been here in the memories of the dead.

It was exactly as she remembered. The same tall buildings, the same straight wide streets. Everything made of materials no longer in use in Isabel's time, unless when scavenged and repurposed in what small fragments remained. So much metal, so much glass. She was standing *under* a building now, a building that easily weighed as much as every building in Sweetwater combined, but raised up on sturdy pillars, with the streets running uninterrupted beneath. It hulked over her like some gigantic animal. She was tiny in the shadow of its underbelly.

The streets themselves were a mess. Torn up in massive jagged chunks. Littered with glass blown out of windows. Pocked with bulletholes. Bloodstained. Half-blocked with vehicles that had flipped, all in a row, as if the street had been yanked out from under them like a rug.

Ayres was there, and Foster, and the ghost. Another operative whose name Isabel didn't know, a girl with skin the same shade of brown as Isabel's, but a ponytail so black the light shone off it blue. Isabel didn't know her name, but knew that Latchkey paired its operatives, and guessed this one to be Ayres's partner. *Or*, she thought, *the one they'd partnered him with when both of their original partners had died.*

All around fifteen or sixteen years old. Isabel had seen enough dead operatives to suspect that these, at the time of this memory, might be the only four left alive.

They were in the process of clearing the main road for something, moving those flipped vehicles down side-streets. By hand. Isabel was well acquainted with the ghost's absurd strength, and Foster's, but that didn't quite prepare her for the sight of teenage kids pushing these huge hunks of metal hard enough to send them *skidding* down the alleys, or picking them up and *tossing* them like snowballs.

Stories had taught Isabel that in the Before, people had machines to do things for them. She realized that these four kids must have been chosen to clear this road because they could do it *faster.*

On either side of the street flanking the operatives, rows of uniformed men and women—not operatives but other soldiers, as Isabel had seen before—stood with guns at the ready. Waiting to provide cover fire for the operatives, shielding them from something they obviously were expecting to come down those streets. The operatives would clear a stretch of road, and then the uniformed soldiers and the four operatives would move together down to the next part to be cleared. While the operatives were working, the soldiers stood stock-still, waiting with the patience of stones, in a sleety downpour.

They made their way down the street like that, toward that weird raised building and Isabel underneath. Whatever they were clearing ground for, they were doing it in a hurry.

Then it came.

Way up the street, glinting in the rain, Isabel had only the vaguest impression of some kind of massive vehicle, itself the size of any six of the vehicles the operatives were tossing like wadded trash. But this one was *floating* maybe half a foot above the rubble of the street, all the unguessable pounds of it, gliding on a gently glowing cushion of blue light.

More of that light pooled and swirled in the open barrels of the thing's three massive guns, pits of blue light each the diameter of a catchment barrel.

Almost as soon as the vehicle appeared, something started falling from the sky, hailing down in long arcs from the far end of the street. Aiming, Isabel thought, for the vehicle, but not making it that far. Landing instead among the operatives. Maybe it wasn't the vehicle they were aiming for at all.

Isabel didn't know what was falling. Only that it landed on the street in a peppering of metallic *ping*s and began to glow, like dozens of fist-sized fireflies lying in perfect stillness on the rubble, cheeping softly.

The operatives were picking them up as soon as they landed. Catching them in mid-flight when they could. Pitching them back down the street with throwing-arms like cannons firing. When the things started glowing, everyone froze involuntarily, fear taking over for a second before their directive kicked back in.

"Shit," Ayres whispered.

"Oh *no*," said his partner.

"Five!" the ghost shouted, and all four operatives started throwing faster.

The uniformed soldiers were looking down at the glowing things with immense dread, but they held the line. A few splintered off to help with the effort. Several looked like they'd rather just run.

"Hold formation!" the ghost yelled. "Let them imprint! *Four!*"

Isabel wasn't sure she'd heard that right. *Imprint?*

Without missing a beat, Foster picked up what Isabel realized was a countdown. But a countdown to what?

"Three!"

Ayres loaded several into a bag he'd found on the street, whirled it over his head and sent it sailing. Foster dropkicked one, and Isabel heard it *ping* off of something in the invisible distance. *"Two!"* the ghost shouted, and picked up a couple of the things in one hand and hurled them so far so fast Isabel lost their glow almost immediately against the paste-gray sky.

Ayres's partner had a kind of handheld device that attracted the things to it with a low humming sound. She'd been holding the device out at waist level and the things had been hopping up off the street to attach themselves to it. She pressed a button on the device, and the glowing and cheeping of the attached things stopped at once. Another button, and they fell to the street, apparently deactivated. *"One!"* she shouted.

Foster screamed *"Against the walls!"* and the two rows of soldiers broke formation. Dived for the walls, plastered themselves against them, as the cheeping of the few remaining things grew quicker, louder, shriller. The things eased themselves up off the street and began to *hover*, spinning at incredible speed at waist-height in midair, and then shot off toward the exact locations where the soldiers used to be—and the operatives still were.

They were fast, but the operatives were faster, swatting them out of the air, kicking them away down the street with one last burst of effort.

Ayres, as his boot connected with the last one, began to cough. Hard. The sickness that followed the operatives' treatment had gotten him in the end, Isabel knew, but she hadn't known *when*. Adrenaline had pushed the symptoms away, but as it wore off, Isabel could plainly see them gaining on him. Catching him back up. He choked and gasped, and his kick went wide. Sent the thing flying with some force straight into the chestplate of one of the soldiers along the wall. There it stuck.

That soldier looked down at the thing, then up at Ayres, gray with horror. Ayres took one step toward him, one hand outstretched like he could reach out and physically take back the mistake. But there was nothing he could do. The soldier began to shake all over, as though having a fit, but faster, impossibly fast, more like a vibration that went on and on. A single high-pitched sustained note was coming either from him or the thing stuck to him, and it was soon joined by a long sequence of sudden snapping sounds as every bone in his body was broken by some invisible force, into halves, quarters, eighths, and yanked inward toward the thing stuck in his chest.

The high-pitched sound stopped when the ghost put a bullet through the soldier's head. The snapping sound went on.

Foster blurred across the street and barreled into Ayres, pinning him forearm-to-windpipe against the wall, denting the metal behind him. "The *fuck*, Ayres," she was hissing into his face. Beside herself. Too furious even to yell. "We *had this.*"

Ayres was staring past her, through her, at the quivering pile of soldier steadily turning to paste inside his skin, crack by crack, as the first outliers of the next wave of things rained down.

"I'm good," Ayres was whispering, wide-eyed and ashen, struggling not to cough. "It's all good. I got this. Back off, Foster, it's okay, I said I got this."

Chapter Thirteen

Back in the tunnels. Disoriented. Queasy. Cold sweat down her spine. The fading back in was the worst.

She took stock. Everything looked exactly as she'd left it. She must have only been gone for an instant. The only difference she noticed was that the ghost now had Ayres pinned to the wall with one hand around his neck. Expressionless, unhurried, his head tilted slightly, as if daring Ayres to provoke him. Swordpoint resting in the hollow of his throat.

Sairy, one good sway from a topple, was nevertheless backing up his effort with a fistful of ghostgrass, gently repelling Ayres toward the ghost's control. Caught between them, Ayres was still, his ghost-energy draining along the thread to Foster.

"Isabel?" Sairy said. "You okay? You fell over."

"Lost my balance," she said.

Isabel stood before Ayres again, an idea taking vague shape in her head. She knew, now, the moment Ayres's ghost couldn't move past. She'd seen it. The field notes had never specified exactly what those moments were supposed to signify for ghosts, only that they were what ghosts got hung up on, what drove them to say a few words or reenact a single moment over and over for eternity.

She'd seen Foster's version of that moment before. She'd seen the ghost's. She'd seen Ayres's.

But now, for one of these at least, she'd seen what came *after*.

Sairy lifted her chin at Ayres. "What's he doing?"

He was flickering at intervals of about two seconds, as the moment he couldn't move past played on loop, dragging him with it like a dead squirrel caught in a cart wheel. Still whispering *I got this*, over and over, staring at a spot around Isabel's hairline that would've been the exact level of Foster's eyes if she'd been standing there instead, leaning in. Her forearm to his windpipe. A wall at his back.

He didn't move. He was wedged deep in that memory now, as mired as in quicksand. Whisper, pause, flicker, repeat.

It was either the best idea she'd had in a while, or the worst. In a minute she'd know.

"Foster, stand here."

She took Foster by the shoulders and guided her into place, which Foster allowed. The ghost stepped aside and stood by in silence, hand on hilt, awaiting trouble.

"Gonna need you to do what I say when I say it and not ask any questions, okay? I'll explain as soon as I can." *If I live through this.* "I promise."

A pause, and then Foster nodded, her mouth pressed into a line.

"Put this part of your arm against Ayres's throat—like this—" in demonstration she held her own forearm up toward the ghost, who raised an eyebrow at her over her sleeve but said nothing— "you're not going to hurt him, okay, nobody's going to hurt him—just—put your arm there and push him back against the wall."

For a second Foster looked like she was going to literally choke on her unasked questions, but then she set her jaw, put her forearm to Ayres's windpipe, and walked him back against the wall. He bumped against it, seemingly weightless, and stood there flickering, staring through Foster across the dead centuries at something none of them could see.

"Good. Now say: *what the fuck, Ayres, we had this.* Sound really, really mad."

Foster looked at her sharply, opened her mouth, thought better, shut it. Blinked. Turned back to Ayres. "What the fuck, Ayres, we had this."

At *had this,* Ayres, who'd been whispering to himself this whole time, reached the end of the loop and the loop kicked over, as it had been doing for minutes straight.

Except that this time it started earlier.

"I'm good," he said. "It's all good. I got this." His voice was wobbling out and in, all waver and echo, like he was calling out with the last scrapings of his strength from the bottom of a well. It cut out for a second, came back in. "—off, Foster, it's okay, I said I got this."

But he wasn't looking at Foster.

He was looking at Isabel.

He'd been looking at Isabel this whole time. Like she was the only thing in this whole place he *could* see. Isabel couldn't help remembering just before she'd fallen into the ghost-place river, the swirls of visual disturbance in the halls with one clean point in the center.

Except that Ayres's field of vision had been centered on Foster, and he'd turned from her to Isabel like Foster wasn't even there.

"Tell him it was an accident," Isabel said. "He was sick and it was an accident. Tell him you know it wasn't his fault."

"Doesn't matter," Ayres said to Isabel, from that far-off, way-back, caught-in-between place. "Still killed him."

"Yeah," Isabel said, shaken. "You did. Foster, let go."

Foster let go.

"This has gone on long enough," the ghost said, but halfheartedly. Staring with thinly-veiled fascination at something even Isabel had only seen twice before. A ghost broken free of its loop. It was how they'd found Foster, saved her from the sinkhole of her own mind, long ago. He knew perfectly well what was at stake.

"Just give me a minute," Isabel told him. "Keep an eye on him but don't engage. Sairy, stand clear."

Sairy nodded, shifting her weight to spring away if needed. "Clear."

"Wasp—" the ghost said.

"I got him," Foster said. The flow up the thread redoubled and Ayres wilted visibly. "Okay," she told Isabel. "Go."

"One minute," the ghost said. "Then it's my turn."

"More than I need," Isabel said.

But eye to eye with the guilt and anger and pain in Ayres's face, all her words dried up. What could she say to him that would make any kind of difference?

"Better to lose one than risk two," Ayres said, and the nimbus of his light started juddering, churning, spitting sparks.

Sairy started. "What?"

But Isabel wasn't listening to her. She saw her way in. She'd just about had her fill of *better to lose one than risk two.* And all the other crap that Latchkey had shoved down its operatives' throats. Partnering them up to inform on each other. Encouraging them to stand back and watch their partners die, because it was easier and cheaper for the people in charge. Less wasted funding. Less effort put forth in removing—whatever it was she'd seen them remove from Salazar's corpse's brain, in secret, having lied about her burial. Impossible to guess where the body had ended up when they were done with it. Isabel's best guess wasn't *buried.*

"That was a lie," she told Ayres. "That's what the Director wanted you to think. And it got a lot of people killed." She held her arms out to either side, indicating the wide empty expanse of the tunnels. "Do you see the Director here?"

Chooser knew if he even remembered the Director. It probably wasn't likely. But Ayres's whole person gave a stutter and seemed somehow to reset. "I'm with you, Foster," he said. "Just tell me what I have to do."

Foster's gaze whipped from Ayres to Isabel. "Why does he think you're me?"

Isabel wished she had an answer. "He doesn't *think* anything. He doesn't even know where he *is,* let alone—"

"Foster," the ghost said warningly, gesturing at the thread. Foster's attention had lapsed, allowing the grayscale lightbleed of the thread to reverse. Ayres, strengthened by the memory, was sucking energy back down it. Foster didn't seem to notice. Nor was she listening to the ghost.

"I'm standing *right here.* Why the *hell* does he think you're me?"

Projecting such angry betrayal. Like she'd landed in a trap she'd have to gnaw her way free of and she couldn't decide which leg to leave behind.

What must it feel like, for someone whose memories were fading, to be effectively erased from the sight of someone who was looking right at you?

"I find out, you'll be the first to know," Isabel told Foster. "I promise." She double-checked her grip on the jar and nodded. "Okay," she said shakily. "I'm done here."

Foster looked like she had a lot more questions where that one came from, but she swallowed them. Instead she shut her eyes, concentrating, and Ayres's ghost-energy went zipping up the thread in huge gulps of light. Within a ten-count he'd silvered and collapsed completely, drained but intact, reverting to the position in which they'd found him, slumped with the side of his face against the far wall of the tunnel.

"So fast," Sairy whispered, echoing Isabel's own thoughts.

But Foster wasn't done. She kept drawing ghost-energy until Ayres had crumpled and shrunken to the size of a mouse. It was how most ghosts looked in the living world, with only enough energy to project and maintain a vague tiny person-shape. But to see a ghost with Ayres's strength so dramatically changed, so quickly, and *on purpose*? Isabel was so impressed that it took her a minute to realize that Foster was glowing.

She'd never seen Foster's ghost-energy before. She had no idea why there were those tiny variations in color between one ghost's energy and another's. Silver-blue. Silver-violet. Silver-gray. Foster's was silver-orange, a color like a thrown spark.

"He's ready," Foster said, cupping that little ghost-form in both hands like a candle she was protecting from wind.

Together she and Isabel coaxed Ayres into the bottle. Isabel lidded it up and handed it to Foster, who set the bottle gently in a little nest of rubble along the wall. Ayres's thread trailed out from there to join the bundle at Foster's chest. Now, including the broken one that had been Salazar's, there were eight. Without being asked, Sairy set a few blades of ghostgrass around the bottle, just in case.

"Okay," Isabel said. No time to rest. Time to look at the map. "A little farther along this way, and then it looks like we make a right. Should be about—" her heart sank— "halfway to the hatch."

They set out. Foster in front, then Sairy, then Isabel and the ghost.

Sairy made it maybe five steps before she dropped.

They got her laid out on the tile as best they could. The floor was mud and rubble here, but Foster and Isabel made a flat place while the ghost lifted Sairy off her face and over onto her back in a grip that looked like it hadn't the first clue how to hold a person without breaking said person's arms.

"Off," Sairy pronounced.

"You're awake," Isabel said. Sairy blinked at her like Isabel had just shaken her from sleep in the middle of the night to take watch. "I need to see your hand."

"How far to the hatch?"

"We're taking a break. I need to see the cut on your hand."

"It's fine," Sairy mumbled. "I slipped in the mud is all. Let's go."

"And blacked out? Makes total sense to me. Happens all the time. Show me your hand."

After a moment Sairy seemed to realize she didn't have enough energy left to argue with. She held up her arm, wincing. "See? It's not that bad."

Isabel took Sairy's hand as gently as she could. Not daring to remove the ghostgrass braids, she slid them gingerly to either side of the bandage as she and Sairy hissed pain between their teeth for different reasons. Then she began to unwrap the bandage. It was soaked through with old blood and new pus, grimy with tunnel-dirt, and Isabel's breath caught when she saw the wound underneath. It had stopped bleeding, but the skin around it had puffed and reddened, and dark streaks trailed from the bottom edge of the wound the whole way to Sairy's wrist.

Isabel had seen this kind of infection before, but never setting in so soon after the initial wound. And she'd never seen it end well. Then again, she didn't know what happened when a ghost bit a person and was stopped before that person was dead. This was unknown territory.

Whatever this was, it was going through Sairy like a hurled rock through a paper window-screen. It was a long walk back to the medical supplies, and Isabel knew at a glance that they had brought down nothing that was going to fix this.

"We'll get you to the midwife," she heard herself say, though she had no idea how to even begin to keep that promise. "She'll know what to do."

"She'd need to be carried," the ghost said. "Look at her. That is a person who has gone as far as she is going to go."

"Your midwife," Foster said, dubious, "can fix *that*?"

"I don't know," Isabel hissed at her. "All I *do* know is that *I can't.*"

"She needs *antibiotics,*" Foster said. "She needs a *hospital.*"

"What?"

Foster was squatting on her heels, sizing Sairy up, head tilted slightly sideways like a hawk's. Like she couldn't make up her mind whether to bargain with Sairy or eat her. Then she looked sharply at the ghost.

"No," the ghost said. Holding up one black-gloved finger. "That's not happening."

Isabel looked from the ghost to Foster and back. "What's not—"

"We change her bandage," the ghost said. "We clean the wound. Field medicine buys time to get her to proper medical attention. I'll carry her myself. But I'm not—"

"Clean it?" Isabel said. "With what?"

"Don't do this," Foster told him. "She needs—"

"Hey," Sairy said. Her voice sounded weird, like it wasn't really hers. Like it'd traveled a long way and was now coming back to her from that distance. She was glaring down the hall into the dark like she could propel them all toward the hatch with her eyes. "Quit wasting time arguing. I've gotten hurt worse in training."

Foster shot to her feet. Took the ghost by the shoulder. "Can I talk to you a minute."

They retreated a few steps, arguing in urgent whispers. The words *help her* reached Isabel's ears, and *selfish,* and *deal.* The ghost didn't seem to be saying much of anything.

Sairy was still muttering under her breath. When she fell silent, Isabel glanced down to find Sairy staring up at her, her eyes huge and luminous with fever. "Don't you dare let them carry me."

But Foster had taken off somewhere, and the ghost came back alone.

"Wasp," he said, and at the sound of that name Isabel started like something had grabbed her in the dark. "Foster is scouting ahead to clear a path and see if the hatch is viable. Have your subordinate rest until she returns, and if the way is clear we'll get her to where she needs to go."

"Okay," Sairy said. "Two things. First—"

"You should rest also," the ghost told Isabel. "I'll keep watch. Foster won't be long."

"*First,*" Sairy said. "It's my hand, not my legs. Nobody's carrying me. And second—"

There was a pause. Isabel and the ghost exchanged a glance.
Sairy had fallen asleep.

Satisfied that Sairy was only asleep and not unconscious or worse, Isabel finally let herself sit down. Stationing herself near Sairy, she began the tedious process of kneading out her leg. Back braced against the wall, staring at the floor in silence, rooting her fingers into those old knots of scar tissue like she was trying to dig a hole to nowhere.

Focusing all her attention on the pain, because it helped distract her from the lightheaded nearly-puking awfulness that was worsening the longer she lingered in the tunnels. At least she hadn't dropped into the ghost-place again, though the threat of it remained: lurking in the dizziness and nausea, the burn of the ghostgrass on her skin, the hum of the harvesting-knife, tiny and low and just *there* enough to notice.

Twice now she'd already passed through the ghost-place, or the ghost-place through her. The contrast between that world and the living one was not, for her, as high as it once was. She didn't reckon it'd get any better from here.

This was all easier when—

But if there was one lesson the past three years had hammered into her head, it was that *easier* and *less complicated* did not always equal *better.*

As if on cue, the ghost approached. Stopped before her. "May I?"

Isabel kept her eyes on the floor. "I own this place now?"

The ghost sat beside her, barely stirring the dust. Even now, even on the periphery of her vision, the inhuman quality of his movement was mesmerizing, so alike and yet so different from Foster's. Foster embracing her power, explosive and expansive, and the ghost with his on lockdown, like one wrong move and it'd either tear him, or everything else around him, into shrapnel.

There was something he was very pointedly not saying.

Isabel didn't have the mental energy or inclination to probe this. All her worry right now was being spent wholesale on Sairy. She wasn't even angry anymore, or at least her anger had been bodily shoved into the box in the back of her mind where it'd lived for three years.

"About Foster," the ghost said, and paused, gathering either his words or the resolve to say them. Finally he spoke.

"Her memories. We . . . after we got her out of that *place*," spitting the word like poison, "I thought they'd . . . "

"All come running back to her?" Isabel said. Already knowing the answer. The one thing she thought she'd truly succeeded at had finally found a way to go wrong. Of course it had.

The ghost looked like he desperately needed to break something into a million pieces. "I was mistaken."

"This is what you wanted to talk to me about," she said. "Back by the room with the child-ghost."

Silence.

"There's nothing you can—"

"No."

"Do you have any idea what's—"

"*No.*"

"Shit." Isabel let her head fall back against the wall. "That's . . . shit."

All they'd been through to find her, and for what? For Foster to lose everything—the ferocious compassion, the burning loyalty, the cocky chase-the-Chooser's-cape attitude—that defined her? What did that leave? Meat, like any corpse. Or the faceless, mindless ghost equivalent that stood in place of death for what could no longer die.

As Archivist she could easily pick out them out, the ghosts who'd forgotten that much of themselves. Their faces would fade. All the colors of their clothes and hair and eyes and skin began to melt back to silver. At last they'd revert to shapes like paper cutouts, empty eyeholes in a silver mask, mouth agape, nothing inside. Formless blurs of light and rage and sorrow. And as Archivist she'd destroy those too-far-gone ghosts on sight. Put them down like Waste-crazed shrine-dogs. Before they got somebody hurt.

All too well she remembered the improbable strength of this ghost when he'd fought her up on Execution Hill the day her life had been turned inside out. He'd been powerful, and confused, but still under control, more so than any specimen she'd encountered before or since. What would happen to Foster's ghost when she, starting out from the same place of strength but without that icy calm to temper it, came untethered?

When Isabel tried to picture it, her mind fixated on one image from the songkeeper's picture-book. *Ember Girl burns the world to ash.*

"Well," she said slowly. Thinking of those ghosts weakened just shy of silver oblivion. Their minds like patterned fabric sun-bleaching to white. "She still seems like herself. She hasn't lost that. Just her memories."

"*Just* her memories," the ghost echoed, with such bitterness that Isabel relented.

"Okay, okay. Bad choice of words. But you know what I mean. She remembers you. She remembers me. She remembers the Latchkey ghosts."

The flip side of this last part, though, was: *Does she? This is Foster you're talking about. Someone who got herself killed putting her ass on the line trying to save people she didn't know and had no personal reason to care whether they lived or died. What makes you think she's doing anything different now? She didn't even remember Salazar's name.*

The ghost nodded impatiently. "There seems to be a cutoff point. Things that happened to her after we found her, she remembers. Everything before that? An almost perfect blank. Bits and pieces. Nothing solid. No continuity." He paused. He looked like he was working up to saying something it was going to cost his pride to admit. "Worse than mine," he said, and paused again. "Don't misunderstand. I'm not blaming you. Far from it. You went above and beyond, and I'm indebted."

"Slag that. Did you not hear me before? You. Do not. Owe me."

"That isn't what I meant."

"Then what—"

"I've been telling her all the things I still know," he said, ignoring this. "About Latchkey. What I have left of it anyway. About you, and how we found her. But she doesn't *remember* any of that. It's like I'm telling her stories. Like I'm handing her things she doesn't recognize." He gestured vaguely and lapsed into fuming silence.

"You tell her how you couldn't find her without me?" Isabel said, because she had to say something stupid or it was all too much, it would knock her over and sweep her away. Her voice was doing something weird, she couldn't modulate her tone for crap, it kept swooping and sinking and she couldn't hold it still. She was desperate to pick a fight with him and she had no idea why. "Or did you cleverly leave that part out?"

The ghost fixed her with the same even look she remembered, the look that came out when most people's tempers would, and it was like a spike being hammered in where the thread in her chest used to be. "I think that was her favorite part of the story," he said, deadpan, and Isabel laughed, though it felt like broken glass in her throat. What was it called when what you were homesick for wasn't a place? Whatever it was, for the first time in years it was gone.

"But it's been a long time," the ghost went on, "and I've forgotten more than I recall, as you're aware. The emptiness of that place, it—" here he gestured, one gloved hand drawing something unseen from the other— "it pulls on you. You lose so much. You can't let yourself forget."

Oh, she knew. She remembered overhearing the ghost reciting to himself the story of the moment when Foster began to be lost to him. *There was a hostage. A child. Foster's orders were to take him to the rendezvous point for extraction, where he'd be—*

"I need you to promise me something."

Isabel had a pretty good idea where this was going. She shook her head. "Not happening."

"When it's your time down there. If you see us. If we're—if we're past saving. If we've lost too much to get back. I need you to end us."

Past saving. Isabel knew what that meant. Unlike in the living world, it was hard to totally destroy a ghost in the ghost-place. A ghost's only strength and currency was its memories, and the ghost-place was *constructed* of memories. Down there, you could cut a ghost into pieces and the pieces would keep moving toward wherever it had to be. Or thought it had to be. The two didn't always overlap.

But the longer a ghost remained in the ghost-place, the more it forgot. Almost like the very landscape of the place was siphoning memories through unseen threads from those who wandered it, draining them to silvery nothing. Reclaiming its faded ghosts the way a forest will reabsorb its rotten trees.

If Foster'd already forgotten her whole life, and the ghost wasn't far behind, how much time did they realistically have left before the ghost-place got the better of them?

"Did you not hear me say no?"

"Foster agrees that it would be for the—"

"Look, I knew what you were going to ask, all right? And the answer is I'm not doing it. I can't do that any more than—" she hesitated, briefly— "than you could kill Foster when she asked you to."

The ghost went very, very still, and she felt filthy for bringing it up, for using that memory as a lever to turn the argument around. But he needed to understand what he was asking of her, and she didn't know how else to say it.

"There's another way. There has to be." Did there, though? Since when was she so blindly optimistic?

The ghost's light flared up, darkening, as his control briefly faltered. Then just as quickly faded, and his demeanor was back to its usual guarded, serene hauteur. Like flipping a switch. Like dropping a rock into a lake. "And what would that be?" he asked her, every syllable cut with slow precision. "Please. Tell me. You know what it's like down there. It scrapes away at you. It doesn't give anything back."

How weird it was, being caretaker of someone else's memories. Being the only one able to access them. The only one who even knew they existed anymore. The gatekeeper and arbiter of someone else's knowledge of their own mind.

If she died down here, in a way, these ghosts would die with her. Risking herself was risking them all. Like she was carrying them above her head as she struggled through swift water up to her mouth. If she lost her footing it wouldn't be just her who was swept away.

"I can't deal with this right now. Okay? Sairy's all messed up, Foster's gone off Chooser-knows-where, my town is under attack, and I haven't really slept in days. What were you and Foster fighting about just now anyway? Not sure what's so important that in the middle of all this you think it's—"

The ghost reached into a pocket of his jacket and pulled out a healing device.

For a split second, Isabel's breath caught in her throat. But she knew better.

"Yeah, you're every bit as funny as I remember," she said. "It's broken."

The ghost held the device lightly, thumb-and-forefinger. Over it, he watched her levelly. Treating her to that long slow appraising stare that made her want to throw things at his head. "Is it?"

For one second she was afraid he'd actually forgotten. But no. She knew that tone. That look. He might not remember everything, but he sure as hell remembered that. Well, his sense of humor had always been a little . . . odd.

"We're seriously doing this. You're seriously going to pretend you don't remember using it up healing me before."

"Did I?"

From edge to edge of the Waste, Isabel was certain, there was nobody alive who could rile her like this dead thing could. She had to shove both hands into her coat-pockets or she was going to punch him. There was nothing for it but that she was going to bust her fist open on the unassailable unendurable calm of his face, frostbite and vertigo and puking be damned.

Even though, deep down, if she was truly, finally honest, she was only angry at herself.

"Don't. Just . . . whatever you're doing? Whatever this is? Stop."

But the ghost had pressed the black film on the side of the cylinder, and it was now beeping softly. Lighting up.

"Fine," he said. Shut the device off and pocketed it. "I am willing to accept I misjudged your priorities."

It was a moment before Isabel found her words.

"That one's Foster's," she said.

"It is."

"She didn't use it up when she healed me before."

"She did not."

"That's what you were arguing about."

Silence.

Isabel swallowed. Thinking about Sairy, of course. But about something else too. "How much—"

"Enough to finish what we started."

"Is that an answer?"

"We healed you, the damage was worse than our hasty field estimate suggested, we didn't finish the job at the time. An oversight we can now correct." A delicate pause. Then, all studied mildness: "If that is what you choose."

"Choose."

Easy enough for her to translate the silence that followed.

"It doesn't have enough power left for both of us. Does it. Sairy's hand. My—" she gestured down at herself like she was flicking something away— "everything the ghost-place did to me."

"Foster is of the opinion that the remaining power would be best spent on your subordinate."

"Then that's where she should use it."

"It isn't Foster's anymore. It's mine." The barest sketch of a shrug. "And your subordinate isn't really my concern."

Isabel steeled herself against horrible temptation. She never in a million years would've imagined she'd be faced with this choice. Never in a million years would've guessed she'd be in a position to turn it down.

"Use it on Sairy."

The ghost shot her a look like she'd been sick on his boots.

"Sairy *needs*—"

"I didn't bring it for *her*," the ghost shouted. Then, tightly, the pristine mask of his calm shoved hastily back into place: "I brought it for *you*."

Isabel was a moment in processing this.

"When?" Although she dreaded the answer.

"I don't know. Does it matter?"

"You tried to come back," she said. "You tried to bring it back." She swallowed. "You couldn't get through the barricade."

For a long moment the ghost did not reply. Staring a hole through the floor, his gloved fingertips pressed together in front of him with a bizarre exactitude, at an apparent impasse with himself. Training all his focus on one point, one thing he could control, like the keystone that holds up an arch. Until the keystone gives way and the arch comes down.

Weird how you could forget someone's mannerisms until they were back in front of you. Weird how it felt like they'd never left to start with.

He measured his next words with even more care than usual. "We didn't expect that you would have shut us out. It was . . . surprising to find."

Unbidden, against her will, Isabel's brain was making another list. *I'm sorry* was on the top of it, followed by *it wasn't what I wanted* and *nothing in the past three years was what I wanted* and *I did what I had to do* and *I'm sorry.*

She wanted to say it. Any of it. All of it. Something. She opened her mouth and what came out instead was: "Use it on Sairy."

The ghost stonewalled her. "This is disappointing. You said yourself that your midwife could heal her. Where does that leave you? Can she fix *you*?"

"I don't need to be *fixed*. And I don't even know *if* the midwife can help her. We don't have magic Before-relics just *lying around*."

"Magic Before-relics?"

"How'd you even get that thing off of Foster in the first place?"

The tiniest, most telling of pauses. "We made a deal."

It was too much. "Really."

"Yes."

"A deal."

Silence.

"A deal, like, what, like the one you made *me* with *your* healing thing, which turned out not so well as I—"

"It was the only way I could get him to help me capture the ghosts we found down here," Foster called, striding toward them out of the dark. She could hear every word of this. Of course she could. From that distance she could probably hear Isabel's breakfast digesting. "He destroyed one first thing, when we came through the waypoint into the tunnels looking for you. I had no idea so many of us were stuck down here."

Not *them*, Isabel noted. Not how many of *them*. How many of *us*.

The ghost would have said *them*.

"You stayed to help them."

"*I* stayed to help them," Foster said. "*He* stayed because he was after that device. He'd lost so many bets trying to get me to hand it over." She paused a beat, amused. "So many bets."

"I don't understand," Isabel said. "You know I put up the ghost-grass barricades. You're pissed at me. I get it. But then why go to that kind of trouble to help me? You have literally no reason to want to—"

"I thought," the ghost said, dangerously softly, "you were smarter than that."

"What the hell is that supposed—"

By then Foster had reached them. "We ready to move out?"

"You're going to have to carry Sairy," Isabel said. "And she's not going to thank you for it. Talk to me about the hatch."

"Well," Foster said, "the good news is I didn't run into any trouble, and the hatch opens easy."

For you, maybe, Isabel thought.

"And," the ghost said, "the bad news?"

Foster glanced at Sairy before she spoke. Then, in a hushed voice: "It's a real mess up there. You go out that way, you surface right beside a lake about three-quarters of a mile outside of the town, and—" she hesitated— "even from a distance, it's not pretty. I don't know where this midwife's office is, but it looks like about half the town is on fire."

"*What?*"

"It isn't over," the ghost said. He was *listening* to the ceiling, Isabel realized. "When it goes quiet is when things have gotten bad."

"I'll get you to the exit," Foster said, "and we'll figure things out from there. But you're going to have to prepare yourself for the possibility that the place you think you're going back to might just be gone."

Chapter Fourteen

From there they took a few more turnings, and then a few more, until Isabel was completely lost. She'd given up on the map. It was taking all her energy just to keep putting one foot in front of the other without dropping facefirst onto the floor. If it weren't for Foster leading the way, she was sure she'd never be heard from again. She'd be bones in the dark for a future Archivist to trip over.

The ghost was carrying Sairy, though at least she was strong enough to protest it. Barely. Infection aside, the dizziness and nausea from constant contact with a ghost must have been intense.

"This is the fastest way to get you to the midwife," Isabel called up to her. "Quit squirming. Be happy your feet are dry."

And it was definitely fast. Isabel had to hustle and block out a great deal of pain to keep up.

There wasn't a whole lot around to take her mind off of it, though. Constant dripping from the ceiling at this point, beading up in condensation on the walls. Muddy lakewater pooling in the gappy tile of the floor. She fell behind a little, then caught back up.

"That," Sairy announced, pointing at a finger-wide runnel of gray water issuing steadily from the ceiling, "I do not like the look of. Is that not bothering anyone else?" When nobody replied, she turned her attention to the ghost. "Thanks," she said grudgingly. "I didn't mean for you to *carry* me like a—"

"No worries," Foster said. "We've carried worse."

But Sairy was on her feet now, Isabel noted. When had that happened? Still thrashed-looking, if not so bright with fever as she'd been . . . just a few minutes ago.

This scared Isabel maybe even more than the leaky ceiling. More than once she'd seen wounded upstarts whose systems had rallied just hours, or minutes, before shutting down for good.

"Sairy," she said, coming level with her. Trying to keep the alarm from her voice. "Hey. Let me check on your—"

Isabel glanced down at Sairy's hand and blinked, then exhaled hard, realizing what she was seeing.

The bandage was gone. The wound was gone.

Behind her, the ghost's silence was thick enough to cut.

Isabel opened her mouth, then closed it.

She fell back to walk beside the ghost.

"You're impossible," Isabel told him.

"You're welcome," he replied.

All at once Isabel could feel something unseen between them click invisibly back into place, like a couple of rusty gears grating against each other until, improbably, they meshed. On they walked in silence, shoulder to shoulder, two old friends in the dark among the sunken bones of a dead world.

Sairy, meanwhile, was practically bouncing on her toes with nerves.

"I was supposed to be helping in the fight this whole time," she was explaining to Foster. "I can't wait to get up there. Going to find Lissa and Meg and *unleash holy hell.*"

"Just a little farther," Foster was saying. She glanced over her shoulder at the ghost and Isabel. "When we get to the hatch, you two can clear a space and relocate the townspeople. It looked pretty stable up that way. Then once everything's over, we'll come back for them."

"I don't think anyone knows where that second hatch is," Isabel said doubtfully. "At least I never heard of it. You said it's by the lake?"

"It's practically *in* the lake. It was under about a foot of wet sand."

"How'd you open it?" Sairy asked.

Foster shrugged.

Even if I'd gotten there, I never could've gotten it open from below, Isabel thought, skin prickling. *And nobody above would have known where to look.*

"Don't worry," Foster said, misinterpreting Isabel's look of horror. "We're going to win." She nudged Sairy. "You ready?"

Sairy made a face. "What do you think?"

Foster grinned. "I think you were born ready."

"Wait," Isabel said. "We?"

But she knew. Foster heard everything, saw everything, missed nothing. She knew exactly what had to happen to make this work.

Foster looked insulted. "What do you think, I'm just going to dump her up there and cross my fingers that she doesn't get herself killed? I'm going with her."

O n and on they went. The lamp-oil was getting visibly lower, the walls and floor visibly wetter.

The harvesting-knife never stopped doing its thing, and Isabel never stopped feeling ill, but she didn't drop through the floor into the ghost-place again. When she started to feel that weird sensation like she was starting to slip through, the ghost always noticed, and always knew what it signified. He'd fall in step close beside her in silence, and she knew that if she did slip through he'd catch her, the way he'd fished her out of the river before.

Eventually they made their way into another stretch of little rooms. This whole sector seemed to be nothing but those, evenly spaced, each one maybe five long paces by five if Isabel stopped and went inside to measure, which she didn't. There was a good bit of distance between them, though, and the walls were extremely thick. This far down the tunnels there was evidence of fire. Scorched walls and ceiling, and the smell was different.

Soon they encountered a huge heavy door, half-open, spanning the hall. They went through it, took maybe a half-dozen steps and reached a second door, identical but closed. The thing looked to be the density and weight of the hatch door they'd descended through, but the ghost slid it open easily and they walked through it and on.

At one point they passed a larger room, fronted with a bank of thick plate windows. Despite herself Isabel slowed as she passed it. Remembering the four Latchkey operatives ducking down below those exact windows, angling bits of mirror as Salazar had her head cut open and a tiny silver square dug out. It'd said something above the door once. Like the rest of the lettering on the walls, it was black on white and mostly illegible. The doors were sealed.

Hit by a sudden compulsion, she put the lamp down under that bank of windows. Hoping to see—she didn't know quite what. Salazar laid out on a white table, maybe. Some evidence of what that thing in her head had been, or where it'd gone.

Cupped her hands to the glass and peered in. Took a second to realize what she was looking at. Jumped back a step, startled. Dropping her hands from the glass like it'd burned her.

Water. The room was totally submerged in the muddy darkness of the lake. The leaks they'd encountered so far in the ceiling must've devolved into a full-blown rupture somewhere beyond this wall. Somehow, whatever those windows and door were sealed with, it was containing the flood to that room.

You've held for this long, she thought at them. *Just a little longer. Please.*

The ghost was beside her. "Those doors we passed a while back," Isabel said. Still staring at that bank of windows like it'd explode in a torrent of Sweetwater and glass if she dropped her gaze.

She didn't need to say anything else. He just nodded once, whistled up the hall to Foster, signaled incomprehensibly, and took off back the way they came.

After three years of giving orders to the ex-upstarts, negotiating with the high seats, forcing appropriate words out of her mouth at appropriate times, all for the sheer stupid sake of fitting in, how refreshing and *comfortable* it was to be able to be silently, absolutely, immediately, flawlessly understood.

A grinding noise echoed up, and then a crash, and then the same again, as both doors were hauled by main force across their runners and rammed shut. Within thirty seconds the ghost returned.

Soon they reached the hatch. Isabel could hear nothing of the fight above, but if Foster's grim expression was any indication, things weren't sounding like they were getting any better.

This hatch looked much like the first, except that the door at its entrance was in somewhat better repair, as were the rungs laddering up.

Under the hatch, it felt like Isabel stood in the world's last bubble of calm and it was about to pop. It reminded Isabel of the instant before she'd step out onto the sand, knife drawn, on the Archivist-choosing day. Only on a much larger scale. Maybe this was what it'd felt like to live in the last moments of the Before, Isabel reflected. Right as it was about to stop being the Before and start being whatever came next.

Idly and not for the first time, she wondered what that must've been like. *Foster wasn't there for it, obviously*, she thought. Then caught herself glancing over her shoulder toward the ghost. She'd always assumed he hadn't been alive at the time of the old world's death. Surely he would have at least remembered *that* much. Even if—

"Here's how this is going to go," Foster told Sairy. "I don't know my way around up there. You do. Anything I need to know, you tell me. Don't wait for an invitation."

"Okay."

"We move fast and we move smart," Foster went on. "I take point, you stay close. We only engage after we measure risk."

"No Ragpicker's gambits," Sairy said. "Got it."

Foster stopped, boot resting on the bottom rung, and looked over a shoulder at her strangely. "No whats?"

"A gamble," Isabel translated. "A crappy hopeless gamble. A Ragpicker's gambit to beat Chooser's odds. Usually a bad idea. Sometimes the only idea you have."

"Last trick up your sleeve," said Foster.

"Sure," said Isabel. "I guess."

"I need you to be my eyes. I don't know the friendlies from the hostiles. More importantly, they don't know *me*. I don't want to start messing up the wrong ones. That'd be bad news for you. I'll tell you someday what it looks like when your side thinks you've jumped to the other one."

A noise came out of the ghost that might have been a laugh, but probably wasn't.

"So once we get up there, I'm your weapon. Point and shoot. In that order. Your people aren't going to like the look of me up there any better than they would've liked the look of Salazar down here, and you're not going to have time to explain, so *prove*, fast as you can, beyond a shadow of a doubt, whose side you're fighting for. Clear?"

"Clear."

Sairy turned to Isabel and Foster stopped her with a gesture. "None of that. Goodbyes are bad luck. You're going to see her again real soon."

As if in demonstration, she turned to Isabel. "Hey." Faster than Isabel could track, let alone block, Foster's hand moved. Isabel glanced down and there was a black-gloved pointer finger poking her in the sternum. When Foster saw her looking, the finger swept upward to bop her gently, incomprehensibly, under the jaw. "Chin up," Foster said, and winked, leaving Isabel to stare after her in bewilderment.

For the ghost, Foster only had a glance and a nod. Whatever passed between them passed in silence.

They all watched as she scaled the rusted remains of the ladder easily and lifted the hatch door up and out like it weighed nothing. Damp globs of sand plopped down from above, and summer morning light streamed in. It seemed somehow wrong that Isabel could hear birds out there, and a breeze in the stunted trees, and lakewater gently lapping at the shore . . .

"Clear," Foster called down.

Then Sairy was on Isabel, squeezing the life out of her lungs. "Don't you fucking die," she was practically snarling in Isabel's ear.

"Me? I'm stuck down here where it's safe. I'm not the one diving neck-deep into the shit." Isabel pushed her back gently, held her at arm's length. "Go on," she said at last, giving Sairy an awkward little shake. "Get out of here."

"Already gone," Sairy said, and followed Foster up into the light.

Isabel and the ghost stood side-by-side and watched her go. That close, frostbite-and-vertigo blasted clean through her sleeve, zapping straight up her nerves to her teeth and the backs of her eyeballs. Like getting stung, or burned, she always forgot how much it hurt until it happened again.

What did a ghost feel when it came into contact with the living? The same? The opposite, whatever that was? Nothing? Mentally Isabel tossed it on her pile of questions she'd maybe ask the ghost someday. Along with *what did you do with Foster's remains?* and *what ended up killing you?* and *you knew that the only bridge between you and your memories is me, and that bridge washes out the second I die*

and turn ghost, so what I can't figure out is, knowing all that, what the
hell kind of sense did it make, offering to take me with you?

Foster shut the hatch, and the dark returned, barely cut now by
the dying lamp.

"I want to check out the rooms in this hall," Isabel said. "Ghostgrass over a doorway worked with Salazar, it'll work against anything
else down here. And—"

At that moment her eyes finished adjusting to the dark and her
gaze fell upon the thread emerging from her chest.

"No," she whispered, rounding on the ghost in a blind panic and
a dead certainty that the tunnels were about to spit her out into the
ghost-place again. Almost-drowning once was plenty, and there were
nastier things in the ghost-place than that river, promising quicker
deaths for her if not more merciful.

But no. She wasn't dizzy, at least no more than she always was
down here, and her vision was clear, free of interference. And unlike
the other threads, she could see where this one was going.

It emerged from her coat-front to run in a clear line up and up
to join the bundle of threads that passed through the hatch, trailing
Foster like a comet-tail, linking her to the Latchkey ghosts she'd captured.

Isabel's thread connected to her chest at the exact place where
Foster had poked her. *Chin up.*

She inspected the thread. It looked different than the one that'd
connected her to her body before. Glossy and cold, pale and fine, but
with a springy strength like scorchweed tendrils. Her best guess was
that it was only the combination of the liminality of this place, her
nearness to death three years ago, her travels through the ghost-place,
and her ability to flicker in and out between the real world and the
ghost one, that allowed the thread to gain purchase on her at all.

Light seeped visibly along that thread, pulsing in infinitesimal
pure white flares.

Ghost-energy. Foster was . . . *fueling* her, the way oil fuels a
lamp, along the wick of the thread. She was standing straighter. It
didn't feel like there was a stick being jammed deeper in her side
every time she inhaled. Experimentally she dumped her weight onto
her bad leg and held it there, reflexively gritting her teeth against the

agony to come—but it never came. There was pain, just as there was still thirst and hunger and exhaustion, but it was dull and muted, like a pillow held over a scream.

"She didn't. Can she even—she didn't *really*—"

"It's Foster," the ghost said drily. "Of course she did."

"But *why*?" Isabel asked, but then fell silent, because something even stranger was happening to her. It was like falling through into the ghost-place, a *here* and an *elsewhere* overlapping. Except that now, the *elsewhere* was the outskirts of Sweetwater. As if, without having climbed out of the tunnels herself, she was now on the lakeshore above, kicking wet sand over the hatch-lid to hide it from view, and Sairy was beside her, staring off toward the smoke and noise in the middle distance.

No: she wasn't *seeing* it at all. The true evidence of her eyes was: tunnels, hatch, ghost. It was like a daydream. Something she was imagining. But she knew it wasn't.

You can see *the ghosts through those?* Isabel had asked Foster.

The ghost touched her sleeve. Frostbite and vertigo, snapping her back.

She drew him into focus, stricken. "I can see her."

Chapter Fifteen

I sabel watched as Sairy and Foster emerged on the shore, kicked wet sand loosely back over the hatch, and paused to get their bearings.

They stood on the edge of the shore where four hundred years' worth of upstarts and Archivists had risen and fallen. Chooser only knew what Sairy must be thinking. And Foster—

It was like when Isabel had read Foster's memories in the ghost-place, except at a closer remove. Those were more like a scene she'd walked into and was witnessing as it played out before her. This, though . . .

She'd heard ridiculous Before-stories of ghosts possessing people. This, as best as Isabel could tell, was very nearly the reverse. She wasn't hearing Foster's thoughts *precisely*, or seeing through her eyes *exactly*. It was much more complicated than that. Like Foster had become the lens through which Isabel experienced the aboveground world.

And all Foster was seeing—perhaps all she knew *how* to see—was a battlefield.

Noise. Screaming. A seesawing rush of sound. All of it much clearer and much closer-sounding than it would have been to Isabel's ears. Without stopping to think she immediately knew the town was twelve hundred-odd yards away, east-southeast. The breeze blew smoke back off the town, causing Sairy beside her to wince and knuckle at her eyes. They stood in a slight dip in the land, a low place beneath the higher ground of the town itself, so Foster couldn't see precisely *what* was burning, only that something was, and it was big. Isabel thought it might have been the meeting-hall.

"We're too late," Sairy breathed.

"No," said Foster, who could hear the noises of the town in layers and read them with astonishing clarity. There was death, and there was dying, plenty of both, but the fight raged on. "It'd be quieter than this if we were." She listened another few seconds. There were two hot spots where the most noise was centered: the middle of town and a point on one edge, away and out of sight. The raiders weren't just trampling over. There was a narrow place at which they—at least some of them—were being repelled. "They're defending a . . . gate?"

The Waste-road, Isabel thought.

"The Waste-road," Sairy said, drawing her knives. "Come on."

Then she saw which way Foster was pointing. "The Waste-road's not that way."

"Well, something sure is."

Isabel realized what Foster must be pointing at. Way off to one side of town, surrounded by its own outbuildings but otherwise kept at arm's length from Sweetwater proper . . .

"The shrine," Sairy breathed, and took off sprinting.

No trouble at all for Foster to catch up with her. Harder not to blast effortlessly past her, leaving her in the dust.

A little shudder racked Foster, like a sudden chill, but not at all unpleasant. Isabel understood. This was what Foster was made for. It was a part of her life she'd died trying to escape, but it was also a thing she was *literally created to do.* It was written into her on a cellular level. Her work, her life, her prime directive, irresistible as instinct. A thing of which she was, and remained, terrifyingly capable.

And now something—not memory exactly, not with that clarity and specificity, but something both vaguer and deeper—was clicking back into place within her. Something long buried was stirring awake after a deep dreamless sleep.

"Two people I need to get to," Sairy was saying as they ran side-by-side toward the town, Foster glowing brighter than before. "Lissa and Jen. They'll be who's in charge until I show. Lissa's big, tall, looks like she can break a bear in half. Lost a bet and had to shave her head so she's been painting it green instead. Jen's little and wiry with short hair. Looks like she can fight but can't for shit so she'll probably be giving orders from somewhere safe. Her skin's a little darker than Isabel's, more like yours, and Lissa's is a little lighter, but still darker than mine. Same scars on their faces as me. Same clothes as me." She paused for breath. "In fact, you see anyone dressed like me, tell them you're who healed Isabel so she could take down the Catchkeep-priest. They'll follow you through six hells after that."

"Really?"

"Six at *least*."

Foster kept careful pace with Sairy toward the village, her mind rushing out ahead. Tracking and triangulating the fires, the skirmishes, the defenses that held and the ones that failed. There was a burning building with screaming people barred inside. There were at least two separate groups of captives under guard. There were girls who moved like Sairy, knives in hand, glimpsed in the distance, there and gone. Someone was screaming words that were spat like curses, so slurred together as to be unintelligible. Someone else was laughing unkindly.

It all splayed out ahead of her in panorama, so laughably slow as to be almost frozen in time. She could rip through this whole place with her bare hands if she so chose, gut it and leave it for dead, and they'd never know what hit them. Corpses before they hit the ground.

It felt like something huge was trying to work its way up out of her. Like her body was made of lightning.

"Remember," she gasped at Sairy. "Point and shoot."

Another shudder escaped her, harder than the first, and if Sairy'd been looking she'd have seen the silvery corona of Foster's ghost-light brighten, deepen, kick up little shining spikes of energy, then settle like a tremor soothed as Foster regained control.

But that power had to go somewhere. As when Isabel and Sairy had trapped Salazar with ghostgrass, Foster's excess ghost-energy didn't just dissipate.

Trailing behind her, the bundle of threads gave one soft pulse and began to glow.

"Y ou can . . . see her?"

"It's hard to explain."

"Imagine my surprise."

"It's almost like when I read her memories. Except it's not."

"That was . . . overwhelmingly informative."

"Thank you."

The ghost studied her a moment. "You seem less anxious. About the fight above."

Isabel considered this. "Well," she said, "Foster's there now. I've seen her fight a *whole* lot worse than raiders."

"Point taken."

They'd walked out from under the hatch and were scanning the immediate area for a room large enough to safely house the towns-people. "I want one with one of those heavy sealing doors on it, like the ones we passed in the hall," Isabel said. "They're going to need to walk lightly past that flooded room, and assume there are others that are flooded too. And we need to put them right by the hatch so if the tunnels do start to flood we can get them out fast." She paused. "I mean, they'll all be huddled up on the lakeshore trying to hide in plain sight from Carrion Boy's entire raider army, and they won't be able to light a fire so they'll pretty much have sand and corpseroot and a hatch-lid to eat, but at least they won't—"

"But you can *see Foster*."

She gave up. "Yes."

"Clarify that for me. You're conscious. You're present in your surroundings. When you read memories, or when you fade into the ghost-place, it's more . . . dramatic."

"It's okay, you can say it. I fall over." But the ghost still seemed troubled. "What?"

"It's more than that. When I pulled you out of the ghost-place earlier, you looked . . . it reminded me of when we were searching for Foster, and your thread was about to break, and I didn't know where you'd go when it did, or how I'd even begin to find you. Or . . . " He trailed off.

Isabel wasn't used to seeing him grasp after words and come up empty. "Or," she ventured, "whether you'd be able to?"

The look he gave her could have peeled paint. "Is that the version of events you remember?"

The corner of her mouth quirked. "No." She pushed the door open on what the map had labeled *RECEPTION*. "Let's check this one."

The room beyond was huge and bare and in decent condition, all things considered. There was a wide heavy desk in the center of the room, and little broken chairs arranged in rows. Frames on the walls here and there, their contents black and rotten. A bigger, more irregularly-shaped frame dominated the wall behind the desk. A kind of symbol, all glass and metal. It looked like someone at some point had thrown a chair through it, and Isabel had no way of making out what it had once depicted. She approached it, squinting in the gloom.

Then she stopped dead.

Flowers. There were blooming flowers in a vase on a table a little ways away. Flame-colored lilies, their leaves the deepest green Isabel had ever seen. They were the only bright thing in the room.

"Plastic," the ghost informed her as he passed, gliding ahead to make a perimeter sweep of those shadowed far corners.

But it was so incongruous that she still needed a moment before she could pull her gaze away. She thought of the ghost-place, of looking for things that were out of place, somebody's misplaced memory jammed sideways into the fabric of the surrounding landscape. She went to join him, shining her lamp under a bank of those little chairs.

She almost dropped it as a sudden jolt of power, intense but not quite unpleasant, went fizzing through her veins, and she shivered with delight. It felt like she'd slept a week. Like she'd been handed a cup of clean water after a week's piss-drinking slog into the Waste.

She shifted her focus back to Foster. Strange how easy it was to just *see* in her mind, like a daydream, something happening concurrent to her present reality, no matter how far away it was.

"*Two people I need to get to,*" Sairy was saying as they ran side-by-side toward the town, Foster glowing brighter than before. "*Lissa and Jen.*"

The thread caught her eye. Like a firefly, it now glowed with its own light, cleaner and brighter than even the lamp. It stood out like a white-hot filament against the dark.

So much power, and this was what Foster could *spare*. They'd be able to mulch the gardens with what was left of the raider army when she was through with it.

The ghost was watching Isabel with close concern. After a moment she realized why. "Oh. It's not that. I'm fine. I'm here. It's . . ." She held out the thread. "Foster's in her element up there."

"Yes," the ghost said. "I imagine she would be."

Isabel gestured widely at the room. "I think this is clear. Let's check the door."

It seemed solid enough, and waterproof insofar as the ghost's estimation. So Isabel gingerly arranged some ghostgrass in the doorway and they began the long walk back to the townspeople for relocation.

By then she'd had some small chance to put her thoughts in order.

"It's like . . . it's not even that I can *see* her," she said as they walked. "Not like you're thinking. It's more like I can see *with* her. Like you tell someone you trust to do something for you because you can't, you say, *you're my eyes, you're my legs,* whatever. Except she . . ."

"You can keep track of her actions remotely, even as you're in control of your own person."

"Yeah. Exactly. Like Foster was doing with the ghosts she caught, I guess. It's confusing though. It's like being in two places at once." Then, as it struck her: "And she's keeping track of *eight* of these?"

"She's had a long time to collect them."

Isabel sighed. "Yeah. I guess she has." She waited for the next round, but it never came. "What, no more vague accusations? You think you have something to say to me that I haven't already—"

"How long has it been?" he asked, surprising her. "Up there."

Almost four years since we went down into the ghost-place to find Foster, Isabel thought, trying desperately to clamp down on it and failing. *But since you came back and offered to take me with you—*

"Three years," she heard herself say. "Two months. Fourteen days."

The silence that followed was so long she thought he might not have heard her. Which was, of course, absurd.

"Three years," the ghost repeated at last. Filing it away, like Foster had filed away *Salazar* earlier. Syllables. Sounds. She could have throttled him. But then he paused again. "It felt like longer."

Yes, she thought. But for some reason she couldn't say it. All at once, her anger had broken and scattered from her, and the calm it left behind was almost overwhelming.

"After this is over," she said, "I'll find a way to help you."

A scornful sound. "Help me. There's nothing left of me to help."

"Shut up and listen. No matter how bad it gets, I'm not going to be able to destroy you. I'm just not. But here's what I'm offering instead. We get out of here, I'll read your memories, I'll read Foster's. I'll write them all down. Every word of it. Every day if I have to. I'll draw *pictures.* Okay? Just—after the fight, when I get out of this Ragpicker-taken place and go back home—" *Don't say it,* she warned herself, *don't you say it—* "come with me."

The ghost made a kind of slow-motion recoil, then stared her down with the wariest, most skeptical specimen of hope she'd ever seen. There was a very long pause, during which he didn't appear to trust himself to speak. "You'd do that."

What she thought was: *I've been waiting three years to undo the biggest mistake of my life.*

What she said was: "Hey. I'm the last of four hundred years of dead Archivists. I take *spectacular* field notes."

A pause, and then he said, deadpan, "Haven't you figured out by now not to make bargains with me?"

"Yes," she said. "But I guess I could say the same."

"What's in it for you?"

"Nothing," she lied. Then, pointedly: "Just like last time." When he said nothing, she glanced up at him. "Come on, you deserved—"

The look of wretched disbelief on his face stopped her cold. "Why are you doing this?"

"Doing what exactly?"

"Helping me. Trying to help me. You're not Archivist anymore, correct? Having dealings with ghosts is no longer your responsibility."

"Destroying ghosts *was* my responsibility as Archivist, like it was *literally*—"

"You know what I mean. Why refuse that and offer this?"

Oh, there was so much she could reply to that. Except . . . she couldn't. She'd spent so long swallowing the words that they'd gotten stuck in her throat, like a handful of thorns.

What came to her then was a ridiculous thought. She could barely protect her townspeople. She wasn't even sure she could protect herself. The idea that the ghost would want or need her protection was absurd. And yet all at once, with every atom of her being, she knew that if this went bad—if it was the last ground she ever stood, the last fight she ever picked, the last worst idea she ever had—whatever either world had left to throw at them, it'd have to go through her to reach him.

"I thought," she said at last, carefully, "you were smarter than that."

For a moment he said nothing. When at last he opened his mouth to reply she plowed over him, louder and faster than strictly necessary.

"*Besides*. The Catchkeep-shrine is a lot better than this shitty place, and it will amuse me to have ghosts over to visit. Especially when I think about how much the Catchkeep-priest would have hated it. You and Foster can stay with us as long as you like. I could tell you that we make decent soup sometimes, and Meg's bread is delicious, and Jen gives honey to the brew-mistress who makes it into wine, but you're dead anyway so you don't care about any of that. So I'll take your share of the wine and I'll read your memories."

"Is this the hard sell?"

"Is that Before-talk for *thank you*?"

I'm babbling, she thought. But she couldn't shut up. "Actually, no. Don't thank me yet. We still have to win this fight. Not to mention getting you and Foster all the way across Sweetwater to the shrine. That'll be fun, the whole town is warded against—"

Ghostgrass.

Hanging from every door and every window of every building in Sweetwater.

A kind of strangled shout came out of her, and before she knew it the ghost was in front of her, gripping her shoulders so tight the feeling had gone totally out of her arms before she could figure out why.

"Wasp," he was saying. "*Wasp*. Talk to me. What is it?"

"They're in trouble."

* * *

Well before they hit the Waste-road, Sairy stumbled over her first corpse. Only the sturdiness of the back of her shirt, and the speed at which Foster grabbed it, stopped her from faceplanting in the second one. Still, Sairy had the presence of mind not to cry out, just gasped out a string of curses as she was hoisted free of the mess.

"Not ours," Sairy said, once she'd caught her breath.

Foster surveyed the scene before her. "None of them?"

Sairy swallowed audibly. "No."

There were five, spread out over a span of thirty yards or so, two together and the other three spaced out. To Foster's eye, developed to distinguish ally from enemy even faster than she could lock onto a target to engage and mow down, pattern recognition did not serve here. These combatants were dressed not unlike Isabel or Sairy, in too-often-mended clothing made of something like leather and some kind of rough knitting, and she was baffled and impressed that Sairy could tell the difference at a glance.

They'd been killed by arrows, within reasonable firing distance of the hills above the town. Reasonable for an exceptional archer, anyway. And they hadn't been dead for long.

Sairy pointed. "See?" Two of the bodies were missing multiple fingers. One had lost an eye. Another had carved a slab out of one cheek, and the fifth one's nose was gone. The cheek wound was maybe a week old, and horribly infected, but the rest of the injuries were older, some by obvious years. "Carrion Boy's followers do that shit to themselves."

There was a certain grim, thin-lipped, grayish look about her that didn't escape Foster's notice. "You need a minute?"

"I absolutely do *not*," Sairy snapped. "I just . . . haven't seen this. Up close. Before."

"Identifying marks," Foster offered.

"That's right," Sairy said gratefully. "Watch out for them. Anybody stupid enough to mess themselves up on purpose like that is not one of ours." A sudden furious grin, and she tapped her own scarred cheek. "Ours messed up little kids instead."

Foster's mouth twisted. "Yours too?"

"What?"

"Long story."

Sairy kicked the nearest corpse and said: "Come on. They want to get cut up so badly, let's oblige them." Then she caught sight of Foster, who had whipped her head around and was staring off toward the town like she could see straight through the walls. "What've you got?"

Foster's gaze snapped back around to Sairy, who literally startled back a step.

"Ragpicker slag me, has anyone ever told you how creepy it is when you—"

"Who's Ruby?"

"What? Ruby's the—how do you—"

"Somebody just said *Get Ruby to cover.*"

Sairy stared across the distance to the huddle of buildings on the nearest edge of town. "Somebody said that in *there.*"

"Yeah. Now—"

"And you *heard it?*"

Foster shushed her with a gesture. Sairy visibly strained her ears and Isabel knew she was getting nothing for her trouble but an impenetrable thicket of sound: shouts, clashing of weapons, the odd scream. Something that sounded like a building incrementally collapsing, which might've been one of Jen's barricades being rushed by a wave of bodies, or—

"Lissa, right? Lissa's your primary objective?"

"I have to *get* to her, if that's what you—"

"Sounds like you're not the only one," Foster said. "Point and shoot, remember?"

"Just get me there."

They stayed low and ran. The fight seemed to have shifted toward the center of town, so the outskirts were pretty quiet and they slipped in undetected. Soon they were glued to the back wall of a house as Sairy tried, as silently as she could, to catch her breath. Beside her, alarmingly, Foster seemed to be doing much the same.

It's the ghostgrass. Isabel tried to propel the thought toward Foster forcibly along the thread. It didn't seem to take. *It's on that house. It's on every house. That whole place is rigged to poison ghosts, Foster, get out of there.*

"How are *you* out of breath?" Sairy gasped at her. "Do you even need to breathe?"

In response Foster just put a finger to her own lips. *Hush.* Pointed.

Another hundred yards distant, partly obscured by a row of houses, a group of captives knelt, clustered together against a wall. They'd been bound and gagged, and many were injured. Effectively managed by four armed guards. Two axes, a spear, a long junk-metal blade.

The prisoners' own confiscated weapons had been piled a little ways away. Clubs and slings and spears, and the heavy hacking scrap-made blades carried by the Waste-road guards.

"Assuming the ones on the ground are yours," Foster whispered.

Sairy nodded. "That pale girl dressed like me is Meg."

"She can fight?"

"Cut her loose and see."

As if on cue, Meg tried to struggle to her feet and was bashed back into place. She sat there, nose obviously broken, drilling holes in her captor with her eyes.

"I'm going in," Foster said, shoving up off the wall. "Stay close but don't engage."

"The hell I won't," Sairy said, but Foster had already closed the distance. She fell on the four guards like a hawk on mice. Not even bothering to draw her sword, she clotheslined the first guard on the edge of her hand with the force of a controlled explosion, crushing his windpipe and snapping his neck simultaneously. Chooser knew *what* she did to the next two guards, but it was too fast for Isabel to figure out. Only that one of them went down with the whole side of his skull caved in like a stomped windfall plum, and the other one was sliding on her own red trail down the rear wall of the house across the road. The fourth she dropped to the ground with both collarbones broken and both ankle tendons ruptured. When Sairy caught up with her, Foster was half-kneeling on that last guard's chest, smiling serenely at him as he blinked up at her in shock and terror and something almost like recognition.

Before the pain kicked in and he started screaming, Foster reached in and gave him a tap on the side of the head that put him straight to sleep. She got up neatly, brushing off her sleeves, and strolled over to retrieve the captives' weapons from where they'd been seized and piled.

"What—" Sairy was panting— "in—the absolute—*shit.*"

"Triage the prisoners," Foster told her. "First untie the ones who can untie the others."

"I *am.*" Hands shaking, Sairy drew one of her knives and cut Meg free.

"Oh," Meg said, eyeing Sairy. "There you are. Who's your friend?"

"I'll explain later," Sairy said. Cutting the others free as they shoved their bound wrists at her. The fruit-preserver and his daughter. One of the yarn-spinners. Three Waste-road guards. "You seen Lissa and Jen?"

"Not lately. We were holding the street in front of the meeting-hall. It was bad. We got separated." Meg nodded toward the freed captives. "They're doing this all over town. Taking prisoners." Grimly: "I guess the stories are true, huh?"

"Yeah, well." Isabel watched as Sairy shook off the image of the captives being sorted. Too easy to play that guessing game: who'd be raider army material, who'd be food. "Their mistake."

Two of the freed Waste-road guards grabbed their weapons back from the pile and didn't return with them to the fight. Instead they pointed them at Foster. If Isabel was in the business of naming fighting stances the way Lissa did in training, she'd be calling this one Terrible Idea.

Except that Foster was *really* starting to not feel so great. She wasn't *exactly* out of breath, and not *exactly* sick, or tired, because she was dead and that was not possible. But Isabel had seen upstarts bleed out before, seen their eyes go glassy as their hearts faltered to a stop, and that was what Foster put her in mind of now.

"So this is Foster," Sairy was telling the two guards. Loud and clear. The others needed to hear it too. "She's here to help us."

Half a dozen people started talking at her at once. Which was six more than she had time for. *Where'd she come from? She's not one*

of ours. Where was she when the fight started? She come with the raid-
ers? She's playing both sides? What the hell is she wearing? What the hell
is she carrying? We've never even seen her before and we're supposed to
trust—

"You're supposed to trust *me*," Sairy said. "And trust Isabel. Or
how about just trust your *eyes*. Were you not paying attention when
she got you out of this? Didn't see any of you getting out of it yourselves."

"Whatever she is, for now, I'm with her," Meg said. Fishing her
knives out of the pile, jamming them into the sash at her waist. "Explain it tomorrow. Today I'll take what keeps me alive."

"Same," Sairy said.

There was a pause while the others chewed this over.

"How many of you can still fight?" Foster asked them.

Several nods, a few raised hands. Some more tentative than others. "Good. Grab your weapons and get back to it." She tilted her
head down toward the unconscious guard. "He'll wake up in a second. I wasn't sure if we were taking prisoners."

"No," Meg said, hefting the spear he'd dropped and driving its
point through his throat. "We're not."

One of the Waste-guards spoke up. "You said you're looking for
Lissa?" he asked Sairy.

"And Jen," Foster said. "I'm escorting Sairy to them so she can
relieve them of command."

Meg was staring at Foster like she was a talking tree. "How the
hell do you know Lissa and Jen?"

"I don't," Foster replied.

"Let's move out," Sairy said. "Meg, stick with us. Foster leads.
We shadow her close and we—" Sairy trailed off. "Foster?"

"I'm fine," Foster said. "Let's go."

Easy enough for Isabel to read the creeping doubt in Sairy's face.
She'd know quite well what it looked like when someone felt like
shit and was trying to tough it out. And if Foster were alive, Isabel
would've bet a week's chores on her either puking or passing out in
the very near future.

Isabel could see the moment Sairy put it together.

"Where's the worst of it?" she asked Meg.

A despairing little laugh. "Everywhere. Look around. It's all gone to shit."

"So point us to where it's deepest."

"I don't know. Outside the meeting-hall was still really ugly when we got grabbed."

"Then that's where we're going. We need the shortest path between here and the meeting-hall. All the ghostgrass between here and there needs to go."

"What? With all this blood around? That's suicide. Why would you even . . . " Meg paused. Really took in Foster's uniform, her sword and gun, the sudden queasy-looking wooziness that had her very nearly leaning on a wall. She seemed to finally notice the pale twist of threads, invisible in certain light, emerging from the front of Foster's jacket. "Ragpicker slag me. She's a *ghost*?"

"Whatever happened to *answers tomorrow, stay alive today*? Right now we clear a path."

"Okay, but let's get back to the part where *she's a ghost*?"

"Okay. She's a ghost. I don't care if she's the Chooser Herself. We lose her, we lose the town. You think Lissa can do what you just saw?"

Silence.

"We clear a fucking path."

"What do you mean, *they're in trouble*. Define *in trouble*. Define *they*."

"Ghostgrass," Isabel said. "The town is *covered in it*. What the hell was I *thinking* letting her go up there."

"I wonder how you think you'd have stopped her," the ghost rejoined.

"Not helping."

"Give your subordinate some credit. She'll figure out the problem."

"She *did*. That *is* the problem."

"I'm not sure I follow."

"They're going to try to take down the ghostgrass to help Foster fight. Which they need if they want to win without a whole lot more casualties. I just saw her rip into a bunch of raiders like nothing. They need her. What they *don't* need is—"

"—more ghosts to wander up from the facility," the ghost finished, understanding immediately. "You never planted ghostgrass outside that second hatch. You didn't know it was there."

"And in the town," Isabel added, "there's blood everywhere." She shook her head, remembering. "*Everywhere.* It's going to draw them. All of them." She glanced down at the thread. Bright as ever. "She's still powering these. She doesn't have the strength to spare. Not surrounded by ghostgrass. She's weakening visibly. But she's not cutting the threads. She needs to, but she's not."

"And this surprises you," the ghost said drily.

"She wants to help the ghosts *and* the town," Isabel said. "And me. I get that. But at this rate, this is going to end with some very powerful Latchkey ghosts coming up out of the tunnels and Foster powerless to stop them. They get much stronger, that little bit of ghostgrass she locked them in with won't even slow them down. So either the town gets overrun by raiders or it gets overrun by ghosts."

"Or both," the ghost pointed out.

"Still not helping." She blew out a frustrated breath. "The funny part is, right now, the people I left down by the first hatch are the safest people in town. And that's *with* Salazar and a cave-in right beside them."

It dawned on her even as she said it. "So we leave them exactly where they are." She turned on her heel and started tearing ass back to the second hatch, the ghost walking easily beside.

"I thought," he said, "the plan was—"

"New plan." Counting on her fingers. *Here's a list for you, Sairy.* "The people we put down here have a solid ghostgrass perimeter. They have supplies for a few days. And now we know the route to get them out when it's clear topside."

"You're still leaving them unattended. Your subordinate was already attacked. She almost lost that hand. I have nothing left with which to heal the next one who picks a fight they shouldn't."

"She didn't *pick* a . . . never mind. We cut Foster's threads, we don't just help protect the town, we also clear up the possibility of any more ghost situations in the tunnels. Cutting Salazar's thread stopped her dead in her tracks."

The ghost raised one skeptical eyebrow at those four upheld fingers.

"Well, it's a longer list than what Sairy and Foster have right now. I'm cutting those threads and then I'm going up there. I'll help Foster link her ghosts back up after but for now I have to take them out of the picture. We just—"

Isabel broke off, skidding to a halt in a sudden cold patch in the hall. Frostbite-and-vertigo, blasting up from the depths. Disorienting as opening a door in the middle of summer and walking out into the snow.

She turned to the ghost, wondering if it could be coming from him—and from somewhere deep down the hall there came a sound, huge and metallic, a grinding shriek followed by a dull distant *whump.*

Isabel couldn't see what was up there. But the ghost could. Already he had drawn his sword, had stationed himself between whatever was down there and her.

"How many?"

"Two."

Whatever—whoever—was down there, they were between Isabel and the hatch. Which meant they were between Isabel's knife and the bundle of Foster's threads.

Ghostgrass in one hand, knife in the other. *Only block,* she told herself, tensing for the attack. *Block and ghostgrass. Box them in like Salazar and slash the threads. Don't cut the ghosts. You cut them, you black out, you die.*

"You get the threads," the ghost said, low and steady. "I'll cover you."

"If I accidentally cut one—"

"I know. I've got you."

Isabel drew in a deep breath, held it, slowly released.

"Say when." Then, remembering her mistake earlier with Ayres: "Don't mention their names."

He glanced back over one shoulder. "That won't be a problem."

"Well. Finally that crappy memory of yours is a help to us."

But almost immediately she wished she hadn't chased the Chooser's cape by saying anything, because the ghosts had approached close enough that she could make out which Latchkey operatives they'd been. One, a girl with a cloud of frizzy dark hair, was Martinez.

The other, a tall boy of maybe fourteen, was Tanaka. From Foster's memories, from the ghost's, she recognized them.

Both had died younger than Foster or the ghost, younger than Isabel was right now. Compared to her, they looked like kids.

She knew better.

We're not special. Martinez was special. Tanaka was special. Salazar was special.

And here they were. Both visibly stronger than Salazar had been when Isabel had taken her on. There wasn't a lick of silver to either. They moved smoothly, not with the stuttering here-and-goneness of a typical ghost, but with the graceful proficiency of a Latchkey operative. Their threads were bright enough to notice the whole way down the hall.

They looked convincingly, terrifyingly *alive.*

And this close to the blood above—

"Don't underestimate them," she blurted. "I've seen them in Foster's memories. They're two of the top Latchkey operatives."

The ghost blinked, then looked the ghosts up and down with renewed interest. "Really."

"I mean it. They're dangerous."

He readied his sword and, Ragpicker slag him, actually *smiled.* "Excellent."

Isabel decided to ignore this. "They're getting too close to the hatch," she warned. "We need to intercept them before they—"

"Let them come. The closer they get, the more room you have to get behind them safely. I'll keep them busy. Cut the threads at the source. Don't engage."

Tanaka and Martinez reached the place where the hall T-junctioned out to the second hatch. They stood there a moment, scenting at the air, wreathed in their own silver light. *They can smell that blood from here,* Isabel realized with a chill.

"They're not going to come to us," she said in a rush. "They're locked onto the blood. They get out that hatch it's too late, I'll never catch them up over open ground, we have to take them out *now.*"

The ghost nodded once.

"Stay behind me," he told her—and vanished.

Chapter Sixteen

Foster, Sairy, and Meg emerged into the grassy area around the meeting-hall, into a solid wall of sound. Within a split second, Foster had it parsed and decoded into individual events.

Three of the Clayspring raiders, disarmed and chased down the street by five townspeople wielding heavy sticks.

A woman who almost fit Sairy's description of Jen, grabbing a kind of makeshift axe from a fallen body and rushing at someone or something down an alley out of sight.

Another group of prisoners, smaller than the first but under heavier guard. "Where are the children?" one of the raiders was screaming at them, his knife held to the throat of a woman Isabel barely recognized as the high seat Yulia. "Go fuck yourselves," she shouted, and the knife flashed, and down she went.

A pair of men carrying torches and running between houses, setting roofs alight. Already the meeting-hall was lost to the flames, door boarded shut, high windows vomiting oily smoke. If anyone was in there, they'd long since stopped screaming.

A slight figure dressed all in black, fighting dirty with knives strapped to its wrists, wearing a bizarre crown-like thing that shed feathers as its wearer wove and slashed between three Waste-road guards. It dropped one guard and darted away to the east, the remaining two guards giving chase.

The grassy area itself was strewn with bodies, dark and slick with blood.

"I just watered those flowers," Meg said, dazed. "Six buckets of lakewater me and Kath carried up, and now look at it."

The air was full of smoke here, not just from the meeting-hall, but everywhere. Foster could pick out the individual smells of scorched rusted metal, woodsmoke, burning flesh, singed hair. Also something she couldn't identify, the spicy-sour green scent of it needling through the other smells of burning, blood, shit, and sweat. Whatever it was, it lifted from the rooftops, blanketing the town.

It hit Foster like a sledgehammer. Her skin was on fire. Her whole body fizzed with pain. Her veins ran poison. She hadn't felt this awful since—she couldn't remember exactly. Something bad had happened to her once, some deliberate, methodical infliction of damage. She knew it had happened. She just couldn't remember. She thought it must've felt something like this. She—

"It's *burning*," Sairy said, her voice gone high and tight with dismay. "The ghostgrass. It's in the smoke, it's airborne, we'll never— *that's* why you—*Foster, look out*—"

Someone ran at Foster, knives flashing. By sheer force of will, Foster shoved herself into motion. Before Sairy could so much as blink, Foster had disarmed her attacker and was holding her up off the ground by a fistful of shirt-front. "One of yours, I think," Foster gasped at Sairy, letting go and stumbling, dropping the knives in the grass.

Sairy took in the attacker, the scars and long red braid and blood-drenched upstart garb, the pair of little knives. "Kath!"

"*Sairy*? I thought you were *dead*, I didn't . . . "

She trailed off. Smart enough to not let go of those knives once she'd retrieved them, Kath still looked like she wanted to run at Sairy and hug her until her ribs cracked.

Her guard dropped for a second too long.

A Clayspring raider came at her from behind, whirling his club. Another couple of steps and he'd be sinking the spikes of it into the back of Kath's head.

Foster tried to move, but her body wouldn't listen. She shot upright and flopped back listlessly, totally spent.

It was like a spike of ice in Isabel's spine. She'd never seen Foster this thrashed. Not after she'd marginally survived the illness that had killed Salazar and Ayres and so many other operatives, not after she'd been tortured by Latchkey.

Move, Isabel thought at her fiercely. *You have to move.*

Foster couldn't. But Sairy did.

Seeing one of the ex-upstarts in trouble—true immediate life-threatening deep shit, for the first time since the Catchkeep-priest was alive—seemed to snap something in her. Like something broke open in Sairy's mind, cracked like an eggshell, and pure molten rage poured out.

One moment she was staring frozen in shock, the next she was on the raider's back, twice her size or no, spiked club or no. She looked unsure how she'd gotten there, or when she'd drawn the knife, just vaguely aware that she had one arm wrapped around his neck while the other fist started jamming her little blade into any soft target within reach. Meanwhile, Meg slashed the backs of the raider's knees and he toppled forward, Sairy riding him down and shifting her grip to smash his face into the ground with both hands as he fell. Jumped up neatly and Kath lifted his head by a fistful of hair and cut his throat.

"Who's she, then?" Kath asked, nodding up at Foster. "Wait. Is that a fucking *ghost?*"

"Her name's Foster. She's a friend of Isabel's. She's on our side. I know—not now—Kath, I *know*, I'll explain later. For now, she's on our side, and she can fight like ten of us put together, and if anybody asks you, you tell them—"

"Ten of us, huh," Kath said, crinkling her brow at Foster skeptically. "Yeah, okay."

"Look, I didn't trust her at first either, but she just took out four armed guards in the time it took me to *get* there, okay? Ask Meg. Right now the ghostgrass is poisoning her, she's like absorbing the smoke or something, we have to clear it out some—"

Her words dried up as she followed Kath's line of sight to Foster.

Foster had stabbed her sword into the ground and was leaning her full weight on it with both hands, hitching up shallow unsteady breaths. Her eyes were downcast, staring at the ground with a vacant, dreamy, distinctly un-Foster-like expression. For one bewildered second Isabel thought she might've found somebody she recognized, lying there on the grass. That man with his guts torn out, maybe, or that woman with the nearly-severed arm.

But no. Something else must have snared her attention. She'd been dead for ages, she was a *ghost* for Catchkeep's sake, she didn't know any of these—

Then it hit her.

Foster was staring at the blood. Yearning toward it openly. It put Isabel uneasily in mind of what Sairy had said earlier: *They're not going to go all crazy hungry ghost on us like the last one?*

"Clear out the *smoke*?" Kath was shouting. "How the hell exactly are we supposed to do that?"

"I don't know," Sairy said, staring after Foster helplessly. "I just know we have to figure it out before she—"

In deep horror, Isabel watched Sairy's face light up. She had a very, very bad feeling about where this was going.

"Go find Lissa," Sairy told Kath and Meg. "I'm going to try something, but I want you out of the way in case it goes wrong."

"Goes wrong how?"

"Find Lissa and back her up. That's an order."

Sairy watched them go. Then she turned back to Foster. Muttered under her breath, so fast and low that Isabel didn't at first recognize it as a prayer to the One Who Got Away. Set her shoulders like a person bracing for trouble.

No, Isabel thought. *Sairy, you wouldn't—*

"Your name is Catherine Foster," Sairy said carefully, watching Foster go even stiller than before. Began to work her way over. Not raising her voice. She knew Foster could hear her. "You're a ghost. You've been a ghost for a long time. You used to be some kind of fighter in a war in the Before, with Salazar and Ayres and that pissy-looking one hanging out down there with Isabel now, but something bad happened to you, I'm not really sure what. You helped Isabel, healed her at some point, and there was something about you being lost in the ghost-place and they found you . . . "

Even from her distance, Sairy could make out the shudder that rippled through Foster's body. Her edges began to glow, flaming white against the black of her uniform. Light shuttled down the threads' length in rapid bursts. With it came a sound like cloth tearing free of scorchweed brambles, a smell like summer rain.

"Sorry, she didn't tell me a lot of details," Sairy mumbled, embarrassed and suddenly nervous to stand before this destabilized superweapon alone. Flashes in Isabel's head of what Foster had done to those four guards earlier. Sairy hadn't even seen her *move* before the blood started spraying. "Just—" she faltered— "memories made Salazar stronger—in the tunnels—I couldn't clear out all the ghost-grass so I—"

"Thanks," Foster said.

"Hey." Sairy swallowed. Trying to stop her voice from shaking. "Point and shoot, right?"

Foster essayed a bleary grin. "Pissy-looking one?"

"Yeah, maybe don't tell him I said that?"

"I don't know. I mean, it's not like you're wrong."

All at once Foster snapped to attention. Listened. Lifted her chin at something across the way. "Somebody over there just said *Lissa*."

Over there. Loose impression of skirmishing, little clusters of bodies sloppily fighting around the burning meeting-hall, some fleeing off screaming through the smoke. Isabel spotted Jen and Lissa, Kath arriving at their flank. Brawling their way through a knot of raiders in formation to surround something she couldn't quite make out.

"Those combatants are expendable," Foster said. "Whatever they're protecting, it's something that isn't."

"Let's get a closer look at it," Sairy said. "You good now?"

"Good enough," Foster said, but from Sairy's face she knew it was a lie. The memories Sairy had reminded Foster of weren't anything the ghost hadn't told her already, and the little burst of energy they had given her was already wearing off.

"If Isabel had just *told* me more about you," Sairy began, and stopped. Looked down at the blood-slicked grass. Seemed to weigh something in her mind.

Sairy—Isabel thought at her. *Sairy, you can't be*—

But Sairy had bent down and was swiping at the ground. Walked over and smeared her hand on Foster's glove.

"They're not gonna miss it, you know," Sairy said quietly.

Foster looked at the blood. Then she looked at Sairy.

Two things happened at once.

The first was that off near Lissa and Jen, someone in that knot of raiders started screaming. "Fall back! The Crow! Protect the Crow!" and there was a huge rush of noise and a surge of bodies and that black-clad figure Isabel had seen earlier was now lifted onto shoulders and borne away at a run. Raised up, she got her first good look at it. A small woman, armed with two knives like the ex-upstarts, except these were strapped tightly to the backs of her wrists and hands. Her clothing was of some kind of scratchy weaving, dyed blue-black, stuck through with black feathers, a few of which had molted in a kind of patchy trail, indicating which way she'd gone. "Stay on them!" Sairy shouted. "They're heading for the shrine!"

The second was that Foster hesitantly, deliberately, raised her bloodied glove to her mouth and licked.

The rush of energy was quick-burning but amazing. It was like a part of her brain being plugged back in. Like a fog had lifted from her, throwing silver sparks.

She barely registered straightening, sheathing her sword, breaking into a dead run, plowing into that knot of raiders like a meteor. She was moving out of time with the living world, half here half gone, and they didn't even see her coming until she was already among them and they were falling around her like autumn leaves.

Fighters from both towns attacked her, unsure which side she fought for. Isabel couldn't make out quite how Foster was determining which were Clayspring and which were Sweetwater, but her success rate was flawless.

Sairy trailed her at a sprinting, panting, never-closing distance, dodging fallen bodies. Each one taken out with a single clean blow, dead before they landed.

"She's with us," Sairy shouted to anyone who could hear her, "she's one of ours, she came to help us, let her through—"

Some of them listened and backed off, but others either didn't hear or were too worked up to register or believe what Sairy was saying. They ran at Foster, and Isabel could see that she was trying to ignore them, let them glance off of her like pebbles pattering off a window, but she was just too fast, too strong. Right now, all keyed up like she was, the gentlest touch from her was like a battering ram.

Three of the Sweetwater townspeople went down howling, holding a broken shoulder, a bloody mouth, shattered ribs. Seemed like the more Foster tried to regulate this sudden upwelling of strength, the more it threatened to burst unstoppably out of her. As if that strength itself was wearing Foster like a puppet, making her shatter windpipes and break spines. Working its way up to leaving her standing alone in the center of a ring of fallen bodies, like in "Ember Girl Tells Catchkeep *No.*"

Sairy trailed Foster the whole way to the Catchkeep-shrine, bobbing along behind her like a kite on a too-long string. On the final approach out of town and among the shrine outbuildings, the sheds and bread-oven and beehives, it became clear that the Clayspring raiders had looked at the shrine, the holiest place in the town, and seen nothing but a fortified building, a defensible site. They'd barred themselves inside and were firing arrows and unidentifiable projectiles through the windows. The townspeople were outside, firing back, but severely disadvantaged. One man had dipped a spearpoint in something, set it on fire, and was trying to jab it through the window-slots. A couple of teenagers were ducking under those windows, slashing at the raiders' arms when they poked through, picking up the dropped objects and hurling them back inside. This seemed to be working until one girl got an oil-jar shattered over her head and the flaming spear caught her unawares. She went up like a torch and ran off screaming.

When Sairy caught up with Foster, she was ringed around with Clayspring raiders, sword and gun still in her belt, not moving as they sized her up. Was the blood wearing off, or was Foster giving them a chance at mercy? Isabel wasn't sure. All that was obvious was that any second they'd rush her, pile onto her, and die. Like moths at an open flame.

But they didn't.

A few dropped their weapons and stared, one or two muttering something that Isabel couldn't catch. The rest turned tail and tore out of there like Foster was the Chooser Herself, all bone cape and famished eyes. Straight back into the fray.

Barely time for Sairy to choose and lock onto a target before there were three raiders coming straight at her. Whatever they thought they'd seen in Foster had spooked the hell out of them and they barely seemed to register Sairy as they broke and ran around her like creekwater around a rock.

"Oh no you don't," she said, and clotheslined one on the side of her arm as she passed, crouching with her as she dropped. A woman a bit older than Sairy, one ear missing, shoulders huge with muscle. Shot one arm up, grabbed Sairy by the throat and squeezed. Trying not to draw blood was a lost cause at this point, but training was training. Sairy caught her knife in a reverse grip and slammed the heavy handle into the woman's temple. It didn't seem to take so she did it again, more frantic now. She looked to be a few last gasps from blacking out. Isabel watched, helpless at her distance, as the raider's free hand drew a knife.

It was going to be somebody's blood, training or no. Sairy fumbled her knife into position. Buried it to the hilt in the raider's eye. Worked it free, labored to her feet and assessed.

Jen was hanging back, issuing orders to a group of townspeople. Kath and a heavy club were doing cleanup on a succession of fleeing raiders, one set of kneecaps at a time. Meg had shouldered a badly wounded child and run off in the direction of the midwife's.

Foster stood unmoving, glowing bright as a full moon. The halo of her light was shuddering hard now, spiking and settling as the blood and the ghostgrass battled it out within her. The ground beneath her feet began to tremble.

Just in front of Sairy, the man carrying the Crow began to topple and went down, harried by a pincer attack courtesy of Lissa and a Waste-road guard. The Crow herself jumped free, pivoting into a midair lunge, slashing with her wrist-knives at Sairy's eyes.

She was fast. Improbably, achingly fast. It was all Sairy could do to twist away from the worst of it, waiting for the impact. But it never came.

There in front of her was Foster, with one of the Crow's hands, shiv-blade and all, caught in each fist. Bones audibly cracking, the Crow dropped to one knee, staring up at Foster in anger and disbelief, hissing wordlessly. It came to Isabel that in her dedication to Carrion Boy she may well have cut out her tongue.

"Still not taking prisoners?" Foster asked. She'd gotten the waves of ghost-energy under control, but now something was wrong with her voice. Like she couldn't regulate it. Like her teeth were chattering with cold or nerves. Then Isabel realized it wasn't Foster's *voice,* it was Foster *herself,* vibrating like a bowstring while the arrow flies.

The noise from Foster's grip on the Crow's wrists was less of a cracking now and more a kind of squelch. Foster, noting either this or the full-body cringe Sairy was making, let go.

And, crushed wrists or no, the Crow leapt. Both shivs flashed out simultaneously, aiming to collide and cross somewhere in the region of Foster's heart. She caught both wrists before the blades so much as snagged her coat-front, yanked them down to one side, and at the same time shot her leg up to bash the Crow to the ground on the downswing, bootheel to neck.

Isabel knew she'd meant to be gentle, but could see at once she'd failed.

At the barred doors of the shrine, half a dozen raiders were making their stand, shoulder-to-shoulder, bristling with weapons. Darting their blades out at arm's length but unwilling to break the line. Some of them had shields made of wood, or salvage scrap, or bones, or a combination of the three. They held the shield-wall and did not attack.

Breaking the line, Isabel realized, wasn't all they were unwilling to do.

"They're down too many fighters," Sairy shouted, earning herself a burning lungful of smoke. "They're not going to go for the kill if they don't have to."

By reputation, they all knew what Carrion Boy's raiders did to the people of a conquered town. They wouldn't needlessly damage fighters they could conscript into their army. Or kill outright the ones they could only injure strategically, clean to prevent infection, and keep for food.

"That's our *home,*" Sairy shouted to the ex-upstarts. Leveling a knife at arm's length at the shield-wall and the shrine beyond. Coughing and choking and wringing the words out anyway. "I say we show these shits they picked the *wrong* fucking ground to stand."

But the townspeople were practically bouncing off that shield-wall. Charging up yelling, trying to poke their weapons through gaps in the formation. The raiders weren't even engaging them, really. More like they were waiting for something.

Then Isabel made out what Jen was yelling.

The leaders are in there.

In the shrine. Barred in and guarded. They didn't have to fight. They only had to stay alive long enough to inherit the town off the backs of its dead.

That's what the shield-wall raiders were waiting for, Isabel realized. The rest of the Clayspring army to finish clearing the town and come here to the shield-wall's aid. At which point the barrel-scrapings of the Sweetwater defense would be caught between the incoming raiders and the shield-wall itself.

Sairy saw it too.

"Foster," she said.

"On it."

Foster looked at the depth of the press of bodies around the shrine. She looked at the height of those huge doors. She listened to what they sounded like when the shield-wall rocked back against the front of the building. The weight of them. The density. "Keep them back."

She approached the shield-wall and the raiders behind it took a step forward in tandem to meet her. She centered on those doors and charged. Jumped lightly up, pivoting in mid-air, reaching down to clamp one hand onto the top edge of a shield and sail over the head of the shield-bearer, slamming into those heavy doors with both boots. They splintered and gave, banging inward hard enough to shatter one door off its fastenings.

The raiders turned and rushed in to guard the leaders, but Foster and her sword were in the way. She spun among them, whirling and flashing. Bodies fell, leaving gaps, and she waded in, the ex-upstarts at her side.

Together they pressed ahead into the depths of the shrine.

Past the door that led to the altar. Sairy peeked inside and signaled with a shake of her head: nobody in there but Catchkeep.

Through the long main room, past the long table and fireplace. Blood and bodies but no active combatants. One or two wounded, near the windows where a spear or arrow or projectile must've nailed them. None of Foster's doing, or they wouldn't be alive enough to moan. Sairy beckoned to Kath and she scuttled among them, cutting throats. Past the row of curtained sleeping-alcoves, which Kath threw open one by one while Sairy and Lissa stood to either side, knives at the ready for whatever ran out, but nothing did.

Foster stopped Sairy before she went through the curtain to the big room at the rear of the shrine, the one where the Catchkeep-priest used to sleep. Gestured *hush*. Gestured *stay back*. Threw the curtain aside.

Three door-guards stood there with spiky clubs. Foster let one come at her and swept his legs, dropping him onto his own spikes, then planted her sword through his heart with surgical precision. The other two fled into the back room. Foster followed and cut them down with ease.

Behind them stood what they'd been guarding. The leaders of Clayspring.

There were two of them: one man, one woman. Both dressed in long-sleeved jackets and long pants, all in black like the Crow before them, though these ones were without feathers. Both with all their visible skin cut and scarified as per Carrion Boy's devout. Both with their weapons raised to attack—until they laid eyes on Foster, standing in the doorway with her sword in her hand.

They dropped to their knees, weapons clattering to the ground before them. Long knives, longer than Sairy's, almost the size of Isabel's, made of sharpened lengths of salvage-metal. Once dropped, neither the man nor the woman made any move to pick them up. They were looking up at Foster, not so much scared or angry as *expectant*, like they were waiting for her to rescue them.

"Why are they staring at you?" Sairy hissed at Foster.

Foster shook her head. "I don't live here. You tell me."

These two were leaders, but they weren't fighters, that much was obvious at a glance. Those long knives were sharp, but clean. They'd drawn no blood. They'd been waiting in here this whole time.

Sairy looked about ready to spit. "They're like the Catchkeep-priest," she said in a kind of disgusted wonderment. "They want this town but they're not even going to get off their asses and fight for it. *Are you?*" she shouted at them. "You want a fight? I'll give you a fight. We trashed your army. We killed your Crow. Don't you want revenge? Pick up those pretty knives and come at me." She considered them, practically shaking with controlled rage. "No? Then I'll bring it to you."

"Wait."

Sairy stared, disbelieving, at Foster's glove on her arm. "What do you mean, *wait.*"

But Isabel could understand Foster's hesitation. It must be unnerving being stared at by perfect strangers at a remove of centuries with what looked so much like recognition.

"Look, I have my orders," Sairy protested. "No prisoners. They'll get loose, they'll escape, they'll come back and try again with more."

Foster nodded. "I know." She tore her gaze from the Clayspring leaders, the unaccountable look of betrayal dawning on their faces. What had they expected? "Make it quick."

"I will."

"Do you want me to—"

"No."

As Sairy and Lissa circled around back of them, one knife out, one hand free to hold each head still as blade slashed throat, both of the leaders of Clayspring began, in unison, to pray.

Sairy wouldn't've been able to make out what they were saying, spoken as it was in the familiar, breathless delivery of memorized words by voices about to be silenced. But Foster could, and so Isabel could too.

Ember Girl protect me, I have been weak, I have kept my head down, I am no hero. Use me as kindling for Your ever-growing fire. I will find glory there.

Ember Girl. Not Carrion Boy. Given everything Isabel knew about these people, this confused her.

What confused her more was that they weren't closing their eyes as they prayed, or looking at the floor, or the suggestion of sky past the ceiling. They were staring straight at Foster.

Chapter Seventeen

O ne second the ghost was there beside Isabel, the next he was the whole way up the hall, slamming into Martinez and Tanaka, keeping his sword between them and the way to the hatch. It was like he faded out of existence, then came back in, and it was all Isabel could do to fling herself up the hallway after him.

Drawn by the blood, Tanaka tried to shoulder past, but the ghost intercepted him, picked him up by one handful of his uniform jacket and flung him easily at Martinez. In the split-second of distraction that provided, the ghost drew his gun and unloaded three bullets between Martinez's eyes, aiming to lead her movements even as she dropped to the floor, sword held aloft. Tanaka sailed over her, two bullets in his back and the third in a shoulder, and fell in two pieces as he cleared the edge of Martinez's blade. Martinez rolled and came up sword-first, deflecting the next two shots into the tunnel wall. The ghost drew his own sword, slashing down as Martinez leaped—

—and Tanaka was upon Isabel. He was missing an arm and a shoulder and a big chunk out of one side, but the rest was still joined up to its thread.

Tanaka blurred, and by now she knew enough to lead the strike. Threw the harvesting-knife up two-handed to block the sword before she'd even seen it move. *Don't cut him,* she screamed at herself, *you can't cut him,* and they clashed and her knife slid free and she twisted aside and spun to give him an elbow in the face.

This seemed to get his attention. Slowly, still holding the sword, Tanaka touched the back of his hand to the busted corner of his mouth. Made a show of examining the blood on the glove. Looked

Isabel dead in the eye and gave his hand a deliberate downward flick, spattering the knees of Isabel's Archivist-coat with syrupy silver.

"Stop it, Foster," he said.

It shocked her into dropping her guard for a fraction of a second she couldn't afford.

Tanaka slashed and she leapt back, tripped over rubble and went down. Already he was on her. She rolled, and Tanaka's swordpoint shattered tile where her head had been. Without hesitating, he pulled it out of the mud and tile and stabbed again, and Isabel rolled, and he stabbed again, and Isabel rolled, and then she was out of floor. She shot her heel out at Tanaka's knee, forgetting for a second that this wouldn't work on a ghost—but he sidestepped neatly and readied for another lunge.

The ghost had other ideas. He took hold of Tanaka again and flung him at the ceiling, cratering the brickwork, then spun to reengage with Martinez, who slammed into him, blade to blade.

Both the ghost and Martinez were moving too fast for Isabel to get a clean lock on either. They were a blur of dark uniforms and silver ghost-light, swords ringing against each other with the speed of raindrops hitting a window.

"Wasp," the ghost said. There was an edge of true alarm to his voice that she didn't often hear.

"I know."

"You have—to—cut—them—*now.*"

"I *know.*"

As if on cue, Tanaka put his hand on the floor, vaulted up neatly and rushed her.

She scrambled for the twist of threads on the floor by the hatch entrance. Easy enough to spot them. Against the darkness of the tunnel they burned like silver fire. Drew the harvesting-knife in one hand. Fumbled up the threads in the other.

At the last second before Tanaka rushed into her sword-first, she realized that all the threads were not in fact in her hand. Her own thread still hung down loose from her coat-front, joining the bundle several feet closer to the hatch.

No time.

Please let this work, she thought to nobody in particular, and slashed the remaining threads.

At the same time, Tanaka dropped his sword entirely and made a grab for them. The knife went through the threads, through his sleeve, raked a deep furrow up his arm.

And she was ripped away.

Tanaka, roughly the same age as his ghost, lay shivering on a cot, flushed and feverish, treading sleep like water. A half-moon of Latchkey operatives sat on the floor beside him. The room was so tiny their backs were pressed against three walls. Six kids on the floor in total, between the ages of twelve and fifteen. Theirs was the somber expectant silence of upstarts awaiting the Chooser when one of their number had transgressed and was unlikely to survive her punishment.

Isabel recognized Ayres there, and the black-haired girl Isabel thought to be his partner, and Salazar. Notably, Foster and the ghost were absent.

There was a pitcher of cheery orange liquid sloshing in the margin of floorspace between the half-ring of operatives and Tanaka's cot. Next to that was a clipboard evidently standing in for a plate. On the clipboard was a stack of crumbly discs, tilting precariously. Most of them were grubby and broken, as if they'd been smuggled around in somebody's pocket for a while. Someone had jammed a twist of paper into the topmost disc. It stuck up and out from the tower like a stubby fuse.

On the cot Tanaka stirred, and his eyes bleared open.

All six kids started talking at once. Their voices were rich with that fruity brightness that aimed to be comforting and fell flat on its face somewhere along the way.

"Hey, Tanaka."

"Hey, man, you feeling better? It's your birthday!"

Three at once: "Happy birthday!"

"We made you a cake—"

"Well, it's actually cookies, dipshit, but—"

"From the *Director's stash*."

"And juice! Salazar swiped a whole pitcher. And it's the good kind. Not from powder."

Salazar gazed at her bare feet with the distinct glow of a person basking in her own uncharacteristic disobedience.

"No cups though."

"Hey, before I forget. Can you hear me? Tanaka? I'm supposed to say happy birthday from Foster. She says she hopes you like the cookies. She, uh, said to say she wanted to be here, but she was *unavoidably detained.*"

"Means she's in the box—*ow!* The hell was—"

"Oh my god shut *up.* This is a *party.* It isn't about *her.*"

"Fine, but all I'm saying is, a little respect. She isn't in the box for stealing cookies. She's in the box because—"

"All *right,* okay? I *know*—"

"—because she covered for *your* ass, Salazar, when *you* got caught stealing the fucking *juice.*"

"So *what.* I never told her to—"

"But you never told the Director it was you either."

"Can we shut up about Foster now? She'll be out tomorrow. Tanaka's *sick.* On his *birthday.*"

And they lit a little fire on the paper twist and murmured over it and blew it out. They put the least mangled-looking cookie on Tanaka's chest, having nowhere better to put it, and set the second-best one aside for Foster, in the manner of a living family leaving an extra place at table for their dead.

"**A**nd *that,*" Sairy said, "is what we call a Ragpicker's gambit." Caught sight of Foster. "What?"

Whatever it was, it was hitting Foster with a shock like a bone breaking. She didn't know what was about to happen, but she seemed to have a pretty good idea, and it scared her worse than the entire Clayspring army arrayed before her.

"She cut the threads."

"Foster," Sairy said. "I don't know what that means." Trying to stay calm and failing utterly in the face of whatever Foster was staring down the barrel of. "Listen, it's okay, we beat them, it's over, you—"

Foster grabbed her wrist, and Sairy gasped. That weird ghost-sensation would be blaring up her arm, Isabel knew, the dizziness and nausea and cold of it, but there was something else. Isabel brought her focus in on Foster and *felt* it. Like Foster was transmitting lightning through her touch. She was utterly rigid, seized into place, radiant as a star about to explode. Her sleeves, hands, whatever of Foster Isabel could see—was glowing.

She's trying to say something, Isabel realized. But it was like her mouth wouldn't work. Like she couldn't remember how to make the tiny, delicate, precise movements that would shape words. They were too small for her, for whatever was ripping out of her.

All the raw energy she'd been shuttling down those threads had found itself abruptly cut off from those destinations. It was clashing and running together like streams joining a river, and began to back-fill into Foster. Without the ghostgrass weakening her, without the threads draining her energy, surrounded by blood and suffused by memory—*your name is Catherine Foster, you're a ghost, you used to be some kind of fighter*—that power kept on generating, welling up from somewhere deep within her. Her eyes, ears, nose, mouth, soon the pores of her skin leaked silver. Her face worked, as if in overwhelming pain.

Eventually, Sairy found her voice. "Jen!" she screamed. "Get everyone out of here *now!*"

Foster clubbed Sairy to the ground, bouncing her head off the floor. Sairy looked up, dazed, and there was Foster standing over her, both arms locked, palms out and down, containing that outpouring of energy with what looked like colossal effort. Like she was trying to hold up a collapsing building with her bare hands.

Foster's eyes were pits of silver light, drilling through her. *"Run."*

With that, she filled and flooded. Black light exploded out of her, sheeting off her in a ring. It went shearing through the walls of the shrine with no resistance.

There was a horrible sound and the ceiling slid sideways, bringing the entire top half of the building with it. Fast as she could, Sairy tucked into a ball, arms clamped over her head. Kept her eyes shut for a twenty-count.

When she dared to look, Foster was still standing over her. Here and there, pieces of black rock from the shrine walls were falling around them. Where they hit the black light of Foster's energy halo they vaporized. The bodies of the Clayspring leaders had been lost beneath the rubble. There was a weird smell in the air, like a summer thunderstorm moving off away.

The dust lifted and there were townspeople staring in at Foster through the broken walls. Jen was there, and Meg, and Kath and Lissa. They were giving Sairy concerned looks. Over Foster's dead body she'd let them come in here. But how could she stop them? She couldn't even move.

Foster was flickering in place, caught in the overload. Another flare threatened to burst from her, it was rising up in her like bile. This time the walls of the shrine wouldn't be there to absorb the strike. It'd flare out, unimpeded, taking down everything in its path. Other buildings. The Sweetwater survivors. Sairy, if she got up. Standing, that blade of light would shear off the top of her skull.

Sairy hustled up into a crouch, gesturing *stay out* for all she was worth.

"Get back," she tried to yell at the people outside. But they couldn't hear her over the sound of Foster's ghost-energy, the grit and dust in Sairy's voice. Small mercy, the townspeople didn't look too ready to come in there after her. They just stood there gaping.

"She's one of ours," Jen was screaming at anyone who'd listen, screaming above that seething thrum of energy with her hands clamped over her ears. "She fought for us."

"The raider leaders are dead," Lissa was hollering at her side. "We killed them. It's over."

Foster, still hemorrhaging power like blood from a slashed throat, fought with all she had to suppress the flow. The next flare was coming, there was no shutting it down, only containing it. It was like trying to bottle a storm.

The ground beneath her boots began to shake. Something cracked under her and threatened to give way. Dirt began sifting down through an opening in the floor that hadn't been there before.

The next flare, clamped down upon with all the colossal force of Foster's will, did not erupt. But it had to go somewhere. It sought and found and rerouted itself toward a new outlet.

The one thread that remained.

* * *

I sabel opened her eyes. She was alive. Tanaka hadn't killed her when she'd snapped away into his memory. She'd cut the threads. It was over.

Already Martinez had collapsed into a silver mess, her ghost-glow blown out like a candle. A few feet away, the ghost had taken up the fight with Tanaka. Mid-swing, Tanaka's remaining borrowed energy ran out. He froze in place for the barest splinter of a second and was skewered. The ghost blinked in surprise, once, and then unceremoniously planted his boot on Tanaka's chest and hauled the sword free, slinging an arc of silver into the growing dark.

Isabel shook her head to clear it. Being in two places at once, and then getting pulled away into a memory, and then thrust back into the here and now, was exceptionally taxing. Her brain struggled to translate those separate realities even as they crumbled around her in pieces, a scaffolding of dreams. Pieces of puzzles she couldn't reassemble. *She cut the threads,* Foster had said. Why had that seemed to scare her? Wasn't that what Isabel had needed to do?

"This may be of interest to you," the ghost was saying. "Someone up there is loudly proclaiming that the raider leaders are dead. That, and I quote, *we killed them, it's over.*"

Isabel squeezed her eyes shut, reopened them. Only tunnels, thank the Chooser. She tried to focus on Foster but didn't understand what she saw. Everything was brightness. There was a sound like her ears were ringing, a smell like the air after it rains. She almost dropped the harvesting-knife, her hands were shaking so badly.

"They're . . . okay?"

"Evidence suggests. Sounds like Foster and your subordinate didn't save us anything to do."

"I told you," she said distantly, "she's not my—"

And doubled over, retching for breath like she'd had her throat kicked in. Unlike anything she'd ever felt. Worse than anything she'd ever felt. Like she was being turned inside out. Like her blood was trying to boil its way free. Like someone was trying to cram a bucket of water into a ladle, and the ladle was her. Frantically she wondered if this was what that soldier in Ayres's memory had felt in the moment before his bones had begun spontaneously snapping into fractions.

The ghost was at her side. The look on his face scared her maybe more than anything. Until he spoke, and that was much, much worse. The sheer level of icy calm in his voice was terrifying because she knew it by now for what it was: his version of anybody else's blind screaming panic.

"Wasp," he said. "I don't know what to do."

She shook her head, helpless, frantic, as pain howled through her like a wind. Clawing at herself like the agony was something she could peel off and cast away, but it *was* her now, and she was it. Like a suit of red-hot metal there was no squirming out of. Tears of pain stood in her eyes. It was like her face was melting, running down like candle-wax. "Get back," she choked out. "I can't—"

She cut off, unable to keep herself from crying out as something ripped free inside her. Ripped free and shoved its way up and out until she was sure her eyes would rupture with the force of it escaping. Her ears popped and she tasted blood. The harvesting-knife dropped from her hand and was flung away in the force of what was erupting out of her. Distantly she was aware that her Archivist-coat had caught fire.

No—not fire—it was *black*, edged and lined with silver—

"Oh *fuck*," she sobbed, and an invisible hand wrenched her head back, pried open every hole in her head, and Foster's ghost-energy thundered through her with the force of a hurricane being rammed down a gun-barrel. She stood—no, she *lifted* inches off the ground and hung there—no, part of her was dragged free of another part, and one part sought to rise while another tried to sink, but both were pinned on that thrumming blare of energy. She froze there, the ghost-self and the pain-self. Weeping, bleeding from the nose and ears, pissing down her leg, fountaining light.

Where that light hit the ceiling it started drilling through. Bricks fell and struck her face and she prayed to the Chooser, the One Who Got Away, the Ragpicker, whoever was listening, that one would hit her hard enough to cave her head in like an eggshell and she could be done, but that was a mercy she was not accorded.

They're safe, she told herself, shutting her eyes and waiting for whatever came next to receive her. *It worked. It's okay.*

And then—it was over.

The connection was gone. The ghost-energy roaring through her was gone. She went limp, incapable of movement as the ghost sheathed her knife for her, lowered her to the floor, propped her head up at a sickbed angle as pieces of something pattered down around them.

The ceiling. Isabel struggled to draw it into focus. It felt like she'd been kicked in the head and her eyes weren't cooperating. Chunks of white brick were falling, chunks and then bigger chunks, and then sudden motion as the ceiling unzipped down the length of the tunnel as far as she could see and all at once there were no more bricks to fall in, there was no more ceiling, only the black mud of the lakebed, which quivered for the briefest instant and fell in.

Chapter Eighteen

Isabel was drifting.

Black mud. Black water. The ghost-place?

No. She'd have sensed the crossing-through. She didn't feel half-here, half-there. *Think.* The ceiling had fallen in, vomiting lakewater, and—

A pressure on her back, her chest, her everywhere. Her brain took a moment interpreting *cold, wet.* Her face was in it. She'd better hold her breath.

Something pulled her along.

The ghost-place. Black water. The river. This time her thread had tangled in a swimming fish, a shark, a thing along the shore, and was unraveling her like knitting as she whisked wrongways, upended, unspooled, the current winding up her silver skein.

But her thread was gone. Without looking, she could feel the lack of it. *He cut it?* Besides, the pulling was in her arm, inexorable, her shoulder liable to pop. Familiar. Where'd she felt this pain before? Pulling *down.* She couldn't hear a thing. Her ears were stopped. Her mouth. Worse than drowning, maybe, if she tried to speak. To breathe. The lake would stomp her ghost down into the tunnel floor.

The tunnel floor. She could feel it, there, beneath her hand, against her cheek. Shards of tile grinding at her face.

A tremendous concussion rocked that floor, once, twice. Again. Dulled beneath the mud, but with her body pressed full-length against the floor, the thumps shook down along her bones like aftershocks of detonations.

The fifth, or maybe sixth, sounded different.

At the seventh, the floor dropped out from under her. She fell and fell.

L anded. Same steady puke of lake-stuff, tumbling through a narrower gap. Like water being poured down an anthill. How deep did this place *go*?

The map. Lost now. She struggled to summon it to mind. Those colored lines, one per level of the tunnels. She'd fallen through the floor of the blue one, *SUBLEVEL A.* Which put her, presumably, on the—green?—one below it, *SUBLEVEL B.* About which she knew precisely nothing. For starters, how to get back out of it.

Different room, empty, set with one of those heavy doors. She could just make it out through the sorry small glow of the whatever-it-was on the floor. Something she'd landed on and now scrambled off of in the dark. Something bigger than her, vaguely person-shaped, sprawled out on the tile. Something completely clotted over in mud, glow striving through where the cover was patchiest. Something not moving.

A distant rumble sounded, up and over, seizing the walls and giving them a single warning shake. Something above let out a long low squeal and buckled. The ceiling rained down a smattering of junk—and held. Further creaks and pops suggested it wouldn't hold for long.

She hurt all over. The thing on the floor still didn't move.

It must have been Tanaka, or Martinez, or some kind of debris. It couldn't be the ghost because he was fine, he could've gotten clear of the cave-in no problem, he wasn't weakened like Salazar, he wouldn't get caught out this easy, all he'd have to do is turn and run.

She drew the harvesting-knife, because best case still meant a fight, a ghost to put down. And worst case—

The thing stirred, or twitched, not rising, and something in the way it made even that tiny movement sent her guts into a barrel roll, because she knew in that instant that the broken thing on the floor was not Tanaka. Not Martinez. Not anything she could begin to accept.

She got hold of both his arms and started dragging. Her hands were slimy, his coat-sleeves were slimy, she lost her grip and fell back, spiking pain from her tailbone out the top of her head. Wiped her palms on—there was nothing to wipe her palms on that wasn't already covered with mud. Dug in and pulled.

In a fair world he'd weigh nothing, absolutely nothing, the way a weak ghost should. Frostbite and vertigo, a smear of silver and light. In a fair world she could bring herself to leave him here to save her own skin, maybe light a little candle to Catchkeep so She'd find the mud-soaked silver rag of him in the blind reeking Ragpicker's bowel of this place, She'd take him to a ghost-place door and shove him through, and meantime Isabel would be aboveground. Safe. Alive.

It crossed her mind for a second. But a lot of things crossed her mind every day that she didn't mean at all. That was just a function of minds. The rest of her was busy struggling with the motionless weight of the ghost along the floor, slipping and skidding and hauling toward the doorway, which was open, though starting to sag along the upper edge, bearing unaccustomed weight. The room was filling. The walls wept black water.

Up to her waist now. Every old ill-healed injury screeching at her while she, without breath to scream herself, mentally cursed the ghost roundly as she muscled him across the threshold of the open door and out into the hall.

There, the floor tilted downward to the left, just enough that the water and muck ran down that way. For now. Eventually it'd hit a blockage and backfill up to here, and she'd drown. Or suffocate. Or asphyxiate. Or whatever it's called when you keel over in the dark with a double lungful of lake-slime, countless tons of mud grinding your ghost into your waterlogged corpse for eternity.

It sludged on by and she turned to the darkness in the other direction, wishing with all the hope left in her that it wasn't a dead end.

Fought her way toward it, pain blooming across all her senses simultaneously. The ghost's faint glow caught a spark on something distant and metallic. Dead end, all right, but with a door at the end of it, thirty or forty feet off. Staggering under the ghost's weight, it looked like a mile.

Isabel paused a second, sucking in huge lungfuls of dank air. Behind her, in the room she'd just left, the ceiling crumpled in like a sheet of paper in a fist, plowing tonnage of mud into the floor. Her breathing break was officially over.

She squatted down, readjusted her grip on the ghost, and stood, shakily, half-shouldering him, dragging them both down that endless little stretch of hall. Muttering under her breath: *slag-for-brains, should've run, the hell told you to save me, what's wrong with you, die anyway down here, there is no damn reason you should be this heavy, I hate you, I hate you, I hate you.*

Knew she shouldn't waste her air. Couldn't stop, all the same.

Made the door, inched it open, digging in her feet and shouldering hard. Adrenaline shoved her through. Just enough fight-or-flight left in her to heave them both in and wrestle the door shut again behind them, cranking the inside wheel to lock it as the lake surged up behind. The door creaked and whined as the tunnel filled—old hinges, old bolts, a *lot* of bolts, no window—but held ground, its seals standing off against the lake and repelling it. For now.

She had to find another way out. But her legs had other ideas. They went out from under her and she collapsed, smacking her cheekbone on the toe of the ghost's boot on her way down. Saw stars. Didn't care. Lay on the floor—clean dry unbroken floor here, wherever *here* was—and breathed the delicious disgusting air.

After a while she opened her eyes. Everything felt wrong. Her skin felt hot, her blood sluggish, her muscles sapped, her bones loose. The dark was gluey, airless, heavy and thick, pressing down on her like the mud that waited for her above. The ghost's glow was barely denting it anymore.

The ghost.

For a sickening instant she knew he'd been damaged beyond repair, was a deflated silver rag with empty eyes, she'd tug on his boot and it wouldn't be attached anymore, the leg would slide free of it like a faintly glowing string of spit and she'd suffocate down here in that dying light alone.

She shuddered. Couldn't make herself pull on that boot so she brought a fist down on it instead. Seemed solid enough. The ghost mumbled something unintelligible, like a person drifting into peaceful sleep, or a person going into shock.

"Get up," she said, her voice unsteady. Brought her fist down again, harder this time. No response. Opened her mouth and her throat caught. Swallowed. Tried again. "You have to clear some of the mud off you. I need the light."

"Request acknowledged," the room said. "Activating."

There came a tinny humming sound from above, and a fraction of the ceiling lit up.

Isabel shouted, scrambling back and gasping, knife out, shoulders to the wall. It was a miracle her heart didn't short out on her right there. "What," she whispered, more hard exhalation than voice. "What."

"Tertiary auxiliary power supply at five point five percent," the room said, and a few of the lights fluttered dimly and blinked off. "Emergency conservation mode engaging." Its voice was smooth as milk, but also choppy, like the words were being read off a long strip of paper with holes punched through it at random intervals. Like listening to Ayres.

"Registering extensive systems damage. Temperature control no longer operational. Humidity control no longer operational. Archival seals no longer operational. Primary archive no longer secure. Please remove all records and materials in accordance with archival protocol to the secondary—"

The voice, still talking, dissolved into an incomprehensible fizz, like a beehive tied up in a sack. More of the ceiling blacked out.

But the water still hadn't made its way in. Isabel could tell the construction of this room was different. The floor was made of different Before-stuff than the floor of the hallway. Same with the walls. The door was heavy, with sealing latches on both sides. Like the sets of doors they'd shut and sealed between the cleared area and the second hatch, she realized, and was briefly faint with gratitude that she and the ghost had thought to shut them on their way down the tunnels.

All in all, the impression this room gave her was of a box that, once closed, could only be opened deliberately. The heart of the maze. The last part standing when all else fell.

"Get up," she said again, either to the ghost or to herself, but she was the only one that moved. Made her way back over to him, gingerly. As if her footfalls would shake him into sparks, like the seed-fluffs of suns-and-moons at summer's end. Knelt gently. In the room's light his glow had vanished, the way the sunshine hides the stars.

She wanted to move him, assess the damage, look for wounds that she could maybe patch. The way he'd stayed sprawled wasn't promising. What did they say about a person with a broken spine? Move them in a certain way? Don't move them at all? Did a ghost *have* a spine to break?

She sat her heels a moment, chewing her lip in impotent fury.

The healing device in his pocket. She fished around. Amazingly, still there.

Less amazingly, it was dead. He'd used it up on Sairy. She hurled it at a bank of metal doors on the far side of the little room. It struck with a muffled clang, slid down, was caught in a handle. Profoundly unsatisfying.

"Tertiary auxiliary power supply at five percent," the room informed her.

Isabel had never wanted to punch a wall so badly in her life. But the last thing she needed now was a busted hand. "Get your shit together," she hissed at herself. "Think."

She had as much basic first-aid experience as could be expected of someone who'd spent years being regularly thrust into, and surviving, ritualized single combat to the death. What she lacked was the first clue how to heal a ghost. Lure one, yes. Banish one, yes. Destroy one, yes. Fix one—really *fix* one—no.

Strengthen one enough to hopefully get a read on what was wrong with it, though? *That* she could just about manage. Wasn't ideal by a long shot, but she was in no position to be looking down her nose at damage control.

She scooted up until she was kneeling beside the ghost's head. His eyelids were open the barest slit, so Isabel waved a hand in front of his face, receiving no response. Lissa slept like that, eyes partway open like she was keeping vigil, expecting to get jumped if she dropped her guard. But Isabel didn't guess the ghost was sleeping.

She tilted his head back and opened his mouth. Or tried to. He had his jaw clenched so tight she'd have to break his teeth to pry it loose. Of course he did.

"Can you hear me?" she said. "I'm trying to help you. Open up."
Nothing.

She drew the knife. Realized she was covered in ghostgrass,
which probably wasn't exactly helping. Emptied her pockets and removed the braids at her wrists and neck and ankles, and pitched the
lot of it across the room.

Brushed her hands off for good measure and carefully made a shallow cut on one finger. She didn't need a repeat of what had happened
this morning—had that only been *this morning?*—with Salazar. Just a
little blood would do. Probably. Really she had no idea. Her experience
of damaged ghosts in the living world was limited. But she got the
ghost's mouth open as best she could and dripped some in. It didn't
look to be accomplishing much beyond reddening his teeth.

After a minute Isabel got up. If she sat there, waiting for infinitesimal changes while the lights gradually died, she'd lose it, the end,
and that would be that.

Besides, even if the ghost somehow ended up completely fine, they'd
still have to find a way out of here. Back the way they came wasn't looking good. Whatever the door seal was made of, she reckoned it wouldn't
hold the lake off forever. Water, like trouble, always found a way in.

"Tertiary auxiliary power supply at four—"

"Yeah, I get it," Isabel yelled at the ceiling. Then, struck by a long
shot: "Hey." Tentative. Ridiculous. "You up there. Whatever you are.
Can you . . . hear me?"

If it could, it didn't deign to reply. In a few minutes, though,
it'd tell her how much longer the light would last. It'd loop that one
thing for however many iterations it had left in it, and then the lights
would go out and the voice would go out with them.

It's a ghost, she thought, grimly amused. *The ghost of this place.*

It'd responded to *light,* though. There might be a few other
phrases it recognized. Perversely tempting though it was, she wasn't
about to test it by saying *door. Get me out of here* would've been a long
shot even by her standards, and she didn't want to drain what little
remained of whatever was powering it by screwing around.

She thought back on what it'd said earlier. She had a mind for
stories, for field notes, for call-and response, for ritual words passed
down. Even under duress, its tendency was to retain.

Archival seals, the room had said. *Archival protocol. Primary archive.*

The room labeled *ARCHIVE* on the map had been almost directly beneath where the ghost had apparently busted them through the floor. Almost directly beneath and two levels down. No wonder the ghost had taken such a thrashing. This wasn't *SUBLEVEL B* at all. It was *C.* The second floor they'd crashed through must've been almost completely rotten for them to have gone through it so easily, barely breaking their fall. Must've been like falling off a building. Like falling off a building with the added bonus of Isabel landing on him. She winced.

Back to the ghost. Was the blood starting to kick in? Wake him up? She couldn't tell. Gave him another dose, kneeling beside him. Burning another minute she couldn't afford. She wasn't entirely sure exactly what would happen when *tertiary auxiliary power* reached *zero percent,* but she had a pretty good idea she didn't want to be here when it happened.

"I'm getting your useless ass out of here," she informed him, and levered herself to her feet. "Somehow."

Archive, she thought. *But what does that mean?*

For her it meant a box of field notes, collected over four centuries by countless ghosthunters, all dead. But she knew better than to expect to find one of those here. If her dealings with the ghost had taught her anything, it's that the world Before worked different than her own. Different tools for different jobs. Different ways to fight, to live, to die, to get from place to place. Words were passed down generations, hand to hand, twisting their meanings slightly out of true. The way Catchkeep's up-self wasn't always Her. *People used to call it Ursa Major,* the ghost had told her, long ago, back when the stars of Catchkeep's up-self were still inset on the blade of the harvesting-knife. *A bear.*

Archivist, he'd said to her. *You're an archivist.* Dubious. As if she'd said she was a fish.

But he was out cold, or worse, so this room was her only clue to decipher the word, and the word was her only clue to decipher this room. Outstanding.

Only one thing for it. She'd have to toss the room. But most of what it seemed to contain was empty shelving. That, and the usual garbage of these tunnels. White brick and tile and the twisted metal wreck of something in one corner. More shelving, maybe, mangled into shapelessness by whatever had destroyed the doors in the tunnels above. She made her way around it in the almost perfect darkness. Not even really knowing what she hoped to find. A door that magically didn't open onto a flooded sector of the tunnels? Some Before-relic that would let her breathe mud?

All she found at first were a few sheets of what might have been paper, which crumbled to dust at a touch. A few broken pieces of something unidentifiable. That was all.

Reaching up blind on tiptoes to swipe the higher shelves snagged her another weird little Before-device, larger than the healing one but flatter, most of one side of which was nothing but a glossy black panel. Nothing that looked like it was going to keep them from drowning, so into a pocket it went.

Then she turned to investigate that bank of doors along one wall. The doors were a couple of square feet apiece, each with a pull handle running the length of the bottom. Stacked on top of each other, four by three, to the height of the ceiling. She'd never seen doors this shape and size before and had no idea where they might lead.

They all looked to have locked, once, but someone had at some point pried them open. All were dented on one side where they'd been assaulted and given way. Most stood very slightly ajar. One was missing altogether, leaving a square dark hole.

Come on, she thought at them. *Give me something to work with.*

Closer, each door had a metal plate bolted to it, about the length of her palm and a bit narrower. Each engraved with some kind of label that Isabel couldn't make out in the poor light without squinting. Those plates, and the doors themselves, were in surprisingly good repair. Like the room itself, whatever they were made of was made to last. The only part that really showed its age was the panel set into each door beside its plate. Once glossy black, now spider-webbed with cracks, set with buttons and dials and things Isabel couldn't name, all busted. *Temperature control, no longer operational,* she thought, leaning in to read one of those plates. *Humidity control, no longer operational. Archival seals—*

"Tertiary auxiliary power supply—" the room said, but Isabel didn't hear it over the sudden pounding in her ears.

Deep in her chest of field notes there'd been a list. One of the oldest sheets of paper in that box. On it was the series of questions an Archivist was supposed to ask a ghost, in the event she found a ghost who could answer them. A template by which Archivists could eventually piece together what had killed the dead world Before. *Name of specimen. Age of specimen. Place and manner of specimen's death. Manner of the world's death, if known—*

It was looping through her head, over and over, as she read and reread the engraving on the plate.

SUBJECT #2122-28-A

SALAZAR, MIA

There were other words, or maybe numbers, engraved below, but those were smaller and less deeply set, and mostly worn away.

"I don't have time for this," she muttered. "This isn't the way out."

But she couldn't make herself let go of that handle. When the room flooded, whatever was in those drawers would be lost to the lake forever.

She glanced at the ghost, then back at the drawer.

She took the handle in both hands and pulled.

Stuck.

She pulled harder and the door lunged out at her, dragging a long narrow drawer behind it. She fed it out beside her until she was standing next to it, looking down into an opening longer than she was tall.

Most of the drawer was taken up by a box, about six feet by two, made of some thick clear synthetic, set with another black panel. Presumably this panel was also broken, because whatever had been in that box, unspeakable age had rendered it down to a pink residue lining the bottom, furred with mold.

Isabel stared at that a second, her skin prickling, before turning her attention hastily to the smaller box at the outer end of the drawer. This one was made of some kind of black material indeterminate to her—she wasn't sure whether it was synthetic or metal. She lifted it to the floor.

On the top was a smaller plate. It was grimy, but cleaned off well enough with a quick swipe of a sleeve. SUBJECT #2122-28-A, SALAZAR, MIA. Like the drawers, the box had been forced open at some point, but then put back where it was. Looters, probably.

Isabel sympathized with the apparent compulsion to replace what hadn't been taken from this room. Next-best thing to never setting foot down here at all. The place was creepy, lousy with ghost-energy, though no ghosts appeared. But the frostbite-and-vertigo sensation was thick in the air here. That, and the taste in the back of her mouth, a sick-sweet tang like she was about to throw up, gave it away.

For a moment she'd thought it might be coming from the ghost, but no. By now the signature of his ghost-energy was unmistakable to her, the way she'd recognize her own handwriting even in field notes she didn't remember taking. This was something different. Knife or no knife, she'd tread lightly. Already the tunnels had proven porous to her, like the ghost-place remembered her, was calling her back to it. She'd fallen through more than once in the span of a day. And this time he couldn't help her. She was on her own.

Just a quick glance. Was he brighter? A little, maybe. What the hell was taking so long?

She opened the box like she expected something to leap out. But it was just a couple of folders stuffed with sheets of paper, all rotten. There, at the bottom, a little black box, labeled with name and number like the drawer and the larger box before it. As if she'd peeled back the false layers and this was the tiny pure essence nestled at its core.

What's more, she recognized that box. Sure enough, when she raised the lid, there was the little silvery thing they'd taken out of Salazar's head, looking exactly the same as when she'd seen it in the ghost's memory. Only cleaner.

Instinctively, she pocketed that too, box and all. To the tune of *tertiary auxiliary power supply at three percent*, she hustled down the bank of drawers. The dark was almost complete, and she was out of time, so she shoved Wasp back to the back of her mind and didn't let her waste time climbing up to the high drawers in order to clean their plates off and squint at them. The same information would be on those little cases, and she could stop to read those when she was out of here. Whatever was on them would be of no use to her corpse. So she eased the drawers open, removed all the tiny black boxes, pocketed them for later inspection.

Ten in total. She swiped inside the square hole in the dark, but there was nothing where that missing drawer should be. Another drawer, high in a corner, seemed empty, but when she pulled it open she could hear something sliding around inside. It sounded different than anything she'd found in the other drawers. Maybe something she could use to escape.

A lower drawer, pulled partway open, made a step. From there she could reach in but not see in. Swiped around inside, cursing exasperation. Snatched her hand back, stung. Dripping blood. Something had cut her.

She shut the drawer she was standing on, opened the one above it, opened the bottom one to the right of it, stepladdered her way up, careful not to touch any of those long pink-smeared boxes.

She reached into the dark and drew the thing out carefully, then stood blinking at it.

It was the last couple feet of a sword-blade, snapped off unevenly.

The legend was skipping through her head again. The first one any upstart learned. The one about the harvesting-knife, found deep in a ruin underground, given to the girl who would become the first Archivist . . .

Isabel, here, now, was standing on the nexus of two stories, in the place where they grated against each other like a badly-set bone.

Slowly, she slid that high drawer shut on its runners. Then she reached up and wiped the plate clean.

Sometimes knowing what you're about to see still isn't enough to prepare you for actually seeing it.

SUBJECT #2122-06-C
FOSTER, CATHERINE

Back on the floor, she touched the two blades together, break to break.

The fit was almost perfect.

Chapter Nineteen

P lenty of time to think on that later. For now she had an unconscious ghost and an inescapable room to deal with. She didn't know what would happen when the *tertiary auxiliary power supply at two point five percent* failed. The lights would go out, sure. But what about the door? What was it sealed with? Did it need *auxiliary power supply* to *stay* sealed?

She could deal with the dark. But she wanted out of there, ghost and little boxes and blade and all, before she got an answer on the door.

First things first. She got the broken blade situated in her belt in a way she hoped wouldn't end up gutting her before the day was out. Then she went to the ghost, gave him some blood from her fresh cut. That began to brighten him noticeably, almost counterbalancing the gradual extinguishing of the room's lights as the last of the power was diverted to wherever the room deemed it most necessary. *The door,* Isabel thought, and mentally gave herself another kick. *Shut up.*

Brightened noticeably but not moved. Or not much. He might have shifted a little, as in sleep. Hard to say. He wasn't breathing, but did he usually? Isabel couldn't remember. The cut she'd gotten from the broken blade was still dripping steadily, so she gave the ghost a fourth quick dose and moved on. If she couldn't find a way out of here, he could wake up right now and it wouldn't make any difference.

But no matter how optimistically she tried to study that room, it stubbornly remained the same dead end. Four walls, ceiling, floor. Some junked old shelving and eleven long drawers, plus the hole where a twelfth would be. If she could get the big clear synthetic box out of one of them, she'd fit inside. Best-case scenario, it was airtight, and she'd suffocate instead of drown. She could climb to the highest drawer, which would still get her drowned, but she'd get to watch the whole room fill with water first.

Really. This is the best you can come up with.

"Tertiary auxiliary power supply at two percent."

Isabel stopped pacing and stared at the door like she could barricade it with her eyes. The shelving could be dragged over and propped against it, but that would do precisely nothing against water and she knew it.

"If I had any sense I'd leave you here," she told the ghost. "Leave you and swim for it."

But she didn't move.

She couldn't stop thinking about the ghosts caught in the black river in the ghost-place. Already dead, they couldn't drown *exactly*, but they could fill with water, ballooning until they burst. No blood, no thread, would fix a ghost that broken.

Not only would she die, she'd die in a way that she'd never get across to the ghost-place, she'd be stuck in this room until Catchkeep ate the world, or Ember Girl burned it down, or Ember Girl and Carrion Boy sectioned it out like an orange between Them.

Maybe someday some future Archivist would open up this weird little room—whatever *Archivist* would mean in another thousand years or so—and study what she'd discovered, not knowing what it was. Both halves of a sword, some little black boxes. Two drifting silver ghost-rags, caroming off each other like blind fish in the murk . . .

Isabel shivered, which she wrote off as dread. Then reconsidered. She started paying more attention to the nausea. It was the very specific kind of nausea that came of being near an upwelling of ghost-energy. If she hadn't just explored this entire little room, she would've been convinced there was a ghost-place waypoint in it. No other explanation for—

The edges of her vision started shifting, rippling like wet clay. Terror seized her between its teeth and shook.

"No," she begged. "Not now."

Like she could command the floor not to open up and swallow her again. Like she could convince the ghost-place to reject her. The river not to drown her, or whatever it would be this time. And this time she'd be lost there for good, because the ghost couldn't pull her back out. He'd be stuck here, on the wrong side of that accidental passage between worlds, in the same facility in which Foster had died. Which made her vision go momentarily white with rage.

She had to anchor herself. A list, she needed a list.

There was a list in her pockets, a list of names and numbers on little boxes. She pulled one out and glanced at the label. Too dark to read it now.

Trying to focus on her senses just made it worse. She was nauseous, dizzy, covered in cold sweat. Even from across the room, the ghostgrass she had thrown away was burning her. The world around her bent and rippled, sickeningly malleable. How could she anchor herself with the evidence of her senses when all her senses were doing was proving she was straddling two worlds at the same—

Wait.

Maybe she could *use* that. If this place was that near the ghost-place, if the veil between those worlds was that thin here, then rules she'd learned in the ghost-place might well apply. And *that* was a territory she had some idea how to navigate.

Or not, and she was *tertiary auxiliary power, one point five percent* away from drowning like a field mouse in a catchment bin. But at least when the Chooser came to claim her ghost, She wouldn't find it sitting numbly on the floor, waiting to hear that clacking cape of bones approaching.

Just like in the ghost-place, she told herself, and drew the harvesting-knife. *Just like before.*

She felt her way over to the ghost in the dark and parked herself beside him. The ghost-place would open to receive them both or they'd be destroyed together. Either way, this was a one-way trip for her.

"I'm getting you out of here," she told him. Ignoring how her voice snagged in her throat. "You Ragpicker-taken utter pain in my ass."

She didn't even have to make a new cut this time. The one she'd got on the broken blade was still bleeding. She just drew the flat of the knifepoint carefully along it, trying to disturb the clotting as little as possible.

When the knifepoint was bloodied, she paused. Took a deep breath. Let her eyes come unfocused. Forced her thoughts to dissolve. Concentrated on feeling like a basketful of mud, oozing through the weave. A stack of papers shuffled into another one.

She let that awful dizziness build around her, let it sluice through her. She went completely still, like a hunter in a blind, like she'd had to do when the ghost separated her from her body to go questing in the ghost-place to begin with. The edges of her vision were going dark. *Not yet,* she thought. *Not yet.*

The room gave a shudder, rippling from one side to the other like heat-mirage, and through it she saw . . . she wasn't sure. Somewhere not here. But wherever it was, it wasn't dark there. She could see it, whatever it was, and that made it better than this.

"Okay," she whispered to the ghost-place. "Come and get me."

She pushed the whole of her will toward that other place and began to feel herself come unstuck from the tunnels. She was floating, she was sinking, her field of vision was pure interference, like walking a night road in a snowstorm.

The worst of the mirage-stuff looked to be in the direction of that bank of long drawers. Effortfully, muscles screaming, she heaved the ghost up and stumbled with him toward that wall. Found the strongest distortion near the leftmost drawers, in the column that contained the missing drawer on the bottom and Foster's on the top, with a third drawer in the middle. She shouldered the ghost as best she could and readied the harvesting-knife.

The unbreakable Before-stuff of Foster's drawer parted like flesh beneath the blade.

As before, only the bloodied part of the harvesting-knife went in, but that was all she needed. As before, elongating the cut was slow going, as though it was meeting unseen resistance, even as it passed through the middle drawer and into the empty hole of the missing one below. It gave her the same sensation as walking into a strong wind, or through deep water, but with what felt like the last crumbs of her strength she dragged the knife up through the missing drawer and the one above it, across the middle of Foster's drawer, and back down, giving her a shimmering imperfect rectangle, a vague approximation of a door.

She had no idea what was through there. It could be anything.

She hit the doorway shoulder-first. Gelatinous and cool even through the dogleather sleeve of her coat. The resistance had grown as the cut in the wall scabbed over, but she fought through bodily, digging her feet in, both hands white-knuckled on the ghost's arms.

"Tertiary auxiliary power, one percent," the room said, but nobody was there to hear it.

All at once, they were through. She almost expected a popping sound as the far side of the door spat them out, but there was nothing. Just a new bizarre sensation, one that put her weirdly in mind of scooping the yolk out of a raw egg. She turned just in time to see the faint blue outline of a messy rectangle as it vanished altogether. No way back. At least, not here.

Wherever here was. She drew the knife and assessed.

At a glance, they'd come through into a building, or the massive ruins of one. A wide sweeping staircase led up to pulverized walkways. Windows all along one wall of the main room, each one bigger than a whole side of a Sweetwater house. Floor covered in a thick layer of *stuff*, more varied and colorful than the broken debris of the tunnels. All the windows were blown out, littering the floor with glass. Light poured in through gaping holes in the roof. Broken doors led to what looked like outside but probably wasn't. There was nobody around.

Satisfied that nothing was going to leap out of this open space and attack them, she sheathed the knife and turned her attention to the ghost.

And froze.

Silver was pooling steadily on the floor around him. An alarming amount of silver.

Isabel felt her own blood drain out of her face. Felt her mind snap blank for a second, a minute—some rushing space of time wherein her plans, her ideas, her strategies, all packed it in and fled. Heard someone saying, over and over, soft and low like a prayer, "It's going to be okay, it's going to be okay." Then she realized it was her.

But where was the wound? Under the jacket somewhere. She got it unfastened and inched it open cautiously, dreading what she'd see.

It wasn't hard to find.

He must've taken a nasty hit in the fight above. Too much blood and damage for Isabel's inexpert eye to tell whether he'd been stabbed or shot, but whatever Martinez had done, she'd really nailed him. It almost looked like—

Sudden image in her head of the uprushing vortex of ghost-energy that had busted the ceiling above Salazar, much the same as Isabel's failure to contain Foster's ghost-energy had done to the ceiling above her. Sudden awful suspicion that it hadn't been Martinez who'd injured him so grievously at all.

"You're in the ghost-place now," she said into the silence. "The ghost-place will heal you." But what was that based on? Field notes. *A ghost will strengthen in the proximity to a ghost-place door.*

But she'd *been* in the ghost-place since, and she knew better. She'd never seen the ghost-place heal a ghost. If anything, she'd seen the opposite. All the ghost-place did was make a ghost dissolve a bit slower than it would in the living world. It would do nothing to help her now.

Damage control, she commanded herself.

She found the cleanest piece of cloth she could: an extra length of bandaging from her pocket. She pressed it to the wound with all the strength left in her arms.

Soaked through in an instant, leaving her plunging her hands into a morass of homogenous silver slop. *I can't see how deep it goes*, Isabel thought wildly. *No guts. It all looks the same in there.*

He hadn't moved an inch throughout any of this. Not when she'd exposed the wound earlier, not when she bore down on it now. He was helpless, she was practically wrist-deep in him, it was extremely undignified, he'd hate it, she wanted him to get up and stop her.

"Fuck you," she said, her face twisting. "Wake up."

Deathgrip on the harvesting-knife. Slashed her palm. Cut too deep. Barely noticed. Made a fist so most of the blood would drip out one way. It dripped slower than it had in the archive room. Like it had somehow immediately congealed to the thickness of honey. Opened her palm in frustration, ready to hack a Ragpicker-taken *finger* off if she had to—and her breath caught.

Not only was her blood alarmingly close to the *texture* of ghost-blood, but it was shot through with rich veins of silver.

But her arsenal of ghost-strengthening techniques was rapidly diminishing, and it was all she could do not to grind that blood into his closed mouth, as she'd done with the salt when she'd captured him, way back when she was an Archivist and he was a specimen and her life was a much simpler thing. Instead she aimed it in, a steady dribble of silver-streaked red, the other hand pressing the wound.

The position was uncomfortable at best. Kneeling, back hunched, tipped forward, arms spread wide, like a crow mantling carrion.

Bent her head to crack her neck—and noticed the thread emerging from her coat-front. It crossed over her left shoulder, traveled a few feet, and there vanished in midair.

It wasn't like the one Foster had given her, not anywhere near that vibrant with ghost-energy. It was frail and gray, like gathered ash one flick from crumbling, attached as it was to something that lacked the energy to power it. Her body. In that little room, in the dark. Only the bare fact of its presence suggested she hadn't yet drowned.

Although, she thought helpfully, *I could be drowning right now and not know.*

For a long moment she sat there, eyes shut, concentrating on her breathing so she wouldn't lose her mind. When she opened her eyes again, they fell on the thread, and she felt something in her chest give a little kick and settle.

The thread.

More than once she'd watched Foster attach threads to ghosts. It'd looked easy, a nothing kind of job, like paying out string from a reel. And it strengthened ghosts a whole lot better than blood.

With trembling fingers she pinched the base of the thread where it disappeared against the front of her coat. Braced herself and tugged.

The pain was outrageous. But an inch of thread unspooled.

She set her teeth and pulled again, slow and steady. The last time her thread had broken, she'd been forcibly ejected from the ghost-place and dumped unceremoniously back in her body, which had been left out in the elements without food or water until it was within easy arm's reach of death. A sack of cold meat lit with the faintest possible pulse.

If this thread broke now, it'd slingshot her back to the archive room, along that dissolving silver trail. She'd be right back where she started, waiting to drown in the dark. Except now she'd wait alone, because the ghost wasn't bound to the archive room and so had no reason to reappear there with her.

She had one chance—at most—to get this right.

A few more inches ripped free from somewhere deep in her and wormed out between her fingers. Felt like yanking arteries from her beating heart. A shudder escaped her and she clamped down on it, tiptoeing the barest edge of blacking out.

Another few slow pulls and she'd generated enough slack to reach the silver of the ghost's wound and watched, wide-eyed, as it fused.

After that, it was easier to push aside the most part of the pain. She pulled slack and fused it, pulled slack and fused. Wiped her hands, caught her breath, cursed a bunch, pulled slack and fused. Gripped in a dreadful certainty she could feed thread into the wound forever and it would never fill, but after an unguessable time it began to look shallower, then narrower, and at last it drew shut.

But now he was attached to her thread, and she didn't know how to cut him free without cutting hers as well.

For a long moment she pondered this. Then she pulled out more slack, so she was holding her thread in both hands, with the slack length of thread between them angling down toward the ghost in a shape like a T-junction, like the map-drawing of the tunnels on their way to the hatch.

She thought about what ghosts were made of. Pure energy, as far as she could tell. No kind of earthly material she could hold in comparison. A ghost could reassemble its shape based on its memory of itself and the strength of its will. She'd seen it a million times as Archivist. She'd just never *used* it before.

This is me, she thought deliberately, feeling silly but hefting the thread in her left hand anyway. *And this is me,* hefting the thread in her right.

She brought them together and they stuck.

Ragpicker slag me, it worked.

She pinched up a length of each thread-path and squeezed them together, rolling the twist between her fingers for good measure. Kept on doing that until the distinct strands had melded to a waxy thickening. Then, keeping them pinched hard in her off-hand just in case, she cut the ghost free, already flinching as the detached thread began to smolder into silver ash. She double-tied the fused thread off and waited, but nothing happened.

"Stay put," she told the ghost needlessly. "I have to find a way out of here."

But she couldn't even find the strength to stand. When had she last been this tired?

She had to be alert. Vigilant. She'd seen what sorts of things tended to go rummaging through the ghost-place, stirring up trouble. The ghosts of all the upstarts she'd killed were here somewhere. The same went for whatever remained of the ghosts of all Catchkeep's shrine-dogs, bred to keep Archivists in their place, drawn to a living Archivist in a place where one did not belong. Last time, the landscape itself had almost killed her at least once. Hell, the idea of the Catchkeep-priest's ghost alone was enough to keep her on her toes.

For now, though, no other ghosts were here. No ghosts of shrine-dogs. No ghosts of vengeful upstarts. All the better—right now, Isabel wouldn't've bet on herself in a brawl. It was all she could do to stay awake. A few more minutes and she couldn't even do that anymore. She crashed into sleep still kneeling, her bloody fist resting on the ghost's face.

Chapter Twenty

When she woke, she was lying on her side, curled in fetal position around the thread. Sunlight warmed her through the coat.

Then she remembered where she was, and her eyes flew open.

The ghost was still beside her.

Beside her, sitting on some kind of crate he'd found somewhere. Leaned forward, boots apart, elbows on knees, eyes downcast.

Barely even disheveled. Unbelievable. Isabel felt like she'd been dragged twenty miles through the Waste from the back of a cart. She wasn't sure how it was possible for a person to feel so irritated and so jubilant in such an even split, but there it was.

"Hey," she croaked.

The ghost's attention snapped to her. He said nothing, just exhaled very slowly, and something in him seemed to settle.

It came to her that he'd been afraid to try to wake her. In case he hadn't been able to.

"Does *that*," he asked, watching her face as he hooked a thumb sideways at the place where her thread disappeared into nothing, "have anything to do—" prodding the air just above the faded silver tail of remaining thread, hanging down from where his wound used to be— "with *this?*"

Somehow it stood in for all of the other questions she knew he kept in waiting. She knew also that the one question he would never ask straight out—*why don't I remember what happened?*—was the loudest.

"You were unconscious for a while," she told him. "I brought us here because I would have drowned if we'd stayed, and we'd both be

241

stuck in the facility with no way out, and I couldn't—" She paused. "What's the last thing you remember?"

Isabel could practically see the walls go up. Not that she didn't see that coming, or sympathize. Most ghosts didn't even remember enough to realize the extent of what they'd lost.

Three years ago he would've stonewalled her. This time, he spoke.

"There was a skirmish," the ghost said slowly. "The tunnels flooded. I had to force a way through the floor. You—" He went utterly motionless. Isabel found she could pinpoint the moment when the oppressive quality of that unblinking stare changed, ever so slightly, from *what the hell is going on* to *what the hell did you do.*

"Wasp," the ghost said carefully. "Did you—"

The words hung unspoken between them. *Die. Turn ghost. To save me.*

Of course not, she wanted to say. *Don't be stupid.*

But she opened her mouth and, like Ember Girl in "Carrion Boy in the Sinkhole of Gentle Deceits," could not get the lie out. Isabel was no Ember Girl. She lacked a certain spiky empathy, a certain noble, bruising, alien generosity of spirit. Though she was quite good at torching everything she set her hands to, so they had at least one thing in common. She couldn't even bring herself to tell him about the broken half of Foster's sword.

"I don't know," she said. Sort of limply gestured toward the spot in midair, now some distance behind them, where the slack of her thread paid out and out and disappeared. Would it dissolve slowly as her body died, or snap all of a sudden when her heart gave out? "Maybe a little. Anyway, don't get the wrong idea. I was saving both of us."

The next thing she knew, the ghost had stood and set her on her feet. "Which way to the exit? If your body is in the flooded facility, getting back to it will be a time-sensitive operation. It'll be faster if I carry you."

"Okay, first? I have no idea. Second, no. Third, I thought you wanted to know what happened after—"

"Then tell me while we're finding a way out. Or later. Or never. It doesn't matter."

"It *doesn't matter?* I thought you just got wounded in the fight, but I'm starting to think you hit your head or—"

The ghost rounded on her.

"I. Am not. Leaving you. In this place."

She couldn't help it. She busted out laughing. Once she'd started, it was very hard to stop.

The look he gave her was pure murder. "Yes?"

"It's just—that's exactly—" She gestured helplessly at the thread— "*exactly* what I—"

The ghost strode off toward that distant door and it was all she could do to heave her exhausted self after. Distortions of distance and time in the ghost-place, by this point, surprised Isabel about as much as sunrises and sunsets in the world of the living, and she had a bad feeling this walk was going to be a lot longer than it looked.

She walked in silence a while, not even attempting to keep up with the insane pace he set. Whole lot of good it was going to do him, too, if this room was anything like the rest of the ghost-place she'd encountered. You didn't get nearer to a landmark in here unless it wanted you to, or you figured out a way to outsmart it. He of all people should know that.

So she followed at a distance, and she looked for clues.

Close up, the floor was littered with discarded Before-relics, randomly abandoned. Clothes, dolls, backpacks, bags. Bottles of water, cans of food. Even single shoes that their owners hadn't stopped to put back on. And many, many objects that Isabel wouldn't've been able to name with a knife to her throat.

The brick and mortar of the ghost-place, Isabel knew, was memories. Everything in it, no matter how big or small, was something that at least one ghost had been struck hard enough by in life to remember clearly in death. Usually the instrument or circumstance or setting of that death. The ghost-place was basically just one big interconnected web of these memory-pockets. Some were rooms or buildings. Others were whole cities. Or clearings in forests, or snow-fields patterned with the staggering footprints of the lost. All honey-combed together with waypoints. These doors did not all look like doors. And they did not always open onto the same place twice.

This room, so big and rich in detail, strongly suggested that it'd been brought into being by many ghosts together. Something bad had happened here.

They picked and crunched their way across the field of it. What they stepped on broke beneath their heels and reformed again behind. She picked up and drank from a bottle of something that looked like bright pink water. It tasted, surprisingly, like salt.

As she walked, she thought back on her escape from the archive room, replaying it over in her mind until she snagged on the detail of the black boxes in her pockets. Those inscribed names and numbers. There'd been no box in Foster's drawer, and the missing drawer was Chooser knew where, but—

The ghost. His name. It had been lost to him for countless centuries, and it might be *in her pocket right this minute.*

She jammed both hands into her pockets and—nothing.

The boxes were gone. Foster's broken blade was gone.

Of course they were. Only an extremely strong ghost could bring objects between worlds with it. On their search for Foster three years ago she'd managed it, but this time she was so thrashed she was amazed that even her harvesting-knife, even her Archivist-coat, even her *clothes* had come through.

It shouldn't have disappointed her, really. It wasn't like she had any idea what purpose those tiny silver squares could possibly serve. She'd only taken the things out of a sense of—she wasn't sure what to call it. Only that she hadn't wanted to leave them there for the lake to digest. Those silver squares, along with a tunnel full of ghosts beside themselves with confusion and loss, were all that remained of a dozen lives otherwise erased, lost forever to this gods-fucked place.

Isabel sighed. Then called up ahead: "You never asked me what I saw."

The ghost's stride hitched minutely, regained its mechanical smoothness.

"When you fished me out of the riv—"

"I know," he said tightly, "what you meant."

What she wanted to say felt like the kind of thing she had to wind up to. Ease her way in. But the more Isabel thought about it, the more she felt like she was teasing out the loose end of a tangle. She could pull it one way and snarl it further. Another way might untie the whole thing.

"I saw a weird little silver square. Some kind of Before-relic. Something they used in Latchkey." Remembering the white-coated woman's expression when she'd worked the thing free of Salazar's brain, Isabel said: "I think they were important to whoever—" she discarded verbs and settled on "—was in charge of the operatives." Another face swam up from memory, a face and a title. "The Director. I think they were going to use them for someth—" The ghost glanced over a shoulder at her, went ankle-deep in something that looked like a heap of laundry but probably wasn't, kept walking. "You don't care."

"Those people," he said, "are none of my concern. They were not then and they are not now."

Expression kept fragilely blank as an egg. Just beneath the surface ran that ice-cold fury, so exacting, so unlike Foster's. Hers leaked out to maintain equilibrium, but he leaned on the lid of his, a jar with a monster inside.

Walking around the edge of the room now. Isabel inched her way along, one hand always in contact with the wall in case it tried anything funny. She knew this place better than to trust it. The door, somehow, looked just as far away as before.

"When I saw . . . what I saw. Those silver squares, they came *out* of the operatives. I saw it. People in white coats were cutting one out of Salazar's *brain*."

The ghost halted so abruptly Isabel almost smashed into him. He didn't turn. He stood there like she'd just told him he was surrounded by venomous snakes that would bite him the second he moved.

Well, she was in it now. May as well splash around.

"When I saw your memories before. Yours and Foster's. I saw you cut a different kind of silver square out of the back of her hand—here—out of yours too. You said it was so they couldn't follow you. So those things—and these things—they must have some kind of information put in them somehow. The ones in your hands to find you, the ones in your brains to . . . do something else. Right?"

With agonizing care, the ghost turned.

"So," Isabel continued. "All these ghosts are stuck in the tunnels, just like Foster was stuck when we found her. They can't remember anything. Sure, part of that is because they're ghosts, and ghosts forget. But maybe another part of it is because they, you know, *had things taken out of their brains.*"

A sudden mental image came to her: broken old skulls lying in the dust somewhere, corpseroot growing through the eyeholes. Silver slivers rattling around inside.

He said he buried Foster, she thought. And then, linked to the back of that, a thought she immediately wished she hadn't had. *Just like the Director said she'd buried Salazar. But there's a silver square in a black case and a big clear box in a drawer that says otherwise.*

"I wonder," she said, as carefully as she could say such a thing, "if the reason why I didn't find one for Foster is because they never got a chance to take hers out."

Finally the ghost spoke. So quiet she barely made it out. He sounded tireder than she felt, which was saying something. "I don't remember." Then, his tone sharpening off as what she'd said sank in: "Wait. Didn't find one *what* for Foster exactly?"

"Well," she said. "Here's the interesting thing. In the room I just got us out of, I found these drawers. Eleven of them, with names and numbers on them, and a space for a twelfth that was missing. Inside were little black boxes, also with names and numbers. And inside *those* were the same little silver squares."

The ghost blinked. Lifted his gaze, brought the precise point of it to bear on her. There was a certain hesitant, suppressed radiance in his face that it took her a moment to recognize as hope.

The unasked question was written in every strained, silent line of him.

"Ten," she said, so quiet the word barely made it out of her mouth. "Twelve drawers. Ten boxes. No box in Foster's drawer."

"And," he said, with feigned indifference that did not fool her for one second, "these drawers are all labeled with the names of their . . . " He trailed off, visibly sifting through all the possible ways to end that sentence. *Owners,* maybe, or *occupants,* or *prisoners.* "Their . . . contents?"

"I don't know. Most of them, definitely. I read one, saw it had Salazar's name on it, and got all those little black boxes out as fast as I could so I could get a good look at them later. It was dark, and I wasn't trying to stick around in there. I was trying to do the opposite, actually."

"And these black boxes?"

"Back with my body," she admitted. "I tried, but . . . " She patted her empty pockets.

He was a moment in processing this. "You got out of there," he said at last. "And so far you've managed not to drown. Everything else is of secondary concern."

"But," she added quickly, because she had to give him *something*, something that wasn't just more screwups and more pain, "I did find the other half of Foster's sword."

"You did?"

"Yeah."

"In the room with the drawers?"

"Yeah."

The ghost narrowed his eyes at that, like a person reaching after the receding edges of a dream. But it outpaced him, and he sighed and shook his head a little, irritated. "Secondary concern," he said again, quieter this time. Then, louder: "We need to keep moving." He resumed walking toward that distant door.

Isabel walked alongside him, remembering.

"It was the weirdest thing, fitting that broken blade to the harvesting-knife. It was like . . . I mean, holding Before-relics is always weird. It's like looking down into a dark hole in the ground with no bottom. But this is the *harvesting-knife*. I knew what it was since I saw Foster with her sword before, back when we found her stuck in the ghost-place, but it still . . . " She trailed off. "She would've hated what we did with it," she said softly.

"Her sword?"

"Yeah. I mean. This is a thing she tried to get rid of. It was broken in half and buried in three levels of underground tunnels, for Chooser's sake. But then it came back *up*, like—like a bag of shrine-dog puppies you mess up trying to drown. And we just kept giving it to kids and making them spill more blood. The exact thing Foster wanted to stop doing. The exact thing she *died* to stop doing. Her sword kept doing it without her for four hundred years." She drew the harvesting-knife and turned it over in her hands as she walked. Now that the dogleather grip had been removed, the ancient synthetic one underneath was identical to the one on the ghost's sword, blue-black and shiny. "Four hundred years of blood."

There was a pause. Then: "A bag of *what*?"

Isabel kicked an object in mysterious crinkly packaging and watched it sail off, then reappear at its exact point of origin. "Never mind."

But he surprised her.

"You're right," he said after a moment. "She would have. But consider this. If it had remained in that drawer, you wouldn't have found her before. You wouldn't have freed your people from further oppression. You wouldn't have earned the authority to protect them now. And we'd never have—"

"Are you trying to say she'd think it was worth it? Because I highly doubt—"

"I'm *saying* she'd think it's a start." The ghost raised his chin at something off ahead. "It's closer."

Isabel glanced up. The door was maybe twenty yards ahead of them now, visibly nearing with each step. Strange. They'd been walking toward it for minutes without closing any distance, and now this. She eyed it skeptically, unsure what had changed.

Isabel studied it. It wasn't even one door, it was four, two sets of double doors side by side, all set into a wide recessed arch. They all might lead to the same place, or each might lead someplace different. Impossible to say until they stepped through.

Within a moment they stood before the doors. They both knew better than to pick one at random and hope for the best.

"Don't look at me," the ghost said with bland self-deprecation. "I'm not the one who figured this out last time."

"Last time I knew where we were trying to *go*," Isabel said. Then she thought a moment. Last time, when they were searching for Foster, she'd tried saying as much aloud before going through a waypoint. But had it worked at that time, or had it been another dead-ended attempt at navigating the ghost-place? She couldn't remember. There had been a lot of false starts, but she couldn't bring to mind the particulars of each. The learning curve of this place was brutal.

Better safe than sorry, she decided. "Okay," she said. Making sure her voice was clear and firm. Worst case, she'd feel stupid, and she had bigger fish frying just now. Best case, the ghost-place was listening, and would decide for reasons of its own to cooperate. "I have to get word to Sairy or Foster or somebody that the tunnels have flooded. We have to get the people out of there."

"No," the ghost said. "Top priority is getting *you* out of there."

"I will," she told him. "Later."

"There may not *be*," he gritted, each word measured, "a later."

"If that water comes in, there might not be time for both. I can't—"

"Exactly."

She waved this off. "Right, yeah, none of your concern, I get it. But there's fifty of them and one of me, and yours isn't the only concern on the table. Anyway, look." She held up the thread, which by some miracle was still intact. "You Before-people might've killed the world, but you sure knew how to make doors. Plenty of time for you to lose this argument on the way back to Sairy."

She gestured at those four doors in frustration. "They should really put *signs* on these things or something."

Then, because it occurred to her that the ghost had never been around to have this explained to him: "I'm not sure *I* even found the right path last time. Every time we got close to the right waypoint, or where the right waypoint *could be made*, the harvesting-knife started acting weird . . . "

The ghost glanced down at the harvesting-knife in its sheath. Contrary to Isabel's very reasonable expectation, there wasn't so much as a trace of skepticism in his face or voice when he spoke. "So what's it doing now?"

Isabel drew the knife and held it out in front of her, waiting a moment to see what it would do. "Nothing," Isabel said, frustrated. "Nothing at all. It was doing more than this when I wasn't even *looking* for anything, I was just walking around in the tunnels, it makes no sense."

"What was it doing in the tunnels?"

"Not anything as noticeable as in the ghost-place before," she said. "It just kind of—shivers? Sometimes? It's hard to describe. I don't think it really *moves*, exactly, it just . . . " She trailed off, at a loss for words. "Since I came into the tunnels it's been pretty intense. At one point it got really bad." When had that been? Everything was blurring together, and her little journeys in and out of the time-distorting ghost-place weren't exactly helping. It felt like she'd been in the tunnels for at least a week, but it couldn't have been more than a day or two. "Right before the time I fell into the river, I think. And then since then it's been worse than before. I've been trying to ignore it, honestly."

Eyeing the knife closely: "But it's not doing this . . . shivering . . . now?"

Isabel paused to assess. Deliberately, she held the knife out two-handed toward each of the four doors in turn, feeling silly. Nothing. She sheathed it, annoyed.

Shook her head. "Not since the tunnels."

"And before the tunnels, not since we were looking for Foster?"

She hesitated. Then, because it was high time she consigned her embarrassment and awkwardness to the Ragpicker and chose to be openly honest for once, she told him how she used to follow the harvesting-knife around the roads and fields and Waste-edges of Sweetwater, taking its weird behavior as reassurance that he and Foster were out there in the ghost-place somewhere.

"Except you weren't," she said slowly, the implications clicking into place. "You were in the tunnels the whole time . . . "

She fell silent. It was a delicate idea, what was hatching in her mind. Too delicate to handle without crushing it.

Last winter, Jen and Bex had built a little game. A handheld frame like the lid of a box, with a floor made out of sturdy scorchweed-nettle paper. On the floor Bex had drawn a maze, a bird's-eye view of a town, zigzag streets and squares of house-roofs. There was a little silver metal person-shape, stubby-limbed and faceless like an unformed ghost, that sat in one corner of the maze. You'd move it without touching it, scooting it through the maze by way of a piece of different metal held hidden underneath. And if you took the two pieces of metal out of the game and set them on a table an inch or so apart, the under-the-maze piece would draw the person-piece to it, snapping audibly together as the ex-upstarts murmured in astonishment.

Right before she'd fallen into the river, she'd said. That's when the harvesting-knife had acted up worse than it had in years. And who'd approached as she lay dead to the world on the floor? Who'd been there when she'd woken up?

The same person it had led her to before, unerringly, as soon as she'd set her rational mind aside and gave the harvesting-knife the reins.

She thought of the map she'd drawn aboveground, the dots indicating where the knife had been the most insistent. She'd expected them to cluster around the ghost-place entrances she knew, which they hadn't. But if she had a map of where Foster had walked in the tunnels beneath the town, it might well match up to *that*.

"Ragpicker slag me," she whispered. Then, louder: "Wait."

"Are you saying that you—"

"I don't know what I'm saying yet. Give me a second."

The ghost fell silent and watched her draw the harvesting-knife, hold it out in front of her. There was a tingling in her fingers where they touched it. She'd assumed that was from where the ghostgrass had touched the hilt, before she'd removed it and thrown it away. But what if it was something else?

Again she held it pointed out toward each door in turn. Again nothing.

She turned around to aim it back toward the field of Before-stuff scattered across the floor, panning back and forth for good measure. Nothing.

She turned toward that long bank of broken windows, and the sensation ever-so-slightly intensified. Like static electricity, but not. Like the certainty that someone is watching you across a crowded room. Like the prickle of your flight instinct kicking in.

Back toward the doors and the sensation dropped away almost entirely.

"Okay," she said under her breath. "Okay."

It came to her the ghost was staring at her, waiting.

"Everything in the ghost-place is made of memories, right?" she said. "So maybe the knife remembered what it used to be, and it was *trying* to get back to her. Somehow. I don't know. All I know is that, for whatever reason, it led me there. I just . . . " She shrugged. "Paid attention."

"And you're paying attention now."

"I'm paying attention now." She nodded toward that bank of broken windows. "And I'm about halfway sure that this'll take us to Foster."

* * *

Close up, the broken windows were slowly cycling through somebody's memory of disaster. They were whole. They were clouded with the breath of countless tight-packed bodies. They were smudged with the palmprints of countless restless children. They were lit with a sudden burst of blue fire. They were blowing out, inward, crumbs of glass melting before they hit the floor. Then the glass-melt ran up and together and leapt back into the window, a perfect pane, and the loop began again.

One of these windows was a waypoint, Isabel was sure of it. She recognized it at once from the way its loop was staggered out of sync with the others. *Out of place,* she thought. Glass in the frame when the others' was on the floor, and vice versa. Also from how, when the blue light hit it, it silhouetted a form in the center of the pane, the shape of a person reaching.

The question was, was it the *right* waypoint. It could well one-way them into certain death.

Isabel stilled, concentrating on the harvesting-knife. She could swing it toward the window easily, but as soon as she tried to pull it away it put up resistance. And trying to take a step backward from the window felt like walking through water up to her neck. "Okay," she said again, inanely.

The ghost wasn't even looking at the window. He was looking at the harvesting-knife. "Even if she *is* through there, that still leaves the question of how to return you to your body."

"First thing, Foster and Sairy have to know the second hatch isn't viable. Then we find a way to get the people out of the tunnels. Foster's somewhere in town. If this takes us to a waypoint near her, then we know where we are, and we can figure out the rest somehow." Then she saw his face. "What?"

"A waypoint near Foster."

"Yes."

"Foster, who is somewhere in your town."

"Yes. It—*oh.*"

Of course. The ghostgrass barricades.

"Well," she said, "it's either I try this or they all drown."

The ghost looked like he wanted to say something, then didn't. Instead he looked at the windows. Then he looked at her. "Tell me what I have to do."

"We're going to step through this waypoint," Isabel said, leveling the harvesting-knife at the smudgy window like she was issuing it a challenge, "and Foster's going to be there on the other side."

The ghost looked doubtful. She elbowed him.

"*Picture it.* I did that before and I think it might've helped."

"You *think* it—"

"Foster. Through there. Wondering why we're not in the tunnels anymore."

"And why you suddenly look so much like a ghost," he said, acquiescing.

"She'll be busy helping Sairy tend to the wounded after the fight."

"She won't have left any wounded to tend to."

"She wouldn't have wanted it to go down that way," Isabel said slowly, realizing it aloud word by word. "But she would've done what she had to do to help me."

"Yes," the ghost said simply.

Isabel swallowed past the sudden tightness in her throat. Sighted along the blade at armslength and long-vanished glass sprayed past her like water, leaving a jagged-edged mouth of blue light. "She's through there."

"She's through there."

The ghost took a step toward the waypoint and stopped, gazing coolly back at her like he was waiting for something. It came to Isabel that she was holding his sleeve.

Her mouth was about to say something. She just wasn't sure quite what.

"If we come through into someplace bad," she heard herself saying, "get out. However you can. Don't—do what you did back there. In the tunnels. I mean it. I'll be fine." *Better to lose one than risk two,* she thought, and *I'll let the Ragpicker eat me and shit me back out before I let you get stuck down here like Foster.* "Promise me."

"The same goes for you," he said. "If you have to make that choice. Don't hesitate."

She scoffed, but her voice caught like her throat was full of fish-hooks. "Like I would."

"Then there's no problem."

Briefly, silently, they sized each other up.

They walked through and the broken window reformed behind them, piecing and healing like a wound.

Chapter Twenty-One

They stepped through into a muck-scented darkness that Isabel immediately placed as *tunnels*. Her thread was intact, at a glance neither brighter nor duller than before.

The lake was not immediately apparent. That was the good news. The bad news was: neither was Foster.

"Well," she said sullenly, "there goes that theory."

They began to make their way around the room, looking for a door. A map. Something.

The air in this part of the tunnels was comparatively fresh, and what Isabel first took for a waypoint in the ceiling was actually moonlight, bleeding in from above through a wide fissure in the ceiling. No greenery trailed down through it, though, so whatever had made that crack was recent.

Standing underneath it, vague noise reached her from beyond. Lots of voices. Weirdly close. Was this sector of the tunnels even still below Sweetwater? Did they reach to other towns, stretching out under the Waste like the roots of some impossible tree? They were definitely in the topmost sublevel, what with the moonlight pouring through the ceiling, though Isabel didn't recognize this room at all.

Then, all at once, she did.

It looked different here than it had in the ghost's memories of it. Different than its rendering in the ghost-place. A long dark room, its running lights long since broken, no longer with its double row of child-sized beds lined up, feet pointed inward. Though the platform where the beds had been remained. It stood in deep shadow on the far side of the room.

"Hey," she called to the ghost, who was making his way briskly over to the platform and the darkness beyond. Thought about telling him where they were, then thought better of it. "This leads outside. Can you get up there and see where we . . . "

She turned just in time to see him stop so fast he rebounded a little, like he'd collided with an invisible wall. A kind of voiceless, strangled little noise came out of him.

Isabel drew the knife and headed over. Then she saw what he was looking at.

On the platform a chair lay toppled over sideways. Like the chairs in the reception room, whatever synthetic it was made of was shockingly resilient. Two neat holes were punched in its back, one high, one low.

The ghost-place version of this room—that platform, that chair—was where they'd found Foster's ghost, locked in the pitiless loop of her own final memory. Those holes were from bullets that had gone through Foster first.

That's why they didn't shoot her in the head, Isabel realized for the first time. *They didn't want to destroy that silver square in her brain.*

Isabel was beginning to get the distinct impression that the knife was messing with her. Foster wasn't through that waypoint. Foster hadn't been here in some time. But it'd brought her directly to the exact place where she'd found Foster *before.*

The ghost stood beside her, fists clenched, deliberately taking measured, ragged, even breaths. Clutching after the rapidly fraying extremity of his calm.

"So," he managed. "Looks like we just missed her."

Isabel was staring at that chair, seized by a bizarre imagining. What happened to the relic of a ghost's broken loop? Any minute the chair might stand itself upright, bullets zipping through it backwards, holes sealing up behind. Foster might reappear in it, her uniform exchanged for a jumpsuit. Clamped into that chair at intervals: chest, waist, upper arms, wrists, thighs, ankles. Then she'd tear free of her restraints. Say something to the ghost. Hand him a sheet of paper, her dying wish. And the shooting would begin.

But it didn't. The chair was a piece of garbage resting on a high place in the floor. The ancient stain on the platform was almost faint enough to ignore.

What the hell was it even still doing here? Why had nobody removed it after Foster died? It put Isabel in mind of the condition of the rest of the tunnels. Not the great age of the place, or the encroachment of the lake, but the older damage, which she'd seen earlier, unable to explain. Heavy doors ripped off their hinges and flung into walls. Fire damage blackening long stretches of hallway. The missing drawer and mangled shelves in the archive. Now this.

It's like this whole damn place went down with Foster, she thought, and shivered.

"Come on," she said. "Let's keep—"

The ghost saw it at the same time she did. Flickering in the darkness beyond the platform.

They stood behind their weapons, waiting to see what it would do. It flickered again and faded. Flickered and reached. Isabel squinted but couldn't get a lock on it.

Whatever it was, it was bright. Not humanoid. There was a violent stop-start stuttering quality to its movement, as though it was only tenuously tethered to the world Isabel could see. It was along the wall, it was emerging from the shadow, it was already on the platform, trailing threads. Lots of threads, sunbursting out behind it, floating on the empty air like the long hair of someone drowned. Shimmering silver filaments, scouring Isabel's eyes with light.

Closer, *not humanoid* was not exactly accurate. Humanoid once. Long ago. Still somewhat recognizable as such, now that it'd settled into place. Isabel's mental box of field notes left her at a loss to classify it. It didn't have the strength to retain its shape—*no, it isn't that*—it looked to have been broken apart and *reconstructed.* Reconstructed, but slightly wrong, as if its person-shape had fallen to the floor and shattered, then been glued back together by feel. Pieces askew, pieces missing, pieces cobbled together. Most of a blue skirt, part of a white coat, a single shoe making crisp sounds like soft gunshots as the thing shifted its weight back and forth on the platform, left heel to right ankle-stump.

Not glued, Isabel realized, staring at it. *Stitched. All those threads . . .*

"Did Foster—?" she whispered, gesturing. Already knowing the answer. She'd *cut* Foster's threads. And yet here these were.

"We've never been down here," the ghost replied. Then he seemed to realize what he was saying. "Well," he added, with a bitter irony. "Not for a while."

Which made Isabel realize something. She knew that blue skirt. Knew that white coat. Knew the sound of that one remaining shoe. Even recognized some of the items in the armload of debris the broken ghost was clutching to itself. She might not have known their names, but she'd seen them. In the memories of the Latchkey dead.

Long ago, searching for Foster, Isabel had thought to look for the ghosts of the people in charge of the Latchkey Project. Glean clues from them. *Those ones I found,* the ghost had told her. *We won't be finding them again.* Because he had destroyed them. Eventually. Once he'd realized they'd be no help to him in his search for Foster.

Well, they'd found one. Or what was left of one.

The Director.

The ghost of the Director was carrying more stuff than she could hold. Objects slipped from her arms, one by one, and each time she picked something up another thing would drop. This task seemed to engage the whole of her attention.

The ghost was watching the Director with a kind of fascinated contempt. "What's it doing?"

"That's the moment she got stuck on," Isabel whispered. "She's looping."

"Like Ayres?"

"Like Ayres. Like Salazar. Like Foster." Glanced over. "What are *you* doing?"

What the ghost was doing was raising his sword. Surveying the platform and the swaying, bending, scooping, fumbling thing on it with a sort of nonplussed derision. It wasn't clear whether he recognized the Director's ghost. Either way, Isabel knew the first move the Director made toward them, he'd go up there and finish what he'd started. The sheer number of pieces he must've cut the Director's ghost into in the first place was both mind-boggling and faintly nauseating. He must have pinned her down and diced her, meticulously, into squirming confetti, while she—

"Wait," Isabel breathed. "The threads."

Tension radiated off of the ghost like the visible heat over a fire. "I know."

"If Foster didn't put them there—"

"I know."

A folder of papers tumbled from the Director's arms and fanned across the platform. The Director dropped to one knee, unsteady on the ankle-stump, and began to gather them one-handed. Moaning under her breath in soft frustration: *no no no goddamnit no—*

Oblivious to her audience, the Director got the papers squared back into their folder, flipped it under an arm, rose smoothly—and a glossy-paneled device fell and cracked.

It looked an awful lot like the kind of device Isabel had found on the high shelf in the archive room. It lay there, broken. When the Director picked it back up, it was whole.

Isabel didn't notice what fell next. All her awareness was locked on that device, because as the Director retrieved it from the floor the light had fallen on and cleanly illuminated an opening near its bottom edge. A shallow square imprint about the size of her thumbnail.

The right size to fit a little silver square.

The Director dropped the device, half-knelt to pick it up—*goddamnit no*—and as she did, Isabel could see over the white slope of her shoulders. Could see those countless threads trailing away into the darkness behind. Could just make out what was back there along the wall, maybe thirty feet away, lit only by its own faint glow. A shapeless silver roiling.

Isabel had wondered earlier why she'd only seen Latchkey ghosts in the tunnels. No sign of any that'd just happened to wander through the ghost-place waypoints. She was formulating a pretty good guess as to where they'd gone. Who'd brought them here to assemble and power the Director with was another question entirely.

"I've seen enough," said the ghost. Readying sword and stance for a clean kill. "I'm taking the one in the front. We'll deal with the ones behind it after."

"Wait," she shouted. All her attention locked onto that device. "I have to try to—"

Suddenly she felt the quality of the ghost's stillness change.

"Wasp," he said, with perfect clenched evenness, easily translated as *trouble*. "I thought you said you trapped . . . "

He nodded at something emerging from the dark beyond. Something whose name he trailed off before saying. Something Isabel was supposed to have trapped.

Only one thing that could mean.

She followed his line of sight—and there was Salazar. Drifting up out of the darkness behind the platform. Attached to the Director by a brand-new, gleaming silver thread.

She must've picked that up from watching Foster, Isabel thought, stunned. *There's enough of her mind left in there that she can still learn.*

"Well," Isabel said shakily. "I guess she got out."

She pictured Salazar, cut off from Foster, escaping the cave-in and crawling blind down the tunnels until she'd found enough material to create another energy source to link up to, and burned it like fuel.

But why would Salazar go to the trouble of putting the Director back together?

As soon as she wondered it, she realized she already knew. Salazar had been the Director's favorite, or one of them. Isabel had seen as much reading Foster's memories before. And it had been the removal of Salazar's silver square that had convinced the other operatives that things weren't quite what they seemed. Salazar *herself* wasn't around to benefit from the knowledge. As far as she was concerned, the Director was probably more like a teacher. A parent. Someone who had the child operatives' best interests at heart.

That still didn't settle the more pressing question, though. Salazar had been direly weakened. The Director was a wreck. The amorphous roil of lesser ghosts behind her wouldn't have given her enough power to create those threads from. Isabel was missing a piece of this puzzle, and she wasn't yet sure what it was.

Then Isabel saw—really saw—what she was looking at.

Two other Latchkey ghosts, about half-formed, were detaching from the silver turmoil. Isabel recognized the black-haired girl from Ayres's memory, but not the other. A few shapeless silver ghosts detached with them, deflating even as they fumbled their way forward after Salazar.

Two Latchkey ghosts, Isabel thought, looking at the Director and her bundle of threads. *Yeah, that'd do it.*

Isabel squinted. For the state they'd left her in, Salazar looked pretty good now. The other ghosts, meanwhile, looked like hell. Worsening by the second. At the edge of the platform there was now a silver puddle ten feet wide, and even the two other Latchkey ghosts were beginning to weaken visibly.

And Salazar's thread was brighter than the moon through the crack in the ceiling.

"Shit. She's sucking ghost-energy out of *all* of them. Look at her thread."

"I'm looking at it."

A humming sound as Salazar's thread drew more power down it, silvering and crumpling the other ghosts even as her own ghost-energy roared up around her, lashing at the high shadows of that room, bright enough to see by.

Light lingered on Salazar's blade and the glistening pits of her eyes. "Why isn't it killing you?" she was saying, again and again, under her breath, in a voice like a wet sponge stuck in her throat. Silver blood dribbling down her chin as she spoke. "Why isn't it killing you?"

"Disengage," the ghost said, not taking his eyes off of Salazar. "Get out. I'll cover you."

Isabel took a step backward and Salazar was there, intercepting her, already so close Isabel could see her own startled face reflected in Salazar's blade.

Clumsily, she launched herself out of range, shielding her thread with her body, knowing full well she was about a million times too slow. *I'm going to die,* she thought experimentally. *I'm going to die today.* It felt like poking an arm that had fallen asleep. She knew it was there, knew she should feel it. Couldn't. Something had hold of her, some dark little hook in her heart that was yanking her forward through a veneer of perfect calm—

—and Salazar was skidding backwards across the floor on the ass of her uniform and the ghost was stalking toward her, swordpoint intended for the soft of her throat.

Salazar sprang lightly to her feet, unfazed, and tried again to get at Isabel. Again the ghost got in the way. Backhanded

Salazar across the side of the head with a gloved fist that would've dropped a bear. Followed the punch with the sword. At the last possible second Salazar feinted out of the way, close enough to crop one of her ears into a silver mess. Popped up already lunging forward, slicing at the ghost, her blade an unseen whistle on the air.

The ghost was faster. Swatted Salazar's strike away, and the one after that. The next one bit deep into his arm, which ran silver like a ditch runs meltwater. This exchange took, all told, less than a second. They paused and stared each other down at a distance of ten paces. Salazar, to all appearances, was unharmed.

The ghost glanced with that unbreakable false serenity at his rapidly silvering sleeve. Something in his face shifted, was crushed back into place. For the briefest instant he settled to an eerie perfect stillness, as if gathering something to himself. Then, all at once, he rushed Salazar, even faster than before. Hopelessly, breathtakingly, *invisibly* fast. They clashed and broke, and Isabel could literally no longer tell them apart, only hope that the blocks she heard were the ghost's, and the silver she could see spattering the floor was Salazar's . . .

It came to her that she'd taken a step forward, was frozen in the act of reaching out. Mouth hanging open idiotically around all the words that knotted, scrabbling for purchase, in her throat.

Chooser turn a blind eye, she thought, clenching her whole mind like a broken fist around that halfassed prayer. *Chooser look anywhere but here.*

She'd failed to stand against Salazar before. Her inability, her sheer outclassedness, had nearly gotten Sairy killed. And now—

Get to the platform, Isabel ordered herself. *Cut her threads. Shut her down.*

She tore her gaze away and hurtled toward the platform, knife already drawn.

There were more threads than ghosts, as if other ghosts had once been attached and drained, or cut away. The remaining threads were bundled into an accidental cable, densely packed enough that ghost-energy hemorrhaged from the loose ends and visibly dissipated across the floor. It hit the knifeblade like ghost-blood, but diluted, assaulting Isabel with a sputtering pinhole leak of memories. Disembodied whispers frail as spiderweb that bypassed her ear to be caught somewhere in her brain.

—*told you he wouldn't*
—*one than risk two*
—*catch me!*
—*gonna get worse before it gets*
—*makes you think I*
—*green one or the*
—*so smart now, huh?*
—*away. All of you. I said*
—*over now. Come on. Let's get you*
—*keep doing this*
—*or dare?*

Some threads parted for her blade with no resistance, but others had grown in wiry and tough, had twisted up with their neighbors into a brambly thicket of silvery light.

She sawed and cursed and heaved a massive sigh of relief as she finally broke through.

"I cut her off," she shouted at the ghost in triumph. "I cut her off, she's done."

As expected, the tailings of the Director's borrowed ghost-energy slipped off down the last few slashed threads, through the Director and into Salazar. Who drank it down like water, then seemed to realize she was down to her last drops of stolen energy and decided to switch up her tactics.

Without a discernible pause, Salazar ripped a new thread free of her own chest and attached it to the ghost.

Isabel couldn't pinpoint that thread. They'd blurred back into the fight too quickly. But she knew it was there from the green-white brilliance of its whip-arc, the tracers it left on the air, the single high pure note that was torn from the speed of its passage. A note that rang her bones like a tuning fork but only registered as the faintest itch in her ear.

"Cut the thread, you idiot," she screamed at the ghost. "Cut it before she—"

Too late.

Dark lightning forked up and out of Salazar, searing Isabel's eyes. She winced violently, wrenching away as if from a great wash of heat.

Recovering, she squinted, furiously blinking streaming eyes. A power surge, stronger than anything she'd seen from Salazar before, stronger even than the one that'd blasted along Foster's thread to Isabel and blown a hole in the tunnels. She could *hear* it, a sound like thunder overhead, like tons of ice cracking all at once under spring thaw.

You underestimated her. He underestimated her. And now—

Half-blind, panicked at imagining what her eyes couldn't see, Isabel started shrieking at Salazar like she could call her out, fight her, trap her, put her down. Something. Anything. Like Isabel could yell herself a line in the sand, a place where she could plant herself in the path of what was coming.

But Salazar paid about as much attention to Isabel as Isabel might to a mildly irritating bug.

Right now she had bigger problems.

That light—the piercing, suffocating, monstrous, crystalline, full-on coldfire onslaught of it—wasn't coming from Salazar at all.

It was coming from the ghost.

*H*e reversed it. Isabel gaped at the ghost, astonished. *He reversed the flow. He's drawing power off of Salazar.*

Light like black fire kicked up behind the ghost, rushed in a ring around his boots. No blue, no violet, but shot through with the same glacial green-white as his thread, silver's uppermost register. If it were a sound, it would have shattered glass. So bright it silhouetted him in the heart of it: a paper cutout that held its sword lightly aside, raised its off-hand with an exploratory languor, set it just below Salazar's throat, gave the gentlest of pushes, and watched with bland interest as Salazar sailed back a dozen yards easy, cratering a wall.

A crack appeared in that wall. Started zigzagging up it. Hit the busted ceiling. A new smattering of debris rained through that wide crack, peppering the floor. Something in the ceiling groaned.

"Stop! She's done, okay? Just *cut that thread* before you bring the ceiling down on—*what the hell are you—*"

The ghost had reached Salazar's point of impact and slung her down easily. He stood over her now, boot to chest, and was making delicate, precise, comprehensive slashes with his sword as Salazar thrashed and fought ineffectually.

Isabel had seen him dispatch a ghost before, cutting it into pieces like he was butchering an animal for meat. Effectively trapping it in place for eternity. She hadn't known then what his aim had been. Whether he'd done it out of cruelty or mercy. She didn't *know* now either, but she sure knew where her guess was going. Pieces of Salazar peeled off and scattered like petals, silvering as they fell.

Foster's not going to like that. This thought reached Isabel at low volume from a vast distance. Thinking was suddenly very, very hard. Her thoughts felt heavy, limp and deadweight, and she had so far to carry them.

A change in the Director's movements drew her attention back.

She'd dropped the folder again, was kneeling to retrieve it. Except now she was . . . unraveling? Isabel didn't have another word for it. Like she was coming untethered to herself, crumbling to pieces at her own feet. Well, her one foot. That too was fading fast.

"Wait," Isabel said. Not daring to look away. Like she could hold the Director together with her eyes. All her attention locked on to the pocket from which that device would appear.

The Director dropped a pencil. Cursed, scrabbled, retrieved.

After that went a clipboard. Then a folder. Papers flew from it and the Director knelt—*no no no goddamnit no*, scatter gather square stand. Then the device. It fell, broke, mended.

The Director lifted the device through the light and that shallow square opening became glaringly visible.

Gently, Isabel tried to lift it out of the Director's grasp. Holding her breath as the device dissolved into black sparks for a second, jumping the gap between the Director's hands and hers. There it reassembled, flickering, blurry, weightless. Already, removed from the Director's hands, it was beginning to fade. If she squeezed it, her hand would pass through.

Upon hasty inspection, she was surer than ever. That opening was the exact shape and size of one of those little silver squares. Tilting it into the light she could make out tiny perforations lining the opening's inner edge that would fit the little nubs of the square's stubby spider-legs.

Heart pounding, she held it up. "What is this?"

But it dissolved into silver mist and was gone, leaving Isabel staring at her empty hand. "No," she whispered, "no no no—"

The device subtracted from her junk collection, the Director wasn't holding one too many things anymore. Slowly she straightened. Gained her balance on the remains of the ankle-stump. Like Ayres, her loop had broken.

She stared, eyes lit with forlorn and terrible hope. "Catherine?" Her gaze raked the darkness, alighted on the middle distance, slid off like rain down a window. Touched on Isabel and locked on. "Is that you?"

No, Isabel had to stop herself from shouting in frustration. *I'm not. Why do you all keep thinking that?*

Then she realized she had a better idea.

In a voice like edging out onto a frozen pond that might or might not hold your weight, she said: "I caused you a lot of trouble."

The Director gave her the tiniest, weariest smile imaginable. Her face was flaking off, blowing away in a nonexistent wind. "That you did." She looked like she wanted to say more, so Isabel waited. One cheek and down that side of the neck was totally eroded now. The Director looked like a victim of her own treatments gone wrong. She looked like Salazar. "I wasn't at all fair to any of you children. I should have . . . " and her voice crackled into slurry, cutting out and in as Ayres's had done. " . . . stick their *funding.*" Her rueful headshake said *too late, too late.* "One can be proud of the work one is doing," she said, lapsing into sudden clarity, "and less so of one's methods."

Ragpicker's gambit, Isabel told herself, and rushed to say, "I found the silver squares you took out of our brains."

The Director's face darkened. "Good. Burn them. I *never* approved . . . phase of the project. It was directly . . . my vision of . . . insult to those children . . . through so much. I wouldn't . . . light of day again."

Isabel swallowed. "What are they?"

"A glorified salvage operation," the Director spat. "Desecration . . . dead." Then something angrily unintelligible. Then, calming somewhat: "A failsafe."

Failsafe, Isabel mouthed, committing the unfamiliar word to memory.

" . . . much of the project was handled so badly. Too rushed, too uninformed, too . . . desperate unfortunate decisions . . . my watch. After . . . point, all I could do . . . archive the results. Those data chips . . . that archive."

Data chips, Isabel thought. Recording the syllables in her mind the way Foster had recorded *Salazar.*

This broke off into a blur of white noise that lasted a couple seconds. " . . . losing subjects. So many . . . fast. Side effects . . . treatment. What better . . . learn from our mistakes than . . . the inside? The first stage . . . hallucinations . . . night terrors . . . early warning system . . . cascading organ failure. The results were catastrophic. We partnered up . . . remaining operatives. Encouraged them to report . . . unusual behavior . . . witnessed. We needed more. We . . . see what they were seeing, when . . . seeing it."

Another sizzle before the Director's voice cut back in. "Vision isn't . . . eyes. It's in the brain. The eyes . . . information relay . . . more. To find where . . . system broke down . . . deeper in. Hopefully . . . avoid . . . same mistakes next time."

Next time.

Something returned to Isabel in that moment. Something the ghost had said, long ago.

They kept us on, but Latchkey was disbanded. Its methods were too expensive, its success rate too low. Its funding was cut, and no new subjects were recruited for treatment. Latchkey was dead in the ground. Foster put her life on the line to keep it there.

She thought of that room full of children. She thought *four percent survival rate.* She thought of Salazar, her skin and nails and eyeballs sloughing away like her own body was rejecting them.

What Isabel wanted to ask the Director was: *What the slag hell do you mean* next time.

What she said was: "Director?"

The Director's face was nearly gone, along with much of her body. No eyes, no nose, just mouth and chin, bridged to the patchy back half of her skull by a narrow spit of silver. "Yes, Catherine, what is it?"

Isabel had time for one question, maybe, before it was too late.

"What happened to my . . . chip?"

Even with two-thirds of her face gone, the Director managed to convey surprise. "How on earth . . . I know?" she said. There was an unmistakable bitterness in her voice, which Isabel couldn't begin to make sense of. Not until the Director nodded the remains of her head in the direction of the ghost and said, "Ask him."

Chapter Twenty-Two

Isabel stared, speechless, unable or unwilling to process what she was hearing. Finally she found her words. *"What?"*

But the last of the Director's head had already flaked away. What remained of her body, tenuously held, now collapsed like a house of cards to scatterings of silver.

Isabel turned toward the ghost in a kind of betrayed outrage. He looked to have finished up with Salazar and was now methodically, dispassionately pacing through that pile of silver scraps, kicking it apart the way children will kick apart a pile of autumn leaves. Dirt rained down around him from the crack in the ceiling. He didn't seem to notice.

Isabel wanted to kick him in the shins.

Is it true? Did you take Foster's chip? Do you know where it is? What the hell did you do?

But she never got the chance.

A horrible sound came from above, from the place on the ceiling where the new damage met the existing crack. A sound like some vast thing under vaster stress. Something creaked and buckled, then gave. Above, beyond the crack, somebody screamed.

Then there was nothing, only darkness and dust.

Isabel, racked and helpless with coughs, could do nothing but wait for it to clear. Her eyes and nose were running what she hoped was only tears. It felt like she'd swallowed a bucket of burning ash.

She'd fallen. No. The ghost had pushed her out of the way? It was like he'd vanished from his post across the room and reappeared in front of her, standing between her and whatever had dropped down from the sky. Her ears were ringing. If he was talking, she couldn't make it out. She rubbed at her eyes, blinking furiously, until she could force her eyelids open against the irritation. Pain or no pain, she had to see what had happened.

A nearly-full moon hung directly above her, huge and vibrant, and her eyes took a moment to adjust to the sudden brightness. When they had, there was stuff at her feet that hadn't been there before. Greenery that didn't grow underground. Clots of roots and grass. Summer flowers: three-eyes, rainstealers, suns-and-moons. Ghostgrass. She felt it before she saw it. Even from paces away, it felt like her memory of the Catchkeep-priest's whip across sunburned shoulders, except over every inch of her body, and deeper than the skin.

Was that what was making her so dizzy, so disoriented? Or was she going into shock? Still so much *screaming*. Or maybe the echo of it had gotten trapped in her ears, was looping there, the way a ghost's last—

She grabbed blind for the thread.

It swam in her vision and gradually focused. Like she'd plucked it and the vibration was stilling as she watched. Dull, gray, thin—but there. Still there.

"Wasp." The ghost was shaking her as gently as he knew how, which was not very. "Hey. Stay with me."

"I'm good," she lied. Even her voice sounded off, like there was a delay between her mouth moving and the sound of it reaching her ears. It sounded like her head was full of whining mosquitoes. Maybe forty feet away in deep shadow was the massed shape of a huge pile of rubble. She squinted toward it. "What *is* that?"

"I don't know," the ghost said impatiently. "Look, we have to—"

"Enough, okay?" She shook him off and stumbled toward the pile. It was like the fallen building at the corner of the garden, miniaturized. But still taller than most Sweetwater houses, a hill it would take her some effort to scale.

But it was a route to the surface. "I can climb that."

"That thread isn't going to hold much longer."

"I *know*."

"You didn't do this," he said quietly.

"No," she said, rounding on him. "You did." It wasn't wholly fair and she knew it. The ceiling had been partway broken when they'd gotten here, and he might not have had such a hard time with Salazar if they'd just taken out the Director immediately as he'd suggested.

Still, though. "Come or don't. I'm going."

She powered forward a few more steps—and stopped.

That ghostgrass on the floor wasn't fresh. It was dried, bundled, tied off with string. Older, smaller bundles than what they'd brought down into the tunnels. More like what the people of Sweetwater would hang in the topmost corners of a door.

Gripped in a chill that wasn't cold, Isabel looked—really looked—at the ground at her feet. Stones had been flung free of impact, scattering wide of the main pile. Regular, evenly-shaped stones, perfect for building with. And dark. Very dark. Almost black.

There were only two places where she'd seen rock that color. Execution Hill. And the building that had been pieced together out of rock chiseled, painstakingly, centuries past, *from* Execution Hill. Because that high lightning-blasted peak was sacred to Catchkeep, and its rock could only be put to use in Her name.

Chiefly to build Her shrine.

A few yellower, rounder stones had also fallen. Isabel toed one over and its eyeholes gazed up at nothing. A green stone rolled out from between its jaws.

Oh, she thought. *Oh no.*

She twisted past the ghost and scrambled toward that pile of rock. The hole in the ceiling was much bigger than before, the moonlight streaming through blinding after so long in the dark. By the looks of it, the entire shrine had fallen in.

Surreal to see people standing above her, squinting into the gloom. They stood there, silvered in the moonlight, and for one brief addled second Isabel thought they might be ghosts, the fresh dead of the day's battle, drifting above the burned-out buildings, waving goodbye to the world. Passing time until they heard Catchkeep's Hunt thundering across the sky, come to claim and carry them to that far green shore.

They were yelling something down at her. She couldn't hear it. Her ears still weren't quite right. It sounded urgent. Two people weren't bothering with yelling. They'd gotten a rope tied onto something and were sliding hurriedly down it, alighting on the rubble-heap. Lissa and Jen. She looked up at them quizzically. She felt so out of it, so detached. *I'm going into shock*, she told herself. *Can a sort-of-ghost do that?*

Several people were frantically pointing at something off to one side, trying to get Isabel's attention.

She turned. The ghost was already there. "Wasp," he said quietly.

Then she saw the bodies.

The fight had been over for a while now, and a lot of them had been corpses before dropping thirty feet to the floor with the Catchkeep-shrine on top of them. Isabel saw people from Sweetwater—the baker's wife, then the brew-mistress's nephew, then one of the men who boiled and strained the lakewater for drinking—and some that must have been from Clayspring, because Isabel didn't recognize them. Most of the previously dead were Clayspring people, which made sense. Invading Sweetwater, they'd only killed the townspeople they must. They had uses for most of them.

But some of these bodies hadn't died in the fight. Some had bandages over wounds they'd gotten earlier. Some were freshly dead. Some were moving brokenly in the rubble.

One of them was Sairy.

She must have been near the ruins of the building when it fell in, because some of it was on top of her. One arm was badly gashed, and her cheek had been ripped open. Everything from her midsection down was either concealed beneath the rubble or missing. A blackred stain soaked upward from where the black rock blanketed her, darkening the blue of her shirt.

She dyed that cloth, Isabel remembered, inanely. *Some of them got rid of the upstart outfits, burned or bartered them, but she dyed hers blue and made it hers. But she screwed up and it bled dye every time it got rained on . . .*

Isabel didn't later recall clearing the distance, only arriving, the stonework jabbing at her as she dropped to her knees. "Sairy," she said. "Sairy, hey."

Sairy opened her eyes. The moon was in them. Twisted away—and couldn't. Something was holding her in place. "Foster?"

"It's me, Sairy, I'm right here."

"But you . . . " Sairy's gaze traveled from Isabel's thread to the silvery wash that edged her. "You're a ghost?" Coughed. Winced. "Thought I told you not to . . . not to fucking die."

"Look who's talking. I'm not the one lying here with the shrine in my lap."

Isabel listened to herself, horrified. Those four days while Aneko's body rotted around her, they'd all sounded like that. Waiting for her ghost to pop free, like a sprout from the mush of a windfall. Empty words like a too-short rope paid out to a drowner. You threw it anyway because it was all you had.

When she spoke again her tone had changed. "We have to get her out of there."

"If we move her," the ghost said quietly, "it'll be over very, very quickly."

"So, what, we let her suffer? We just sit here and do *nothing* and *wait for her to die?*"

"Wasp—"

"Where the hell is Foster, she was supposed to protect—"

"She went back into the tunnels," Sairy said. "To let everybody out." She blinked up at Isabel. "You didn't see her?"

"Long story."

"I might need the . . . " Sairy coughed. Something popped audibly in her chest and she spat blood. "The short version."

The smell of Sairy's blood shouldered its way relentlessly toward the forefront of Isabel's notice. No—it wasn't the smell exactly. But something. She could *sense* it. It *called* to her. She wanted to spit and spit until her mouth stopped watering.

Jen appeared beside Isabel, hugging herself. Like she was the one whose guts needed to be held in from spilling. "Look, maybe I can get something from the midwife."

"No," Sairy managed. "Be a waste. Others need . . . more."

"Slag it," Jen said. "I'm going."

Lissa rushed over, going *no no no* like she'd forgotten other words. Reached Sairy's side and her legs went out from under her. "But we won," she was saying, all shocked disbelief. "We *won*."

She set to clearing away some of the rubble from Sairy's hips and belly. It looked worse underneath.

"Find the survivors," Isabel shouted over her shoulder at the ghost.

"On it," he replied, and he was. Though he didn't seem to be finding many.

"We need to move her," Lissa said. Shouting toward the ghost: "Hey—"

Isabel looked down and Sairy was holding her wrist. Her eyelids labored open. "No," she mouthed. Tried again. Coughed. Winced. "No." Whispering now. "Help the others."

"Screw the others," Lissa said. "We're getting you out of here. We won, it was supposed to be over, why was there a second earthquake *now*, this isn't fair—"

Second earthquake, Isabel thought. *Oh, Ragpicker slag me.*

"Isabel," Sairy whispered.

Hurriedly, Isabel leaned in.

"Listen. Don't let my . . . my ghost turn bad. Like the one . . . like . . . in the tunnels. Thing was . . . seriously an asshole."

Small chance of that, Isabel thought, but didn't want to think about why. Far more likely, Sairy would go the way most ghosts went. No threat. No strength. No memory. Just a silver cutout, almost indistinguishable. The kind of specimen that, as Archivist, she'd be able to fit in a jar.

"I won't," Isabel said. "I promise."

"And hey. Foster did . . . protect me. Not her . . . her fault. Just. Wrong . . . place." Sairy coughed, spraying the Archivist-coat with blackish red. "Wrong time."

Chooser, a body had a lot of blood in it. Isabel suppressed a shudder. For one horrible second she'd thought she was about to lick her sleeve. Then Sairy seemed to rally. "Tell you a secret."

Isabel nodded. "I'm listening."

"When I stayed too long in the tunnels and . . . and Jen shut me in with you. I lied. I wasn't . . . wasn't settling people in. I went down to the barricade. I wanted . . . I wanted to see if . . . it's stupid, but . . . "

"You wanted to see if Aneko was there," Isabel said, hushed.

How could Isabel tell her that no, she wouldn't find Aneko in the ghost-place, no matter how hard she looked? How could she admit the reason? She wished she could open her stupid mouth and say *I think Aneko's ghost destroyed itself to help me, I'd probably be dead now if it wasn't for her.*

"Remember her," she rushed to say instead, because Sairy's eyes were glazing over now, full of moonlight. "Remember all of us. Remember everything. And when that place pulls on your mind you pull back harder. It's the only—"

Sairy was furrowing her brow toward the hole in the ceiling, at something Isabel couldn't see. "Catchkeep?" she said.

Isabel glanced up too. This time of year She was too low, resting behind the hills, regaining Her strength for the winter, when cold and illness and famine would give Her twice as many ghosts to carry.

No, slag her luck, that up there watching Sairy die was Carrion Boy. Blade in hand, reaching out to Ember Girl in betrayal even as He turned His face away.

Isabel wanted to say something comforting, but she couldn't think of the words. She was unequipped for what happened on this side of death.

And then it was too late.

I sabel reached down and shut Sairy's eyes, tracing a star over each lid. *She's strong,* she told herself. *She'll remember. She'll find her way.* The idea lifted something from her, something she didn't reckon she deserved to be lightened of.

"We need to help the others," she said. "She'd want us to help the others." Stepped down too quickly, rolled her ankle, was steadied by the ghost. "She's strong," she told him, though he'd said nothing. "She'll remember. She'll find her way."

Then, knowing it would go nowhere, knowing it was used up, knowing she'd pitched it away in the archive room, Isabel's mouth said anyway, as if of its own accord: "That healing device—"

"It only expedites the curative process. You know that. It can't bring back the dead." Such a light cool tone from someone who Isabel knew had attempted precisely that, and failed.

Around them, one by one, each ex-upstart set a hand to her Catchkeep-scars and raised it in salute to Sairy, then trudged off to help carry the injured.

"Find Foster," she told the ghost. "Tell her—"

But he was already gone.

Isabel picked her way across the rubble toward Lissa, who was struggling to calm a screaming girl with a visibly broken leg. Midway there, she stopped. The blood-smell, or blood-whatever, was stronger here. It made her intensely uncomfortable on a personal level, but was bad in a whole lot of much bigger ways too. All it would take was one of the other Latchkey ghosts making its way down here, drawn by the blood. Tanaka, maybe, or Martinez. And all hell would break loose.

She took Jen by the shoulder. Jen flinched at her touch. *Frostbite and vertigo,* Isabel thought, and drew her hand away, strangely embarrassed. "There's a lot of blood here." She tilted her head toward the silvery rags that used to be Salazar, the Director, the ghosts off which they'd fed. Weak now, but she wasn't taking any chances. "Get as much ghostgrass as you can and block them in. Then look for entrances and block those too. I want this fucking room locked down. Remember ghosts can shrink. I want it *airtight.*"

Jen nodded. Then she kept nodding. She looked like she was trying to put a puzzle together in her mind. Her eyebrows shot up as it clicked. "You're a *ghost?*"

"Yeah," Isabel said, because it was easier than *soon.*

"What *happened?*"

"I'm fine. Don't worry about me. Ghostgrass. Perimeter. Get it done."

"Won't I be blocking you in here then? If you're a . . . " Jen trailed off, like she'd be chasing the Chooser's cape just by saying it. She tried again. "If I put ghostgrass . . . "

"Secondary concern," Isabel said, suppressing the reflex to glance in the direction where the ghost had gone. The next—last—part of her plan was coming up fast, and if she lost her nerve now she wasn't sure she'd get it back. "Go."

Jen knew better than to press. She shut her mouth and hustled off.

More people had come down from above by now. The midwife had been summoned and was patching wounds on-site, setting bones, readying the last of the dozen or so wounded for transport. Isabel did a double-take when she noticed Rina was with her.

Isabel turned so fast she cracked her neck. Scanned the room—and there were Onya and Andrew, working together to move rocks from somebody's trapped foot. There was Glory, checking the knots on a rope before a wounded body was ferried up into the night, Bex shouting instructions at her from above.

So it was true. Foster had gotten them out of the tunnels somehow. It was over. For better or worse, it was over.

That just left her with one more thing she had to do.

First she had to find a quiet place, away from everyone. The ghost especially. He understood her—almost too well sometimes—but he was absolutely not going to understand this.

I'm sorry, she thought at him. *This is the only way.*

Off along the wall behind the platform, there were some metal staircases leading up to a kind of walkway that ran the whole room's perimeter. She climbed them and found that the walkway used to be enclosed in glass, long since shattered.

She located the most secluded corner, sat herself down, and drew the harvesting-knife. With her off-hand she picked up the thread.

It was silver, pure silver, without the blackish violet of Salazar's, the searing white-orange of Foster's, or the glacial greenwhite of the ghost's. It was of the gauge and tension of strangling wire. Right now it was the surest path she knew to anywhere.

She wrapped it around the blade.

"Wasp." She jumped. The ghost was at her side. Where the hell had he come from? "A moment."

"Look," she said, flustered. "Can it—"

"No. It can't. I've waited long enough. This is important. Because the water is going to find its way into that room eventually, and I'm not sure you've fully considered what will happen when you drown."

"You don't think I've—"

The ghost raised one black-gloved finger. "*Fully.* Considered."

"I'll die. I'll turn ghost. Obviously."

"And if your ghost gets stuck in the room where you left your body? If it can't find a clear path to a waypoint? You've seen what happens to trapped ghosts. You would have been one yourself if I hadn't managed to pull you out of the ghost-place river yesterday.

You're welcome for that, by the way." Then, when no response was forthcoming: "I would have thought you'd be aware of the risks."

In light of everything, this weird angry solicitude struck her like a fist. The ghost's appearing here was not supposed to happen, had shoved her resolve off-balance. She struggled to right it.

"Pretty sure if I wasn't *explicitly* aware of what happens to a trapped ghost, I could have left you in the archive room no problem and spared myself this little talk." she said. "*You're* welcome, by the way."

For a few seconds they just glared at each other. Then she realized this might be the last conversation they ever had. She took a deep breath and relented.

"And I don't plan on drowning."

At last he noticed the harvesting-knife in her hand. The thread wrapped around the blade.

Very slowly, he drew himself up and back, like a snake. "You can't be serious."

"It's the only way that makes sense."

"The hell it does."

"Think about it. Because I have. And I *do* remember the ghost-place river, and I *do* remember what happens to a ghost that's destroyed beyond repair. And I can't let that happen. Not like that. Not to you. And not in this place. Of all places. I couldn't in the archive room before and I can't now."

And I'm getting those little black boxes, she could have added but did not. *Foster's wasn't there but there's a chance yours might've been. Whatever ends up being on those chips, that black box knows your name.*

"But I'm just, what, going to sit here and let the same happen to you. Do you honestly think—"

"I have to go now," she said, though it felt like ripping herself in half to do so. "If this works, I'll be back soon."

"And if it doesn't? What exactly is the plan here? How exactly do you—"

"Hold my breath," she said, and cut the thread.

Chapter Twenty-Three

This time she is not in the ghost-place when her thread is cut. So no whirlwind came to claim her, deposit her in the living world. Instead, she walks.

At some point she'd realized she wasn't in the big room where she'd left the ghost. Nor is she in the little room where she'd left her body. It might not really be a field where she is now, though it looked like one. Some other kind of wide open place, same suggestion of unbounded emptiness. She's been *flickering*, like the lights in the archive room running on *tertiary auxiliary power supply, emergency conservation mode*. Like stars viewed through an ash-pall. Like a ghost half torn free of its loop. Not here, not there. Not anywhere.

Teetering on the boundary between two worlds. Her feet didn't touch the ground. *Caught in between*, she'll think, and keeps walking. Everything was hazy here, as though she walked in thick fog, but shapes materialize from it, shooing her silently along. They had the wide-sleeved silhouettes of upstarts. *Sairy*, she thought. When she turns her face to them they vanish.

Time has long since abandoned her. She'd been here a minute, an hour, a year, before she'll realize this. None of these words meant anything to her anymore. *Minute, hour, year*. Her tenses are jumbling together.

A few useless inches of thread-end hang out of her chest. Nothing she can follow. There was no landscape, no road, no sky. Only fog. She couldn't hear her breath, her heart. *In between* go her steps, *in between in between*. There was nobody around. There'd never been anybody around. Someone might come, if she only waited. She'll wait. Nobody comes.

She knew what's happening to her. The process that had started in the tunnels was finally complete. How many times can you fall back and forth between the ghost-place and the living one before you get stuck half-in half-out for good? It'd be like straddling a fence, one leg in each world. Perfectly balanced there. Impossible to fall.

Was this what Foster had felt like, her ghost trapped in the room where she'd died?

Soon she'll start running toward nothing in particular. She's already been running forever. It was the slow-motion shambling of a nightmare, her soles striking air six inches above unseen ground. *In between*, go the tempo of her footfalls, *in between in—*

At some point, one hand drops to the hilt of the harvesting-knife. The knife wasn't moving exactly. Probably it never has been, and *moving* was just the best translation into words her brain has for the impulse it lays on her now and again. To turn around. To head in the direction it compelled her in. Certainly, now as before, it's doing *something*.

She held the knife out in front of her.

She's going to follow it home.

I sabel opened her eyes to darkness so complete she thought at first there was something covering her face. Winced. Her whole body was one great slug of pain. Everything from her nose down her throat and deep into her chest felt like it was smoldering. Her coat was soaked. She was lying in three inches of lakewater. The boxes and device were still in her pockets. Foster's broken blade was missing somewhere in the dark.

The thread was gone.

"Light?" she hazarded, but nothing. The room was silent, its ghost run down.

Up, she told herself, and levered to her feet, hauling her weight by main force up the drawer-handles, splashing her way by feel around the wall back toward the door.

There she paused, both hands on the wheel. Reviewing in her head: *swim out, down the hall, through another door, room with a hole in the ceiling, then swim up, up, and back as far as you can go toward the hatch before—*

She couldn't face the rest of that thought head-on without losing her nerve entirely. Already she felt faint. She was shaking so hard it set the harvesting-knife audibly rattling in its sheath. Nothing for it. At least if she drowned near the surface they might find her ghost. Nobody would get trapped down here coming after her. Chooser's odds, but her only hope.

"I'm sorry," she said aloud, because nobody was there to hear it. "I didn't want—I wanted—"

Taking the deepest breath she could, she dragged the door open. Braced herself for impact as the lake rushed invisibly in. Water crashed against her, swirled around her shins and knees and thighs.

And stopped.

The muggy dark was so thick it was nearly tangible, so it was a moment before she could translate the evidence of her other senses into a scene in which she stood.

There was water up to her hips. Dank air above them. The flood—had stopped? She pictured the sublevel beneath this. Had it all drained down there?

Slowly, painstakingly, lake-mud suctioning at her shoes, then barefoot as her shoes were lost, collapsing with exhaustion, she battled her way back up the hall, Archivist-coat bunched and hoisted in both hands to keep the contents of the pockets dry, one foot in front of another, moving forward.

When she reached the doorway to the room with the hole in the ceiling, she stopped.

There was light coming from somewhere, so faint she might not have noticed it if the darkness wasn't so otherwise complete. She'd stopped shaking, but the harvesting-knife rattled on.

She slogged her way into that room and stood under the hole, peering up. The light was definitely coming from far off up there.

Voices made their way down with it, growing louder as the light brightened. She held her breath and listened, convinced she was losing her mind.

"—drive a bus through the hole in this floor," one voice said. "The hell did you *do*?"

"Down two levels through the hole," the other voice replied, ignoring this. "Then out the door and to the right."

You memorized this map at a glance, she thought incoherently, *and you can't even remember your name.*

"I'm here," Isabel shouted up to them. Half-laughing, half-crying, voice cracking to shit under the strain of bearing such unexpected, breathtaking, selfish elation. "Here, I'm down here, I'm okay."

Up through the ceiling, then another. Both ghosts climbed down to the hole just above Isabel's head, then the ghost dropped down to her level to help her up. She was too tired to protest as he handed her up to Foster, then climbed up so that Foster could hand her up to him.

From there it was, of course, only a short distance to the second hatch, and soon they were standing on the lakeshore under the stars.

"I'm not sure why you look so surprised to see us," the ghost said. "I told you before that I would find you. I would have thought I'd made that clear."

"You could've been trapped," Isabel said. "Both of you. I've *seen* drowned ghosts, you idiots, they fill with water and they *burst,* okay—"

Foster reached down and picked a clot of rotten vegetation off Isabel's cheek with practiced tenderness. "Ragpicker's gambit?"

Isabel coughed. "Last trick up your sleeve."

With a jolt, she remembered. "Look," she told them. Reaching into her pockets. Pulling out the device. Then one of the little black cases at random. She held it out to Foster like an offering. SUBJECT #2122-33-A, TANAKA, SHIRO. Her hands were shaking. Somehow she got the case open and removed the chip.

It slotted into the device without resistance. The fit was perfect. The box must have been water-resistant in the way of Before-things, or else she'd done a fantastic job of keeping the pockety part of her coat out of the flood, because the chip was dry. The spider-leg nubs fit down into the perforations, exactly as she'd guessed. She located the button that would power on the device. Held her breath and pressed it.

Nothing happened.

* * *

Ruby found her before she'd made her way fully into town. Isabel staggered a few steps away from the ghosts, and Ruby came forward and clasped hands with her, paused, then pulled her into an awkward embrace. It was a measure of Isabel's exhaustion that she tolerated this.

"We were wrong to have ever doubted you," Ruby said.

Isabel wasn't so sure. The fallout of the day was crashing down on her, and from where she was standing, it seemed like everything she set her hands to turned to shit. She'd lost Sairy. She'd lost the Catchkeep-shrine and the meeting-hall and the rest of that pile of dead. Now she'd lost Foster's ghosts as well. Whatever was on those chips. The ghost's name, probably. Without even going through those boxes she was already upwards of ninety percent sure that the missing one was his. That was just the way this day was going.

Her mind was turning inward on itself, curling up, blowing out the lamps in its windows. *Nobody home*, she tried to project at Ruby. *Go away.*

"I want to show you something," Ruby said.

"Anything you want me to see, they can see too."

Ruby submitted the ghosts to an inquisitive once-over. "One of you must be Foster." Foster lifted her chin at her, guardedly, and Ruby went on: "Isabel's shrine-girls have a lot to say about you. I'm given to believe we would've been lost without your help. You saved a lot of lives today."

For a moment, Foster stared at her. Then, with a note in her voice Isabel had never heard before, she gave Ruby a strange little salute and said, "It was my pleasure."

Ruby led them through the torchlit town. Past rows of bodies, from Sweetwater and Clayspring both, laid out for burial or burning, respectively. Past the red-stained mudpit that used to be somebody's flower-garden and the back half of their house. Past a boy sitting on a violently tilted roof, something motionless cradled across his lap as he stared out at the moon. Past people looting the invaders' corpses, and at least two ongoing fistfights, apparently over items found there.

The baker's, the songkeeper's, the midwife's, the tradehouse, the meeting-hall. All ruined. There were streets where one house in maybe three was untouched, its neighbors burned out or broken or mired in mud. It would rain through the roofs of some. Others had halfway nosedived into the earth and gotten stuck there. People scurried between doorways like ants around a disrupted hill. Carrying clothing. Food. Blankets. They were packing these things onto themselves as if preparing for imminent flight. Away to the side of town there was a black mound of something recently burned, an oily plume of smoke still rising.

Once Isabel glimpsed Lissa at a distance. She'd put together a crew and they were reallocating ghostgrass bundles from broken roofs to whole ones.

It put Isabel in mind of the ghostgrass barricades. Of Sairy standing where Foster and the ghost had stood before, silently calling Isabel's name from beyond that impassible sea of gray-green vegetation.

As they walked, Foster and the ghost gave her the mercy of silence. Also the mercy of remaining at her side. A certain numbness had settled deep into her. A kind of bone-deep chill that locked in and preserved everything she'd rather let go of. She couldn't walk far enough or fast enough to get out from under what was hanging over her. She had nothing left to offer anyone. The bottom of that barrel had been scraped, and she was done.

When Ruby took her near the black yawn in the earth that had once been the Catchkeep-shrine, Isabel hit her limit. She stopped walking.

A line had formed there, townspeople lowering a lamp on a rope to gawp down into the depths. That sort of drop would smash their heads in like eggshells and they accorded it the same fascinated respect they'd pay a tornado.

Foster bled out down there, Isabel thought bleakly. *Now Sairy has too.*

"Okay," she said. Her voice sounded like a dead thing rolling down a hill, only gravity and momentum shoving it along. "What did you want to show me?"

"That," Ruby said, gesturing expansively.

"What?"

"All of it. Everything you just saw."

Isabel's patience was wearing thin. Her leg ached, she was beyond exhausted, she just wanted to find a quiet place to lie down and sleep for a week. Not that she had a bed to sleep in anymore.

"Which part? The trashed town? The bodies? The way the lake is coming up through the streets? I get it. The whole place has gone to shit because of me."

"These people are *alive*," Ruby said, "because of you. Because you spoke with Catchkeep and She granted us counsel which She would speak only to you. Because you and the shrine-girls put in remarkable work. On every level. In every way." For one horrible second she looked like she was going to reach out and touch Isabel's face. "The Ragpicker's favorite sweet is should-have-dones," she quoted instead. "Don't give Him yours."

But Ruby's words were glancing off of her. They wouldn't sink in. "I need someplace to sleep," she said dully.

"My house is yours," Ruby said, "for as long as you need it."

"Where will you sleep?" Isabel asked.

"Oh, don't worry," Ruby said, in a tone that said *there are other beds that will welcome me, and I don't mind having an excuse to visit them.*

Isabel thought of all those burned houses. All those bodies in need of beds. "What about the others?"

"Don't be silly. You're the hero of the hour. You and your—" she gestured at Foster and the ghost— "friends. I'm not crowding you out of a well-deserved and proper rest. Honestly it's the least I can do." Ruby paused. "Do they . . . sleep?"

"No. And I just need enough space to lie down in. Send in some others. They're not going to bother me. I plan to sleep like a corpse."

"Isabel, please, I am doing you a favor here—"

"Send in some others or I will *sleep right here in this street.*"

Ruby opened her mouth, then shut it tightly and nodded.

She led Isabel to her house and left her there, not even hesitating, at least not visibly, at the prospect of inviting ghosts into her home. The town knew what Foster and the ghost had done for them, no question. The word of it would have spread very, very quickly. They would all have to rearrange their mental field notes after this.

Ruby's house was one long low room divided into four sections with curtains woven of what looked like scorchweed-nettle yarn. Isabel staked out the smallest of these sections for herself. A small table was in there, and a couple of stools. On the table was a Before-relic, a kind of game nobody had any idea anymore how to play. A plastic board with black-and-white squares, and a few little plastic discs in black and red. The board had been broken and repaired in at least two places. Moonlight came in through a single window. There was nothing else of note in the room. No bed. No cushions. Nothing comfortable at all. This suited Isabel's mood perfectly.

"You sit," Foster said. Not so much pushing Isabel onto a stool as guiding her collapse toward it. "I'm going to find Jen."

"Don't you dare. I don't want to see anybody. I'll talk to them tomorrow, I promise. Just . . . not now."

Halfway out the door, Foster turned. "Oh, I'm not getting *her*. I'm getting whatever was in that jug she was carrying around back there. You look like you could use it."

"I don't—" Isabel called after her, but Foster was already gone.

Isabel sighed. Shut her eyes. Her head felt like a boulder. She let it crash back toward the wall behind. Unexpectedly, it hit something soft. Some kind of thin cushion? She opened her eyes.

The ghost had fetched a quilt from somewhere and had draped it behind her at some point in the past few seconds without her noticing. "Put that back wherever you found it," she said, shutting her eyes again. "I don't want it."

Even with her eyes shut, she could practically see the ghost's not-quite-shrug. "Make me."

The bare idea of getting up was daunting enough. She decided to ignore him instead.

Methodically, Isabel's foot was swinging out and banging back against the stool-leg. How long had it been doing that? She looked at it and it stopped. "Listen, tell Foster it's nice of her and I appreciate it but I'm just really, really tired."

Isabel wasn't quite numb enough to feel comfortable sleeping in that quilt, but her aching body was protesting that it *did* look very thick and warm. She piled it on the floor and shucked off the Archivist-coat, not caring when she heard objects rattle out of the pockets to the floor. A few of the black cases, the device. It didn't matter. What were they going to get, more broken? She kicked them aside, dropped the harvesting-knife to the floor, and settled into her nest, feeling wretched and hopeless and done.

The ghost observed this process in silence, sitting on the floor with his back to a wall, feathered in a soft silver luminescence. As the boxes fell, he reached to turn them label side up, but none of what was written on them seemed to jog his memory overmuch.

"Subject #2122-21-B, Patel, Nida," he read aloud, in a tone like the songkeeper telling the old stories. "Subject #2122-33-A, Tanaka, Shiro. Subject #2122-17-C, Deegan, Zachary."

Isabel buried her face in the quilt. It was a whole lot softer and cozier and nicer-smelling than she deserved. She stayed there for a time, too keyed up to sleep, listening to the ghost recite this litany of the twice-lost dead. When he ran out of boxes to read, she pulled the quilt away from her face and looked out.

There he was, exactly as she'd left him. Except he had her harvesting-knife held loosely in one gloved hand, was tapping the knife-point lightly, pensively against his boot.

Pure dumb reflex, her hand dropped to her sheath. As if there were two knives that looked like that in the world. *There would be if he broke his sword,* she realized, and pushed the thought away. "Hey. Do I steal your shit?"

He raised his gaze to her, tapped the knife, said nothing.

"Why did you ask me to come with you?" she asked suddenly.

The tapping stopped.

"I mean." She paused, grasping after the thought, miserable. She couldn't even formulate the question, though it had burned in her mind for three years like a coal. "I don't think I can read your memories when I'm dead." She coughed out a bitter little laugh, hating herself. "But I guess you realized that. No wonder you keep putting so much effort into keeping me alive."

She hadn't meant to say it aloud, but then it was out, she'd said it, there was no going back.

She let the silence stretch on. She had no idea what she wanted anymore. She wanted to disappear into the floor. She wanted him to get up and leave. She wanted to fight him. She wanted to sleep for a week. She wanted him to come over and punch her out so she wouldn't have to think anymore.

"I would rather destroy this thing right now," the ghost said icily, "than leave you under the misapprehension that I—" He trailed off. Then a blur, and the harvesting-knife had vanished to the hilt in the packed dirt and woven matting of Ruby's floor. "You," he spat, "should *know better.*"

Right then she hit her limit. She was just too damn exhausted to hold it in anymore.

"I'm sorry," she said. "For everything. If I'd just . . . I wouldn't . . . I would've been . . . "

It took her a second to work up the nerve to look the ghost in the eye, but when she did she was met only with that deliberately mild, deceptively open, almost scholarly consideration that could have meant anything.

"Are you finished?"

"Yeah. I'm finished."

With infinite, pointed care, the ghost removed his gloves.

"What the hell," Isabel breathed, seeing what had happened to his hands. But she knew, immediately, horribly, exactly what she was looking at. Foster had shown her the same, earlier, down in the tunnels. *We tried to leave through the southern exit, but . . .*

A wide swath of each of the ghost's palms was completely silvered with profound damage. Foster had scars that would never fully heal, but this—this was *wreckage.* Like someone had gouged a gaping furrow into each hand. The same along each finger, silver flaking up like birchbark. It came to her that he'd never taken his gloves off in the tunnels, even when cutting his palm on the harvesting-knife. It was a wonder he could even still hold the sword.

"Looks like maybe you should have tried the second hatch instead," she said at last, instead of everything she was thinking. "No ghostgrass there."

"Maybe," he said evenly. "Foster wanted to. But at the time I thought this one made your intentions clear enough."

Isabel almost laughed, it was so outrageous. But it was very much the logic by which *this particular ghost* operated. Three years ago she'd found his stubborn pride incomprehensible, infuriating.

Today—she still did, honestly. But if he'd forgiven her for shutting him and Foster out of Sweetwater, it was the least she could do to let this slide.

"No," she replied, so soft she wasn't sure he'd heard her. "It really didn't."

There was a long, long silence. Slowly, deliberately, the ghost put his gloves back on. Even then it was another moment before he spoke.

"Do you want me to go?"

"I don't know. No. No, I don't." Isabel paused. "I very much do not."

So the ghost resumed his post against the wall, tilting his head back like he could see the whole circuit of the summer stars through Ruby's ceiling. "All right."

Eventually Isabel must have fallen asleep, because she dreamed that she was perched on the Catchkeep-priest's high seat, dropping little silver chips into the Ragpicker's open maw, one by one by one.

She woke to full morning, sunlight blasting through the window. She was thirstier than she'd been maybe ever, and ravenous—for about one second, before she remembered where she was, and why, and her appetite receded from her like the tide.

She lay a moment in that empty room, staring at the ceiling. She could hear morning sounds from elsewhere in the house—Ruby had been true to her word after all—and work sounds from outside. Rebuilding efforts, she guessed. She really should get out there and help.

Sitting up, her body informed her in no uncertain terms that this was not going to happen just yet. So she lay back and listened to the noise coming through the window. There was Bex's voice, bantering with Lissa. It sounded like they were betting on something. Then several voices in unison began chanting Foster's name, and there came a huge noise that Isabel couldn't identify, and then cheers. Over them, Lissa: "Chore tokens for a *week*, enjoy!" and Bex groaning in dismay.

Once she'd gathered her strength she dragged herself to the window and looked outside.

Sure enough there was Foster, helping a group of ex-upstarts rebuild a house across the street. Mostly they were shouting encouragement while she and the ghost slung entire walls into place and braced them, bending their shoulders to a ton or more of stone and scrap and whatnot at a time.

For what felt like a long time she watched them. Their speed, as always, was unreal. In half an hour they made the kind of progress that would take a week for a team.

The way they worked together was mesmerizing, almost impossible for Isabel to look away from. Watching them, she thought back on the paper the ghost used to carry on his search for Foster. On it was printed the only image she'd seen of them alive. They'd been standing in an obviously posed manner—posed by someone else, and against their will, from the look on the ghost's face—in front of the smoking ruins of a building. For a second it was almost like that picture was the loop they'd been cut from and this, what Isabel was seeing now, was its rightful continuance. They'd busted a building, they were making buildings whole. And when they were finished, this time they could walk away.

Foster caught her looking and winked.

Foster. After everything that had happened, Isabel could only hope to face today with that kind of attitude. Foster was far from stupid. She knew she'd inadvertently done almost as much damage to the town as she had fixed. She might've been kicking herself in the ass just as hard as Isabel was. Might be mourning her mistakes and the collateral damage of those mistakes just as keenly. It wasn't for Isabel to say. But was Foster moping around feeling sorry for herself? No. Foster was out there rebuilding Isabel's town for her.

And Isabel could do nothing to pay her back for everything she'd done. The device was broken. She hadn't been able to find a black box and silver chip for Foster. She'd even managed to screw up something so simple as bringing back the other half of Foster's sword. All she had to do was picture Salazar to get a crystal-clear image of Foster's eventual destiny. Pure, uncontrolled, directionless, destructive power. It was only a matter of time.

Which only made Isabel feel worse. She was aware she was wallowing but she didn't know how much further than that her options extended. She wanted to be able to kick herself in the ass until she felt motivated or shamed into usefulness. Instead she turned back to her quilt-nest and the promise of oblivion.

And paused.

Something, somewhere was beeping faintly.

She tracked the sound across the room, wondering what kind of bizarre salvage whatnot Ruby was hiding. Something that still worked after all this time, it was incredible, Before-relics in the Waste never worked, they got too scoured by the elements, they were—

She stopped dead, right at the edge of a band of bright sunlight on the floor. The sound was definitely coming from pretty much exactly here.

She looked down. In the middle of the band of bright sunlight was the broken device she'd found in the archive room.

She picked it up.

At first she didn't see it over the glare on the device's glossy black panel. Squinting helped her make it out. When she did she almost dropped the device all over again.

Up in the top right corner, pulsing faintly in time with the beeping noise, a tiny, dimly glowing, pale green light.

Chapter Twenty-Four

Isabel worked until late afternoon, helping the ghosts and ex-upstarts as best as she was able, past the aches in her body and the self-doubt in her head. It felt like the best and only apology she could genuinely make.

Around midday Jen took her aside to explain how Foster had led the ex-upstarts into the shrine to take out the Clayspring raider army leaders. How Foster had saved them all, and destroyed the shrine in the process. "I've never seen anything like it," Jen told her. "It was like a storm of light just . . . coming out of her. It cut through everything it touched. Do they have some kind of Before-relic that does that, or . . . ?"

"You and your Before-relics," Isabel said. Awkwardly forcing out the teasing tone, the bantering words. When what she was really thinking about was how the timeline of the prognosis between Foster's condition and Salazar's might be rather shorter than Isabel had thought.

When the workday was done, she thanked Ruby for the use of her house and took up residence in one of the empty outbuildings of the Catchkeep-shrine, a storage shed that had, by a wink of the Chooser's good eye, withstood the fight for the town unscathed. The ghost and Foster came with her.

"At least keep the quilt," Ruby said, and wouldn't take no for an answer.

So later that evening they sat, leaning against the outside wall of the shed, the quilt bunched under them like a cushion, and Isabel explained to Foster about the device, the silver squares, the one she'd seen removed from Salazar's brain, and—after slight hesitation—the broken blade she'd forgotten in the archive room.

Nothing for that now. That whole sublevel was lost. The tunnels beneath Sweetwater must've spanned acres. The lake was visibly lower, the shoreline extending fifty feet further inward than it should. Even the big room where the shrine had toppled in had finally flooded, sometime in the night. Isabel didn't know whether those massive doors across the tunnel hall had failed at last, or the pressure of the water had breached new gaps elsewhere in the maze, only that she'd walked out there that afternoon to find the shrine-rubble lost beneath the water.

Now, summer night-breeze brought the sound of the ex-upstarts from somewhere in town, a few wine-jugs into a very noisy drinking-game. "Sure," Kath was laughing at someone, "you say that *now.*" The air still smelled like a warn-fire from all the burned wood of the houses. Also like lakewater.

Isabel was holding the device out in both hands. "The sun powers it," she explained to the ghosts. "I think. Jen told me once a long time ago that there used to be Before-relics that worked like that. And then I left it in the sun by accident and, well."

She'd brought out one of the little black boxes at random. SUBJECT #2122-02-C, KHOURY, SAFIYAH. She slotted the silver square into the device.

"Safiyah Khoury," Foster read off the box. Listening to the words leave her own mouth, like she hoped in that way to find them familiar.

Isabel was gripped by a sudden image: Foster and the ghost attached to Salazar's threads as the Director had been. Salazar, regrown and somehow hideously strengthened, feeding them tiny sips of power the way Foster had done with the others. Just enough to keep them alive and observe them. Keeping them manageably small, and silver, and shapeless. Ghostgrassed into some room. And if they'd lost enough of themselves by that time, they'd be powerless to stop her.

She pressed the button, harder than maybe necessary, and the device powered on.

What appeared on the device was a long, long string of numbers, marching down and down the screen. 15 01 2122. 16 01 2122. 17 01 2122. And so on.

Isabel frowned at this puzzle. Then, remembering somewhat-similar devices in Foster's memories, she reached out and slid her finger up the screen. The numbers scrolled along obediently until she poked one at random: 29 04 2122.

For a second, nothing happened. Then came a jumble, a mishmash of moving images sped up faster than real life, as though Isabel was looking out from what were presumably the eyes of #2122-02-C Safiyah Khoury, as she did . . . nothing much of note. Spooned up breakfast. Walked down a long white hall. Laced a child-sized pair of boots. Cleaned her teeth. Isabel made particular note of Khoury's face in the mirror, quickly sketching and labeling it as the images rolled on.

All the while, all along one side of the display, there was a constantly changing column of numbers, different numbers than the ones before. These were beside multicolored lines that changed as the numbers did. They reminded her of the maps of the tunnels, except these only traveled up and down, like waves.

There was also a cute little image of the cross-section of the inside of what must have been Khoury's head. It didn't look like anybody's real head, just that basic shape, like a child's drawing of one cut sideways in half to reveal a stylized brain.

Different-colored areas of the drawing-brain brightened at different times in inscrutable patterns. It reminded Isabel of the long tendrils she'd seen detached from Salazar's chip. She pictured them worming through Salazar's brain, or Khoury's—*or Foster's*, she thought, *or the ghost's*—poking each of these areas to light them up red blue green.

They watched as, under the Director's eye, Safiyah Khoury sparred with an operative who looked like a nine-year-old Ayres, and the peaks of those wavy lines spiked higher. Later, the session over, she retreated to her cot, pulled a book out from under the mattress, and began to read, and the numbers bottomed out. Then, later still they spiked again—when she slept, and dreamed.

Night terrors, the Director had said. *Early warning system . . .*

The screen blinked, and the device kicked over to display 30 01 2122. Wake, clean teeth, lace boots, eat breakfast, so forth. A quick glance at 31 01 2122 and 01 02 2122 revealed much the same.

"There's no sound," Foster observed. "There, right there, that kid she's looking at, his mouth is moving and there's no sound."

"Broken, I guess," Isabel said. How long must it have sat in the archive room? Surprising enough that it worked at all.

As if on cue, an inexplicable little symbol flashed three times in the corner of the screen and then the whole image—currently, a room of children sitting at desks, the Director standing at the head of it, holding a device of her own—went dark. Isabel watched the screen long after it powered down, unsure what she expected it to do.

"You were both in that room," she said. "I saw you both in that room in one of Foster's memories before, but it was—" she stopped herself just short of saying *real*— "right there."

"I saw," the ghost said, hushed and uncharacteristically unsteadied. At least Isabel had seen these memories before *somehow*, and they weren't hers to forget. "That *was* us. Wasn't it?"

"You must have been, like, eight years old," Isabel said. "You were practically *babies.*"

The ghost shook his head slowly, like he couldn't even imagine. The way Onya would shake her head at you if you told her that one day she would grow old.

Isabel didn't dare ask whether seeing themselves in someone else's memory was helping to bring back memories of their own. Intellectually she realized it was probably a bit of a stretch. But she was hoping it in silence with all of her being all the same.

If it was, the ghosts gave no sign.

"We really did spend our whole lives in that place," he said. Eyes cast toward the grass like he could see through twenty feet of soil and four flooded sublevels beneath. "Didn't we."

"Yeah. Right down there," Isabel said, and shivered a little, considering it.

"So those things," Foster said at last, in a voice like she'd just discovered a worm in her bite of apple, "were in our *brains?*"

"Yeah," Isabel replied. More unsettling the longer she thought about it. It was like the Catchkeep-priest keeping tabs on his upstarts and Archivist. Only from the inside, and without their knowledge, and comprehensively.

Isabel had lived for years with upstarts. A dozenish people, in rotation as they died off and were added in, all crammed into the same quarters, curtained alcoves the only halfassed nod to privacy. She had walked in on a lot of things. Overheard a lot of things. Somehow, she'd never felt so much like she'd intruded as she did now.

"Well," she told Foster, unsure whether she was making things better or worse, "there wasn't one in *your* drawer. Maybe they never gave you one."

It was anybody's guess what the chips had been meant for in the first place. From what the Director had said, Isabel didn't reckon this device was their final intended destination. The device didn't seem to be anything except a kind of display.

Still, that night she curled up in Ruby's quilt right there in the grass and slept, and the next morning she set the device in the sun and waited. Frustrating. A full day of powering up would give her a few minutes of use at most. It put her in mind of the archive room, the last dried-up dregs of power remaining to it.

But she set out those black boxes and separated the names of operatives she could match faces to from the names of those she couldn't.

In one pile:
SUBJECT #2122-08-B, AYRES, NICHOLAS
SUBJECT #2122-28-A, SALAZAR, MIA
SUBJECT #2122-05-A, MARTINEZ, ELENA
SUBJECT #2122-33-A, TANAKA, SHIRO
And in the other:
SUBJECT # 2122-02-C, KHOURY, SAFIYAH
SUBJECT #2122-42-C, SORENSEN, EMIL
SUBJECT #2122-21-B, PATEL, NIDA
SUBJECT #2122-11-B, SONG, JIN
SUBJECT #2122-17-C, DEEGAN, ZACHARY
SUBJECT #2122-38-B, HALE, TIFFANY
She surveyed her handiwork, then moved Safiyah Khoury's box from its pile to the other. It was a start, anyway.

Still, she was without a clear idea of what exactly she wanted the chips to teach her. These ghosts were lost in the tunnels beneath the lake. Even if she'd been able to retrieve them, she had no idea how to use this information to help them. Break them out of their loops somehow, as she'd done—temporarily, semi-accidentally, and at great risk—with Ayres? But she had no idea how to go about that. A few minutes here and there of watching an operative eat lunch or sit at a classroom desk or get poked and prodded by white-coated people in Medical wasn't going to give her the kind of information she needed to rehabilitate a ghost.

Not that the rehabilitation of ghosts had ever appeared on her list of duties as Archivist.

Not that she had any ghosts *to* rehabilitate. At least, not any whose chips she'd found.

Or did she?

"Did you ever end up moving Ayres from where we captured him?" she asked Foster on a sudden surmise, not really daring to hope but asking anyway.

"I left him in the tunnels so I could go up with Sairy," Foster said ruefully. "I figured he'd be safer there."

"Oh," Isabel said, crossing that idea off her list too. "Okay."

I'm the last of four hundred years of dead Archivists, she parroted at herself, sardonically. *I take* spectacular *field notes.*

Use that, she thought, and developed a strategy. Ration those dwindling crumbs of power. Cross-reference. Extrapolate. Be meticulous.

She knew just who to go to for meticulous.

She found the ghost sitting on a rock at the edge of the floodplain, boots in the mud, staring out across the black water where the shrine used to be. "Look," he said, not turning.

"What?"

He gestured *hush*, then pointed at something that had not yet, to her eyes, appeared.

Looking at that accidental pond, the ghost beside it, Isabel's brain chose that moment to remind her of something she'd overlooked.

The damage to the tunnels. All those doors ripped off their hinges and flung. The pulverized walls. And then, in the archive room, that missing drawer. That junked metal ruin in the back corner she'd at first taken for broken shelving. Who *could* have gone through the facility, breaking everything in sight, with no other operatives to stop him? Who, more than anyone, would have had both the ability and the motive to finish what Foster had started and try to bring that whole place down?

Four percent survival rate, but in the end, only one left standing.

And it was terribly easy to picture him ripping his drawer from the wall and destroying it utterly, the way he'd destroyed the Director utterly, or Salazar. As if to say to Foster's corpse: *they can't get both of us.*

His drawer, his name and number. Lost now. It was beyond the reach of any scrap-diver, and that heavy gnarl of metal wasn't about to float up on its own.

As if to underline her point, there soon came distant tiny bubbling. "Wait for it," the ghost said.

"How long have you been—"

"There."

Isabel shaded her eyes. An object had drifted up from the depths. A little flake of something, like a fallen leaf, but gray. It stayed where it surfaced, bobbing up against several other identical objects, not nearing the shore.

"I believe that's Salazar," the ghost said conversationally.

"Does Foster know you—"

"No."

For a while Isabel stared out at that smattering of gray flecks on the water, a thought taking shape in her mind. "And they were all just *down there* when you and Foster showed up? Salazar, Martinez, Tanaka, all of them?"

"Yes," he said. "Why?"

"Well. Ghosts don't usually get stuck where they died. Unless something is physically stopping them from reaching a waypoint into the ghost-place."

"So you've said. Such as your ghostgrass barricades. Or the way you would've been trapped in the room where you left your body, had you drowned."

"Right. And, I mean. You weren't stuck in the tunnels. Before, I mean. Neither was Foster. She was stuck in the ghost-place. But the others were right down there, in the actual tunnels in the living world." She pointed at the flood, the vanished tunnels below. "You said they'd been there all along. Right there where they died. And I don't get it. It doesn't work like that."

"Why?"

"I don't know, it just doesn't. Think of Ayres. I saw the memory he was stuck on, and it wasn't the moment he died. Same goes for Salazar, and that little-kid ghost. The memory Ayres was stuck on didn't even take place in the facility. That was the moment he couldn't move past, there's no reason his ghost should've been in the tunnels if . . . " She trailed off. *"Unless."*

"Their data chips were in the facility," the ghost said. "Mine wasn't."

"Their memories," Isabel said slowly. "It's *all their memories* on those chips."

"But Foster did die in the facility. We know that definitively. If her chip wasn't in her drawer, where was it?"

"Yeah." Shrugging hard, like she wanted to dislodge the idea's sticky weight. Nonetheless, it clung. "I know." She paused, deliberating, then said: "About that. I asked the Director about Foster's chip." Another pause, and then: "She told me to ask you."

This startled him into turning. "She what?"

"And you told me before that you buried Foster."

The ghost narrowed his eyes, like he was trying to focus on something in the distance that he could see through Isabel's head. "I did?"

The alarm in his voice was tamped way way down, but Isabel heard it. He didn't remember. He'd told her three years ago about that memory, but since then it had been lost.

It made her think, again, of Salazar. Of the shapeless melted child-ghost. Of the ghost's words the other day: *if we're past saving. If we've lost too much to get back. I need you to end us.*

She plowed over it all.

"So if her chip wasn't with the others, they probably never took it out," Isabel said. "But if you don't know where you buried her . . . " She blew out an exasperated breath. "That chip could be anywhere."

"Is that what you came out here to ask me?"

"Even better," she said, grateful for the change of subject. "I have a proposition for you."

So they sat in the shed together, a stump of lake-driftwood serving as table between them. On it were the device, the chips, and a modest stack of papers: Isabel's brand-new field notes on the Latchkey ghosts. There was a sheet of paper for each operative, name and number. Several by now—Salazar, Ayres, Tanaka, Martinez, Khoury—had faces sketched in beneath.

One sheet—Foster's—had a name but no number.

One sheet—the ghost's—was blank.

"Do you want to go over the names one more time?" she asked him. "See if any of the ones we haven't matched yet sound—" *like they might be yours*— "familiar?"

He just looked at her, then removed one glove and laid it on the table.

It'd been a long time since she'd sat down with the ghost like this, reading his memories. Prying into all the parts of him he'd lost. How had this managed to be less awkward when they *weren't* doing it by choice?

"Okay," she said. "You ready?"

In response he spidered his fingers on the tree-stump: *am I not waiting?*

"Now," she said, aware she was stalling. "You might not like what's in there to see."

He breathed a little humorless laugh. "You don't say."

"I mean it. It might be bad. I need you to tell me, right now, no bullshit, if it's bad, I mean if it's *really* bad, if it's something you'd be happier *not* knowing, if it's *that* bad—"

"—do I still want to know?"

Isabel nodded.

The ghost picked up the nearest thing to hand—an empty cup—and winged it at her. She caught it and pitched it back. Recently she'd noticed both ghosts practicing adjusting their strength, their pure power output, to pass among the living. Good thing, too. Catching that cup would otherwise have shattered her hand.

The ghost was shaking his head at her in mock disappointment. "What do you think?"

"All right," she said. "But no sulking if it's bad news. Hear?"

He held his hand out like he wanted her to shake it. She put the blade in it instead. Just before he closed his fist around it, he said: "It's all bad news. We both know that."

Isabel took the hilt and braced herself, waiting to be shaken from the fabric of the world. But she was not. All that came to her were whispers, there and gone, and the vaguest hint of something just glimpsed and now receding.

The ghost was watching her carefully.

"Is it because you're not in the ghost-place?" he asked her, at the same time as she said, flatly, "I'm not in the ghost-place," and forcefully sheathed the knife, then threw up her hands in frustration. "Well, there goes that—"

Then came the knock at the door.

"That'll be Ruby about the meeting," she said, and made herself answer.

Already, the weather had changed. That morning had been crisper, the evening cooler and less oppressive. Summer was beginning to turn its face toward fall. In light of that, and of the coming winter, the high seats had called a meeting to decide how the people of Sweetwater would proceed from here. There was no meeting-hall in which to hold one anymore, so they'd gathered on the lakeshore beneath the lowering sun.

By now seventeen new buildings had gone up, pieced together from the busted parts of old ones, courtesy mainly of Foster and the ghost. Four roads had been repaired. They'd sealed both breaches in the garden perimeter fence. Whatever damage Foster had inadvertently done to the town seemed to have been widely forgiven in light of this.

On top of twenty-nine townspeople lost in the fight, another ten had since perished of their wounds, bringing Sweetwater's total count to one hundred fifty-seven. Given the current state of the town, even half that population was insupportable.

To Ruby's credit, she didn't ask Isabel why she hadn't been at the meeting, just launched into what she had to say without preamble.

"Some of us have decided to leave," she said, putting Isabel immediately in mind of the statue of Catchkeep, the candles burning in Her eyes. How Isabel had tried, and failed, to disobey Her counsel. *You win,* she thought at that statue, lost or sleeping beneath the lake. *Of course You'd win.* "And some will stay. Watch over the wounded. Try to rebuild."

Most, Isabel figured, would leave. Inch by inch Sweetwater was drowning, melting, returning to the earth. In a year it would be overgrown, digested wall by wall into the greenery. Most potential supplies having been buried or burnt, a hundred-odd exhausted townspeople, six ex-upstarts, and two superpowered ghosts could only do so much. Salvaging building material from these upended houses was the kind of job you draw straws for, and start praying to the One Who Got Away before your foot so much as touches mud.

"The ones who are leaving," Isabel said. "Where will they go?"

Ruby gestured vaguely southward. "Grayfall, mostly. A few want to strike out for a place they're calling Waterside. I've not heard of it myself. I gather there's a river?" Ruby drew herself up, a full head taller than Isabel. "I will stay. I have no intention of forsaking the wounded. Here we have fresh water—more of it than we need these days!—and reliable means of food production, once the perimeter fence is repaired."

"Next year, maybe," Isabel said. "There's nothing left to harvest."

"Well. Jen and I spoke with Cora. She leaves tomorrow with a cart of weapons and trinkets and whatnot off the Clayspring dead. She's taking it to Stormbreak, thinks she can trade it along with the things Jen's finding from the tunnels for enough food to see us partway through the winter. Especially with our somewhat . . . attenuated numbers."

"We trade in corpse-loot now?" Isabel said, impressed.

"We trade in what we have for what we need. I didn't guess that would bother you."

"It doesn't bother *me*."

"Well, we all make compromises if we want to eat," Ruby said. "Which looks more inviting to me than a Waste-slog any day, Grayfall or no Grayfall. Though I do hear it's lovely. My aunt used to run a scav crew down that way . . . " She tilted her head at Isabel. "What about you? You're young and strong. Take your chances in the Waste? I understand some of your girls are throwing their lot in with that group."

"I heard." Kath and Bex were going, but as far as Isabel knew, the rest planned to stay. The high seats had put Jen in charge of rationing and distributing and storing what remained of the town's food supply for winter, with Glory as her number two. Lissa was to begin holding regular combat training sessions, aided by Meg. They wouldn't be caught unawares again.

It was interesting to see how, after the fight for Sweetwater, the ex-upstarts had adopted Foster as one of their own. Sometimes she'd go out into the fields with them while Isabel worked with the ghost, exchanging sword-lessons for knife-lessons. Their styles were well-matched. They all fought dirty.

"They're planning to come back," Isabel clarified. "They just want to see what's out there."

"You say that like someone who's not going with them."

"I'm not," Isabel said. "I have work to do here."

"You've really poured yourself into the rebuilding effort," Ruby said, nodding. "We've all noticed. You and your—friends. Those two ghosts. I know you've been hard on yourself, but the fact remains, we'd've been lost without the three of you."

Stupid that after everything she'd been through, one lousy compliment could still make Isabel squirm. "Thanks," she made herself say, and shut the door, then fell back against it, utterly exhausted.

"It was in the ghost-place," she said, gesturing tiredly at the table, the harvesting-knife, the ghost who sat and watched blandly as she shook her head at her own stupidity. "When I read your memories, or Foster's. It was always in the ghost-place. I don't know why I never realized that before."

The ghost said nothing. Whatever disappointment he felt, he had the grace to hide it well.

"I'll get back in," she promised. "I'll find a way."

But she wasn't so sure. When she'd gone to the ghost-place to find Foster, it'd nearly killed her, and that method wouldn't work again. The tunnels, so full of ghost-energy, had been porous enough for her to pass back and forth within them, having been partly a ghost for so long herself, but they were under the lake now. There had to be other places that were like that, were possessed of that liminality. She just had no idea where. Or how, short of dying, she'd persuade them to let her in.

So she couldn't read the ghost's memories. She couldn't read Foster's memories. And the chips and device were looking more and more like a dead end.

Her aggravation must have been visible on her face.

"Like I said. It would've been bad news anyway," the ghost said lightly, which somehow only made it worse.

* * *

Still, together Isabel and the ghost developed a system, and over the next days fine-tuned it. Each chip had about a million times more information on it than they had any hope of combing through at a stretch before the device needed to be recharged. So they'd pick a chip, pick a random chain of numbers off the initial list—a list of days, the ghost explained to her—and skip around the mess of images it showed, hoping to hit upon something that seemed maybe slightly more important than the rest. When they got there, Isabel would match each operative in the scene up with their field notes, and make note of what they were doing. She also wrote down what each one was doing in each memory of the ghost's or Foster's she'd read before, to the best of her recollection.

By comparing all her information methodically, she'd inferred that the child-ghost she'd found in the tunnels was #2122-17-C, DEEGAN, ZACHARY, the first in that last wave to die. That the girl with the blue-black ponytail, Ayres's partner, was SUBJECT #2122-21-B, PATEL, NIDA. That Salazar had initially been partnered to Safiyah Khoury, Martinez to a boy whose name Isabel hadn't yet figured out, and Deegan—briefly—to #2122-42-C, SORENSEN, EMIL, before Deegan had died in the early stages of his treatment, cutting Sorensen adrift until the next operative died and her surviving partner—Tanaka—was paired up with him. Process of elimination strongly suggested that the dead girl had been #2122-38-B, HALE, TIFFANY, but there was something wrong with her chip and it wouldn't run at all, so her life remained in large part a mystery. That left #2122-05-A, MARTINEZ, ELENA partnered with SUBJECT #2122-11-B, SONG, JIN, presumably lost to the tunnels with Sorensen, Khoury, and so on.

Isabel and the ghost mapped this all out together. No detail left out. *Be meticulous*, she chided herself when her patience flagged. *Do the work.*

So she wrote down how the child operatives would all play seek-and-find in the lower tunnels, and barter chores for the brightly-wrapped candies that the white-coated adults would reward them with after each round of treatment, and tell each other stories after lights-out. How they could make games out of found trash and desperation. They raced bugs, adopted rats they found in the deep tunnels. Drew pictures on each other's bandages when they emerged from under the knife, playing tough but crying in their sleep, cradling new wounds. Each of them wanting to be a normal kid in the way an outrageously beautiful topiary might secretly desire to be an ordinary tree.

She also recorded, diligently, the deathbed-birthday party the operatives had thrown for Tanaka. The weird fight in the streets she'd seen when she'd accidentally cut Ayres. The way the kids had all played together in that big room before the Director had divided them up into groups. One to become the first wave of Latchkey subjects. Where the other went, she didn't know.

They were like upstarts, she thought, not for the first time. *All thrown into the same crap together, knowing they wouldn't all survive. Climbing up onto each other to get out.*

She got a lot of useless information. The memories were viewed piecemeal, and without context, and out of order, and with no sound. Trying to curate such overwhelming volume of information was like wading into a stream with a minnow net in one hand. A little water ran through the net at once, and maybe a minnow if she was very, very lucky. But most of it rushed on by.

And none of it could help Foster or the ghost reclaim their memories. That was, by far, the worst of it. She found she carried on with the work anyway. She'd cut Foster's threads and lost those ghosts. She owed at least a bit of effort. And it wasn't like there was a whole lot else right now vying for her time.

Every night, after she'd set the device aside to recharge throughout the next work day, Isabel tried again to read his memories, or, occasionally, Foster's. Every night, the most she'd get is a feeling much like waking from a dream, grasping after details that ran through her fingers like sand. Like dreams, sometimes she'd catch disjointed little fragments— *a glowing bank of buttons, a wooden training sword, a needle injecting something into a child's arm, a bottle passed back and forth, a bright light overhead*—but nothing concrete enough to write down. She was all too aware of the damage every cut was doing, and that none of them would heal. Eventually, despite the ghost's objections, she stopped.

But she still had so many questions, and no way of answering them now.

How had the ghost died? Why did all the Latchkey ghosts mistake her for Foster? What was the deal with the harvesting-knife—leading her back to Foster with almost perfect reliability, again and again, in the ghost-place and the living one?

For that matter, why were Foster's remains not in her drawer? Where was her chip? And the ghost's?

And when Isabel'd asked the Director about Foster's chip, what in the slag-blasted fifth hell had she meant by glancing at the ghost and telling Isabel *ask him*?

Meanwhile, Foster fished for ghosts.

Every morning, she and Jen had been going out to stand at the edge of the black pond that used to be the Catchkeep-shrine, skimming float-salvage off the surface as it bubbled up. Lately, Isabel had been opting to join them. It rapidly became her new favorite chore. She didn't have to walk anywhere, she barely had to talk to anyone, and it was fascinating to see the kinds of junk that drifted up from the depths as the tunnels had filled.

Lake-crap, mainly. Plant matter. Aquatic clotweed in its element, and Carrion Boy's Tears well out of its. Also waterlogged bits of paper, dissolving at a touch. Cylindrical orange bottles, each of which she held up to the light, looking for a silver glint inside that might be Ayres. Shards of plastic whatnot. Unnameable antique debris.

Foster wasn't here for artifacts, but Jen sure was. Before-stuff, every bit of it, and priceless. They wanted to eat this winter, they needed to wring use out of every scrap of this new currency.

Glory joined them, aiding Jen with inventory. They'd been working in companionable silence for nearly an hour one day when something bubbled up and spread there on that black water. Something big. Something like a drowned coat. Pale and gray, with hints of darkness on its underbelly.

"Your side," Jen called across thirty feet of water to Glory, who reached with her stick-net to pole the thing over, then dragged it slithering onto land. Jen, inventory notebook in hand, was shouting before the thing had even touched the shore. "What is it? Some kind of blanket, or—"

"*Stop,*" Foster said, in a voice of pure and urgent command. It stunned them where they stood.

Isabel's breath caught and Glory nearly dropped her salvage-pole as Foster turned the thing over in the grass.

It wasn't a coat at all, but something like a person-shape cut out of a sheet. Almost perfectly gray, but silver where the sun hit it. Streaked with smeary black where its clothes would be if it were wearing pants and long sleeves, with darker black where its hair might fall. It had the barest suggestion of mouth and eyes. The vague shape of a sword was at its waist. Its chest was rising and deflating softly with the memory of breath.

"And where were *you* hiding?" Foster asked it, in a tone of fond reproach. To the question in Isabel's face she said, "This isn't one I put a thread on."

"What is that?" Glory was asking. "That isn't *Sairy?*"

"No," Isabel said. "I have no idea who that is."

Within ten minutes Jen and Glory had assembled a ghostgrass ring on the floor of the storage shed, that trashed silver ghost lying rumpled in its center like a discarded skin. A new thread ran from the center of its chest to Foster, squatting on her heels as far away from the ghostgrass as the tiny room allowed. A little ways away the ghost stood stationed in a corner. The sword-hand on the hilt belied the studied indifference in his eyes.

"Put more ghostgrass down outside," Isabel instructed Glory. "Fresh perimeter around the whole building. Maybe ten, fifteen feet from the walls."

"What," Glory said, grimacing, "like the old Archivist-house?"

This gave Isabel pause. But only for a second. "Yeah," she said. "Like that." At Glory's look of alarm she realized what Glory was really asking. "Not *like that* like that. This is just—" she sighed, then opted for honesty— "something I can do."

"She's reclaiming her powers," Foster added theatrically, doing some kind of songkeeperish voice. "Using them for good instead of evil."

Glory snorted. "Before-story stuff."

"Came from somewhere."

"Out somebody's ass." Glory side-eyed Foster, who shooed her toward the door in mock irritation. "Five minutes for the perimeter," Glory told Isabel, all business now. "I'll give you a yell when it's done."

"Remember," Isabel said, "nobody breaches that perimeter. Not Ruby, not anybody. No matter what."

"Yes, Archivist."

"And Glory?"

Halfway out the doorway, Glory turned.

"Thanks."

She shut the door behind.

"You two want out before she lays the perimeter?" Isabel asked.

"Nah," Foster said. "I'm good."

The ghost swept his gaze from the rumpled ghost on the floor to Isabel. "I'm staying."

"I figured you'd say that," Isabel said. "That's why I told Glory to leave some space."

When Glory had given the all-clear, Foster sent a few gentle pulses of ghost-energy down the thread, darkening the silver ghost's uniform to solid black, bringing its face into focus. Sixteen years old, maybe, at time of death, a long-limbed girl with skin the color of Isabel's and a blue-black ponytail.

I know you, Isabel thought, and rooted around in the black boxes until she came up with SUBJECT #2122-21-B, PATEL, NIDA.

Turning to Foster. "You good?"

"I got her." The thread brightened, dulled, stabilized. A warmish silver. "Do it."

"Done." Into the device went the chip. While it powered up Isabel sat at the outer edge of the ghostgrass ring. Mentally preparing a sort of introduction, something with which to anchor this ghost to its new reality. *Your name is Nida Patel. You were an operative in the Latchkey Project. You fought in a civil war. Your partner was Nicholas Ayres. You were two of the last few standing. Everyone around you got sick and died. After a while you did too.*

It scraped the bottom of the meager barrel of Isabel's knowledge, but it came naturally enough. By now she was used to making lists.

She held that little black screen out at eye level with Patel's gaze, half silver half brown.

"Your name," she said clearly, "is Nida Patel. I want to show you something."

Chapter Twenty-Five

E ven after the pond froze over, Isabel tended to slow her pace going past the clouded surface of that water. Waiting for the day she'd glance down and find the silver hands of Sairy's ghost pressed up against the ice from underneath, Sairy's silver face staring up. But this never occurred.

Meanwhile two more ghosts surfaced—first Martinez, then one who Isabel's study of the chips eventually revealed to be SUBJECT #2122-42-C, SORENSEN, EMIL.

Also some more bits of silver flotsam that Isabel collected in a jar labeled SALAZAR, unsure what else to do with them. Martinez and Sorensen, meanwhile, went into ghostgrass rings in the shed as Patel had done. First alone, then together, in the hopes that they might attempt to communicate, or send their own threads questing out toward each other as Salazar had done. They did neither.

The work was a monotonous, painstaking grind. Two steps forward and one step back on a good day, one step forward and three steps back on a bad one. The device only had enough juice to run a chip for maybe a quarter hour at a time when they'd started, but that limit had dwindled down to half that length by now, and the effect of the chips on the ghosts, if any, was not obvious.

Thanks to Foster's thread, Patel had at least strengthened enough to start muttering to herself. "Out of here," she was saying, over and over, to no one. Days of this, incessant. Her voice sounded as hopeless and tired as Isabel had ever felt.

And until Sorensen and Martinez were strong enough to show her the moments they'd gotten stuck on, there was no loop for her to break them free of. And until she stumbled across a clue in Patel's chip that would *explain* the moment *she'd* gotten stuck on, Isabel's hands were similarly tied.

For nowhere near the first time, she found herself wishing the device still played sound to go with the images. She had no idea how to break a ghost free of its loop without hearing what it was saying, then matching the words to the memory in which they'd been said. In her somewhat limited experience of breaking ghosts free of their loops at *all*.

"At least," she confided in the ghost in a moment of downtime, as they attempted to play the mystifying Before-game from Ruby's house, "as Archivist I knew what I was *supposed to do*." When she pictured this new work she saw a sheer cliff of ice, without handholds or footholds, that she was somehow expected to scale. Absently she stacked the little plastic game-discs in a tower, red-black-red-black, until she ran out of discs, and then she flicked the whole thing over.

Each day the Latchkey ghosts stood dumbly in their ring. Patel fully-formed and lifelike, mumbling *out of here* at something long since too dead to hear her. Sorensen and Martinez, silver-streaked and shambling, bumping into the unseen wall that marked the ghostgrass perimeter. Foster tried giving them more power, but either they'd taken too much damage or they'd been drowned too long. They spewed ghost-energy like slashed veins.

"I used to have to put down this kind of ghost," Isabel finally admitted, after about a week of watching Foster frantically regulating her energy output to keep Martinez balanced on the vanishingly fine line between deliquescing entirely and blowing the roof off the shed. "Or send them back to the ghost-place. If I could."

The ghost's boot, tapping out a bored little tune on the floor, abruptly stopped. "And we aren't doing this why?"

Isabel bit her lip doubtfully at Sorensen, at present geysering silver-blue light from both eyes. Sighing, Foster dialed back the energy down his thread and he collapsed like a puppet with its strings cut. *I don't want to give up on them yet,* Isabel thought, and said, "They're not ready."

The next day she left the Latchkey ghosts in their ghostgrass ring and sat in the violet evening light with the device and Patel's chip. "Useless slag," she told the device, but powered it up all the same. She'd chased the Chooser's cape for longer, and for causes less lost.

She caught the black box before she saw who'd thrown it. While she shook out her stinging hand she inspected what had landed in it. SUBJECT #2122-08-B, AYRES, NICHOLAS. Looked up and the ghost was sitting his bootheels beside her. "Try that one." One black-gloved finger motioned: a loop endlessly rolling. "Skip to seventeen oh-eight two-one-three-one."

"Okay," Isabel said. "Why?"

"That's the last date on Patel's chip."

"Yeah, but we ruled out where they die. I told you, ghosts don't get stuck on—"

"Something happens to her feed a full two weeks before that. She stays in one room the whole time, and then out of nowhere she—" he gestured incomprehensibly— "goes dark."

"This is Ayres's chip you just threw at me."

The ghost just looked at her.

"Fine."

She selected a string of numbers a couple dozen places in advance of 17 08 2131.

There was Patel, battling her way up a long street of weird machines.

"What am I looking for?" she asked.

"Not that," the ghost said. "You'll know it when you see it."

"How do you know?"

"I don't," the ghost said. "Keep going."

Next came a training session in which Ayres was sparring with the ghost.

He stared at that a moment, then said, "Next."

Isabel spun ahead a few numbers on the string.

There was the Director shouting directly into Ayres's face, shaking a sheet of paper at him: INCIDENT REPORT.

"Go back one."

There she/Ayres found Patel, hunched over her knees, backed into a corner in a little tile stall with a drain in the floor. Isabel expected the sickness to have disfigured her by now, but she looked healthy enough. Apart from the long ditches of blood she'd gashed into her forearms, presumably with the shard of glass that lay beside her.

There came a pause while Ayres might have said something, though no sound came through the device, as expected. But, for some reason, the ghost was pointing. "There."

"There where? There's no *sound*. The hell are you—"

Then the ghost was tapping at the screen. The image halted, ran backwards a second, resumed. Like any ghost-loop.

"You're not listening. You're *looking*. What's she been saying all week?"

"*Out of here*," Isabel said, with a weird little prickle of disorientation as the shape of Patel's mouth matched up to the words Isabel spoke.

The image skipped back again, replayed. The ghost pointed at Patel's mouth as she spoke. "She just said *until I get out of here.*"

Isabel practically hurled herself back into the shed.

Inside, Foster was overseeing Patel's pacing and muttering with the air of someone intently watching paint dry.

"She tried to kill herself," Isabel shouted. "Ayres found her. He must've said something like, I don't know—" frantically trying to come up with a set of words that fit Patel's, like a puzzle-piece— "something like *how much longer are you going to do this*, because then she said *until I—*"

"—*get out of here*," she and Patel said together.

Patel blinked. Took in Martinez, Sorensen. Tried to walk forward, was rebuffed by the ghostgrass ring. She put her hands up in front of her, palm-out, like she was trying to feel a wall that wasn't there. The ghostgrass singed them and she pulled back fast, wiping her palms on her legs. "What is this? Is this some new test? I want to talk to the Director."

Foster leaned forward as far as the perimeter allowed. "What's your name?"

"Patel," she said impatiently. "Nida Patel. 2122-21-B. Look, tell the Director—" She broke off, peering around her like she'd walked into darkness and was waiting for her eyes to adjust. "Am I in the simulator? What is this place?"

It was all Isabel could do not to start shouting. She had the strongest most unaccountable urge to grab the ghost and shake him. *We broke it*, her mind was blaring. *We broke a loop* on purpose.

But now what?

Isabel found herself staring at the pits of light that were Sorensen's eyes. Pure silver until memory gave them shape and depth and color. As with any part of any ghost. Something rustled at the back edge of her mind.

"You can see us?" Foster was asking, incredulous. "You're *here with us now?*"

"I see *you*," Patel said, annoyed. "What, she can't even come down to run her own diagnostics anymore?"

"Tell me something you remember," Foster demanded. "Something that happened to you before what's happening to you right now."

Patel opened her mouth. Shut it. Opened it again.

"She doesn't remember," the ghost said aside to Isabel.

"This test makes no sense," Patel declared, gathering herself. "I refuse it."

Foster held up the device. Onscreen Patel bled silently. Ghost Patel folded her arms. "Do you know who this is?" Foster asked.

"Should I?" Patel said irritably. "Some girl. I *demand* to speak to the Director. *Now.*"

Isabel wasn't listening. She was thinking back on when she'd healed the ghost. The unvaried silver of his insides.

The unvaried silver of any ghost's anything. A ghost was energy, pure energy, molded by memory into a person-shape. But malleable. You could pull a thread out of the chest of one. You could cut one into pieces and watch those pieces reattach. A ghost could carry items with it, even, out of one world into another. She thought of the ghost's gun and sword. Of her own harvesting-knife. Of the Director's device, which had shivered into sparks upon Isabel's touch.

Isabel hadn't healed the ghost by knowing medicine.

She'd healed him by knowing *ghosts*.

"A girl," Isabel said, watching Patel's face as she spoke, "a Latchkey operative, found by fellow Latchkey operative Nicholas Ayres, #2122-08-B. Her partner." A pause while she hefted the guess in her mind. "Her friend."

Patel looked back at her blankly. "Who?"

I've been going about this all wrong. The device just shows pictures. But the chips . . .

"Listen," Isabel said. Patel's chip in one hand. Harvesting-knife in the other. "So I just had the weirdest idea."

They stood before the snapped spine of the oldest bridge, before the gray-green sea of ghostgrass planted there. It was the easiest waypoint for Isabel to reach on her bad leg, but she still had to hang back, resting, while Lissa and Glory forged ahead, clearing a path to that distant grayscale lightbleed that indicated a ghost-place door. An open wound in the skin of two worlds.

She wasn't in the tunnels anymore, and she wasn't mostly a ghost. So she wasn't going to be able to cut her way through this door. She'd tried, earlier, before escorting Patel out of the shed. Bloodying the knifepoint and setting it to the waypoint, which had, predictably, refused to acknowledge her.

But in the archive room she'd *made* a waypoint. If there was a place in the living world that was permeable enough to receive her, it was here at an existing one. If she only bent her will to it sufficiently.

Foster, the ghost, and Patel stood with her.

Predictably, Patel's loop had resumed, and she didn't seem to so much as notice the waypoint. "Out of here," she was muttering under her breath. "Out of here."

"You really think this is going to stop her doing that?" Lissa asked.

"I don't know," Isabel said. Thinking back to the Director, or Salazar, or Deegan, or Ayres. If it'd been possible to break them out of their memory-loops for more than a few minutes, or Patel from hers, Isabel didn't know how. *Someday,* she assured them silently, though it was a promise she had no idea how to keep. "But right now it's kind of the best I got."

The roil of emotion coming off of Foster was palpable. On one hand, a Latchkey ghost potentially rehabilitated. On the other hand, even if what Isabel was about to try worked, she wouldn't be able to do the same to Foster, or the ghost. Their chips had vanished with the rest of the Before.

Across twenty feet of ghostgrass, Lissa waved.

Truth was, she had no idea how this was going to go down. But it felt like the nearest thing she was going to get to closure. Not for her, not for Sairy, but for *someone.* There were still two more ghosts in her shed, and *their* chips were safe in their boxes. If she could do this much, she could do more.

"If this works," she told the ghost, "I should see at least one of your memories, anyway. Maybe we can figure out a way to use it in future to read more of them."

"Just stay safe," the ghost told her. "We'll deal with the rest of that another time."

Keep moving, she thought, and walked the path her ex-upstarts had cut. The ghosts followed.

Within spitting distance of the waypoint, the ground beneath her gave a little lurch and steadied.

Come on, she thought at the waypoint. *You're going to let me through.*

Then doubt seized her all over again, like a cramp. What if she couldn't get through? What if she couldn't bring the chip through with her? She couldn't ask the ghost to bring it through for her, she needed him here to get her back out. And she pointblank refused to ask Foster. There was no guarantee that the far side of the waypoint would lead back here.

So instead she glanced over at the ghost, who was standing by awaiting his cue. "I'm going to feel pretty stupid if this doesn't work," she said.

"You did it before," Foster reminded her. "This thing's got nothing on you. It's just a door. So open it."

"Okay," Isabel breathed. Her heart was hammering. "Just a door. Okay."

"Count of five," said the ghost, "when you stop breathing. Yes?"

Isabel nodded. "Just like in the tunnels. I don't think I can signal or anything, so, you know. Do your best."

Isabel took Patel's hand and shut her eyes. *I did this before,* she told herself. *I did this before.*

Trying to bring back that feeling from the tunnels, the feeling of being half in one place, half in another. Eventually she felt it, a yearning sort of dizziness like a long drop urging her to jump.

I'm not falling-into, she thought. *I'm crossing-through.*

The here-and-elsewhere feeling was building around her, she was tugging it along the length of her, from the feet on up. When it reached her eyes she opened them.

There was the bridge, blood-red in the twilight. The half-moon sky, the flatlands of the Waste beyond. But also a path, a meadow, a distant city. On second glance, the stars were wrong. Catchkeep, but not. Ember Girl, but not. The One Who Got Away, almost. Carrion Boy, recognizable only if she looked really hard and with an open mind. They were there, but all the stars of their up-selves were arranged slightly *off,* like somebody had elbowed them and knocked them askew, then put them back from memory as best they could.

Count of five, she thought. *Let's do this.*

She concentrated all her will and focus on that other place—and the bridge vanished, though the stars remained.

One.

Time stretched and dilated, irising open. A five-count in this place might last minutes. Or an eyeblink. Chooser knew.

Patel appeared beside her, at the ragged hem of that wide meadow. A road unrolled before them, straight and narrow as a sword. On either side, grass grew to the height of her throat. On the horizon, that unreachable city's lights blinked off and on.

Isabel took inventory. The harvesting-knife was there. Patel's chip was there. At the roadside was a squat stone statue, unidentifiable. Sitting on it put Patel at just the right height for what Isabel was about to do.

Two.

Quickly, carefully, ignoring the pain, Isabel drew a thread from her chest and affixed it to Patel. Then she stepped around behind.

The point of the harvesting-knife parted the non-flesh, non-blood, non-bone of the back of Patel's head like a stick through fog. It made and did not make a tiny aperture, the length of a fingernail. Patel's chip did and did not fit through there neatly. Like the device Isabel had taken from the Director, the chip fizzed into sparks and vanished, and Isabel poured all her focus into that thread as she had done with the ghost before, until the incision sealed shut, its edges oozing slowly together like wet sand.

Three.

"Sorry," Isabel said, as if it had hurt her. "Okay. This is it. Be smart. Stay safe. I'll send the others down when they're ready. You won't be alone. Just make sure you—"

"Is Ayres here?" Patel interrupted.

Isabel stared at her. "Not yet," she said slowly. "But I'll bring him as soon as I can."

"Good," Patel said. "It feels like forever since I've seen him."

"Yeah," Isabel said. "I believe it."

Isabel pictured them, Patel and Ayres and Martinez and Sorensen and the rest of them, wandering the ghost-place together as the dead upstarts had done. Gaining strength from each other. Lending strength to each other. Having each others' backs. In either world, it was the best that anyone could hope for.

In this place other ghosts were wandering. Some were faceless silver cutouts, life-sized or smaller. Some looked like people, only edged with silver. They walked alone, in pairs, in little groups. The ghost-part of Isabel was drawn toward that wide field, those strange stars. But there'd be time enough for that someday. All the time in the world.

Four.

She ought to do something. She was releasing a ghost. The words were there, just waiting to be spoken.

"I am the Archivist," she whispered. "Catchkeep's emissary, ambassador, and avatar on earth. Her bones and stars my flesh; my flesh and bones Her—"

One group of wandering ghosts caught her eye. They carried little knives. They wore the wide-sleeved undyed garb of upstarts. Isabel didn't recognize most of them, but knew at once what she was seeing.

The one in front she knew. Long bloodstains tracked down both of her pant-legs where she'd slashed the big veins in her thighs on the Archivist-choosing eve when Isabel had drawn the short straw instead of her.

"Becca," Isabel was about to whisper, but then forgot about Becca entirely.

She'd spotted the one ghost in that group that didn't match. Like most of them, this one's upstart uniform was stained deeply red.

But unlike the others, under the red this one's clothing was dyed a streaky, patchy blue.

An exhalation of pure stupid relief ripped from her. Something prickled at the backs of her eyes, catching at her throat. She drew breath to call out, not even knowing what she'd say, just to see the look on Sairy's face when she turned and saw Isabel in the—

"Thank you so much, Foster," Patel said, and the ground gave a lurch under Isabel's feet that had nothing to do with the ghost-place claiming her or the living world pulling her back. "Seriously. For every—"

"Wait," Isabel said. "What? Patel, I'm not—"

Five.

F oster was lying on the floor, bleeding from two bullet-holes. The ghost knelt beside her.

Great, Isabel thought. *This one again.*

"No," he said. "Get up. You idiot, you can take worse than this, don't you dare let them break you, get up." He shook her. He slapped her. Blood ran out of her mouth. He lowered her back to the floor, his grip so tight Isabel heard bones crack in Foster's shoulders. "Not like this, Kit," the ghost was saying, softer now. "Not like this."

He let go and knelt beside her, eyes shut, face a blank. He did not close Foster's eyes. He stayed there for a long time. He seemed to be debating something with himself. It looked like the kind of debate that had no winning side, really, no preferable outcome. Just the Ragpicker's own top-shelf shit both ways as far as the eye can see.

The ghost's sword was on the ground beside him. He picked it up.

This part was new to Isabel. When she'd seen this memory before, it'd stopped before she'd reached this point. She'd stopped it there herself.

In one smooth motion the ghost stood and raised the sword. There he paused. Looked down at the awful extinguishment of Foster's face. The depthless nothing in her eyes. The line of black blood that ran out her mouth to pool on the floor beside her cheek. Lowered the sword. Paced the room a few times like a caged predator, wheel and turn, more visibly agitated than Isabel had ever seen him.

He was muttering under his breath to himself. When he passed Isabel she caught snippets: *make me do this, only way, how can I, should have believed you, fucking idiot.*

Fucking idiot did not seem to be aimed at Foster.

All at once he stopped. Looked stonily down at the dead thing on the floor. Raised the sword.

"I'm going to get you out of here," he said, his voice awful. "The only way I can. Thank you for showing me how."

The mask of his face had utterly sloughed off. Beneath it was dread, a deeper dread maybe than Isabel had ever felt. And alongside that, resolve.

Resolve to do wh— Isabel wondered, and then it was happening, and she could only watch.

The sword flashed, and the top of Foster's head slid off.

Isabel couldn't help it. She screamed. Then stared—no more able to speak than if her throat had been kicked in—as the ghost worked his fingers into Foster's brain.

She became gradually aware of a horrible soft choking sound coming out of either herself or the ghost. She couldn't tell which. Possibly it was both.

Many, many seconds of blind rummaging later, the ghost emerged with Foster's chip and pocketed it. Stalked briskly out of the room and returned after several minutes with Foster's uniform, Foster's sword, and more blood on his boots than before. He piled all that stuff on top of Foster's body and picked it all up at once, careful to hold her skull together, and—

I sabel came back shuddering uncontrollably, gripping the hilt of the harvesting-knife hard enough to cramp her whole arm. She almost lost a fingertip cleaning the knife and took three tries to sheathe it. She was having a hard time looking at the ghost. She'd promised she'd tell him everything she saw. But this . . .

The whole time we'd been covering for each other, the ghost had told her once. *Taking turns saving each other.* She knew the rage and shame he'd felt at letting Foster die. And he hadn't even known the rest of the story. What had happened after. What she'd just seen.

No way could she say to him: *if Foster's body had gone into Medical like Salazar's and everyone's, they would've put her chip in the archive with the rest of them, and I would've carried it out of there in a little black box with her name on it. You were trying to help her, save her, keep what was left of her out of the Director's hands, but you—no way you could've known you were—*

She couldn't even mentally finish that sentence without wanting to break things, or throw up, or both.

"It worked," she said weakly. "Patel took the chip. The rest is up to her now."

"Capture and release," Foster said. "Not bad." She punched Isabel in the shoulder as lightly as she could. It still felt like running flat-out into a doorframe. "Sometimes things work out, huh?"

"Sometimes," Isabel echoed. Feeling very small. Very dejected. Very lost. "Listen, I'm not feeling so great, I'm going to take a walk, I'll see you guys later."

She headed out around the edge of the town, going where her feet took her. Years of habit and muscle memory were leading her up the narrow path that tacked up into the hills and dead-ended at the ruined Archivist-house.

The ghost gave her a head start of a quarter-mile or so, then appeared out of nowhere beside her.

"It was bad," he said. "Wasn't it."

"Yep."

If you'd left that chip where it was, it would've ended up in that drawer, and I would have found it. And now I never will.

Her memories aren't lost because of Latchkey. They're lost because of you.

"Worse than—"

"Yep."

This gave him pause.

"It's about Foster."

"Yep."

He stopped. She bulled ahead a few more paces, whipped sideways, kicked a rock off the hillside, instantly regretted it. The ghost folded his arms patiently for the minute it took her to recover.

"You're gonna have to trust me when I say that this time, you actually, truly, no shit do not want to know."

"I know that," he said. "But I need to."

Isabel exhaled hard. "Or, *or*, also an option, I could just, you know, carry it for you. For a little while. Until I figure some stuff out. I'll write it down. I won't forget. I just—"

"It isn't yours to carry," he said softly. "If it's going to eat at one of us, it should be the one who deserves it. You don't need to—"

"I know that," she said. "But I want to."

She started walking. Didn't get far. He caught her sleeve.

She let him turn her around, but fastened her gaze to the stars beyond his head. Carrion Boy's attendant crow, two tiny stars emerging from behind the hill: His vanguard and Ember Girl's alike, taking point for both of Them across the endless empty night.

"Wasp."

"*What.*"

"Please."

Somehow, this above all else was unbearable.

"Sit down," she said, and he did, and she told him.

After, he was quiet for a long time. Long enough for Isabel's curiosity to get the better of her. She glanced at his face and immediately wished she hadn't.

"Because of what you saw with Salazar's chip when you were kids," she heard herself saying. It was like handing a bandage to someone who'd been cut in half. Like trying to put out a bonfire by spitting on it. Why couldn't she shut up? "Because it was all that was left of her. All you could save. All you could get—"

"It's my fault," he said. "Not only how she died, but everything . . . everything . . . "

Isabel swallowed. *Gentle deceits*, she thought, and said: "Yes."

"Where did I—" the ghost said, and faltered. Choking on his fury, quivering with the effort of containment. Every word taut as a tripwire. That desperate misguided precision. "Did you happen to see where I—"

"You want to know why I didn't want to tell you? *This* is why. Because the stupid thing that *this* piece of crap does—" she was drawing the harvesting-knife, holding it out, so much easier if she could just fling the damned thing out into the dark for real this time and be done with it— "all it does is tell me what went *wrong*.

It doesn't give me any way to make it *right*. And it *sure* as hell doesn't—"

She stopped. All at once, the puzzle-pieces in her head were colliding, fitting together into something she could almost see the shape of.

The harvesting-knife, which kept leading her toward Foster, in the ghost-place and the living one.

Foster, who the Latchkey ghosts kept mistaking her for. First Salazar, then Ayres, Tanaka, the Director. Even Patel, *with* her memories restored to her, had *still*—

The realization hit her like icewater.

Salazar *hadn't* been the first.

Something she'd said once, three years ago, to the ghost standing beside her now, who'd drawn his sword on her the day they met.

You attacked me because you took me for Foster.

"What," the ghost said. Unsure what he was reading in her face. She wasn't sure what it was herself. "*What.*" His tone like he'd taken a bullet in a place he couldn't see, was relying on her to report upon it honestly.

Chooser knew how she must look to him. Bringing the knife back in close, turning it over and over in the silvery moonlight. Reaching toward it with her off-hand, slowly, like it'd burn her.

There was so much she hadn't understood. So many questions yet unanswered.

But if there was one thing she understood in this world or any other, it was this ghost. Honestly, given what she knew of him, she was almost surprised it took her this long to figure it out.

The harvesting-knife, the chip, the ghosts all mistaking her for Foster—

A ghost's strength is its memories.

But that didn't mean what it would in the world of the living, did it? In the ghost-place, memories took tangible form. They were a cabin in a meadow of grass higher than her head. They were a well with no bottom, a monster made of leaves. They were a city. They were many cities overlapping. They were a bridge built of the tokens buried with the dead. They were the fabric of the ghost-place, and of the ghosts within. Their only strength and currency. Realer than anything.

Suddenly, horribly, she felt like laughing. *This whole time,* she thought. *This whole Ragpicker-taken time.*

When the hilt-half of Foster's sword had been found and given to the first Archivist four centuries ago, modifications had been made to its design. Sixteen dots of darker metal had been fastened to it, signifying the stars of Catchkeep's up-self. The hilt had been wrapped with a grip of holy dogleather from the first brace of shrine-dogs. When Isabel had realized what the harvesting-knife used to be, she'd removed these modifications, leaving it a naked blade, its hilt wrapped with its original synthetic grip, tougher than dogleather, soft and shiny, the blue-black of a crow.

Now she was picking at the end of it. Now she was prying up a strip, unwinding, unwinding, almost dropping the knife her hands were shaking so hard. There were a good three layers of this stuff wound onto the hilt. She reached the bottom layer, unwound a bit of that, and stopped. The corner of something peeked out, silver in the starlight.

"Hey," she said. "You're going to want to see this."

Acknowledgments

When I wrote *Archivist Wasp* back in 2013 or so, I always had it in the back of my mind to write more books in that world, and with those characters. But I didn't pitch it as a series or trilogy or what-have-you. Honestly I didn't really pitch it *as* anything—the story behind that book's publication is a little weird, and certainly unorthodox.

With *Latchkey* it gets weirder.

I amicably parted ways with *Archivist Wasp*'s publisher, Small Beer Press, in early 2017, but not before going through several rounds of edits. My thanks to Kelly Link first of all. Even if we didn't end up working together on this one, her insights regarding several plot points were invaluable. Also to Gavin Grant for taking a chance on Wasp and her specimen in the first place when literally everyone else told me they were too weird, too cross-genre, too unclassifiable, didn't tick enough YA boxes, etc. I had to walk away from offers because I refused to shoehorn in a romance that didn't belong in that book. Gavin and Kelly never asked for one.

My agent, the fabulous Kate McKean, remains awesome. Kate! Did I mention you are awesome? Thank you for putting up with my weird random questions and messy drafts. Let's make more books together!

Thanks to my first readers! You guys are the best. Unfortunately, I drafted this book so long ago that I don't actually remember exactly *which* of you weighed in on this one. So I'll just go ahead and thank you all. Dan Stace, Patty Templeton, Caitlyn Paxson, Jessica Wick, Julia Rios, Amal El-Mohtar, Grey Walker, Ysabeau Wilce, Dominik Parisien, Autumn Canter, and C.S.E. Cooney. Also to my family and all the friends who helped me along in every stage of the writing and publishing process in more ways than I have space here to discuss.

And thanks to Mike and Anita Allen, without whom I'd probably be putting this book online with a tip jar somewhere. (The *really* weird part? They published the short story *Archivist Wasp* grew out of, in their anthology *Clockwork Phoenix 4*. The world is small.)

Also a huge shoutout to all the book bloggers, handsellers, librarians, teachers, etc. who clicked hard enough with *AW* to champion it to others across the internet and real world alike. Thank you. So much. Here I need to single out Shana DuBois especially. She is goddamn fantastic and I owe her bigtime.

One last massive thank you to everyone who read and loved (or liked, or hated, or was indifferent to, but *read*!) *Archivist Wasp*. It's the book of my heart and I never really expected it to go anywhere. To be fair, a weird little cross-genre novel about a far-future post-apocalyptic ghosthunter priestess, the ghost of a near-future genetically-enhanced supersoldier, and their adventures in the underworld was never going to be an easy sell. Seeing it resonate with readers over and over again has been so, so satisfying.

About the Author

Nicole Kornher-Stace is the author of *Desideria*, *The Winter Triptych*, and the Andre Norton Award finalist *Archivist Wasp*. She lives in New Paltz, New York, where she is currently at work on her first middle grade novel. There is a newly-adopted cat trying to sit on her keyboard as she types these words, and chances are excellent the same cat is trying to sit on the same keyboard as you read them. Visit her website at nicolekornherstace.com.

CPSIA information can be obtained
at www.ICGtesting.com
Printed in the USA
LVHW03s1440171018
593921LV00001B/75/P

9 780988 912489